CW00853118

Anothe
The STABLES on
MUDDYPUDDLE LANE

Heart-warming, uplifting
romance

Etti Summers

For my family…
Love you always x

VALENTINE KISSES

CHAPTER ONE

October Rees eyed the man standing in front of her on this cold and dark January morning with trepidation. She'd met him during her job interview the other day, and she didn't think he liked her much.

Looking at him now, she was even more convinced she was right. In his mid-to-late forties, Nathan Windrush was the stables' general manager and was going to be her immediate boss, although it had been Petra, the woman who owned the stables, who had asked most of the questions. October had a feeling he was going to be a hard taskmaster, and it didn't help that she got the impression he was suspicious of her reasons for applying for the position of groom, since her previous job had been in a prestigious showjumping yard.

But she was here now, and both she and Nathan had to make the best of it.

'Hi,' she said, and Nathan nodded at her, his expression wary. He had been dour at the interview, hardly saying anything, and she'd felt the weight of his assessing gaze throughout.

She felt it again this morning and she hoped he'd leave her alone to get on with things, because she didn't think she'd be able to cope if he didn't. As an experienced groom, October knew what she was doing, but she also realised that she'd have to prove herself, and that she might have to get used to him looking over her shoulder for a while until she did.

His breath steamed around his head in the early morning chill, and the glow of the yard lights cast shadows across his face. He had a short stubbly beard, and a bobble hat pulled firmly down around his ears. An ancient waxed jacket, faded jeans and a pair of steel-toecap boots completed the picture, and October felt overdressed in her clean black breeches, Barbour boots (they looked like wellies but smarter), and padded jacket. Underneath, she wore a Joules fleece, and beneath that she was wearing a long-sleeved tee shirt and a pullover. On bitterly cold winter days it was better to wear too much than too little, and October operated on the premised that if she got too warm, she could always take something off, but if she got too cold and she didn't have any other layers to put on, she was going to freeze.

'If I tell you what's what for today, I'll leave you to get on with it,' Nathan said. 'Charity is working this morning and so is Petra. Charity stables her horse here in exchange for labour,' he added, 'so she knows the ropes. If you're unsure of anything and I'm not around, ask her. There's a whiteboard in the office with jobs on, so if you're at a loose end take a look at that.'

October nodded; she'd spotted the whiteboard at her interview. The tasks were roughly divided into three columns – today, this week, and whenever. The "whenever" heading had made her smile.

Nathan continued, 'We turn the horses out every morning, no matter what the weather, and they all come in at night. I'll be down to the fields in a minute with some silage for them, so if you want to carry on taking those ponies there—' he jerked his head at the row of looseboxes to his left '—I'll start on this lot. Oh, and you'll find a pair of Shetlands in one stall: keep them together because they'll pine if they're apart. And the donkey can go into the same field as the Shetlands.'

October loved donkeys and she couldn't wait to meet this one. There was something very appealing about their long ears and scruffy coats.

Once the assorted equines had been turned out into the fields to graze, October diligently mucked out each stall and re-laid it with fresh bedding. She didn't mind the hard work – she'd been mucking out since she was a tot and she enjoyed the exercise – but she was grateful that Charity was there, so she didn't have to do it all by herself.

Towards the end of preparing the first stall, she had taken her jacket off. During the second she'd removed her fleece, and now she was working in just a tee shirt and a pullover. It was heavy work forking soiled straw into a barrow then hauling it to the manure pile, and it certainly got her heart pumping.

'Fancy a hot drink and a warm in the kitchen?' Charity suggested when the mucking out was done.

She was younger than October, but only by about five or so years, and she'd explained that her horse was the pretty mare called Storm, and that she'd been riding at the stables since she was a teenager.

There had been a bit of a sticky moment when the girl had asked what had brought her to the stables on Muddypuddle Lane, but October had evaded the question by airily saying, 'My mother lives in Picklewick so I'm spending some time with her.'

It wasn't strictly a lie, although it was very close to one. October hadn't come to the village for the sole purpose of spending time with her mother (although it was lovely seeing more of her). October had moved in with Lena because she didn't have anywhere else to go. The showjumping yard where she had previously worked had provided living accommodation as part of her employment, so when she'd left she'd effectively become homeless.

Lena was delighted to have her back, especially since October's grandma had moved into a care home recently. Her grandma had lived with her mum, and Lena had told October she felt as though she was rattling around in the house on her own since, so she welcomed the company.

3

October felt a little despondent about having to move back in with her mum. When she'd left home ten years ago, she'd had big plans and driving ambition, but none of it had come to fruition. However, it was nice being fussed over and having meals cooked for her for a change; although she did try to do her fair share of the chores, and she loved spending more time with her mother.

Feeling unaccountably nervous, October followed Charity into the house, where a wall of warm air hit her. Her cheeks reddened in the sudden heat, and she hastily took her jumper off.

The kitchen was redolent with the smell of coffee and baking bread, with a slight undertone of dog and horse. Two dogs were cuddled together on an armchair and both raised their heads when she came in, their tails thumping on the cushions. One was a black spaniel and the other was a white Jack Russell terrier with a blob of brown over one eye.

Nathan was already there, his hands curled around a mug, and when he saw October looking at the dogs he said, 'The black one is Queenie, she's Petra's, and the Jack Russell is mine. His name is Patch. They've got more sense than to be out on a day like today.'

An elderly man had his back to the room, but he turned around at the sound of Nathan's voice. 'Hello, you must be October. I'm Amos, and I own the stables.'

October blinked: she had been under the impression that Petra was the owner. 'Nice to meet you,' she said, trying to work out the dynamics.

Amos must have realised she was confused because he added, 'I might own the stables, but Petra runs it. She's my niece.' He opened the oven door and a waft of steam billowed out. Bending down, he carefully lifted out a loaf of golden-crusted bread and October's tummy rumbled.

'Tea or coffee?' Charity asked her, heading over to the kettle.

'Coffee, please. Strong. No milk.'

'How about you, Petra? Would you like a coffee?'

Out of the corner of her eye, October noticed Petra shudder. 'No thanks. I think I'll have tea,' the woman said, and October saw Nathan shoot her a concerned look.

Someone's mobile tinkled into life and Nathan patted his pocket before drawing out a phone. When he looked at the screen his whole face was transformed as he smiled widely, and his eyes lit up.

'I take it that must be Megan,' Petra said, accepting a mug of hot tea from Charity.

Charity handed another mug to October, who took it and sipped it gratefully. 'Thank you.'

Charity smiled. 'You're welcome.'

'Aw, look at him,' Petra chortled, her eyes on Nathan. 'He's gone all bashful.'

Bashful wasn't a word October would associate with Nathan, but he did look a little sheepish.

He glared at Petra. 'Excuse me, I need to take this outside,' he said, striding through the kitchen door and into the hall, and October heard him say, 'Sorry Megan, Petra is ribbing me again.'

'Megan is his girlfriend,' Amos explained. 'They've only just got together.'

Charity giggled. 'It's so sweet, seeing the pair of them – they're like two little lovebirds.'

Nope – "lovebird" was another word October wouldn't use to describe Nathan from what she'd seen of him so far, but what did she know? She'd only met him once before. He might be a veritable Romeo, and even from that tiny glimpse of him as he answered the call, she could tell he was in love.

She didn't begrudge anyone that, despite her own recent unfortunate foray into the realms of romance. At least she hadn't had her heart broken, but she had been quite hurt though.

'Talking about being in love, how is Faith getting on in Norwich?' Petra asked Charity, and October was interested to see the differing play of emotions flitting across the girl's face at the question.

'Just so that you can keep up,' Petra said to October, 'Faith and Charity are twins. Charity's horse, Storm, is stabled here. Faith used to stable hers here too, but she moved to Norwich with her boyfriend, so she's had to sell her horse. He's still here, though. He's the big black gelding called Midnight,' she added.

'She's doing great,' Charity said. 'She's got a new job and she's sent me loads of photos of her house. They're renting at the moment, but I think they're looking for somewhere to buy.' Charity seemed a little downcast at this, but then she perked up. 'Me and Timothy are going to visit them at the end of February.'

Petra said to October, 'Timothy is Charity's boyfriend and he's a vet at the practice in Picklewick. Timothy is also Harry's brother, and Harry is my…' Petra hesitated, then followed it up with, '…partner. Not in the business sense, you understand, more in the living together sense. You'll meet him soon. He'll be back before you leave this evening. There's not an awful lot of shoeing you can do when it's dark.'

'He's a farrier?' October asked.

'That's right'.

'It must be handy having both a farrier and a vet around.'

Petra flashed her a smile. 'It certainly is! Saves me a fortune in shoeing, I can tell you. I have to pay full price for the vet service though, more's the pity.'

'How come Midnight is still here?' October asked.

Petra shrugged. 'He was bought by a guy called Luca something or other…I can never remember his name…and he asked if he could pay livery fees to stable him here. I wasn't going to say no, especially considering those fees pay some of your wages.'

'Does that mean I have to be nice to him?' October joked.

Petra snorted. 'Not if you don't want to. He comes across as a bit of a flash git, but he's okay really. He likes horses, that's the main thing.'

As far as October was concerned, that was the main thing for her, too. She could deal with flash gits – after all, her last romantic liaison had been with an incredibly flash git indeed.

Luca hadn't expected to see a strange woman in Midnight's loosebox but when he noticed how pretty she was, he didn't object. The first glimpse he had was of her behind. She was bending over, scrabbling about in the straw. It was a nice trim behind, and that alone would have been enough to concentrate his gaze, but when she straightened up and turned around, the sight of her focused his attention even more.

She was probably close to his age, maybe a year or two younger, slim but with curves where he hoped to find them, and long shapely legs encased in a pair of breeches. When his attention finally made his way to her face, it was to find her staring at him with a questioning and not particularly friendly glint in her eye.

'Can I help you?' she asked.

'Shouldn't I be asking you the same question?'

'I don't know, should you? Who are you anyway?'

'I own the horse whose box you are standing in. Who are you, and what are you doing in it?'

She blushed and bit her lip. 'Oh, sorry, I didn't realise. I work here as from today, and the reason I'm in Midnight's stall is because I've lost something.'

'Can I help you look for it?'

'No, thanks, I've looked. It's not here. I'll check the loosebox next door.'

'What exactly have you lost?'

'It's nothing. It doesn't matter.'

'Clearly it *does* matter, or you wouldn't be looking for it'.

She shrugged. 'Honestly, it's nothing; it's just a hair grip.'

He could see tendrils of her hair poking out from underneath her woolly hat. They were very dark and curled slightly around her face. Her skin was creamy and clear, and her eyes were brown, possibly with flecks of green in them. It was difficult to tell without squinting, and he thought it best not to do that – he seemed to have made her uncomfortable enough already.

'If I come across it, I'll leave it in the office,' he said. 'What does it look like?'

'It really doesn't matter.'

He waited patiently, hoping that she'd tell him in the end if he didn't say anything.

'It's a claw,' she said finally, demonstrating what she meant with her fingers and thumb. 'It's white and blue, a sort of Mediterranean design. But don't trouble yourself. I can easily get another. I took it out of my hair to put my hat on and it must have fallen out of my pocket. It's no big deal,' she insisted.

Luca couldn't help staring at her as she spoke, and he tore his gaze away from her with difficulty and glanced around the yard at the empty stalls. 'They're still out in the fields, are they?'

'If you mean the horses, then yes. If you're asking about the humans, I'm not quite sure. And the chickens could be anywhere.' Her lips twitched and her eyes twinkled.

He grinned to himself. She was sassy, and he always thought that a sense of humour in a woman was far more attractive than her looks. 'Where's the goat?' he asked.

'In the barn.'

'And Tiddles?'

'I haven't had the pleasure of meeting Tiddles, yet. I'm assuming that's a cat?'

'She certainly is. Sorry, I haven't introduced myself. I'm Luca Dalton. As I said, Midnight is my horse.' He thrust his hand through the open stable door and she stepped forward and took it awkwardly.

As they shook, he noticed how firm her grip was. He also caught a whiff of her perfume, and he slowly inhaled the gorgeous scent.

'October Rees,' she said. 'He's got good conformation and a nice neat head. What's he like to ride?'

Eh? Oh, she was talking about Midnight. 'Smooth, rocking horse canter, pacey trot. Can be a bit headstrong.'

She nodded. 'I prefer them with some spirit.'

Luca got the feeling she might be just as spirited as his horse, and a little bolt of excitement jolted him in the chest. 'Do you own your own horse?' he asked.

'Unfortunately, no.'

She looked crestfallen and Luca spoke without thinking. 'Feel free to ride Midnight whenever you like.'

Why had he done that? He didn't know a thing about her, and he certainly didn't know how well she rode. Petra and Nathan were the only people who Luca had agreed could ride his horse, although Timothy, Charity's boyfriend, had been on Midnight's back once or twice when he'd gone out with Charity for a ride. Horses were valuable creatures, especially when things went wrong, and Luca wasn't in the habit of loaning his horse to just anyone.

However, October must be a decent enough rider or Petra wouldn't have employed her. He'd read the advert she'd put out, and it did say that the successful person would be expected to teach the occasional class so October must be a competent horsewoman.

'Thanks.' October nodded and gave him a small smile which he interpreted as showing her appreciation for the offer. 'I'm sorry, you'll have to excuse me. I've still got a lot to do and I'm not quite sure where everything is yet,' she added, stepping towards the door of the loosebox.

He realised he was blocking her exit and he stood to the side to let her pass. 'I expect I'll see you around?'

'I expect so.' Her smile was polite but her eyes were friendly, and as she walked away Luca's gaze followed her.

To say he was intrigued was an understatement. To say he didn't find her attractive would be a downright lie.

He wondered whether she'd say yes if he asked her out.

Flipping heck, Petra thought. She'd never felt so shattered in all her life! Thank god she'd finally taken someone on at the stables. October Rees was overqualified for the job, but Petra wasn't complaining. Besides, she hadn't had much interest in the advert she'd put out, and she guessed the main reason might be because living accommodation wasn't included. But there was no way she wanted a stranger living under her roof, and there was nowhere else suitable.

She didn't run a big enough operation to warrant converting any of the outbuildings into flats – that sort of thing was reserved for the big racing yards and the like. Little stables such as her riding school had to rely on the local workforce, and being a stable hand (or *groom* as Megan, Nathan's girlfriend, had suggested she put in the advert) wasn't for everyone. It was hard work, the hours could be unsuitable, and you worked outside in all weathers. The wages weren't brilliant either, but Petra was offering the most she could afford and, as she'd told October during her interview, she could have all the rides she wanted. If you didn't own your own horse, that alone was worth a small fortune. Petra had also been delighted when October had told her she'd be able to teach a few lessons, freeing up Petra to do other things. Such as sleep.

Petra headed into the office, wanting to check which jobs still needed to be done for the day and which could be put off until tomorrow, when she ran straight into the woman she'd just been thinking about.

'Oops, sorry,' October cried, reaching out to steady her.

'My fault,' Petra said. 'I wasn't looking where I was going.' She'd been too busy yawning. 'How did your first day go?' she asked, moving around to stand in front of the whiteboard and scanning it quickly.

'It's good; nothing I haven't done before.'

'Are you enjoying it so far?'

'Yes, I am.'

'It must be a far cry from what you've been used to.'

'I suppose it is...'

Petra hadn't delved too deeply into why October had left a prestigious showjumping yard to work in a small stable in Picklewick. Of course she'd checked October's references, and she had been given a glowing one by her previous employer, but when she'd asked why October had left, she had been informed it was due to personal reasons. The man she'd spoken to had been at pains to clarify that those personal reasons weren't a reflection on October's suitability for employment.

As soon as she'd met October, Petra had felt an affinity to her. They were around the same age and they both loved working with horses, although that was where the similarities ended. Their paths had been very different. Petra, although she didn't technically own the stables, knew that if anything happened to Amos she would inherit it. Also, she had carte blanche on how the riding school was run. Amos rarely interfered anymore. Although *he* wouldn't call it interfering, he'd call it "guiding" or "helping out".

October, on the other hand, had worked for some very famous people in the showjumping world. And, although Petra wasn't certain, she'd sensed that October had wanted a slice of that particular pie for herself; but maybe she wasn't talented enough, or maybe she simply hadn't been able to afford it, or she hadn't had the right breaks or the right kind of luck. Petra didn't know. All that mattered was that October was a good rider, a good worker, and cared about horses as much as Petra herself did.

However, she had a feeling October would move on at some point, although Petra hoped she would stick around for a while. It was the only reservation Petra had had when she'd offered October the job. Petra would hate to get used to October, only for her to leave after a couple of months, but she hadn't had a great deal of choice because she'd not had any other applicants.

October said, 'I'm just going to bring the horses in and get them settled, and then I'm done for the day. Is that okay?'

Petra yawned again. 'Sorry, I've been overdoing it. We've been shorthanded for a while. See you tomorrow.'

'Bye,' October replied, and Petra watched her leave.

As soon as she was alone Petra slumped onto the desk, resting her backside on the edge of it, feeling washed out. She'd been feeling like this for a while, and she was fairly certain she'd been fighting off a bug. However, this bug had been hanging around for six to eight weeks and it didn't seem to be going anywhere. She wished it would develop into something proper, so she could get it over and done with. Feeling crap for nearly two months wasn't fun.

Occasionally she caught Harry, Amos or Nathan giving her sideways glances, and she knew they were all concerned about her, but she told them the same thing she'd been telling herself – that she'd had much more work to do since Faith had stopped coming to the stables to help out, and then there had been Christmas and all the fuss leading up to it, so it was no wonder she'd hardly had a minute to draw breath. Plus the winter months were always difficult financially for the stables, so she was also worried about paying the bills. Hopefully, now that October was here and spring was on the horizon, she was bound to feel more like her normal lively self soon.

Wasn't she?

'Is everything okay?' Petra asked. She was snuggled under the duvet with only the top of her head and her nose poking out and Harry thought she looked incredibly cute, if somewhat tired. When he first met her, no way on earth would he have described her as cute – prickly, argumentative, stubborn, defensive, but never cute. She was still all of those things, but he could see the kind, loving, loyal and incredibly beautiful soul beneath. And when she was peering out of the bedclothes at him with her hair all messed up, he thought she was the most gorgeous woman in the world. And she was *his*.

He shrugged off his dressing gown and slipped in naked beside her, still damp from the shower he'd had after doing his usual check around the stables before bedtime.

'It's fine,' he said. 'Everything is locked up and everyone is sleeping. Apart from Fred. I could hear that darned cockerel chundering away to himself in the coop. The hens won't be happy if he keeps them awake all night.'

'Neither will I, because a grumpy hen won't lay.'

Harry turned onto his side and propped himself up on his elbow. 'How was October's first day?'

'Good, I think.'

'Let's hope she'll take some of the strain off you.'

'Let's hope she'll stay around long enough,' Petra retorted.

'Why wouldn't she?' Harry was puzzled.

'There's not enough to keep her here horse-wise, plus the wages aren't great. As you know the problem is that the big racing and showjumping yards have live-in grooms. Having your accommodation provided is quite a perk.'

Harry kissed her on the nose. 'It can't be helped. You can't afford to pay her more.'

'At least she's living with her mum, so she doesn't have a mortgage or rent to pay, although she told me that she's helping with the bills,' Petra said.

'Do you think she'd stay if we had suitable accommodation?' he asked slowly, an idea beginning to form.

'Maybe. I don't know.' She yawned hugely, then gave him a plaintive look. 'I'm starving,' she said, sleepily, 'but I can't be bothered to get anything to eat.'

Harry grinned, guessing she was hoping he'd offer to nip down to the kitchen and fetch her something. 'I'll make you a snack. What would you like? Toast? Omelette? Sandwich?'

'Peanut butter.'

'You hate peanut butter.'

'I don't.'

'You do,' he insisted. He loved it but she'd never been able to stomach the stuff (her words). He felt the same way about Marmite, but she adored it.

'I've changed my mind – I fancy some.'

Harry smiled down at her fondly. 'Okay, peanut butter it is. On toast?

'No, with bananas. And some yoghurt.'

'Really?'

She nodded.

He reached across to give her a squeeze but as he did so she winced. 'What's wrong?'

'My damned bra shrank in the wash and it's been cutting into me all day, so now I'm a bit sore. A few other things have shrunk too. I'll have to have a word with Amos. He still can't get to grips with the new washing machine and we've had it a couple of months now. I'll have no clothes left at this rate.'

Harry got out of bed and put his dressing gown back on. 'I can't say I've noticed any problem with my clothes.'

Petra glared at him. She reminded him of Princess when she was cross. That goat had a mean look in her eye when she was upset. 'So it's just my stuff he's shrinking, is it? Great!'

Chuckling to himself, Harry made his way downstairs. Peanut butter indeed! It was rather nice with bananas, but he hadn't tried it with a scoop of yoghurt dolloped over the top.

After he'd made Petra her snack, he had a quick taste. Mmm, not bad. He must remember to have this for breakfast tomorrow. Healthy and nutritious, and very tasty. Nice one, Petra, he thought, as he carried the bowl and a spoon back to their bedroom.

Closing the door quietly behind him, he began, 'It's quite nice—' Then he stopped.

Petra was fast asleep, bless her.

Harry used his free hand to stroke a strand of hair off her face, love filling him so completely that he thought he might explode from the force of it. He never thought he'd feel this way about anyone.

Smiling ruefully, he put the bowl and spoon to one side in case she woke and was still hungry, then he eased himself into bed, careful not to disturb her. With a contented sigh, he turned onto his side and spooned her, wrapping his arms around her waist and gently pulling her close, then he winced when she half woke up and pushed at him.

'Sore,' she muttered, and he realised he was crushing her to him rather too tightly.

'Sorry,' he murmured, loosening his grip, and was relieved when she immediately sank back into slumber. She looked as though she needed all the sleep she could get.

He hoped she would slow down and be able to take a step back now that she had October to help her. He desperately wanted for them to be able to spend more time together, just the two of them, which wasn't easy when she was running such a time-consuming business as the stables.

Harry wanted nothing more than to spend every moment with this wonderful woman and as he lay there in the cocooned darkness, listening to her soft breathing, he thought how lucky he was to have found her.

CHAPTER TWO

A couple of days later, Luca was leaning against the railings surrounding the gallery, his eyes trained on the woman in the centre of the arena who was teaching a small class of novice riders. Petra was by his side, and she was equally as focused.

'What do you think?' he asked quietly out of the side of his mouth, without taking his eyes off October.

'She certainly knows what she's doing,' Petra said. 'Not that it's any of your business.'

'I was just asking,' Luca replied, feeling slightly hurt. Petra could often be prickly, but she was definitely grouchier lately.

She must have realised how grumpy she sounded because she turned to him and said, 'Sorry, I'm a bit short tempered. Not enough sleep and too much to do. I'm quite impressed with her: she's patient, kind, and calm, and she's got a nice way about her. She'll do.'

Luca was pleased about that. He'd only just met October, and he'd hate for her to be sent away with a flea in her ear. There was no fear of that though, because Luca could also see how good she was. She'd be an asset to the stables and no mistake.

He wondered where she was from. He didn't live in Picklewick himself; he lived just outside, but he hadn't been there all that long, having only bought his house in the summer, and he wasn't fully integrated into village life yet, and hadn't got to know many people so far.

Luca glanced at his watch and was pleased to see there was only another ten minutes of the lesson to go; he couldn't wait to put Midnight through his paces.

He'd done a little bit of jumping with him, but not much, so he was looking forward to getting on the horse and seeing what he could do. He'd already checked with Petra to make sure the arena wouldn't be needed after this lesson, and as long as he put the jumps away and tidied up after himself, she had been more than happy to let him loose in there.

He watched for another few minutes as October gave each young rider another turn over the low jumps then, when she called the lesson to a halt, he left the gallery and went back out into the yard to fetch Midnight. Luca had already saddled him, so it didn't take him long before he was back in the arena, the horse in tow.

'Hi,' he said, nodding and smiling to Charity who had come in to loosen girths and slide the stirrup irons up their leather straps ready to take the ponies back to their respective stalls.

She stopped for a moment to make a fuss of the horse that used to belong to her sister, and the gelding snickered a greeting and nuzzled his nose into her, probably looking for a mint or a horse nut.

Charity duly produced a mint from her pocket and held it out, and Midnight snaffled it up with his mobile whiskery lips and crunched contentedly. Most ponies and horses loved mints, and it was a nice little treat for them without having to worry about additional calories. Luca always had a packet about his person, too.

'There's no need to bother,' he called out suddenly, seeing October starting to put away the jumps. 'I'll be using those,' he added.

Luca tied Midnight to a tethering ring set into the wall and strolled across the arena floor, his boots sinking into the sand, and debated what height he should place the poles at. He decided he'd start the horse off fairly low to warm him up, then he'd give him a bit of a stretch and a challenge.

It took Luca a few minutes to arrange the jumps to his satisfaction and to make sure they were at the correct height, and by that time Charity and October had taken the ponies out and he was on his own.

Swinging himself into the saddle, Luca took his mount on a couple of laps around the arena first, to make sure the horse was paying attention and listening to him when he asked him to trot or canter, and when he was satisfied that Midnight was behaving himself, Luca did one final circuit and then aimed him at the nearest jump.

Cantering slowly up to it, the horse popped over the fence with the minimum of effort, and he did the same with the next three. Happy with the way things were going, Luca dismounted and raised the height on the bars, before moving one of the jumps to allow for the horse's increased stride.

Satisfied, Luca mounted up again, and took him over the new height.

It was as he was approaching the last one that a movement out of the corner of his eye caught Luca's attention, and he glanced up to see October lurking at the back of the gallery, as though she didn't want to be seen.

Luca pretended he hadn't noticed her and he carried on about his business, once more getting off Midnight, raising the bars another notch, and mounting up again.

He'd gone a little higher than he'd intended, and he knew he was in danger of showing off. He wasn't normally like that but he found himself wanting to impress her, and Luca got the feeling that his ability to handle a horse would be more important to the new stable hand than what car he drove or what job he did. He wanted her to think well of him and his ability to handle Midnight.

Luca wasn't a novice jumper and neither was he new to horse ownership. He'd been around horses all his life, having ridden since he was five, but he'd never been seriously competitive and he therefore hadn't joined the Pony Club or competed in any major gymkhanas. He had only wanted to ride for pleasure, but he did get a buzz and an adrenaline rush when he rode over jumps.

He knew he was lucky to be able to afford to own a horse. They weren't cheap to buy, but that wasn't the issue; the problem was their upkeep. A set of shoes roughly every six weeks, plus all the feed, plus the vet bills, plus the insurance – it soon added up. Not to mention having to find grazing, and pay livery fees. It was unfortunate that he wasn't able to see to his horse himself every day, but his job had to take precedence and at least he knew Midnight was well looked after at the stables on Muddypuddle Lane. Petra ran a tight ship, and Luca was more than happy with the care she provided for his mount.

Right, he thought, *let's have a go at this, my boy, and see what you can do.* He hadn't tried the horse over jumps this high before, and he supposed he should put them down a couple of notches. But they were there now, and as he took Midnight for a lap around the arena before he tackled the first fence, Luca risked a very swift glance at the gallery.

October was barely visible in the gloom, but he knew she was watching him.

Midnight pricked his ears as he straightened up to face the first jump, and Luca aimed him at it. The horse knew perfectly well what was expected, and Luca reined him in slightly to allow him to gather his hindquarters under him. Before he gave Midnight his head, he felt the animal's power and knew the horse would have no trouble clearing this height.

The constrained canter lasted for a few paces, then Luca leaned over the horse's neck to give him more rein and braced himself for the jump.

Midnight landed perfectly, and no sooner had he done so than Luca gathered him up again and pointed him at the next hurdle.

Yes! he thought silently as Midnight took this one in

20

his stride too, and Luca turned him into the last jump, going wide to make sure the horse had enough time to both see it and to prepare for it.

That was the point where things started to go wrong.

Midnight, for some inexplicable reason of his own, took an instant dislike to the fence he'd already jumped twice before, albeit at a slightly lower elevation, and just as Luca thought the animal was about to take it, the horse changed his mind and juddered to a halt.

Luca went sailing over the horse's ears and fell unceremoniously on the other side of the fence in a winded heap.

'Oof!' Not the most dignified of sounds.

He sat up slowly, rubbing his shoulder.

Thankfully, nothing was broken, and he didn't appear to be hurt apart from his pride. That'll teach me to show off, he thought ruefully.

Feeling a bit of an idiot, he clambered to his feet, dusted himself down, and went to catch his horse.

Midnight, though, had other ideas. The animal was quite happy to not have a rider on his back and was trotting around the arena with his head and his tail held high, his ears pricked forward and a smug, self-satisfied look on his face. If horses could snigger, Midnight would be laughing his horseshoes off.

It was as Luca was debating whether to run around after the horse or wait for Midnight to get fed up and come to him, that he realised he was no longer alone; October had slipped silently into the arena and was standing just behind him.

'Do you need a hand?' she asked, and he could hear the amusement in her voice.

'No thanks, I can manage.'

'It looks like it.'

'He'll get fed up before I will.

'I don't think so. If you go that way and I go this, we can trap him in a corner.' October was grinning broadly.

'I swear to god he knows what he's doing,' Luca groaned.

'Of course he does. He's having great fun.'

'And you aren't?' Luca asked her, with a raised eyebrow.

'I suppose I am.' She sent him a wicked smile.

Luca caught his breath. The bolt of desire that shot through him was a surprise. He thought she was pretty, beautiful even, and he was seriously attracted to her, but the reaction he'd just had was visceral, felt deep in his gut, and it floored him.

He cleared his throat to cover his confusion and started walking towards Midnight, who was at the far end of the arena. The horse had come to a halt, but he continued to be on full alert, staring at them with his ears pricked forward, daring Luca to come any closer.

The horse let him get within about three metres, then he jerked his head up, whirled on his haunches and trotted off. Luca was positive the animal was looking over his shoulder and laughing at him.

October hadn't moved. She was watching intently, a smile playing about her lips. Then she calmly stuck her hand in a pocket and pulled out a carrot.

'That's cheating!' Luca exclaimed.

'All's fair in love and catching horses,' October retorted. She whistled, attracting the horse's attention.

Midnight, still circling at the far end, turned to look at her, his ears flicking back and forth.

'Look what I've got,' she said to him.

The horse looked, and he mut have liked what he saw because he trotted a few paces, then stopped a short distance away and huffed.

'You're going to have to come a little closer if you want your carrot,' October told him.

Luca could see the exact moment the horse admitted defeat and decided the carrot was worth more than his short burst of freedom. He seemed to slump slightly as if he'd had his fun and he now wanted to eat his treat and return to his stable.

Luca didn't blame him; after the fiasco of falling off with October witnessing his ignominy, he felt much the same way himself.

As the horse walked up to her, Midnight stretched out his neck, delicately took the carrot between his mobile hairy lips and began to crunch on it. October reached around and grabbed hold of his bridle.

Midnight gave Luca a sideways look and Luca narrowed his eyes at him. The horse may have won this round, but there would be plenty of others.

'I'll take him back to his stall if you want,' October said, but Luca shook his head.

'It's okay, I'll see to him. He's my horse and you've probably got enough to do.' He was wishing she'd go away so he could nurse his wounded pride in peace.

'I don't mind giving you a hand.' She lifted Midnight's reins over his head to use them to lead him with and gave them to Luca. 'He was going so well, too,' October said, and he heard a hint of laughter in her voice.

'Do you jump much?' he asked, innocently.

'Some.'

Luca made no move to leave the arena. Instead, he turned to her and said, 'Do you fancy having a go?'

'Me ride Midnight?'

He smiled. 'Of course, you don't have to if you're worried you might come off.'

'Like you did, you mean?'

Luca shrugged, admitting the truth of it. But he'd attempted a decent height, and he didn't believe she would do any better.

'Go on, then.' She held out her hand for the reins and he gave them back to her and stood aside.

'Do you need a leg-up getting on him?' he asked, but even before he'd finished the sentence October was on the horse's back and staring down at him.

'I think I can manage,' she said.

Luca shook his head. That showed him. 'Should I hang around here in case you...?' He trailed off, gesturing towards the jumps and wondering how soon she'd come a cropper. Midnight, Luca had discovered, could be a handful.

'Fall off?' She turned the horse's head and urged him into a trot, shouting back over her shoulder, 'Nah, you're okay. Sit in the gallery and get yourself a coffee.'

Smiling to himself, Luca was impressed with her spirit. If that was the way she wanted to play it...

October took Midnight for a canter around the arena. He was biddable enough now that he'd got his rebellion out of his system, but she could also sense the horse would be quick to take advantage of any sign of weakness on her part.

'Oh, no, you don't, my laddo,' she murmured to him when he tossed his head, not liking the short rein she was keeping him on.

He crabbed sideways and tossed his head again, but when he realised he wasn't going to get his own way and that the rider on his back was in charge and not him, Midnight settled down and behaved himself.

For the moment.

October wasn't fooled. She'd met his sort on more than one occasion and she knew precisely how to deal with him. You had to show him who was boss and take charge from the beginning, or he'd walk all over you.

As she took Midnight around for a second time to make sure he was settled and focused, a thought occurred to her. She *was* referring to the horse, wasn't she? Not the man who owned it?

If the cap fits...

Not that she intended to have any more of a relationship with Luca than she had with his horse. Caring for Midnight was part and parcel of her new job. His owner was, to a certain extent irrelevant, as far as October was concerned.

He was damnably good-looking though, she was forced to admit, as she caught a glimpse of him out of the corner of her eye.

He was in the gallery, leaning nonchalantly against the wall, a cup of something hot in his hand and a smug expression on his face, and she realised that he was expecting her to come off.

Ha! Not a chance. She'd been watching Midnight carefully whilst Luca had been in the arena with him, and she knew precisely the point at which the horse was would be tempted to baulk at the jump. All she needed was to urge him on just as he considered refusing to jump it, and the wind would be taken out of the animal's sails. He'd pop over the fence without a second thought.

Anyway, it wasn't particularly high, and October knew she could get more out of this horse with a bit of encouragement. It would do for now though, to prove a point.

Luca was an arrogant so-and-so and a bit patronising, and she'd love nothing better than to see the smug expression wiped off his face when he realised she wasn't going to be thrown off.

Sitting upright and slightly back in the saddle, she lined Midnight up for the first jump, holding him back with practised ease, relishing the control she had over him. It was exhilarating to think she had half a tonne of horse underneath her, behaving itself impeccably, and she could tell that Midnight was keen by the way he held his head and the bunching power of his hindquarters. His ears were pointing towards the jump, and October stared through them and beyond, still holding him back.

Then abruptly she released him and he exploded

towards the fence, tucked his front hooves neatly underneath his chest and popped over the jump with minimum effort and absolutely no fuss whatsoever.

Then she asked him to do the same a further four times until he'd cleared all the jumps, joy bubbling through her. God, she'd missed this!

Careful to keep her expression neutral (she didn't want Luca to think she was gloating, even though she secretly was), she brought Midnight to a standstill and slid gracefully off his back.

A slow clap echoed around the arena.

October ignored it.

She didn't acknowledge Luca until he was standing right next to her, and even then she didn't dare look him in the eye. Instead, she busied herself by sorting out the horse's stirrups and loosening his girth.

'That was…' Luca paused. 'Clean.'

'Clean is good,' she replied, accepting the compliment. She could guess how she and the horse had looked – controlled, graceful, effortless, neat, popping over the jumps with ease.

When she finally met Luca's eye, she was intrigued by what she saw. Respect – she'd been hoping to see that. But there was also desire smouldering in their depths, which drew an answering response from her as butterflies fluttered into life in her stomach.

After what had happened at her last stables, she didn't think she'd feel anything but a low-key despair when it came to men, but she surprised herself. *Luca* surprised her.

'Good jumping,' he said. 'I'm impressed. You must think me a right jerk after my little stunt.'

She gave him a wry smile. 'Perhaps.'

'I should have known better.'

'Agreed.' She handed him Midnight's reins. 'I take it you're going to bed him down?'

His eyes widened and she could simply tell that he was imaging taking *her* to bed. In your dreams, she felt like saying, so it wasn't unexpected when he asked, 'Will you have dinner with me tonight?'

What she hadn't anticipated was her reply. 'I'd like that.'

And she would – she most definitely would.

'I've been thinking,' Harry said, walking into their bedroom, wrapping his arms around Petra and cuddling into her. He hoped his idea might be the solution to the stables' financial problems, but initially it was going to take money, time and hard work before Petra and Amos would start to reap the benefits. Hard work wasn't an issue – none of them was averse to that; however, time might be a problem because he didn't know how long his idea would take to implement, or how long the stables could keep going without an upturn in their finances; which brought him to the main stumbling block – money.

Petra groaned. 'What about? It had better not be silly.' She had been changing out of her work clothes and into jogging bottoms and a fleece, and Harry saw her give her jodhpurs a grim look. Oh dear, he thought, Amos must still be having trouble with the programmes on the washing machine.

'It isn't silly,' Harry protested, then added. 'Okay, you might think it is, but hear me out before you say anything?'

'Go on…'

'How about we convert the cowshed into living accommodation?'

'For October?'

'For paying guests. Although it might also help to persuade October to stay at the stables if we could throw in somewhere to live.'

'I suspect a certain horse owner might help her do that just as successfully, and without us having to go to all the expense of building a house for her.'

Harry was derailed for a moment. 'What do you mean?'

'She fancies Luca and he fancies her. You ought to have seen them this afternoon. They were in the arena together and they couldn't take their eyes off one another.'

'Interesting… But I didn't mean somewhere for October to live – I was thinking about holiday rentals. We're not using the cowshed for anything.'

Petra slid out of his arms and sat on the edge of the bed to wiggle a clean pair of socks over her toes. 'Do you think my ankles look puffy?'

Harry bent down for a better look. 'Not that I can see. They look the same as usual.'

'Hmm.' She frowned as she rotated her foot, turning her leg this way and that. 'It's being used for storage,' she said.

Harry pulled a face. 'I've seen what's in there.' Some of the stuff had been "stored" since the last World War.

She shrugged. 'It might come in useful one day.'

'When?'

'I don't know, do I?'

'When was the last time you made use of anything in there?'

'Um…?'

'Exactly!'

'It's a great idea, but it's not feasible. What about the expense for a start, and who's going to run it? I've got too much to do as it is.'

'I'm not suggesting turning it into a five-star luxury hotel. I reckon we could get three two-bed holiday lets out of it. It'll take a bit of work but once they're up and running they'll bring more money in for minimum effort than anything else in the stables.'

'What about the initial outlay? It's going to cost a fortune to do the renovations.'

'There is that—' he began, but Petra waved a hand at him, yawning.

'Can we talk about it another time? I'm too tired to discuss it now,' she said.

She did look exhausted. He'd been hoping that now she had October working for her, she would be able to slow down and take some time off. But if anything, she looked even more tired.

'Of course. It was only a thought…' he said. 'Let's see what Amos has made for dinner, then you can veg out in front of the TV.'

He waited for her to finish putting her socks on and held the door open.

As she went to walk through it, she stopped and reached up to stroke his face. 'I really appreciate you trying to help,' she said. 'Have I told you I love you?'

'Not for at least an hour,' he said, pressing his face into the palm of her hand. 'I love you too.'

Her smile took his breath away. 'I know,' she whispered, and his heart flooded with joy.

Luca was unaccountably nervous. This was a meal in a gastropub. Nothing more. He'd taken many a woman on dates in similar places. What was there to be nervous about?

Possibly because none of them had made his heart race the way October did?

Telling himself not to be ridiculous, he pulled up outside the address she'd given him and debated whether to beep the horn, ring the doorbell, or text her to say he was at the kerb.

Whilst he sat there dithering, her front door opened and he stared at the figure illuminated by the hall light. He caught a brief glimpse of her, before she pulled the door closed and was dashing down the path.

He leaned across the passenger seat, cranked the door

handle and October got in.

'Nice car,' she said. 'Is it new?'

'I've had it a while.' He smiled at her, using the excuse of checking that she'd put her seatbelt on to give her a closer look.

What he saw made his mouth go dry.

She looked stunning. Her hair was loose and she'd curled it at the ends, she'd put smoky stuff around her eyes, her lashes looked longer and fuller than he remembered, and her lips were tinted red. Not only that, the boots had three-inch heels and her legs were endless, encased as they were in black tights. She was wearing a short skirt, which she tucked around her thighs as she settled herself in the passenger seat, and a knitted top with a coat over it.

He swallowed hard.

'You've got *two* cars?' she asked.

'Um, yeah? Is that a problem?'

'Not at all. Although you've got to admit, it is a bit greedy.' She grinned at him, and he decided she must be pulling his leg. 'What make is it?' she asked.

'An Aston Martin. It's quite an old one,' he added, as if to justify the expense. He was about to tell her that cars were his one weakness but he'd be lying. He had many weaknesses, and they were all for the finer things in life. Luca usually made no apology for that – he'd worked hard to get where he was – but somehow this woman made him feel tacky about it.

'It's gorgeous,' she said. 'Not very practical though.'

'Which is why I also drive a Range Rover.'

'I've got a Ford.'

'I know, I've seen it in the car park.'

Silence followed, and Luca concentrated on his driving as they seemed to have exhausted that particular topic of conversation.

'What do you do for a living?' she asked eventually, and he wondered if she was feeling as awkward as he.

Maybe asking her out wasn't such a good idea if the only thing they had in common was horses. 'I own a tech company.'

'Do you want to expand on that?'

'It's not very exciting,' he said. At least, not for other people, although he tended to find it fascinating.

'Try me,' she said, and he heard the challenge in her voice.

'Okay, you asked for it,' he replied, and for the next twenty minutes he regaled her with details about how he first started up, what his business was all about now, and where he saw it going in the future. 'What about you?' he asked, when he guessed he must have bored her enough. To be fair to her, she'd asked loads of questions and had seemed genuinely interested.

'I'm a stable hand,' she said. 'You know that.'

'I suspect there's more to you than that,' he retorted. 'Such as, where did you work before?'

'A showjumping yard in Kent.'

'What brought you to Picklewick?'

'My mother moved here a few years ago and now that my granny has gone into a care home, she's lonely. So I thought I'd move back in and keep her company.'

He gave her a sceptical look – there was something in her tone which made him think she wasn't telling him the whole story. But even if that were the case, it was none of his business.

Changing the subject he said, 'You're a fab rider.'

'Thanks. You're not too bad yourself.'

'You're humouring me.'

'I'm telling the truth. It helps if you can stay on, though.'

'Ha, ha.' Luca indicated left and drove into the gastro pub's car park. 'Here we are.'

When they walked inside, Luca having sped around to October's side of the car to give her a hand getting out (the sports car was rather low-slung for elegant exits), he noticed her quick scrutiny of the place.

'Is it okay?' he asked, concerned that maybe he should have taken her somewhere flashier.

'It's nice,' she said, and once they had been shown to a table and were seated, she added, 'When I saw the car, I thought we might be going somewhere really expensive.'

Luca frowned. 'Would that have been a problem?'

'Yes. I intend we go Dutch.'

'I asked you out, so I'm paying.'

'No. You are not. Dutch,' she insisted.

He sighed. 'As you wish.' He'd been about to order a nice bottle of wine, but he thought better of it, and when she asked for water with a twist of lime, he also understood she was being sensible – he'd forgotten that she probably had to be at the stables early in the morning.

So far, this evening wasn't going quite as he'd expected, but then nothing about October was as expected. For one thing, she wasn't particularly forthcoming about herself and it intrigued him.

He had a feeling he was going to enjoy getting to know her better.

Luca might come across as a bit of a show-off, but October had a feeling it wasn't his true self, she thought as she studied him over dinner. Like the way he'd seemed nervous when he asked if the pub was okay. He'd appeared uncertain, as though he might be worried that he'd brought her to the wrong place. It was quite endearing.

He'd also been rather self-deprecating when he was telling her about his business. She guessed it had probably taken a great deal of determination and drive to build it from such humble beginnings, not to mention a considerable degree of business acumen, skill and creativity. He'd skimmed over all those things when she'd mentioned them, and he'd put it down to luck.

Or was it merely an act to get into her knickers? The problem was that she was used to Zeus's false modesty and he'd used it most effectively to get her to sleep with him, that it had made her wary.

Slowly October and Luca discovered more about each other, superficial things mostly such as what kind of music they liked, what bands they'd seen, the films they'd watched, and of course, horsey stuff. She lived and breathed horses, and at least he enjoyed riding and he seemed to enjoy hearing about her adventures in the showjumping world. She hadn't always worked for Zeus Fernsby (she resisted the childish urge to cross herself to ward off his particular brand of awfulness), and she had many tales of behind-the-scenes disasters and near misses.

In turn, Luca told her stories about some of his more difficult and demanding clients, and how some of them expected him to be on call to answer their questions or solve a problem at all hours of the day and even in the middle of the night.

Both October and Luca were discreet enough not to mention any names, and she was glad of this because she preferred not to go into detail about her time working for Zeus. The less said about that the better.

Eventually, though, they'd outstayed their welcome in the pub (the staff were dropping them big hints by cleaning up around them) and after a brief tussle over the bill (she won the argument and insisted on paying half) they found themselves in the car heading towards Picklewick.

'I've had a good time tonight,' Luca said, keeping his eyes on the road.

'Don't sound so surprised,' she shot back.

'I'm not,' he protested, then saw her grin and realised she was teasing him.

Taking pity on him, she said, 'I did, too.'

'I'm paying next time.'

'Who says there will be a next time?' She raised an eyebrow.

'Oh, but I thought—'

'Kidding.' Her voice softened as she added, 'I'd like that.'

'Me paying?'

'There being a next time. I was hoping there would be – but we're still going Dutch.'

'You're a very stubborn woman, October Rees.' He drew the car to a halt outside her house, leaving the engine running.

'Yeah, but you like it,' she retorted.

'I like *you*. What are you doing on Saturday?'

'Nothing.'

'You are now – if you want,' he added, and she heard the tone of his voice change from confident to uncertain.

'I want,' she told him.

'Good…'

She saw him hesitate as she reached for the door handle, and she wondered if he was going to kiss her, so she tilted her face, offering her cheek.

But at the last moment she changed her mind and turned her head, and his mouth met hers and suddenly they were kissing. Nothing heavy, just his lips fluttering against hers, teasing, tantalising, promising much more…

To say she was tempted was an understatement, especially when her pulse soared and a bolt of desire shot through her, but she pulled away, slightly breathless from the force of her reaction, and left it at that.

She'd not long come out of a relationship (such as it was – the relationship being all in her deluded mind, because for Zeus it had been more of an employee with benefits kind of thing) and she had no intention of rushing into a new one, no matter how much she was attracted to Luca. Or how much she enjoyed his company.

But even as she got out of the car and waved goodbye, she was already looking forward to seeing him again. She was looking forward to it a lot.

CHAPTER THREE

Although Petra was convinced that Harry's idea was a pie-in-the-sky one, it was now firmly lodged in her head and she'd been thinking about it all yesterday evening and today, too. If it wasn't for the immense financial outlay to get the conversion done, it could be the answer to the stables' money problems.

The finances weren't in dire straits, but neither were they blooming and it was a constant and daily battle to keep the bank balance in the black. To have a source of income that didn't involve a great deal of daily input from her once it was up and running, would also be very welcome. She'd have to consider change-over days and whether any interim attention (such as bed-making or bathroom cleaning) would be needed during the lets, or whether she could leave the holidaymakers to get on with it, but she could probably come to some arrangement with one of the villagers if necessary.

But she was getting ahead of herself.

The first thing she had to do was to find out how much it would cost. She suspected they'd need an architect, and they'd definitely need planning permission. But after that, a lot would depend on how much work they would be able to do themselves and how much a builder would charge. She'd seen enough property renovation programmes to know that any kind of build always went over budget and over time.

Nathan might be a good person to speak to. He had a decent head on his shoulders and wouldn't pussyfoot around. If he thought it was a daft idea, he'd tell her.

Of course, if she was serious about this, she also needed to speak to Amos at some point. He owned the stables, and the building works would involve some considerable up-front costs – although, at the moment, she had no idea where the money was going to come from, but until she could think of a plan to finance the work there was little point in discussing it with him.

Her thoughts whirling, Petra went in search of Nathan; she wanted to sound him out while the idea was still fresh in her head and before she'd had a chance to talk herself out of it.

Nathan was in the barn when she caught up with him, and she automatically checked the amount of hay and silage, to gauge whether there was enough feed to see them through the next month, or whether she needed to order any in.

'Can I pick your brains?' she asked, satisfied for the moment that she didn't need to place any orders.

'For what it's worth,' Nathan said, stretching to ease the kinks out of his back. He'd been pouring over the baler, and he had grease and oil on his hands.

'Have you fixed it yet?' she asked, hoping that he had. The baler was an essential piece of kit if they were to harvest their own hay.

'Nearly. What's up?'

Petra wrinkled her nose. 'Harry has this idea of transforming the cowshed into holiday lets. What do you think?'

She braced herself for a negative reaction but was surprised when he said, 'I think it's a grand idea.'

She pulled a face. 'I don't know if we can afford it.'

'How much will it cost, if you don't mind me asking?'

'I don't know.'

'Before you go any further, wouldn't it be a good idea to get a ballpark figure?'

He was right. She honestly didn't have a clue how much something like this would cost. Or how she'd manage to fit in supervising building works as well as everything else.

'I think we'd have to get an architect first,' she said. 'Harry thought the shed could be made into three cottages. What do you think?'

'Shall we take a wander over there?' Nathan suggested. His eyes were shining, and he looked quite enthused.

'I suppose.' Petra was both excited and terrified at the same time. It would be a fantastic thing to do and a great boost to the riding school's income once it was completed, but the thought of spending all that money made her feel quite ill. Perhaps they could do some of the work themselves?

It was an option to be considered, but she was exhausted just thinking about it, and she wondered how much longer it was going to take before she felt the benefit of having October around to help – because she was getting more and more knackered by the day.

Luca leaned back in his plush office chair and stretched out his legs, putting his hands behind his head. He should be concentrating on the needs of one of his most prestigious clients, but October was in his thoughts and he couldn't seem to dislodge her.

She wasn't anything like the women he normally dated. He couldn't remember the last time anyone had insisted they pay half the bill when he took them out. What usually happened was that his date ordered the most expensive thing on the menu and was more than happy to drink bottles of wine costing an arm and a leg.

October had drunk *water*, for goodness' sake. And she'd not picked at her food and wasted half of it – she'd eaten more than he had. And neither had she felt it necessary to explain why she was hungry, which one of his dates had once done. October had eaten heartily, had asked for the dessert menu, and had also enjoyed a full-fat cappuccino afterwards.

It made a refreshing change.

She'd also been funny and witty, and had displayed a keen intelligence. When he'd gently teased her, she'd given as good as she'd got. Better, in fact.

He'd thoroughly enjoyed the evening – especially the last part, where he'd kissed her.

He hadn't been sure she was going to let him, so he'd originally gone in for a peck on the cheek, but their lips had met and...Wow. Just wow.

He'd never felt so turned on by a simple kiss. There hadn't been any tongues or petting – just a gentle, tentative touch. But it had sent all his senses spiralling. And now she was stuck in his head and refusing to leave.

Luca smiled. He quite liked having her there, and he reached for his phone.

'What are you doing tonight?' he asked as soon as she answered.

'We've got a date on Saturday, remember? Or can't you wait?' Her voice was teasing and it sent a delicious shiver through him.

He didn't want to wait until Saturday. He wanted to see her now. This evening.

'What are you doing tonight?' he repeated.

'Nothing.'

Once again, that was unexpected; other women might have played hard to get.

'Do you fancy going ice skating?' For some reason, he didn't want to wine and dine her in a stuffy restaurant or a too-posh wine bar. He wanted to do something *fun*.

There was a pause. 'Where's the nearest rink?'

'Not sure. I believe there's one in the West Midlands.'

'It's a fair distance.'

'Do you mind? I'll throw in dinner,' he added, to sweeten the deal.

'You'd better had. After all that exercise, I expect to be fed. But it'll have to wait until Saturday. Some of us have to work.'

'What time do you finish?'

'Four.'

'Hang on.' Luca hurried over to his desk and clicked on a search engine. 'Are you still there?' he asked after a few seconds.

'I'm here.'

'It's open until eight o'clock this evening. I've just booked online. Pick you up at four-thirty? Or do you need more time to get ready?'

'Huh! Four-thirty is fine.'

'You might want to bring a change of clothes,' he advised.

'Oh? Why?'

'Because you'll have a wet backside from falling on it so often.'

'Hah! You wish. Whoever falls over the most gets to buy dinner. And it won't be me, sunshine.'

'Challenge accepted.' Luca was left with a huge grin on his face and excitement in his belly.

October stared at her phone incredulously then she glanced out of the window, wondering whether she'd imagined the message on it. The view from the tack room was dreary; lowering clouds, heavy with rain, the smudged grey of distant hills, and the lights already glowing from the farmhouse even though it was only two-thirty in the afternoon. Typical mid-winter gloom.

She looked back at her phone.

Nope, she hadn't imagined it. Zeus and Minnow had broken up. Again.

And Zeus thought she should hear it from him before she heard it from anyone else. Which was thoughtful of him. It was a pity he hadn't been as thoughtful in letting her know that he and his wife had got back together in the first place, because if he had, October wouldn't have slept with him. And if she hadn't had slept with him, Minnow wouldn't have discovered them in bed and demand that Zeus terminate October's employment. Minnow's language had been far more colourful and far less Human Resources speak, and October still shuddered at the humiliation.

But the question on her mind now was, why did Zeus feel it necessary to inform her? Unless…

Her heart missed a beat and thumped uncomfortably to catch up, as she processed the information and arrived at a disconcerting conclusion; was he telling her this because he hoped October would return to his yard? But if that was the case, why didn't he simply say so?

Although, even if he begged her, she had no intention of going back to him. He'd hurt her, and she would be extremely wary of putting herself in a position where she could be hurt again.

October's stomach churned and she pulled a face, confusion clouding her mind. She missed her life in Kent terribly. She missed the horses, the rhythm of a showjumping yard, the other grooms, and the excitement and busyness of preparing for and going to an event.

But did she miss *Zeus*?

He was a brilliant rider – Olympic gold medal standard – and his was a face everyone in the showjumping world, and many not in it, would recognise.

She wondered what he was doing, whether he was going to the qualifiers in Birmingham, or if he might be off to Germany at the end of next month. Which horses would he take? Which grooms?

Suddenly she had a yearning to be sitting in the living room in the grooms' house, drinking cheap wine and arguing over whose turn it was to wash the dishes.

And, just as suddenly, she understood it was no longer the life for her. She was getting too old for this. Although she missed the excitement and the camaraderie, she didn't miss the incredibly early starts, nor the hours spent travelling, nor having a place to call home. She'd been a groom (and a wannabe professional showjumper in her own right) for longer than she cared to remember, and it was clear now that she was never going to be snapped up by a trainer or an owner who spotted her potential and begged her to ride for them in international competitions.

The closest she would ever come to her dream, had been working for others in their quest for glory.

Was she bitter?

A little, perhaps.

But she was also realistic enough to know that although she might be a competent rider and a pretty good showjumper, she didn't have the same flair as Zeus Fernsby. Neither did she have his money. You needed both in order to make it in the world of showjumping, and now that she'd finally recognised that she had neither, it was time to reconsider her options and her future.

Going back to Zeus's yard in Kent wasn't an option, and he couldn't possibly feature in her future. Not only did she not fully trust him (he should have told her he and Minnow were taking another shot at their marriage) but she didn't feel nearly as heartsore now as she'd done when he'd sheepishly informed her that she had to leave. Looking back, although she'd been incredibly upset, she hadn't been *heartbroken*, which told her that she hadn't loved him, although she had been infatuated with him.

Had it been Zeus the man who had drawn her to him, or had it been Zeus the famous rider...? She suspected the latter, which explained why she felt reluctant to respond to his message.

Anyway, what was she supposed to say? Commiserations? Congratulations? Well done?

October didn't like Minnow and Minnow most definitely didn't like October, but Minnow and Zeus made a striking couple. They were both tall, slim and athletic, with cut-glass accents and bags of style and confidence. Zeus had the talent, Minnow had the money. He had the fame, she had the connections and knew the right people. They looked good together.

They looked like they *belonged* together.

Although October was tall (like Minnow), slender (like Minnow) and had long, dark hair (like Minnow), that was where any similarity ended, and October knew when she was outclassed and outgunned.

Not only that, she suspected that Minnow still loved Zeus, and October would never forget the pain in the woman's eyes when she'd—

Enough of that! she told herself. There was no point in dwelling on the past. What was done, was done, and it couldn't be changed. She had to put it behind her and concentrate on her future – whatever that might look like. The only thing she was certain of was that she wanted to continue to work with horses; she couldn't imagine a life without them. But as for any non-horsey aspects such as romance, she still had no idea…

She did have another date with Luca this evening, though, and as unexpected as it was, she welcomed it. It would help take her mind of Zeus, and Luca *was* rather handsome, even if he was a bit smooth.

October chuckled as she thought about how he'd come a cropper when he'd attempted to show off his jumping skills, and how he'd bowed to her superior ability. It had been sweet and rather endearing. He'd taken his humiliation on the chin, and she respected him for it. And she'd enjoyed last night. He'd been good company – funny, humble, interesting, and his attention had been unwavering.

Zeus had ended his message with "Call me" (which she had no intention of doing) but before she put Zeus out of her mind once and for all, she gave in to the temptation to check the internet. He was a famous guy and there was bound to be some info about what he'd been getting up to recently.

She'd steadfastly avoided doing so until now, but curiosity finally got the better of her (and maybe there was a bit of prodding-at-a-loose-tooth about it, too) so she scrolled and clicked until she found a story reporting that his and Minnow's reconciliation had been short-lived and had ended acrimoniously, due to him being seen on the arm of another woman.

October took a deep breath and sincerely hoped *she* wasn't the other woman the article was referring to. She might have fallen for Zeus's undoubted charm, but she'd only allowed herself to do so because she'd believed that his marriage was well and truly over. There was no way she would have wanted to be responsible for Minnow's heartache.

Oh god, there was even a photo of October and him— Hang on...*it wasn't her.*

October scrutinised it closely. It wasn't Minnow, either, although the woman in the photo had long dark hair, just like October herself.

Huh, Zeus had a type and this was it. The woman in the photo had her back to the camera and was leaning into Zeus, and from the tilt of her head October guessed she was looking up at him. Zeus had one hand on her bottom, cupping a buttock. His left hand. And his wedding ring was conspicuously absent from the third finger.

The article stated that these two had been seen together at an event which had taken place a mere ten days after October left his yard.

He hadn't wasted any time, had he?

October wondered who she could be.

It was rather telling that she felt nothing but distaste when she looked at Zeus, and pity welled up in her mind for Minnow. October and Zeus had both wronged her.

However, October's sin against Minnow had been unwitting; Zeus had no such excuse.

Feeling rather grubby about the situation, October switched her phone off and threw it on the bed. She refused to give Zeus Fernsby any more headspace. It was time she put the whole thing behind her once and for all, and stopped lamenting her misfortune. She needed to concentrate on her future – whatever it might be. And the first step along the path to a new life was her date with Luca.

It might not come to anything (in fact, it probably wouldn't) but he intrigued her and she simply knew she was going to enjoy getting to know him better.

Luca hadn't gone ice skating in years, but he'd been rather good at it once. Good enough not to make a total fool of himself on the ice and fall over every five seconds. He used to be able to go backwards and do a twirl, and he wondered if he'd remember the technique – whether it was like falling off a bike and your muscles never truly forgot and all that was needed was a gentle reminder, or whether he'd be like Bambi, all legs and comedic expression.

He also wondered how well October skated, and he had a feeling she might be pretty good at it considering the alacrity with which she'd accepted the challenge.

It was going to be fun finding out, and he took his own advice and put a spare pair of jeans on the backseat of his car, just in case he spent more time on his bottom than he anticipated. Sitting in a restaurant with wet jeans wouldn't be pleasant.

But when he saw what she was carrying as she got into the passenger seat, he groaned. 'I might have known,' he said slapping the palm of his hand against his forehead. 'You own your own skates.'

'Yep. See 'em and weep, skater-boy.' She grinned at him, and he couldn't help grinning back.

He said, 'Shall we forgo the skating part and head straight for the restaurant, because you're clearly going to win this challenge.'

'And miss seeing you fall over? Not a chance.' She leaned towards him and he caught the subtle scent of her perfume. It made his mouth go dry with desire. 'I'll let you into a secret,' she said. 'I haven't skated since I was a teen. I'm surprised these still fit. When I told my mum where I was going this afternoon, she said my ice skates were still in the attic. Even if they no longer fitted me, it was worth bringing them just to see your expression.'

'You horrid person.'

'I am, aren't I?' she replied cheerfully. 'I'll be even more horrid when I beat you, and no cheating by hanging onto my coat and making me fall over. That's a foul, and will count as a fall on your part.'

'I would never do that. I play fair and square. No cheating.'

He was true to his word, despite October being a better skater than him. It was a pleasure to watch her on the ice once she'd regained her confidence. He was rather wobbly at first, too, but gradually he rediscovered his balance and practiced a few moves, and after a couple of topples he managed to remain upright.

There was one occasion where he came perilously close to running straight over a child who'd fallen right in front of him, but October grabbed his arm and yanked him towards her and he stumbled past the kid, his arms windmilling until she dragged him into the side.

'Close call,' he said. 'Thanks.'

'I didn't want a great big lump like you landing on top of that boy. Mind you, if I wasn't winning, I might have let you fall flat on your face.'

'And risk ruining these good looks?' he teased, pointing to his face, which was probably red and sweaty from the exertion.

October reached up to stroke his cheek, and Luca's heart skipped a beat as she gazed into his eyes. 'Roughing you up a bit might be a good idea,' she murmured.

'Oh?'

'You're far too attractive for your own good.'

Luca was stumped for a reply. He wanted to come back with something witty, but all he could think of was that she thought he was attractive. Lord, he wanted to kiss her: a deep, soul-searching kiss that would rock him to his core.

Then the mood was broken as she pushed off from the side and darted away.

He watched her go, admiring her grace. That wasn't all he was admiring though, as his gaze was captured by the way her hair flowed from side to side with each long, languid glide, her slim legs, and her rounded bottom encased in jeans which were free of tell-tale damp patches because she'd not fallen over once yet.

With a whoop, he chased after her.

When he caught her he had a feeling it might be a while before he let her go.

'What about you? Are you likely to stay in Picklewick?' Luca asked, and October considered the question as she picked up a piece of fried chicken and bit into it.

'I honestly don't know. I've been a stable hand or groom all my working life. I don't know what else I can do.' Or what else she wanted to do. Horses were all she knew.

'You like working at the stables on Muddypuddle Lane, though?'

She nodded, licking her fingers. They were in one of the fast-food places adjacent to the ice-rink, because October hadn't wanted to bother with a restaurant. She knew she was easily pleased but she was hungry *now* and she didn't want to have to drive somewhere, then wait for her food. Luca had argued that as he was paying (he'd lost the bet) he should be the one to choose and he'd wanted to take her to a nice place and wine and dine her. But she'd got her own way, and now he was happily tucking into his bucket of chicken as enthusiastically as he would have tucked into a cordon-bleu meal.

'I do like it,' she said. 'Petra is lovely, but I'm not sure I can see myself working there for the rest of my life. It's meant to be a stop-gap until I sort something else out.' She wasn't sure how much she should share with him, but neither did she want him to think she was staying in Picklewick permanently. If she intended to work for another professional rider, she'd have no choice other than to leave Picklewick.

'What do you want to do?' he asked, licking his own fingers, and she tried not to focus on his mouth and the way it made her feel.

'I have no idea,' she replied, honestly. 'When I was younger, my dream was to become a famous showjumper and ride in competitions all over the world. But I'm thirty now, and I realise that's never going to happen. Don't get me wrong,' she added, in case he thought she was bitter about it. 'I've loved travelling to different places and caring for wonderful horses, but it can be hard. Stable hands often move from yard to yard, and it can be a very unsettled life. I suppose I could have bought a house and stayed in one location and in one job, but I was chasing my dream for such a long time that it took being—' She stopped, wondering if she should tell him the whole story.

'Being what?' he asked, wiping his lips with a serviette.

'Every job I've had, I was either renting a room in a house or living in the accommodation provided for the grooms. Either way, I was sharing with other staff, and barely earning enough to have my hair cut twice a year. When accommodation and utilities are provided as part of the job, the wages are often considerably less than they would otherwise be.'

'I can see how that might happen,' Luca said. 'But now you're ready for a change?'

'I want to have a place of my own someday, to get married and have kids,' she said. 'I suppose being sacked from my last job has acted as a kind of catalyst. It made me re-evaluate my life.'

'Oh, dear. What happened? You don't have to tell me if you don't want to,' he added, reaching out to briefly squeeze her hand.

She wanted to tell him though, so she took a deep breath. 'I was working for this guy called Zeus Fernsby. He was married and we had a relationship, but not until he and his wife had split up. What he'd failed to tell me, was that they had decided to make another go of it. Minnow, his wife, caught us in bed together. I lost my job and my home, so I've moved in with my mum for a while.'

'That's awful,' he said. 'But I'm glad you came to Picklewick.'

So was October. It was time she seriously thought about what she intended to do with the rest of her life, and a teeny, tiny part of her was beginning to hope Luca might feature somewhere in her future.

'What about you – do you want to do the wife and children bit one day?' she asked.

'Definitely.' He became sombre. 'I thought I was close to that once or twice, but it didn't work out. I've had a few disastrous relationships in the past. The women I've dated see the money, not me; which is daft, because although I might own my own company I'm not exactly rich.'

'False advertising,' she said, sipping the dregs of her drink through a straw.

'I'm sorry?'

'So you should be – you drive an Aston Martin, you wear expensive clothes and you take girls to posh restaurants.'

Luca glanced around. 'I don't call this posh,' he laughed.

'It's not where you planned on taking me, is it?'

He shrugged. 'I suppose not.'

'There you go, then. Women see all that and think you're rich.'

He stared into space. 'You're right. Should I ditch the car?'

'I'd ditch the women. You could always borrow Petra's old Land Rover and take your dates to a fast-food place. That would weed the gold-diggers from the ones who genuinely like you.'

'Excellent advice. On that note, what do you think of the food here, and would you consider another date? Or has eating fries and greasy chicken out of a cardboard box put you off me?'

'I think I'll give another date a try. How about a burger van, next time? Or fish and chips out of paper?' She was only half-joking – she rather liked a fish and chip supper.

'I want to kiss you.'

Oh. Okay, she was good with that. More than good, as her leaping heart indicated, and when they returned to the car and he kissed her, October had no hesitation in twining her arms around his neck and pulling him close.

Initially, when his lips found hers their kiss was soft and gentle, but when she opened her mouth to let him in, and she tasted him and felt his tongue play with hers, she uttered a moan of longing.

Deepening the kiss, he held her tight, one hand on the small of her back, the other buried in her hair, and she lost herself in the exquisite sensations washing over her. The feel of him, the taste, his scent, his soft groan as he clasped her to him – all of it made her head spin and her pulse race.

Finally she drew back, pulling away gradually, his lips following to trail kisses down the side of her neck until she shivered with longing.

'I'd better take you home,' he said, even though the night was still young.

And although she was grateful for his restraint, what she really wanted to do was to take him to bed.

Thank goodness one of them could control themselves she thought, because after that marvellous, wonderful, mind-blowing kiss, October wasn't sure she could trust herself to behave around him.

Oh, boy…

CHAPTER FOUR

'Are you sure you're happy riding Hercules?' Petra asked as October saddled the stallion under Petra's watchful eye. 'I'd take him out myself but I've got an architect coming to look at the cowshed.'

October grinned. 'I can't wait,' she said. Hercules was an ex-racehorse and could be a handful on occasion, but she'd ridden much more highly strung animals than this one.

'You will be careful with him?' Petra looked anxious and October hurried to reassure her.

'I will,' she promised. Hercules was Petra's horse, her pride and joy, and October felt honoured that Petra was trusting her with him.

He hadn't been ridden for the best part of a week, and he had shied and bucked a bit when October had placed the saddle cloth on his back and he'd realised he was going to have to work for his keep.

'Luca should be here any minute,' Petra said, and October gave her a sharp look.

'Okay…?'

'Didn't I mention that he was going for a ride this morning?' Petra's face was a picture of false innocence, and October bristled.

'It's not that I don't think you can handle Hercules,' Petra continued, swiftly. 'I thought you might like some company, and as he was already taking Midnight for a hack, I thought the two of you could go out together. It's always more fun when you have company.'

October shook her head in disbelief. 'You're

matchmaking,' she accused. She knew full well that Petra liked nothing more than being out on the moors on her own, just her and her horse.

'I think the matchmaking has already been done, don't you?' Petra replied with a knowing smirk.

October felt her cheeks grow warm, and she bent her head to check the girth in order to hide her face. She and Luca's relationship wasn't a secret, but it was so new, she wasn't entirely sure it actually *was* a relationship. What they had was a couple of dates and a toe-curling scintillating kiss.

Oh, that kiss…

'Speak of the devil,' Petra said, and October looked around to see Luca leading Midnight into the barn.

The horses whickered a greeting. Petra beamed.

October and Luca shot each other shy smiles, and October wondered whether Luca was thinking about the other night. She certainly was. She hadn't been able to get him out of her mind. They had another date arranged for this Saturday, but she hadn't expected to see him midweek even though she knew that he popped up to the stables regularly to check on his horse, so this was an unexpected and very welcome pleasure.

'I'll leave you to it,' Petra said, sauntering out of the barn.

'She seems rather pleased with herself,' Luca observed.

'We've been set up.' October placed her foot in the stirrup and swung herself onto Hercules's back.

A look of confusion spread across his face. 'Did we *need* setting up? I thought we were… um…?'

'Are we?' October wasn't sure, either.

'Going steady, you mean?'

'Er, yeah…'

'I thought we were. I know nothing's been said, but…'

October bit back a smile. Neither of them was capable of completing a sentence, it seemed. 'I assumed…' she said.

'So did I.'

'That we are? Or we aren't?' October wanted to know.

'Would you like to? I mean please don't feel obliged. I've kind of put you on the spot. Sorry.' Luca wore an anxious expression.

'Don't be – I'm not. And yes, I would like to "go steady".'

'That's fantastic! I could kiss you.' He gave her a big grin.

'Later,' she said.

'Is that a promise?'

'It is.' She nodded, catching hold of her bottom lip with her teeth, a shiver of excitement surging over her.

The desire in his eyes made her tummy lurch and she looked away, certain that her own rising passion was written all over her face.

Goodness, all they'd done was banter and she was already shaken and unbalanced.

As if sensing her mood, Hercules pawed the ground and snorted. She pulled his head up and he arched his neck and pranced to the side.

'I think he's eager to get going,' October said.

Luca seemed to blink and shake himself, and she wondered what he'd been thinking, and whether it was as wicked as her own thoughts. As far as she was concerned later couldn't come soon enough.

When Petra had informed him that Hercules needed to be exercised and that she was going to ask October to take him out, Luca had wondered how it concerned him. But on being told that Hercules could be a loose cannon and that Petra would feel happier if October had someone with her, Luca didn't hesitate in offering to go on a hack with her.

It was only when he arrived at the stables that he understood October hadn't needed anyone to accompany her after all.

He should have realised – October was an exceptionally competent rider, better than Petra, and she would have been perfectly fine hacking alone, which Petra already knew.

October was right, they *had* been set up.

Petra didn't realise that they'd already been on two dates and had another lined up for the weekend. Luca wasn't complaining about seeing October today, though; he was positively delighted and he couldn't stop grinning.

She looked delectable, all muffled up in a scarf, thick coat and gloves. She even wore a pair of earmuffs over the top of her helmet and he had a sudden urge to lift one of the fluffy pads and nibble the exposed ear.

Hastily, he cleared his throat and mounted Midnight. It wouldn't do to be having such delicious thoughts when they were about to venture onto the wild and windy moors. It was January and freezing, so there was a fair chance his ardour would be dampened long before they returned to the stables.

It was certainly fresh outside, he decided, as the pair of them made their way along the track next to the fields leading onto the hills above the stables. But there were already hints of spring, and he ducked as dangling catkins from several overhanging branches tickled his cheek. Tiny buds could be seen on an old oak tree, waiting to unfurl, and although the ground beneath was mostly bare, Luca noticed vibrant green shoots poking their heads through the soil.

He also became aware of birdsong; the cheeps and chirps of sparrows in the hedgerow, the trilling voice of a blackbird high in a tree, and there was the unmistakable silhouette of a bird of prey overhead. The land was coming back to life, slowly and surely, and before long spring would be here. The knowledge made his heart sing.

He found he was looking forward to riding with October when the weather was warmer. Maybe they could bring a picnic and a blanket? They could tether the horses, and lay the blanket down in a grassy, secluded spot—

Flippin' heck, he was getting ahead of himself, wasn't he? They'd only just agreed they were a couple and he was already planning trysts in the open air – which made him realise that he was hoping their relationship would continue to grow.

He couldn't wait to kiss her again.

'October? Can we get off for a minute?'

October was ahead of him as the horses were walking in single file, and she glanced over her shoulder, a look of concern on her face. 'Sure. Is anything wrong?'

Luca reined Midnight in and slid off his back. He waited for her to dismount, then said, 'Come here and loop the reins over that gate.' His voice was husky and his heart was thumping. He tethered his own horse and waited, his mouth dry, his pulse racing.

She came towards him, her attention on Midnight. 'Is he okay?'

'He's fine.'

'Are you—? *Ohhh.*' She let out her breath in a soft sigh as he caught her around the waist, pulled her to him, and covered her mouth with his.

Her lips were cold and she tasted of fresh air and the lip salve she wore. He could smell apples in her hair, and coconut and vanilla on her skin, and she felt firm yet soft against his chest as she kissed him back with passion.

It was October who withdrew first – Luca could have carried on kissing her all day.

'As lovely as this is,' she said, 'those horses aren't getting much exercise. And it's cold!'

'I can keep you warm,' he said, raising his eyebrows suggestively, and she batted him on the arm.

'I bet you could. Behave yourself.'

'Spoilsport.'

'That's me. Now, get back on your horse. Race you to the top?' She gestured towards the track. It had widened and levelled off somewhat, but there was a gradual gradient rising to the top of the moor.

Without waiting for a reply, she wriggled free of him and dashed towards Hercules. Startled, the horse jerked his head up, and was already prancing in anticipation as October leapt onto his back. She turned him to face the right way and then she was off, leaving Luca staring after her and shaking his head in disbelief.

Realising he was being left behind, he followed, urging Midnight into a canter. 'Not fair,' he shouted. 'He's a damned racehorse.'

'*Ex* racehorse,' she called back, and her laughter floated in the air.

Whooping, he raced after her, his own laughter bubbling up. When he caught her he'd kiss her so thoroughly she'd be begging for mercy. *If* he caught her…

Damn, she was good!

But when he did eventually catch her (he rather suspected she had let him) neither of them felt the cold for quite some time.

'I'll be in touch as soon as I have some outline plans drawn up,' Isaac Richards said, shaking Petra's hand. 'If you're happy with them, I'll leave a copy with you to use as a basic guide for builders to give you a quote. After that, if you decide you definitely want to go ahead with the build, let me know and I'll draw up more detailed ones for you to submit to the planning department for approval.'

Petra blew out a breath, her cheeks ballooning. 'It's complicated, isn't it?'

'Yes, but I'll guide you through it.'

She saw him back to his car and as he drove off down the lane, she sighed. Even the outline plans were costing money she didn't have, but there was no point in doing this half-heartedly. And for her to have a more accurate picture of how much it was going to cost, she needed to obtain several quotes for the build, and even then Isaac had advised her that she'd need to set aside a contingency fund of twenty per cent on top.

Petra returned to the office and the copious notes she'd made, and she was busy filing them away, her mind full of partition walls and skylight windows, when the phone rang.

'Do you have a woman by the name of October Rees working for you?' The voice on the other end was female and had an accent that would put the royal family to shame.

Petra wasn't impressed. 'What's it to you?'

'Do you, or don't you?'

'As I said, what's it to you?'

Petra wasn't in the mood for this, although she was glad to have an excuse to think about something other than the blasted cowshed, because all this conversion stuff was giving her a headache. Crossly, she rubbed her eyes.

'My name is Minnow Fernsby. I assume you've heard of my husband.'

'If he's Zeus Fernsby, I've already spoken to him.' Was this woman calling about October's reference? If so, she was wasting her time – Zeus Fernsby had provided one.

'So she *does* work for you,' the woman cried. 'Because there couldn't possibly be any other reason for my husband to speak to *you*. He gave her a reference, didn't he?'

Petra didn't say anything.

Minnow took Petra's silence for confirmation, and continued, 'Did he tell you he had to *let her go*—' Minnow emphasised the words '—because she seduced him? That's right, she *seduced* my husband. She's untrustworthy and duplicitous. What I mean by that is, she's deceitful and treacherous.'

'I know what duplicitous means,' Petra said through gritted teeth. Just who did this woman think she was? 'And I don't care.'

'You will when she leaves you in the lurch.'

'What do you mean?'

'She's not going to hang around in a little riding school for kiddies, is she? Not now.'

'What. Do. You. Mean?' Petra was a hair's breadth from hanging up on Minnow Fernsby, and she would have done so if she hadn't needed to know whether October was actually about to hand in her notice. Petra didn't think she could face going through the rigmarole of advertising and interviewing again.

'She's been seen with him,' Minnow spat.

'Who?'

'My *husband*, who do you think? He told me he'd ended it, that he'd sacked her, but it's all over the internet. So you can tell her from me, she's welcome to him.' The woman let out a sob, and even though she was possibly the most annoying person Petra had come across since a delightful parent by the name of Cher had told her how to run the stables and had then set her sights on Harry, Petra felt sorry for her.

'She can have him,' Minnow continued. 'Much good it will do her. Let's see how the pair of them like living on fresh air. And you can tell her that from me, too.'

And with that she abruptly ended the call, leaving Petra wondering whether she should expect a letter of resignation from October, and if so how the hell was she going to manage.

Working at the stables on Muddypuddle Lane was turning out to be much more fun than October would ever have imagined. For one thing, she'd discovered that she enjoyed teaching kids how to ride, and she was happy to split her working day in order to take a class or two in the evening. It meant coming in early to muck out and do any other jobs, then go back home, only to have to return later; but she didn't mind. And for another, she wouldn't have met Luca if it wasn't for this job.

It was quite telling that Zeus had never made her feel quite as giddy as Luca was making her feel. Admittedly, she'd had her head turned by him, but he hadn't had the effect on her that Luca was having, like a hormone-driven teenager with a major crush.

October was singing *I Will Survive* to herself under her breath and making up the buckets of grain ready for this evening, when Petra appeared in the doorway of the feed store.

'Can I have a word?' she asked, and October immediately stopped what she was doing.

'Of course.' She wiped her hands on the backside of her breeches and looked at Petra expectantly, hoping she hadn't done anything wrong.

Petra leaned against the doorjamb and folded her arms. 'I've just had a woman by the name of Minnow Fernsby on the phone,' she began.

October's good mood abruptly fled.

'What did she want?' She could kind of guess… Had she phoned to warn Petra not to leave any stray husbands lying around? To tell her new employer that she was a homewrecker? October felt sorry for Minnow, but if the woman wanted to lay any blame for the breakup of her marriage, it should be at her husband's door.

'To tell me you were going to leave me in the lurch,' Petra stated.

'Excuse me? Why on earth would she think that?'

'Because she claimed that you and her husband are

back together. Is it true?'

'It most definitely is not! I can't think where she's got that idea from—' October froze. Oh, yes, she could. 'Hang on.' She fished her phone out of the pocket of her breeches. 'Here,' she said, after a moment, turning it around so Petra could see the screen.

Petra squinted at it. 'Is that you?'

'No. The photo was taken ten days after I left his yard; it couldn't be me because I was here in Picklewick having an interview with you.'

'He likes women with long dark hair, does he?' Petra said.

'He most certainly does. His wife has got long hair too, but hers has some grey in it now. I get the feeling he's trying to trade her in for a younger model.'

'That old cliché?'

October nodded. 'I feel rather sorry for her. She can be quite obnoxious, but she doesn't deserve to be treated like that. She should kick him into touch.'

Petra smirked. 'I think that's what she intends to do. She mentioned something about him living on fresh air?'

Good for her, October thought. Zeus deserved what was coming to him. She was well out of it, and hopefully that was the last she'd hear from Zeus or Minnow. She had a new life here, and it mightn't be the one she thought she'd be living when she first started her riding career, but she was surprised to discover she was happier now than she'd been for some considerable time.

Harry kissed Petra on the top of her head and sat down to supper. Goodie, sausage, mashed potatoes, and rich onion gravy; he was ravenous. Being outside all day in the cold did that to him, despite the heat his portable forge kicked out.

'I met with an architect today,' Petra said, poking a fork at the sausages on her plate.

'I wondered who you were holed up in the office with,' Amos said. 'Are we going ahead with it?' He pushed the dish of mash across the table. Petra ignored it.

'I doubt it. I didn't realise how many rules and regulations there are when it comes to converting an old building, and the cowshed isn't even a listed one. And the health and safety stuff alone is enough to make me cry.'

'That's the responsibility of the builder, isn't it? Speaking of builders, have you asked anyone to give us a quote yet?' Amos tucked into his food with enthusiasm.

'Not yet. Isaac – that's the architect – said he'd draw up some plans so the builder could give us a more accurate quote.'

Around a mouthful of food Harry said, 'I thought you were going to get a ballpark figure first?'

'I was, but when I looked into it, I realised we need to know what we can and can't do with the shed first. There's no point in asking for a quote for three cottages if the configuration and the available space means we can only have two.' She sighed deeply.

As he listened to Petra speak, Harry smiled fondly; she was already sounding as though she knew what she was talking about, which was impressive considering she hated admin and paperwork with a passion.

'Do you want me to step in?' he offered. 'I don't mind meeting architects and dealing with builders.'

She shook her head. 'Thanks, Harry, but this is down to me and Amos.'

He heard the subtle hint that although he lived at the stables the business wasn't his responsibility. Which was fair enough – he had no financial interest or say in the stables, and he fully understood that if any decisions were to be made, Amos and Petra had to make them. Actually, it was *Amos's* decision, because he was the one who owned the stables and he would be the one who would have to raise the funds needed.

Harry wished he could do something to help. Coming up with ideas was all well and good, but from where he was sitting he seemed to have added to Petra's burden, not lightened it.

She looked as though she had the weight of the world on her shoulders. If only he could help out more…

Suddenly he knew what he could do, and once the idea lodged in his mind, he instinctively knew how right it was, how perfect.

Harry was going to ask Petra to marry him.

CHAPTER FIVE

Petra inhaled deeply and squared her shoulders. She could do this. It was only for an hour – more like an hour and a half in reality by the time she'd chatted to those parents to didn't seem to have homes to go to. Nathan, bless him, had saddled up all the ponies that would be needed for this evening's lesson and they were waiting patiently in the arena for their riders to arrive.

Thankfully this was an intermediate class, and the pupils would be concentrating on the finer controls of horse handling, such as asking their mount to lead on alternate legs and getting them to back up nicely and without fuss.

She didn't think she could face an energetic lesson over jumps, or one where they played games. Petra was so tired she didn't know what to do with herself. Neither did it help that she felt bloated and completely out of sorts. And her jodhpurs were too tight because Amos had managed to shrink them in the wash. God knows what cycle he was using on that blasted washing machine. She was tempted to do her own laundry, but she knew her uncle would be hurt if she suggested it. Since the onset of his angina, the arrangement was that he took care of the paperwork and all the household chores, whilst she concentrated on running the stables. It usually worked well, but not when it came to a new washing machine and her clothes. He'd even managed to shrink her bras, because every single one felt uncomfortable, as though she was spilling out of them.

At least, that was what she told herself – she didn't

want to acknowledge that the apparent shrinking of various garments was probably more to do with the fact she was eating like a horse lately, so had put on weight.

It was because of the cold weather, she told herself as she bent over awkwardly to stuff her feet into her Wellington boots. It always made her hungry, and what with being outdoors so much she was bound to burn more calories at this time of year, therefore it was only to be expected that she ate more to compensate.

One by one her students arrived, and the next few minutes were a flurry of saying hello to everyone, asking how they'd been, listening to tales of what the kids had got up to in the week since she'd seen them last.

Finally they'd all arrived and were mounted up, and she could get on with the lesson. She usually enjoyed teaching, but lately it had become more of a chore and she would be glad when the time came for the little darlings to go home. Not only was she shattered, but she didn't have much patience. They were all so loud and boisterous, and she didn't know how their parents put up with them. Which was one of the reasons why today's lesson featured the basics of dressage – it took concentration and therefore would hopefully keep them quiet.

Trying to remain focused (it would be so unfair on her young riders for her not to give them her best), Petra studied her pupils, providing each one with feedback and encouragement. One girl, Heidi Walker, had reached the limit with this class. She needed to move to the next one where she'd be challenged more, and Petra made a mental note to remember to ask her to stay behind after the lesson so she could have a chat with the girl's mum. Heidi had the talent, the enthusiasm and the dedication to make a competent rider, and Petra wanted to encourage that.

'Can I have a quick word?' Petra said to Heidi's mum, Rose, when the lesson finally drew to a close.

Petra was supervising the dismounting process, encouraging her charges to shorten stirrup straps and loosen girths so she didn't have to, under the guise of trying to teach them some basic horse care, whilst being relieved that it was one less job she had to do herself.

A frown creased Rose's forehead, and Petra hastened to add, 'It's nothing to worry about. I just wanted to chat about Heidi's progress.' Mindful that the child's mum mightn't want Heidi to move up a class (it was on a different day and at a different time, so it might not be convenient) Petra said to Heidi, 'Do you think you could take your pony and May's to their stables? You're sensible enough and Nathan is there to give you a hand if you need it. Is that okay with you, Rose?'

Thank goodness Nathan had agreed to stay on for a while – Petra would have had to have spent at least another hour bedding the ponies down for the night if she'd had to do it all by herself. She'd debated whether to ask October, but she had a hunch her new employee may have had plans with Luca.

Rose followed Petra into the office and Petra slumped against the desk, gesturing for her to sit down.

'I see congratulations are in order,' Petra said, nodding to the woman's gently swelling stomach. She hadn't realised Rose was pregnant until just now.

Rose smiled and rubbed her belly. 'It was a bit unexpected,' she said. 'Neither Jason nor I had talked about having more children, but once we'd got over the shock, we're both delighted.'

Petra thought about the family's dynamics – they were each a single parent with a daughter, and both had custody of their child. Rose and Jason had met at the stables, and Petra had watched their romance unfold over the course of the previous summer.

'How does Heidi and May feel about the new baby?' Petra asked, wondering if she needed to keep a weather eye on any potential behaviour issues in class.

'They're thrilled. They want a brother, but I've told them they don't get to choose.' She paused for a moment, then said, 'It's going to be a pain bringing a baby along to the riding lessons, but I want to try to keep things as normal as possible so the girls don't feel pushed out.'

Petra was about to say that the reason she'd asked for a chat was to discuss Heidi's lessons when Rose said, 'You'll have to start a creche. Or is Amos going to look after your little one when it arrives?'

'Excuse me?'

'I'm sorry, I didn't mean to speak out of turn. You're starting to show, so I thought…' Rose trailed off, and colour flooded her cheeks. 'Oh, dear.'

'I'm not pregnant,' Petra said.

Rose bit her lip. 'I'm sorry,' she repeated. She was clearly mortified.

'We've got a new washing machine and I've been eating like a horse, and…' It was Petra's turn to grind to a halt, as what Rose said took root. 'You don't think…?'

She glanced down at her tummy in shock. Surely it was only protruding a bit because she was slouched against the desk and was hunched over slightly?

'Oh, shoot.' Petra closed her eyes, her heart dropping to her wellies. She couldn't be. *Could she?*

Conscious that she wasn't alone in the office, Petra opened them again to see Rose's concerned and knowing gaze fixed firmly on her.

Abruptly everything made sense: her dreadful exhaustion, her increased appetite, her sore boobs, the way her clothes were too snug, the fact that she hadn't had a period in god knows how long. How could she have failed to notice?

'Didn't you realise?' Rose asked gently, and Petra shook her head.

She felt like crying. How could this have happened? She pulled a face – she knew *how*, obviously, but… Damn. She wasn't ready for this. Babies weren't on her agenda. They never had been. She wasn't the motherly type. Harry had never mentioned it; the subject hadn't come up. She'd just assumed that after being both mother and father to Timothy for so many years since the brothers lost their mum and dad in an accident when Timothy was eleven, Harry would have had enough of parenting.

Petra briefly closed her eyes again. Harry…she'd have to tell him.

Dear Lord, what was she going to do? How would they manage? The riding school was barely hanging on by its fingernails without *this*.

She was scarcely aware of Rose leaving, and when she did notice she was tempted to run after her and beg her not to mention anything to anyone. Because it mightn't be true. Petra prayed it wasn't. She didn't want a baby. And neither did Harry.

But what if it was?

She'd only just found Harry. Their love was not even a year old. How would he take it? Would he still want her once she told him her news?

The thought that he might not sent fingers of ice clutching at her heart.

'Petra? Amos?' Harry almost fell through the front door in his haste to get out of the wind and the rain. 'Anyone home?'

'I'm in the kitchen,' Amos shouted, so that was where Harry headed.

'Is Petra around?' he asked, relishing the warmth as he entered the room.

'She's in the arena – got a class.'

'What time does the lesson finish?'

Amos glanced at the clock on the mantelpiece. One of the things Harry loved about the former farmhouse was the open fireplaces in all the downstairs rooms. The one in the kitchen wasn't lit very often because the Aga kicked out so much heat, but today a fire smouldered and two dogs and a cat were sprawled on the rug in front of it.

'Any minute now, I think. How about you? Are you done for the day?' Amos asked.

'Yes, thank goodness. It's freezing out there. Farmyards and stables are the coldest, draftiest places on the planet.'

Patch, Nathan's little Jack Russell terrier, lifted his head before flopping back down again, and Queenie, Petra's spaniel, wagged her tail but otherwise didn't move. The cat ignored him. He walked over to the fire, careful not to step on any paws or tails, and crouched down, holding out his hands to the flames.

Harry stayed there for a moment, gathering his courage. He wanted to ask Amos a question but it could only be asked when Petra wasn't in earshot, so right now was the ideal time as long as he was quick. He didn't want to risk her coming in at the wrong moment.

However, Harry was fretting that Amos would think it was too soon for such a big step, or that the old fella wouldn't want him for a son-in-law. Not that Petra was Amos's daughter – she was his niece – but to Harry she felt more Amos's child than her real father did. He'd only met her dad once and it had been an awkward affair; the two men hadn't connected and had found little in common.

So if he intended to ask anyone's permission to marry Petra, he was going to ask Amos.

'Er, can I ask you something?' he said. 'It's important.'

'Ask away,' Amos replied. He was rolling out pastry for an apple tart, the contents of which were in a bowl, cooling.

Harry straightened up and turned to face him. The question was far too momentous to be asked in a crouching position. He took a deep breath, held it for a second, then let it out slowly.

'I'd like to ask for Petra's hand in marriage,' he said. He knew it was an old-fashioned thing to do, but he wanted to

69

do things properly. Petra deserved it.

Amos's back stiffened. He stopped what he was doing, put the rolling pin on the counter and turned around.

Harry felt a degree of relief that at least Amos wasn't about to brain him with it. Crikey, he was more nervous about this than he had been when Petra had asked Amos if he'd minded Harry moving in. Petra might run the stables, but it was Amos who owned it, and he had the ultimate say in who lived in his house.

Amos narrowed his eyes and studied him, saying nothing. He might have an air of a friendly Captain Birdseye about him with his weather-beaten face, crinkly eyes and almost white beard, but he was no pushover and Harry wondered what he was thinking.

Slowly Amos nodded. 'Yes, on one condition.'

Anything, Harry thought. If Amos wanted him to sign a prenup, he'd willingly do so.

'I'd like Petra to wear my wife's engagement ring. It's Petra's by rights and I know her aunt would have wanted her to have it.'

Harry almost sagged with relief. 'It will be an honour, and I know Petra will feel the same.' He was touched that the elderly gent felt so strongly about it. It must hold great sentimental value, and instinctively Harry knew it was the right thing to do.

'Wait there, I'll fetch it,' Amos said, swilling his hands under the tap and wiping them on a towel. He walked to the door and was nearly through it, when he hesitated. 'Welcome to the family, son. I know the pair of you will be very happy. You're made for each other.'

Harry believed so, too. He just hoped Petra felt the same way, because Harry was far from certain she'd say yes when he popped the question.

October wasn't the best cook in the world, and for some reason she hadn't expected Luca to be either. So when he'd casually mentioned he liked cooking, she'd suggested that instead of going out for a meal, he might like to make her something.

She hadn't missed the hunger in his eyes when he'd agreed, and she was well aware that food might not be the only thing on the menu this evening.

The thought made her go weak at the knees. Whenever she was with him, her pulse soared and her stomach knotted, and all she wanted to do was to kiss him and be held by him.

She'd had her fair share of boyfriends and she wasn't inexperienced when it came to the bedroom, but October could honestly say she'd never felt like this about any man. Not only did he make her feel faint from pure lust, but she also couldn't stop thinking about him, and although she wasn't in love with him yet, it was only a matter of time before she was head over heels.

The wonderful thing was, he seemed to feel the same way about her.

Therefore she could guess what he was hoping for this evening, but she also knew him well enough by now to realise that he wouldn't push her to go to bed with him, that he'd leave it to her to tell him when she was ready.

Oh, boy, was she ready!

She hadn't been able to think of anything else all day, so by the time she arrived on his doorstep, she was all a-fizz with anticipation.

'Nice place,' she said nonchalantly when Luca opened the door.

'It'll do,' he replied, just as casually, but when his eyes bored into hers she wasn't fooled. He was nervous, and the realisation excited her even more. It was also rather endearing, and she smiled to think he wasn't as cocky and as confident as he appeared. Mind you, she already knew that, because if he had been they would never have had a second date.

'What are we having?' she asked as he led her through the depths of his large house and into the kitchen. 'Wow! It's huge.'

October gazed around the open-plan room in amazement. The island in front of a row of cabinets was bigger than a tennis court (only a slight exaggeration, she felt), and the kitchen area merged into a dining space that could seat a football team, and then into a squashy sofa area with plate glass doors leading onto a terrace. If the house had been impressive from the outside, it was stunning inside.

'Is all this just for you?' she asked.

He nodded, ducking his head, but not before she'd glimpsed embarrassment on his face. 'This is my forever home,' he said. 'I'd like to raise a family here.'

'How many kids were you planning on having?' she cried, circling the huge table, and running her hand across its polished surface. 'I like the décor, by the way.'

'Thanks.'

'Did you get someone in to do it?' It wasn't terribly subtle of her, but she wanted to know if another woman had had a hand in it, and a prickle of jealousy niggled at her.

'All my own work,' he said.

'I can't see you trailing around kitchen showrooms,' she laughed, the green-eyed monster subsiding.

'Ah, but I did. I found it quite therapeutic.'

'That's not what my mum said, when she was looking for a new kitchen. This is lovely, by the way.'

'I'm glad you like it. And in answer to your question, we're having enchiladas.'

'Great! I'm starving.'

'Would you like a drink while I finish up here? If you want a glass of wine, I'll happily drive you home, then pick you up in the morning to fetch your car.'

'Are you trying to get me drunk so you can have your wicked way with me?'

'I wouldn't dare,' Luca replied, and he looked as though he meant it.

'Pity…'

His eyebrows shot up and he stared at her.

'I'll have a glass of wine,' she said,' but there's no need to drive me home.'

'Isn't there?'

Abruptly the air was super-charged and she found it difficult to breathe as a frisson of excitement made her shiver.

'No…' Her reply was slow, languid even, and she watched his eyes darken as her meaning became clear.

'Are you sure?'

It was sweet of him to ask. 'Totally.'

He cleared his throat but despite that his voice was rough and husky when he said, 'I'll fetch the wine.'

'Take me to bed first.' she said, and in two strides he was standing in front of her and scooping her up as though she weighed nothing.

'My pleasure,' he said.

But, as it turned out, the pleasure was as much hers as his. More so perhaps…

'Do you want that wine now?' Luca asked, easing his arm out from underneath her, and propping himself up on an elbow.

'I am rather thirsty after all that exercise,' October said, her tone teasing. 'Hungry, too.'

'Mmm, so am I.' Luca nibbled at that delectable spot where her neck and collarbone met. He'd quickly discovered the secret to driving her wild. One of them…

'Stop it,' she squealed, pushing him away. 'Let's eat, we've got all night.'

'In case you hadn't noticed, half the night has gone already.'

'Really?' October sat up and looked at the clock. 'So it has. It's amazing how time flies when you're enjoying yourself.'

Luca smirked. 'Glad to hear you had a good time.'

'I think you did, too.'

'Hell, yeah,' he breathed. He'd most definitely had a good time. The pair of them had fitted together perfectly, no awkwardness, no embarrassing moments – just pure harmony. And a deep connection. He'd had fantastic sex before, but it had always been on a physical level. Making love with October had touched his soul. And his heart.

He was falling for her hard, and whilst he was excited and thrilled, he was also scared – he'd never felt like this before and it was terrifying.

CHAPTER SIX

October risked another look at Petra out of the corner of her eye and wondered what was wrong. Petra, like Nathan, could be rather quiet, but this morning she was positively morose. The two of them were in the office, October giving the helmets a clean with disinfectant wipes and Petra leaning against the desk, staring into space

Was she unwell? She might be, because she kept rubbing her stomach. Maybe Petra had eaten something that didn't agree with her, or maybe her period had arrived and she had cramps?

No, that wasn't it. Petra didn't appear to be in pain. She appeared to be thoughtful, introspective—

October let out a gasp.

Petra was pregnant! October could definitely see a small bump, at odds with the woman's slim frame.

'Did you say something?' Petra asked.

'Please don't take this the wrong way, but are you pregnant?' October asked.

Petra snapped into focus and the glare she gave her made October wish she hadn't opened her mouth. 'What makes you say that?'

'Erm…nothing.' Oops, she'd gone and put her foot in it.

'I want to know.'

'You're…er…I thought you might be showing a bit.'

'Bugger.'

'You *are* pregnant? Congratulations! That's wonderful.'

'No, it's not.'

'Ah, I see.' October cast around for something to say. 'How far along are you?'

'I'm not sure.'

'Okay. They should be able to tell you when you have a scan.'

Petra pulled a face. 'What scan?'

'You usually have one at twelve weeks.' October saw Petra's expression. 'Your doctor should have explained it.'

'I haven't been to the doctor. I haven't even taken a test.' She swallowed and shook her head. 'I only realised yesterday that I might be pregnant.'

'Crumbs, you really do need to do a test,' October urged. 'If you don't mind me asking, when was your last period?'

'The middle of October. Ish. I can't honestly remember.'

'Okay…' October didn't know what to say to that; she religiously kept track of hers, especially when she had a boyfriend. Like now…

As if reading her mind, Petra said, 'I never needed to keep a record of them, they just happened.' She screwed up her face. 'I can't believe I didn't notice that I haven't had one since before Halloween. I've been so stupid.' She put her hands over her face and October's heart went out to her.

'I didn't think about it,' Petra continued, her voice muffled. 'It's been so busy, what with Harry moving in, and Faith selling Midnight, and all the extra work that caused. Then there was Christmas, and the horse rustling incident…' Petra straightened up, turned sideways and pulled her fleece taut across her midriff. There was a small, rounded bump below her belly button. 'I can't be more than twelve weeks, but I don't know how you work it out.'

'Um, I think you calculate it from the first day of your last period,' October said. One of the grooms had found out she was pregnant last year and had shared all the details.

'Wait a minute.' Petra sat down at the desk and flipped through the diary, her mouth a thin line. 'There, that's when it was!' She jabbed a finger at the page. 'I remember because the kids were about to break up for half term and I was sorting out activities for the following week. Bloody hell, that means I'm possibly fifteen weeks pregnant. How can that be?'

'You need to do a test.' That would be the first thing October would do, if she found herself in the same situation. 'Then if you definitely are pregnant, you should make an appointment with your doctor.'

Petra screwed up her eyes. 'I know. I'll buy one later. I was awake most of last night worrying about it. What if I'm not pregnant and it's something else?'

'Like what?'

Petra stared at her, her face bleak.

October shook her head. 'Now you're being daft.' She wanted to give her a hug, but she didn't dare. Her boss didn't come across as a hugging type. 'You're pregnant,' she stated firmly. 'And the sooner you do a test and put your mind at rest the better.'

Petra didn't look convinced, and October got the distinct impression that she wasn't thrilled about her impending motherhood.

'Keep this to yourself, eh? Please?' Petra asked.

'Of course I will. You can trust me not to say anything,' October promised.

Picklewick's high street was usually busy, and today was no exception. After the conversation with October, Petra decided to strike while the iron was hot and pop into the village to buy a test, but when she saw the number of people waiting to be served in the chemist, she bottled it.

Besides, the staff there knew her. Ditto the tiny supermarket. Petra didn't want to risk being seen, or risk someone idly mentioning to Amos that they'd seen her browsing the aisles for a pregnancy test. If she *was* pregnant, it was only right that Harry should be the first to know. Besides, she wanted to break the news to Amos herself.

She felt sick when she thought of telling them. Maybe if she knew how Harry would react, she could at least brace herself. Amos, she was sure, would be very disappointed in her.

The nearest big supermarket was nine miles away, but at least her anonymity would be guaranteed. There would only be a small chance of her bumping into anyone she knew; she could put twenty tests in her basket and no one would bat an eyelid.

Even so, Petra parked the car at the furthest end of the car park and slunk inside. She grabbed a basket, and on her way to the correct aisle she threw a couple of things into it because she didn't want anyone to think she'd come in for the sole purpose of buying a pregnancy test.

Feeling very self-conscious and a little ridiculous, Petra found the shelf she was looking for and hastily glanced around to check that no one was watching.

No one was, so she moved closer and studied the various boxes.

Flippin' heck, who knew there would be so many to choose from? Did they all do different things? Were the more expensive ones more reliable than the cheaper ones?

Not wanting to ask, Petra grabbed a couple of mid-range ones and dropped them on top of the packet of salad leaves and the half a quiche she'd already put in there, and hurried to the checkout, wondering why on earth she'd shoved the quiche in. She didn't even particularly *like* quiche. Not daring to put it back in the chiller she'd got it from, she joined the queue at the self-service checkout and waited impatiently for a free till.

'Hiya, fancy seeing you here.'

Petra jumped guiltily as she recognised the voice, and her heart plummeted.

Cher Reynolds, who had made a play for Harry when he'd first moved to Picklewick, was standing behind her in the queue.

Petra rolled her eyes – that was just what she needed. *Not.*

Feeling scruffy in her jodhpurs and old riding boots, Petra tried not to look at Cher's glossy shoulder-length hair, long nails, expertly made-up face and immaculately trendy clothes.

Then she realised Cher was examining her basket and Petra hurriedly pulled the bag of salad leaves over the top of the pregnancy tests. Hopefully the damned woman hadn't seen them.

'How are you keeping?' Cher asked, her eyes still on the contents of Petra's basket.

'Great. You?'

'Thalia is doing brilliantly at her new stables. They're simply wonderful with her.'

'Good, glad to hear it.'

'How's business?'

'Fine.' Just at that moment a till became free and with a tight smile, Petra scurried over to it.

'Bye,' Cher called after her, but Petra ignored her. She'd never liked the woman and didn't see the point in making small talk with her. Hopefully another six months would pass before she would set eyes on her again.

All thoughts of Cher were cast out of Petra's mind as she drove home, and were replaced by a steady worry about what the two boxes in her bag would tell her.

She'd do both the tests, just in case. Perhaps she should have bought another one, then she could have had the best out of three, but even as she was thinking it, she knew a false result was unlikely. Both tests would either be positive or negative.

Please be negative, she prayed sometime later in the privacy of the bathroom, after peeing on both of the plastic sticks. But deep down she knew they wouldn't be, and when a second line appeared in the little window, her fears were confirmed.

Petra was unquestionably pregnant.

Harry, I'm pregnant. No, that was too blunt. Petra gathered up the evidence, and as she went outside to pop it in the wheelie bin, she tried another approach.

Harry, you're going to be a father.

Maybe she should start with that? She might finish with it too, if Harry walked out in shock and refused to speak to her again.

That was the issue – Petra was terrified it would spoil things between them. It was going to change everything, regardless of whether he was happy about it or not. Nothing would be the same again, and she didn't think she was ready for that.

She'd tell him tomorrow; which would allow her to indulge in one more afternoon and evening of normality, one more day of his love, because once he knew there was no going back.

There was no hurry to tell him just yet. One more day wouldn't hurt, and it would give her a chance to work out how she was going to cope. She was barely holding things together financially as it was, and that was with her often working fifteen-hour days, even with October's help. Owning horses was hard work. Running your own business was hard work. Put the two together…

Harry's idea of turning the cowshed into cottages was a lovely one, but a pie-in-the-sky one. Especially now, if he ran screaming for the hills when she told him about the baby. Even if he was willing to stand by her, she would have too much on her plate with the impending new arrival to even consider adding another problem. And whilst the income from the cottages might make the difference between the stables staying afloat or going under, she couldn't afford the initial outlay.

What a mess. How could she bring a baby into this?

But that was the issue, wasn't it, because she had every intention of bringing a baby into it. She might still be in shock and she had no idea which way was up, she mightn't have considered a child to be part of her life or never had any wish to be a mother – but she *was* having one and suddenly Petra felt intensely protective of the little scrap growing inside her.

Didn't that man ever give up, October asked herself as she saw another message from Zeus on her phone.

We need to talk, it said.

The hell we do, she thought. He had nothing to say to her that she could possibly want to hear, and he definitely wouldn't like what she had to say to him if ever the two of them met again. Which was unlikely. Zeus and October lived in very different worlds now, and she didn't envy him his one little bit. She was perfectly happy in her own.

She couldn't think what he wanted to talk about, unless his new beau had also dumped him. Zeus was a man who didn't like being without female company for long, so she wouldn't put it past him to expect that if he clicked his fingers October would come running.

She would bet her last penny that he'd assume he would be able to sweet talk her back into his bed.

Hoping to prevent Zeus from contacting her again, she sent a reply back – *We have nothing to talk about* – then she blocked his number.

That would put an end to his shenanigans, and October couldn't think why she hadn't blocked him before now.

One thing was certain though: even if she had been tempted to return to Zeus's yard, October couldn't leave a pregnant woman in the lurch. Whether Petra liked it or not, a baby was going to turn her life upside down, starting from today. The woman was going to need all the help she could get.

And there was also another reason: an even more compelling one.

Luca.

Harry paused and glanced up and down the street before he stepped into the jewellers on the way home from his last client of the day. He was fairly certain Petra was safely at the stables, but he wasn't taking any chances. He wanted his proposal to be a complete surprise and he was determined that she wasn't going to get wind of what he was planning.

'Are you able to resize this?' he asked, taking the ring out of his pocket, unwrapping the tissue he'd folded it up in, and handing it to the lady behind the counter.

She picked it up and turned it over, studying it. 'Eighteen-carat gold. Is it to be made larger or smaller?'

'Smaller, please.' In order to discover whether the ring fitted her, Harry had boxed clever – so he'd thought – and had waited until Petra was soundly asleep last night, and had then carefully slipped the ring onto her finger without waking her.

It had taken a while for her to drop off to sleep, which was surprising considering how exhausted she'd looked. She'd had dark circles around her eyes and had hardly touched the evening meal Amos had cooked. Putting everything together, Harry wondered if she was more worried about the stables' finances than she was letting on. Something was on her mind, because she'd been withdrawn and preoccupied all evening. Maybe he shouldn't have mentioned his idea of converting the cowshed into holiday lets – it was one more worry she didn't need.

Anyway, after Valentine's Day, she wouldn't need to worry any more. What was his would be hers, and the money in his bank account should be enough to cover the renovations, with some left over.

After explaining to the sales assistant what he'd done and being informed that slipping a ring on someone's finger and seeing how loose it was wasn't an accurate gauge for resizing, he also explained that he'd need it back by the 12th February at the latest. It was cutting it fine, but when Harry told the jeweller what he was planning, she took pity on him and assured him it would be ready in time.

Right, he thought, stepping outside, all he needed to do now was to book a table somewhere special, which might be easier said than done; all the best places were probably fully booked for Valentine's Day. But maybe Amos could recommend somewhere?

Before Harry walked back to his car, he gave Amos a call.

'You'll be lucky,' Amos said when Harry asked him. 'Anywhere decent will cost a fortune – it's like the florists, they hike the prices up just because they can. Why don't you eat here?'

'At the stables?' He turned his back on the street and stared at the engagement rings in the window. They all looked the same. The one which had belonged to Amos's wife was striking and unique, and he couldn't wait to see it on Petra's finger.

'Why not?' Amos asked. 'It's the place she loves the best. Don't worry, I'll make myself scarce. Oh, and don't bother with all that nonsense of putting the ring in the bottom of a champagne glass or burying it in a trifle – she won't thank you for it.'

Harry thought about Amos's suggestion. Petra probably wouldn't want to have dinner in a fancy restaurant, so Amos had a point. Anyway, she might suspect something was up if he suggested going out, and he wanted it to be a complete surprise.

'Good idea,' he said to Amos. 'It's going to be tricky keeping it from her, though.'

'We'll think of something.'

'Okay, let's do it. I just hope she says yes.'

'Why wouldn't she? She loves the bones of you, and you feel the same way about her.'

Harry did, at that. Petra was the best thing that had ever happened to him.

He was grinning madly to himself and was about to walk away, when a figure blocked his path.

'Hello, stranger.'

Harry stifled a sigh. The last person he wanted to see was Cher Reynolds. He hadn't forgiven her for being bitchy about Petra when he'd first moved to Picklewick.

'Hi, Cher,' he replied, with a distinct lack of enthusiasm.

'I haven't seen you or Petra for ages, then I bump into both of you on the same day.' Cher gave him a knowing look and smirked. 'I saw Petra in the supermarket earlier. I was surprised to see her, to be honest – I didn't think grocery shopping was her thing.'

Neither did Harry and he briefly wondered what she'd been doing there. Cher seemed to be waiting for a reply, but all he did was shrug, hoping she'd take the hint and go away.

She continued to stare at him and, feeling uncomfortable under her scrutiny, he was about to make his excuses and hurry off, when she said, 'Am I allowed to congratulate you?'

Trust her to jump to the right conclusion. He shouldn't have lingered outside the jewellers.

'Um…' He hesitated, wondering if it was a good idea to ask her not to say anything in case she bumped into Petra again, or whether him mentioning it would only make her want to gossip to every man, woman and child in the village, just to spite him.

Cher gazed at the display of engagement rings in the window, her expression thoughtful, then she looked at him and smiled. 'I'm sorry, have I jumped the gun?'

'A bit.' He didn't want to say much more.'

'I take it the wedding will be before the baby arrives?'

Harry stared blankly back at her. He had no clue what she was talking about. 'I'm sorry…?'

Cher smirked at him. 'She hasn't told, you, has she?'

'Told me what?'

'Petra was buying a pregnancy test when I saw her earlier.' Cher leaned closer. 'I must say, she has put on a bit of weight around her middle already.' She placed a hand on his arm. 'You must make sure she isn't still riding when she's eight months pregnant.'

Harry was frozen to the spot. 'Pregnant,' he repeated, and as he said it, everything fell into place and he knew without a doubt that what Cher said was true. *Petra was pregnant.*

The signs had all been there if only he'd looked, and he wondered how long she'd known. Not long, he surmised. Why hadn't she mentioned the possibility to him? Then he thought that maybe she didn't want to get his hopes up until she was certain. They hadn't discussed having children, but he'd always hoped he'd be a father one day—

'Are you all right?' Cher asked.

'Fine. Never better,' he said, absently.

He couldn't wait to get home, he was so excited. But he'd hang fire until she brought the subject up. She'd probably wait until they were alone anyway – it was unlikely she'd announce it over the dinner table with Amos there, although Harry knew Petra's uncle would be just as thrilled at the news as Harry. Of course, there was always the possibility that it might be a false alarm…

But if Petra *was* pregnant, Harry would be more than thrilled – he'd be *overjoyed*.

'I'm sorry,' October whispered in Luca's ear. 'My mum insisted. She's been going on so much about meeting you, that I agreed in order to shut her up. I hope you don't mind?'

October looked anxious, but Luca didn't mind in the slightest. In fact, he was delighted to think that October had told her mother about him. It made their relationship seem all the more real and solid. He decided he'd take her to meet his parents before too long: they would be delighted.

Lena was an older version of October, with the same shaped eyes and mouth, and the same dark hair, although Lena's sported considerably more grey.

'Hello, I'm October's mum. I'm so glad she's met someone nice.'

'Mum!' October looked mortified and hissed, 'Stop talking. Please!'

Luca barked out a laugh – this must be where October got her forthright way of speaking from. 'Pleased to meet you,' he said.

Lena simpered. 'I don't get to meet any of her friends very often because she always moves around so much. It does worry me, you know, October going from yard to yard. Something went on at the last place she was at, but she won't tell me what. Perhaps she's told you?'

'Sorry, Mum, we've got to go or we'll be late.' October, who was blushing furiously, grabbed his arm and pulled him down the path.

Lena called after them, 'Will you be home later? Or—'

'Gotta run! Bye!' October scampered towards the car, dragging Luca who was chortling like mad.

Her mother was hilarious, he thought, although October didn't appear to think so.

'I'm so sorry,' October began, but Luca stopped her with a kiss.

'It's fine,' he said. No doubt his parents would be just as embarrassing. It didn't matter how old you were, parents always had the ability to reduce you to an awkward teen.

It was only later when he and October were lying in his bed, October asleep on his chest, that Luca had time to muse on what her mother had said about October moving from yard to yard.

October had definitely come to Picklewick under a cloud, and although she had shared the reason with him he wondered whether she truly intended to remain here working at a small riding school, when she'd travelled the world as a groom. She was used to far more excitement than either this village or Luca could offer her.

Would she be content to live here, or would she get itchy feet and want to leave?

Luca prayed he'd be enough of a reason for her to stay, but he had an awful feeling that he might not be.

CHAPTER SEVEN

Petra hadn't said a word last night. Not one single word. Harry had waited on tenterhooks, for her to tell him her news, but nothing, so he'd come to the conclusion that there *was* no news. No pregnancy, no baby, no impending fatherhood.

He had been awake half the night, feeling upset. Which was ridiculous – fancy lamenting the loss of something you never had in the first place?

But this morning everything changed.

Normally Harry would be long gone by eight o'clock, on his way to his first shoeing of the day. But his van was in the garage for an MOT and a service, and without a vehicle he couldn't work, so he was hanging around the stables trying to make himself useful until his van was ready to collect. He'd considered waiting at the garage, hoping his lurking presence would hurry them along, but common sense prevailed and he'd asked Amos to follow behind him in the Land Rover when he dropped the van off. Amos had then brought him back to the stables for a couple of hours where he could at least be of some use. Timothy was due this morning to give the horses their annual booster shots, so he guessed that an extra pair of hands would come in useful.

Last night Harry had forgotten to put the bins at the top of the lane ready for collection, so the first thing he did when he got out of the Land Rover was to drag them to where they needed to be. There were two wheelie bins, one for general waste and one for all manner of recyclable items. But as he manoeuvred the general waste bin, it caught on the side of the fence and to his dismay toppled onto its side

The lid flew open and a disgustingly large amount of rubbish fell out. Thankfully most of it was in plastic bags so at least he didn't have to pick up loose stuff with his bare hands.

There was one thing he had to pick up though, and that was a small white plastic stick. It was about as long as his forefinger and had a bulbous bit on one end with two lines on it.

He immediately guessed what it was, and he stared at it curiously.

It was a pregnancy test.

Sadness pricked at him and as he bent down to retrieve it, he noticed that the cardboard box it came in and the instruction leaflet were lying on the ground next to it.

Tutting because those two things should have been placed into the recycling bin and not the general waste, he picked them up, but as he did so his eyes scanned across part of the leaflet.

It was the part which said "*one line, not pregnant, two lines, pregnant.*"

He carefully looked at the pee stick. Then he read the instructions again.

What the—?

Petra was *pregnant*?

He didn't know whether to leap for joy or thump the nearest fence post.

He was thrilled, delighted, awed, and several other wonderful emotions: but he was also dismayed and upset that she hadn't told him.

Harry took a steadying breath and let it out slowly. Maybe she needed a few days to come to terms with it first? He knew he was going to take a while for the news to sink in, so he empathised with her. She'd tell him when she was ready. He didn't know how he was going to keep a lid on his excitement until then, though.

Putting the evidence into the correct bins, he cleared up the rest of the mess, wheeled them into position and went to find Petra. Even if he had to keep his mouth shut for the time being, at least he could give her a cuddle.

October found she was humming to herself a lot lately. On the short drive to work she always listened to the radio and often a song would get stuck in her head and play on repeat and she'd end up singing it all day. It usually irritated her, but since she'd been dating Luca, she quite enjoyed it. The animals didn't seem to mind either, and she had the impression the hens positively liked it.

They were laying brilliantly, and over the past few days she'd taken it upon herself to release them from their coop in the mornings, then root around in the warm straw for the eggs. It was a soothing and pleasant interlude between taking the horses and ponies to the fields and starting the other jobs that needed doing. She hadn't yet turned the horses out this morning though, because the vet, Timothy, was due to arrive to give them their annual vaccinations so they were still in their stalls. She'd be on hand if she was needed, but Petra would be overseeing the process, so she strolled off to see to the chickens.

Thinking of Petra, October wondered how she was feeling. She hadn't spoken to her since their conversation yesterday, although she knew that Petra had popped out for the sole purpose of buying a pregnancy test. October was convinced it would be positive.

Smiling, she pushed aside a broody hen and felt underneath her for the egg, the bird's feathers tickling her hand.

'Thank you, Rita,' she said. The hen looked at her out of one beady eye.

October added it to the others in the basket and straightened up. She'd take these to the kitchen before beginning the mucking out. Forking up soiled straw wasn't a task she particularly liked, but when you owned or worked with horses it was a fact of life.

At least it was good exercise, and along with riding it kept her reasonably fit, so she was looking forward to a ride later on. Petra had told her she could have all the rides she wanted, fitting them in during her free time. She'd probably go out later, before the lessons started, and maybe Luca would come with her. Him being his own boss had its advantages, and being able to come and go as he pleased was one of them.

Hearing a vehicle on the lane as she walked across the yard to the house, October looked around, expecting it to be Timothy. But when she saw the flash four-by-four, she immediately recognised it and its personalized number plate: ZEUS 1.

What the hell was he doing here?

She waited for the car to come to a halt (in the middle of the yard, for goodness' sake!), her heart in her mouth, tension making her head pound. A small muscle beneath her left eye began to twitch and she blinked furiously.

Zeus slowly emerged from the driver's seat, took his sunglasses off (what a pratt – it wasn't even sunny), leaned against the car door and stared at her, his head tilted to the side. 'Please don't cry. You know I can't cope with crying.'

October stopped blinking and opened her eyes wide, overcompensating. 'I'm *not* crying. What do you want?'

'To talk. Is there somewhere we could go? I'd suggest we go for a drive, but…' He trailed off and glanced meaningfully at her boots. They were covered in manure and mud.

For a man who lived and breathed horses, Zeus was oddly reluctant to deal with the mucky side of equine ownership.

91

October hesitated. Seeing him standing there in all his handsome self-assurance, like a model out of Horse and Hound (minus the horses and the hounds), threw her off-kilter. He was still devilishly handsome and very charismatic, but he no longer made her insides flip or her heart flutter. In fact, apart from the obvious – good looks, fame and wealth – she didn't know what she'd seen in him.

However, she *was* curious. Now that he was here, it wouldn't hurt to hear him out and then she could send him away with a flea in his ear. Anyway, this couldn't take long because she needed to get on with the mucking out or she'd have Petra on her case.

'Please,' he said, plastering a winning smile on his face. He often used it to get his own way, and it usually worked. He was good at turning on the charm.

The feed store would be empty at this time of day, so with a quick glance around the yard, she said, 'This way,' and marched off.

She heard the car door click shut and his firm footsteps behind her as she led the way.

He followed her inside, his gaze scanning the tubs of grains and the buckets stacked to one side and came to rest on a handwritten list pinned to the wall. 'What are you doing in a place like this, Toby?'

Toby? Grrr. Once upon a time she used to love his nickname for her. Now it only served to set her teeth on edge. 'Working,' she snapped. She put the basket of eggs carefully down on the ground and folded her arms.

'You are better than this.' He waved an arm dismissively.

'I needed a job.'

'Yes, but…' He shuddered.

'You sacked me, remember? I took what I could get.'

'I "let you go" – there's a difference. And I had no choice, you know that.'

If he was here to persuade her to go back to him, he was doing a poor job of it. He could at least have brought her flowers or begged her forgiveness. All he'd succeeded in doing was dissing her job and making her cross.

'What do you want? Why are you even here?' she asked with a sigh.

'I need a favour, and you've blocked my number so…' He held out his hands in a what-else-do-you-expect-me-to-do gesture.

'A favour? That's rich considering what you did.'

'I wouldn't ask, but I'm desperate. I need you to tell Minnow a small fib. I could make it worth your while?'

'If you think I'm coming back to you or your yard, you've got a nerve.'

'I think we both know that's not going to happen, don't we? We've moved on since then.'

'Yeah, you certainly have,' she said, thinking of him with another woman only days after he'd "let *her* go".

'Don't be petty. We'd had our fun, but we'd run our course.'

'So you thought you'd run another one with someone else?'

'It was only a quick kiss. It didn't mean anything.'

'Yeah, right. And Minnow believes that, does she?' October saw the expression on Zeus's face and said slowly, 'You haven't told her that it wasn't me in that photo, have you? Do you realise she phoned my boss because she thought you were still seeing me? You need to tell her the truth.'

'That's the problem – I told her it *was* you.'

'Why would you do something like that?' October cried. 'What's wrong with you?'

'I had to. If she knew I was seeing someone else, Minnow would have left me for good.'

'I was under the impression she'd left you anyway? She mentioned something to my boss about you living on fresh air?'

'That's why I need a favour from you. I wouldn't ask if I wasn't desperate.'

'What's the favour?'

'I want you to tell Minnow that it *was* you in the photo, and that when it was taken you'd thrown yourself at me and you were begging me to take you back. She'd believe you. Especially if you said I didn't want anything to do with you.'

October couldn't believe what she was hearing. This was surreal. He'd lied to her, slept with her, then sacked her, and now he wanted her to take the blame?

Hardly!

Zeus stepped closer and took hold of her hands, a pleading look on his face. 'Please, please, please. For the sake of my marriage. You must call her and tell her it was all your fault, that I didn't know you were going to be there, that you were causing a scene and begging me to take you back, and that I was trying to get away from you. Please?'

October was about to tell him where to go, when something outside the door caught her eye.

Luca was standing less than ten feet away. His expression was tight, his mouth a thin line.

Dragging her hands free of Zeus's grasp, she hurried towards him, but before she'd taken more than two steps he turned smartly on his heel and strode off.

'Toby, wait!' Zeus grabbed her sleeve and hauled her back.

'Let go of me,' she snarled.

'Not until you say you'll help. Please, Toby, you don't know what's at stake.'

'Oh, I'm pretty certain I do. Now let go of me, before I scream.'

Zeus released her, and October shot out of the door and hared across the yard.

But she was too late.

The last glimpse she saw of the man she was falling in love with was the tail lights of his Range Rover as he sped down the lane.

'What are you doing?' Harry demanded, incredulously, striding up to the loosebox Petra was working in.

'What does it look like?' she retorted in a clipped voice. 'I'm mucking out.' She was carrying bales of straw into the stall and she looked as grumpy as hell.

Well, so was he, after seeing this. Actually, grumpy didn't cover it – he was furious. Those bales were darned heavy, and she was *pregnant*, for god's sake!

'Do you honestly think that's a good idea?' he demanded.

'I always muck out.'

'I don't care. October should be doing that – where is she, anyway? You shouldn't be lifting bales of sodding straw in your condition.'

He watched her pause as what he'd said sunk in.

She had her back to him, and she stiffened. Without turning around, she said in a small voice, 'What condition is that?'

'Don't play games, Petra. I *know*, okay? You've got to think of the baby.'

Suddenly she sparked into life and whirled around to face him. 'What do you *think* I've been thinking about?'

Harry stabbed a finger at the bales of straw. 'Clearly not our child!'

'How dare you!' She stormed towards him and for a moment he thought she was going to deck him, but she barged on past and he quickly stepped to the side.

'Wait…Petra, let's talk.'

'I'm going to talk, all right,' she yelled over her shoulder. 'Some people need to learn to keep their mouths shut.'

And with that she was gone, leaving Harry stunned.

He debated whether he should go after her, but Petra had a temper and it wasn't a wise idea to try to apologise when she was so angry. He'd give it an hour. Hopefully, she'd have calmed down by then.

Needing to work off his own ire, he did the only thing he could think of – he carried on where she'd left off and mucked out the sodding stall.

October stood in the yard staring after Luca and wishing she'd never set eyes on Zeus Fernsby. The man was a menace. She heaved a sigh and blew out her cheeks. She wasn't sure how much or what portion of the conversation Luca had heard, but he'd listened to enough of it to get the wrong end of the stick.

Oh god, and here was Petra with a bee in her bonnet. She had a face like thunder and she was peed off about something – probably because October was late doing the mucking out. This morning wasn't turning out to be one of her better days.

'Toby?' Zeus asked.

Huh? Was he still here? 'Get lost.'

'Who the hell is this and what's he doing in my yard?' Petra demanded, marching up to them.

'He's no one and he's just leaving.' October glared at him, daring Zeus to contradict her.

Zeus spluttered, 'But—'

'Sod off.' October scowled menacingly.

Seeing he wasn't going to get anywhere, Zeus shook his head sadly, and sauntered towards his car.

Thank goodness he was leaving without a fuss, October thought, but when he reached his car, he paused and smiled at her. It was the sort of smile a hyena might give to an antelope just before he ate it for lunch. 'You'd better hang on to this measly little job,' he said, 'because I'll make sure you never work in a decent yard again. Your name will be mud. Ciao, Toby.'

October poked her tongue out at him. It was more likely to be the other way around by the time Minnow finished with him. He might have the talent, but it was his wife's money that paid for his fabulous horses and their hideously expensive upkeep.

Pulling herself together and knowing there was nothing she could do about Luca right now – she'd speak to him later, and explain – she said to Petra, 'I'll just take the eggs in to Amos, then I'll get on with the mucking out.'

When she saw Petra's expression, her heart sank.

'What have you got to say for yourself?' Petra demanded.

'I'm sorry…?' October was confused. What was she supposed to have done? If it was about Zeus, she hadn't asked him to come to the stables and he'd gone now, so—

'You *told* him.' Petra had her hands on her hips and murder in her eyes.

'Told who what?'

'Harry?'

'What am I supposed to have—? Oh…'

'Well?'

'I didn't tell him anything. Does that mean you're definitely pregnant?'

'It's none of your business whether I am or not. I don't appreciate you gossiping about me. I don't care who it is. You don't go running to Harry after I expressly told you not to.'

As far as October could recall, Petra hadn't issued a direct order – she'd asked. But even if she hadn't, October wouldn't have dreamt of saying anything to anyone.

'I didn't,' she repeated.

'*Someone* did and the only person who knew was *you.*'

'It wasn't me!'

Petra glowered at her and shook her head. 'I'm not going to argue with you. Harry knows, and someone told him. It can only be you.'

Sod this; October had enough. She'd thought she was settling in at the stables on Muddypuddle Lane and that Petra was starting to view her as a friend and not just as an employee.

Obviously not.

The woman had leapt in, throwing accusations around, and was refusing to listen to her protestations of innocence.

'I resign,' October said, slowly and distinctly.

'You what?'

'I resign. I don't like being accused of something I haven't done, so you can stick your job. I'm out of here.'

And with that, she did just as Zeus had done minutes earlier – she left the stables on Muddypuddle Lane. But unlike Zeus, she was trying not to cry.

Where else was she going to get a job working with horses within easy travelling distance of her mum's house?

Hopefully, when she explained why Zeus had been at the stables, her relationship with Luca would be back on an even keel, because she didn't think she could take any more upsets today.

Luca's heart was pounding as he drove down the lane, faster than was wise. He couldn't believe what he'd just heard. That poor man.

He was finding it difficult to reconcile the woman he thought he knew with the woman that Zeus Fernsby had been pleading with. Begging, even. The poor man's marriage was on the rocks and October was still chasing him, not caring who she hurt.

It was despicable that she'd do something like that. He thought she was different, but she wasn't.

Luca shook his head in disgust. She'd been stringing him along, probably using him as a back-up in case she didn't get back together with Zeus. Zeus was the better prospect – Luca was the reserve. What a—!

He was tempted to call her all the names under the sun, but instead he pulled into the side of the road, reached for his phone and blocked her number. Just in time, because she'd already sent him a message which he deleted without reading.

It was going to be difficult stabling Midnight at Petra's place with October around, but he had a feeling she wouldn't be there for long. As much as he was tempted to move his horse to another yard, he decided to hang on for a while. He liked the stables on Muddypuddle Lane, damn it, and it was convenient too. Why should he have to move Midnight, when October was the one at fault?

He'd simply have to do his best to avoid her and wait for her to find some other mug to latch on to.

But even as those thoughts were travelling through his mind, along with the anger and the hurt he was feeling he also felt a stab of pain and an ache in his heart. He could so easily have fallen in love with her.

An incredible loneliness and feeling of loss swept over him, and for the first time in years, Luca felt like crying.

CHAPTER EIGHT

Harry dusted stray stalks of dried grass off his clothes and stood back. He'd mucked out the stall and as he was doing so he'd used the time to practice what he was going to say to Petra when he caught up with her. He knew she might still be mad, but they had to talk. Not just for their own sakes, but for the baby.

He still couldn't believe he was going to be a father. Wow. It was mind-blowing and he was as scared as hell. What if he was a hopeless dad? He might be awful at it. But even if he was, he knew one thing – he'd love it with every cell in his body. He already did. The thought that Petra had his baby growing inside her, made his heart melt.

He wondered how far gone she was. Had she seen a doctor yet? Probably not, if she'd only just found out. What about scans? Would he be allowed to go with her? He wanted to be as involved as humanly possible, to be as supportive as possible.

But first, he needed to find her and apologise.

She was finishing up with Timothy, handing over the lead ropes of the last two ponies for Nathan to take to the field, when Harry veered towards Nathan, and said quietly, 'Can you finish off the mucking out? I need to speak to Petra and I haven't clapped eyes on October this morning.'

'You won't, neither,' Nathan said. 'She quit.'

'Why? I thought she was getting on okay.'

'Petra didn't say why, but I think they've had a bust-up. I'd keep out of her way if I were you – she's got a face like a slapped arse.'

'Erm, that might be my fault.' Harry winced. 'I'll tell you about it later.' He clapped Nathan on the shoulder and walked over to his brother. 'Timothy, are you all done?'

'Yep. That's it for another year.' Timothy picked up a box and tucked it under his arm. 'See you, Petra.'

Petra gave Timothy a tight smile. She didn't even look at Harry.

Harry waited for his brother to move out of earshot before saying, 'I'm sorry. It took me by surprise that's all, and when I saw you humping blimmin' great bales around, I lost it for a minute.'

She sighed and finally looked him in the eye. 'I should have told you. It wasn't fair you having to hear it from someone else.'

'Cher said she'd seen you in the supermarket. I had, erm, popped into Picklewick to pick up, erm, um, never mind. And I bumped into her. She couldn't wait to tell me.'

Her eyes widened. '*Cher Reynolds* told you I was pregnant?'

'Yeah, why? Who did you think it was? Who else knows?'

Petra hung her head. 'Rose Walker guessed, and so did October. Honestly, the idea hadn't entered my head before then, so I thought I'd better buy a test. I did it yesterday afternoon. It was positive.'

'I know. I saw it in the bin.'

She looked up at him from under her lashes, and her eyes glistened with tears. 'I'm sorry. I just didn't know how to tell you.'

She let out a sob and Harry groaned.

Gathering her into his arms, he said, 'It's okay, no harm done. I know now, and that's all that matters. There's no need to get so upset.' He kissed the top of her head and held her tighter.

'Aren't you annoyed?'

'About Cher telling me? It couldn't be helped. But I was annoyed when I saw you mucking out the stable. You've got to look after yourself.'

'I meant, are you annoyed about me getting pregnant?'

Harry drew back to look at her face. 'I don't understand. Why should I be annoyed about that? I'm absolutely delighted. Did you honestly think I'd be mad?'

Petra sniffed. 'Yes.'

'Is that the reason you didn't tell me straight away?'

'Yes.'

'What made you believe I wouldn't want this baby?' He was thoroughly bemused.

'We've never talked about having kids. I didn't think you'd want children after looking after Timothy for all those years.'

'I did what I had to do as far as Timothy was concerned, and I don't begrudge him a second of it. But Timothy is my brother, not my son. I *want* this baby, Petra. I want to be a father. And I want *you*.'

'But how am I going to manage?' she wailed.

'Don't you mean how are *we* going to manage? I'm part of this, too, you know.' He grinned down at her. 'What exactly are you fretting about?'

'The stables, duh.' She gave him a tiny, worried smile.

'We'll be fine. People get pregnant and have babies every day, and they cope.'

'I won't be able to do half of what I did before. And when the baby comes, I'll be spending most of my time looking after it!'

'It'll be okay. We'll work something out.'

'October resigned.' Petra screwed her eyes shut and took a deep breath before opening them again.

'Nathan told me. Do you know why?'

'It's my fault. I accused her of telling you I was expecting. I'm such an idiot. I should never have flown off the handle.'

Harry agreed that she shouldn't have, but he thought it best not to say anything. He kissed the tip of her nose instead.

'I'd better apologise,' she added. 'And not just because we need her, but because it's the right thing to do.'

October threw her phone down on the coffee table and slumped back onto the sofa. Either Luca had turned his mobile off or he'd blocked her. She strongly suspected the latter because none of the messages she'd sent him had been delivered.

Once again, her eyes filled with tears and she brushed them away angrily. She wouldn't cry. *She wouldn't.*

If he chose not to give her a chance to explain, that was his loss.

She rubbed her eyes with her knuckles and gritted her teeth. It had been a pretty awful day all round. Not only had she lost her job, but she appeared to have lost her boyfriend too. She might not have been working at the stables on Muddypuddle Lane for long, but she'd liked it – and she might have only known Luca for a short amount of time, but she was starting to fall for him. Early days or not, she'd begun to harbour a tiny hope that he might be The One.

How silly of her!

He'd baled on her at the first hurdle, which made her wish she'd never taken him up on his challenge when he'd come a cropper the day he'd been showing off over the jumps. If she'd walked away then, she wouldn't be in the mess she was in now.

Thinking that she ought to start looking for another job so at least she'd be able to tell her mum she'd applied for something, she eyed her phone balefully.

The way she felt at the moment, she'd apply for anything as long as it was a couple of hundred miles away from Picklewick. Or Kent. She had no desire to go back there, either.

Suddenly she remembered something Zeus had said, and it made her sit up and groan. Hadn't he threatened to sully her name and make sure she was persona non grata in showjumping circles? Damn it, he had.

He couldn't possibly inform every single yard in the country, but gossip was rife in the horsey community and he was incredibly well known, so news would travel fast, especially since he'd be putting it about that October had ruined his marriage. He'd do anything to salvage it – it was just a pity he hadn't considered how much he'd stood to lose *before* he'd taken October to bed.

If he could have an affair with her and then leap straight into another with this unknown woman in the photo, the odds were that he had slept with other women in the past and had got away with it, so he'd probably assumed he would get away with it this time.

October had been incredibly blind not to have realised what he was like.

She still couldn't believe the cheek of him driving halfway across the country to try to talk her into helping him out of the pickle he'd got himself in. His arrogance had cost her her job at the stables on Muddypuddle Lane and her relationship with a man who she'd been starting to fall for.

Oh, who was she kidding? She *had* fallen for him. Hard.

The sound of the doorbell ringing roused her from her pity party for a second as she debated whether to bother answering it. She was about to sink back into misery, when a thought occurred to her and she scrambled to her feet and hurried into the hall.

'Oh, it's you,' she said, on opening the door and seeing Petra standing on the step. 'What do you want?'

'To apologise.'

'Hmph.'

'I shouldn't have jumped to conclusions.'

'Damned right, you shouldn't have.'

'Can I come in? Or is your mum home, because if she is, I don't want to intrude.'

'She's at work.' October opened the door wider and stood to the side. 'Congratulations?'

A smile lit Petra's face as she nodded.

'I'm happy for you,' October said, coming to a halt in the middle of the living room and crossing her arms.

'I'm happy for me, too. I think.' Petra hesitated, the sudden silence acute, then she said, 'Would you consider coming back to work at the stables? Please? Will it help if I blame it on the hormones?' She made a wry face. 'Scrap that – I'm just a sour cow with a quick temper. I really am sorry.'

She did indeed look sorry, October thought. Although Petra was in a steady relationship with a great guy, October had seen for herself how scared she'd been about telling Harry, so she said, 'Apology accepted.'

'Thank you. Will you come back?'

'Um…' October paused, thinking furiously. 'I don't think so.'

Petra's face fell. 'I promise nothing like this will ever happen again.'

'Luca and I have split up.'

'Oh, dear. Was it anything to do with the guy who was at the stables earlier?'

'Zeus. Yes. Remember that photo I showed you of him and the woman with long hair? Luca overheard a conversation where Zeus was trying to persuade me to tell Minnow it was me in the photo and that I had been begging him to take me back.'

'Pft! If his wife believes that, she must be stupid. He had his hand on the woman's backside, for a start.'

'I know, but he's desperate – she's the one with the money.'

'Can't you go to Luca and explain?'

'He's not taking my calls. I'm pretty sure he's blocked me.'

'Give him time – he'll come round.'

'I don't care if he does or doesn't. I don't want him in my life if he reacts like that at the slightest misunderstanding. I'm done with him. I'm done with men, full stop. I've had enough work-related romances to last me a lifetime. It leads to nothing but awkwardness at best, and an untenable working environment at worst.'

'That shouldn't stop you from coming back to the stables.'

Bless her, Petra looked so hopeful, that October nearly changed her mind. However, she knew she'd regret it if she did. 'I can't face seeing him,' she admitted.

Petra gazed at her quizzically and October squirmed under the woman's scrutiny. 'You really like him, don't you?'

'And that's the problem.'

'I can fix that – I'll tell him to take Midnight elsewhere.'

The generous offer almost made October cry. 'You can't do that. You need his livery fees to pay me. You said so yourself.'

Petra sank into the nearest chair, and October felt awful for not inviting a pregnant woman to sit down. 'What will you do?' Petra asked.

October sat opposite her. 'I honestly don't know.'

'Would you say I'm a meddler?' Petra asked Harry later that afternoon. Harry had just arrived home and Petra had been itching to talk to him. Since she'd returned from October's house, she'd been thinking, and a plan had begun to form. But if she decided to act on it, she wanted to make sure Harry was on board. She also had a suspicion she might be interfering in something that wasn't her business.

On the other hand, she'd seen the way October and Luca looked at each other, and there was definitely a great deal of emotion and passion. It seemed a shame to waste it.

'Is someone accusing you of meddling?' Harry asked. 'It wouldn't be Amos by any chance, would it?'

'No, it would not!'

'Who then?'

'No one, yet.'

'Yet…?'

'It's October and Luca. I've been thinking.'

'Oh, dear.' Harry rolled his eyes and Petra slapped him on the arm.

'I need your help,' she said.

Harry shook his head. 'I'm not promising anything.'

'I'm going to play matchmaker,' she said.

'Again? You'll get a reputation, if you're not careful. And it didn't actually work, did it? If I remember rightly, Megan left Nathan's birthday party early because she was upset.'

'Only because she had fallen in love with him, and she felt she was betraying her husband. She came round in the end, though – Jeremy has been dead two years and it was time for her to move on with her life. Look at her and Nathan now!'

Harry ran a hand through his hair. 'I hope you know what you're doing,' he warned.

'October and Luca aren't speaking to each other, and she's handed her notice in. How much worse can it get? They'll thank me in the end.'

Amos wandered into the kitchen and placed his empty mug next to the sink. 'Who'll thank you?' he asked.

Petra put her tea towel down and leaned against the counter. 'I've got a plan to get October and Luca back together.' She ignored the quick exchange of glances between Harry and Amos. 'Amos, I need your help.'

He squinted at her. 'What do you need me to do?'

'Can you phone October and ask her to come to the stables to pick up the wages we owe her and her P45? Tell her to come after this evening's lesson. If she suggests coming up now, tell her I've got a little gift for her. You can tell her that you want to say goodbye to her, too,'

'What are you going to do?' Amos asked, and Harry groaned.

'Don't encourage her,' he said.

Petra grinned. 'I'm going to phone Luca and tell him we need to have a chat about Midnight. I'm going to ask him to call in after the lesson.'

'What if October's busy? Or Luca's got plans?' Harry argued.

'I'll just have to think of something else, won't I?'

Harry sighed loudly. 'I know I'm going to regret this, but you said you wanted my help?'

Petra rubbed her hands together. 'Yes, my love, I most certainly do.'

Luca could have done without driving to the stables this evening. It was dark and cold, and he wasn't in the mood. Surely whatever it was could have been discussed over the phone? But Petra had said she had to dash because she was about to take a lesson, and had ended the call before he'd been able to ask for clarification.

He'd been tempted to phone her back and tell her it would have to wait until tomorrow, or whenever he decided to return to the stables, but the one thing which made him decide to simply get it over with was her mention of teaching a lesson. If she was taking the class, it meant October wasn't. She'd have left for the day, so there was no chance of him bumping into her.

Feeling lost and rather sad, he drove up the lane, and was about to pull into the car park when he noticed there was tape across the entrance and a sign which said, "closed for resurfacing – please park around the back".

"Around the back" was where the horsebox, the trailer and the Land Rover lived. He didn't think the car park was too bad – if anything it was the lane which could do with new tarmac, but he obediently drove around the back of the stable block and switched the engine off.

Hoping the problem with Midnight wasn't a physical one, he headed for his horse's loose box first, to check on him, and was relieved to see the gelding contentedly chewing on the contents of his hay net.

'Hiya, big fella,' he murmured, slipping his hand into his pocket and bringing out a carrot.

Midnight whickered softly, and reached out to take it from him. Luca stroked him on the nose and the horse nudged him gently.

He sighed, and remained there for a moment, enjoying the contact, smelling the pleasant scent of dried grass and horse, and listening to the animal's crunching. Luca let his gaze roam over Midnight's back and down his legs, checking for any obvious signs that there was something wrong, but the horse seemed contented enough.

Scanning the inside of the stall and seeing that nothing appeared to be amiss, Lucas froze when he noticed a hair grip on a narrow ledge running around the top of the stable. A pang of regret and loss struck him as he pushed Midnight back, opened the door and went inside to retrieve it.

This was what October had been searching for the first time he'd met her, and as he held it his thoughts returned to that day. If he'd had known then what he knew now, he would have run a mile, because her betrayal hurt like hell.

He put the hair grip back. No doubt October would notice it soon enough. He was tempted to keep it as a reminder of her, even though she was lodged firmly in his mind and he guessed it would take a while to shift her. She'd burrowed her way under his skin more than he would have believed possible.

With a heavy sigh, he gave Midnight a final pat on the neck and walked towards the house to find Petra.

Harry watched Luca make his way across the yard towards the house, and felt idiotic as he skulked in the tack room, the door a tiny bit ajar to enable him to peep out.

The moment Petra opened the door and ushered Luca inside, Harry darted towards the car park, and hastily ripped the tape off and grabbed the cardboard sign, stuffing it behind a low-growing bush.

Only just in time, too, he thought in relief, as he heard another vehicle make its way up the lane. Petra had wanted to ensure that neither October nor Luca spotted the other's car in case one or the other of them buggered off before she had the chance to put her plan into action.

As Harry expected, the car belonged to October, and he slapped a sorrowful expression on his face and went to meet her.

'Sorry to hear you're leaving us,' he said, as she got out of her car. 'You fitted in brilliantly, I thought.'

'So did I, but... you know...' She shrugged.

'I've just about finished doing the rounds, so shall we go inside? It's a bit parky out here. Brrr.' He rubbed his hands together and blew on them.

'I would have come tomorrow, but Petra insisted on this evening. I'm going to miss this place.'

'Yes, well...' Harry coughed to cover his embarrassment. He'd never been good at subterfuge and he was certain she must realise there was something fishy going on. 'After you,' he said, gesturing towards the house.

And, as October walked ahead of him, he hoped Petra knew what she was doing.

October had barely stepped over the threshold when Queenie slammed into her legs uttering delighted little whimpers, and she bent down to stroke the dog's silky ears. Which was why she didn't notice Luca at first, but when she did, he looked as shocked as she felt.

'What are you doing here?' she demanded, shooting him an incredulous look.

Her heart clenched and her stomach flipped over at the sight of him. She wanted desperately to throw herself into his arms and kiss him until he begged her to stop. But he'd made his position clear. He didn't want anything to do with her, and despite her swooping emotions she didn't think she wanted to be with a man who had so little trust in her.

'I thought you'd finished for the day,' he replied.

So he was only going to visit the stables when she wasn't here, was he? At least her resignation would solve that problem for him.

'I've finished for good,' she retorted. 'But *someone* wanted me to call in this evening to pick up my wages and P45.' She scowled at Petra. 'How could you? You know how I feel.'

'That's right, I do,' Petra replied. 'You two need to talk. Luca, you shouldn't believe everything you hear, and October, don't cut your nose off to spite your face. Please sort yourselves out, if not for your own sakes, then do it for mine. I need your help more than ever, October. Harry, Amos, let's leave them to it. And while we're at it, Amos, Harry and I have got something to tell you…'

October watched, open-mouthed, as Petra bustled her partner and her uncle out of the room.

111

Then she turned to Luca and was about to tell him she was leaving when she saw his face.

'P45?' he asked.

'That's right.' She folded her arms and glared at him.

'Why? Do you think you'll stand a better chance of wrecking his marriage for good if you get a job closer to him?'

October seethed. 'You don't know what you're talking about.'

'I know what I heard.'

'You heard wrong,' she said, flatly. If Petra didn't return with her wages and her P45 soon, she was out of here. Petra could post it or drop it through her letterbox. She didn't need this aggro. 'Why are you here?'

'Isn't it obvious? I was conned.'

'As was I.' She threw her hands in the air. 'That's it, I'm off.'

She turned to leave but stopped when he said, 'What did Petra mean when she said I shouldn't believe everything I hear?'

October pulled a face. 'You heard half a conversation and jumped to the wrong conclusion. Then you didn't even have the decency to let me explain.'

'You can explain now.'

'I can't be bothered,' she retorted.

'Petra said you're not to cut your nose off to spite your face. Have I been a fool?'

'Sod Petra, and yes, you bloody well have!'

'Are you going to tell me what happened today with Zeus Fernsby, or not?'

October shuffled from foot to foot, wondering if it was worth explaining. Would it make any difference what Luca believed? Their relationship was over, practically before it had begun, so why should she waste her breath?

But she did, anyway. 'What you heard this morning was Zeus asking me to tell Minnow that a photo which had been taken of him with another woman, was me throwing

112

myself at him because I was upset that it was over between us. If you'd stayed around long enough, you'd have heard me tell him to get lost.'

'He's been having an affair with someone else as well as you?'

'I'm not saying he was seeing her when he was with me – although he might have been. But even if he wasn't, he wasted no time in getting himself another mistress once I had been kicked into touch. You see, Zeus likes women with long, dark hair. He also likes his wife's money because he doesn't have a great deal of it himself. Here.' She took her phone out and showed him the photo.

It meant moving closer to him, and she was acutely aware of his cologne. It made her heady and breathless, and she struggled with the urge to wrap her arms around his neck and—

'It does look like you from the back,' he said, gazing at the screen. 'But it's not – your hair curls at the ends, and it's shinier. And your legs are longer.'

October stared up at him. His lips were less than a foot away from hers. She could almost taste him.

'I'm sorry.' His eyes met hers. 'I seem to make a habit of being a prat when you're around.'

'Are you sure you're not a prat all the time?' she replied, archly. Neither of them had moved.

'Probably. I'm sorry – I should have known better. You're nothing like the women I've dated in the past.'

'Glad to hear it.' She might sound sharp, but she certainly didn't feel it.

'Can you forgive me? Start over? Petra has gone to so much trouble…'

'You're incorrigible.'

'Is that a yes?'

'Yes.'

'Are you sure?'

'Shut up and kiss me,' October instructed.

And to her delight, Luca did as he was told.

CHAPTER NINE

Luca put his elbows on the table and steepled his chin on his clasped hands.

'Well?' he asked.

October swallowed her mouthful of wine and made a face.

'Don't you like it?' He'd splashed out and ordered one of the most expensive bottles the restaurant had. For her not to like it was a bit of a blow. He wanted to treat her to a fabulous meal because that's what one did on Valentine's Day, and the wine was part of the experience. As was the candle on the table, the oysters, the Lobster Thermador, and the soft music in the background. He'd even presented her with two dozen red roses when he'd picked her up in his car.

The restaurant itself was small and intimate, a perfect place for a night like tonight, and it was damned expensive.

'Have they got lemonade, do you think?' October asked, and his face fell until he realised she was joking. 'You didn't have to do all this, you know,' she said. 'I'd have been just as happy with lasagne and chips in the Black Horse.'

That was precisely why he wanted to treat her – because she didn't expect it or demand it. Luca wasn't rich by any stretch of the imagination, but he was quite well off and he hated it when his girlfriends in the past had felt aggrieved if he didn't take them to the most expensive places or lavish gifts on them.

October wasn't like that.

October was special – and he was incredibly thankful he'd found her.

He was also incredibly thankful that Petra had stuck her oar in the other evening, because if she hadn't he wouldn't be sitting here now gazing into the eyes of the loveliest woman on earth.

'Um, can I ask you a question?' he asked, his usual self-confidence hiding in the back row, scared to raise its head.

'You can. I mightn't answer you, though.'

'Now that you're working in the stables again and you've very graciously forgiven me—'

'Don't push it…'

'Do you think we can go steady? Boyfriend and girlfriend?'

'Excuse me, but I thought we already were!'

'Oh, I see. That's fantastic.' He'd hoped they were, but he'd had to ask, just to make sure. With October it wouldn't do to take anything for granted.

She grinned at him. 'It is, isn't it?' she said, and picked up her glass of rather expensive wine and drained it in one gulp.

Luca rolled his eyes, her irreverence towards the wine typical of her. She was exactly what he needed to keep him grounded.

She was exactly what he needed, full stop.

And as he stared into her eyes and saw his own love reflected back at him, he realised that physical possessions and money meant nothing when someone owned you body, heart and soul, the way October owned him.

Petra blew on her hands and walked into the kitchen, Queenie darting ahead of her. The dog's tail wagged furiously as she headed for Harry who was standing just inside the door.

He was looking anxious, and she realised why when he bent down to stroke the dog, and she could see beyond him.

'What's all this?' she asked, staring at the battered and well-worn kitchen table, which had been transformed with the aid of a pristine white tablecloth, a candle, a slender vase with a single red rose, and place settings for two.

'Valentine's Day,' Harry said.

Petra narrowed her eyes. 'Is that why Amos asked me to drive him into the village? I thought it was odd for him to visit Honeymead this evening.' Amos had suggested that she bring Queenie with her because several of the care home's residents wanted their fix of flop-eared spaniel. But he'd arranged to go for a drink in the Black Horse afterwards and didn't want to take the dog with him, arguing that Queenie would be better off at home. So Petra had waited whilst Queenie had said hello to everyone, and she'd then returned to the stables with the dog. It had meant she'd been out of the house for well over an hour.

'The pair of you can't be trusted,' Petra said.

'Don't you like it when the shoe is on the other foot?' Harry teased, going to the stove and stirring a saucepan. 'Amos is playing you at your own match-making game.'

'We don't need to be matchmaked – if that's a word. We're already together, if you hadn't noticed.'

'I'd noticed,' he said. 'Wash your hands and sit down. What do you want to drink? I've got sparkling apple juice? Non-alcoholic beer?

'Apple juice, please.' Petra popped to the downstairs loo and washed her hands. Who knew Harry was such a romantic? She hadn't given Valentine's Day a single thought, and she wondered if she should have bought him a card.

Oh, well, too late for that now.

At least he was cooking her a meal at home and not forcing her to go out to eat. She was so knackered these days, she didn't think she'd have been able to keep her eyes open.

The kitchen was full of delicious smells and her mouth watered as she sat down. Thankfully she'd not suffered from morning or any other time of day sickness, and she was looking forward to seeing what he'd cooked for her.

'Mmm, it looks yummy,' she said, when Harry put a plate in front of her. 'What is it?'

'Smoked salmon and pesto tartlet. Then there is steak with chilli butter, followed by salted caramel chocolate pots.'

'Wow. Did you make all this yourself?' She knew Harry could cook, but she didn't realise he could cook this well.

'Er, not really. I bought the tartlets, and the chilli butter. And I bought the chocolate pots. I'm cooking the steak from scratch, though.'

Petra laughed, filled to the brim with love for this wonderful man of hers. 'Have I told you recently how much I love you?'

'You have, but you can tell me again.' He smiled at her. 'Um, before you go all gooey on me, there's something I need to discuss with you. It's to do with the cowshed.'

'I honestly don't think we can go ahead with it, not now.' She glanced pointedly at her stomach. She was seventeen weeks pregnant already, and there wasn't enough time to do even a fraction of the work needed before the baby came – and that was assuming she was physically able to do it. 'It's a nice idea, but even if I wasn't expecting, there's no way we could afford the renovations.'

'What if we could?'

'But we can't, so there's no point in talking about it.' Petra put her fork down, her appetite fading. Why did Harry have to spoil what had been shaping up to be the most romantic meal she'd ever had, with talk of something that simply wasn't possible.

'The sale of the house in Cheltenham has been completed,' he said, beaming at her. 'I want to use my half to invest in the stables, starting with the renovations to the cowshed.'

'What? How? I mean, you can't do that!'

'Why not? It's *my* money. Timothy wants to see if he can buy the cottage he's renting with his share, and he'll ask Charity to move in with him. If he can do what he wants with his, why can't I do what I want with mine?'

'But, what about the risk?'

'What risk?'

Petra paused. How was she going to say this without sounding negative? She had every faith their relationship would last. But what if it didn't? There might be a very grey area indeed if they split up after he'd ploughed in his share of the money he'd made from the sale of the house which had originally belonged to his and Timothy's parents. She couldn't let him do it.

'What if we…you know…split up?' Her voice was small and timid. She hated to say it, but he'd pushed her into a corner.

'We're not going to split up,' he said firmly.

'How do you know?'

'I love you and you love me. Why should we split up? Besides, I want to marry you.' His eyes widened and his mouth fell open. 'Bugger, I didn't mean to ask you like that. Can I try again?'

'What?' Petra's brain was numb. Had she just heard him say he wanted to marry her?

She watched in astonishment as he slipped from his chair and got down on one knee. He put his hand in his pocket, brought out a small black velvet box, opened it and held it out to her.

'Petra, will you marry me?'

'What?' she repeated, her eyes on his hopeful face. She didn't look at the contents of the box.

'Will you do me the honour of being my wife?' He was smiling but there was a hint of strain in his voice.

'Is this about the baby? Because if it is, I don't want

you to marry me just because I'm pregnant. Petra glared at him. She didn't want a pity marriage, or a doing-his-duty marriage. She wanted him to marry her because he loved her, not because he felt obliged to because she was carrying his child.

Harry lurched to his feet. 'Cramp,' he said, hopping about on one leg, whilst he tried to massage the calf on the other. If this wasn't so serious, Petra might have found it amusing.

'I am not asking you to marry me because you are pregnant,' he said through gritted teeth. 'I want you to be my wife because I love you, you silly woman. Ask Amos.'

Petra blinked in confusion. 'What's Amos got to do with it?'

'I asked him for your hand in marriage *before* I found out you were pregnant.' He shoved the box with the ring in it under her nose, forcing her to look at it.

'That's Aunt Mags's engagement ring!' she cried.

'It's yours now. I was taking it to the jewellers to be resized when I bumped into Cher.'

'You want me to marry you?'

'For god's sake woman, that's what I've been trying to tell you for the past five minutes. Now, do you want to be my wife or not?'

Petra raised her eyebrows. 'Since you put it so nicely, how can I say no?'

'You're saying yes?'

She nodded.

Harry snapped the lid of the box shut and danced around the room. 'She said yes, she said yes!'

'Harry?'

Harry stopped leaping about. 'What?'

'Are you going to ask me properly and get down on one knee?'

Harry pursed his lips. 'You are so annoying.' He walked towards the table and gingerly lowered himself onto one knee, wincing as he did so.

'But you love me anyway,' she said, holding out the third finger of her left hand for him to slip the ring on it.

'I must be mad, but I love you to the moon and back, and our little one,' he said, placing his palm on her stomach.

'That's good, because you're stuck with us now. If you try to get out of it, Amos will come after you.'

'I'll never want to get out of it. You're my whole world.'

'I love you too, Harry. More than you'll ever know. Now, please can you get up so I can finish my tartlet – I'm starving!'

'Here I am trying to be all romantic and all you can think about is food,' he grumbled, using the table to pull himself up.

'I *am* eating for two,' Petra retorted primly, but the adoration on Harry's face when he looked at her took her breath away.

Maybe the tartlet could wait after all...

THE PATTER OF
TINY FEET

CHAPTER ONE

Isaac Richards pulled into the car park of the stables on Muddypuddle Lane, grabbed his document case from the back seat, then clambered out and glanced around. The yard was as immaculate as always, with hardly a blade of straw out of place. Despite being about seven months pregnant, Petra ran a tight ship.

It was a short walk across the yard to the farmhouse and as he made his way towards it, he passed several loose boxes with their doors open. A couple of others had an equine head poking over the top, the owner's ears twitching as the animals followed his progress. He could hear music and voices coming from one of the stables and he wondered whether he should let whoever-it-was know he was here, or whether he should carry on up to the house and knock on the door.

The decision was taken out of his hands when a woman reversed out of the stable, dragging a loaded wheelbarrow. As she glanced over her shoulder to see where she was going, she spotted him.

'Petra, your architect is here,' she called, manoeuvring the barrow so that it rested next to the wall.

Out of habit and even though he'd met October on his previous visits to the stables, Isaac held out his hand. October wiped hers on her backside, began to reach out to shake his, then hesitated.

'I don't think it's a good idea,' she said, and she showed him her palm. It was daubed with green-coloured muck and Isaac was fairly certain he knew what it was.

He settled for saying, 'Hi,' and smiling at her.

'Isaac!' Petra emerged from the stable. 'Shall we go into the house? Amos, Harry and Nathan are already there. We're just waiting for the builder to arrive.'

Isaac chuckled. 'I've yet to meet a builder who's on time.' This would be the first time he'd meet the builder Petra and Harry had decided to use, and he was interested to see who they'd plumped for, considering he'd be working fairly closely with the guy.

Petra frowned. 'Actually, it isn't the builder who is late – you're early,' she pointed out.

'You know I hate being late,' he said, following her around the side of the house and into a boot room.

Petra toed off her Wellington boots and shoved her feet into a pair of pumps. He caught a glimpse of horses woven into the fabric of her socks and smiled.

'What?' she demanded, noticing the direction of his gaze. 'Doesn't everyone have horsey socks?'

Isaac thought of his own plain black socks and wished he was wearing more inspiring ones as he began to remove his shoes.

'No need to take them off,' Petra told him, 'Just as long as they aren't covered in mud.'

They weren't, although they were rather scuffed and scruffy, and hinted more towards the steel toe-cap end of the footwear market than the loafer side. He also kept a pair of sturdy work boots in his car for when he was on site, as building work tended to be a mucky business.

Petra led him through a higgledy-piggledy kitchen redolent with the aroma of coffee and baking bread, and into a dining room where three men were already seated.

'Amos, Harry, Nathan...' Isaac nodded to them and sat down. He'd met Amos who owned the stables, and Harry, who was Petra's fiancé, several times over the course of the past few months, but he'd only met Nathan, the stables' general manager, once or twice before.

As he opened his document case, slid out a rolled-up

bundle and spread the drawings out, Isaac wondered which of them was going to manage the build.

'Congratulations on obtaining planning permission,' he began. 'I expect you're relieved it didn't take very long. The process can sometimes trundle on for months, so you're lucky.'

'Luck has got nothing to do with it,' a woman's voice said from behind. 'It's because they've got a good architect.'

Isaac stiffened. Straightening slowly, he turned around, wanting desperately to believe he was mistaken, but at the same time praying that he wasn't.

'Hello, Isaac, long time no see,' the woman added.

'*Nelly*.' His reply was barely louder than a whisper and he cleared his throat, conscious of everyone's eyes on him. 'How are you?'

'Do you two know each other?' Petra asked.

'We go way back,' Nelly replied. Her gaze bored into him, pinning him like a moth to a board.

'It's good to see you,' Isaac said, hastily trying to compose himself.

'You, too.'

Harry half-rose. 'Nelly, take a seat. I was about to make more coffee before we start. Can I get you anything?'

'A coffee would be great,' she said, sitting down.

'Isaac?' Harry turned his attention to him.

'Er, no thanks.' Isaac couldn't drag his gaze away from Nelly. '*You're* the builder!' he blurted.

'I am. Have you got a problem with that?' Her voice was as sultry as he remembered, velvet over steel. She was as forthright as he remembered, too. He could almost see her bristling.

'No problem,' he assured her, but he was lying. He most definitely *did* have a problem. But it had nothing to do with her being a female builder in a predominantly male profession. It was because of Nelly, herself. 'How is your dad?' he asked.

'He died a while back.'

Isaac saw the pain in her eyes. 'I'm sorry to hear that. I know how close you were.'

Harry returned to the dining room and placed a tray containing several mugs of steaming black coffee on the table, along with a jug of milk and a bowl of sugar. Despite Isaac saying he didn't want a drink, Harry had made him one anyway.

Nelly added milk to hers, then picked it up and took a sip, and Isaac's gaze was drawn to her mouth. How many times had he kissed those lips? Would they taste the same, feel the same?

As though she could tell what he was thinking, Nelly caught his eye and he blushed, hastily looking away.

Nelly said. 'Can I take a look?' She gestured to the plans.

'Be my guest.'

While she studied the drawings, Isaac studied her.

The changes the years had made to her were subtle. Shorter hair, but not by very much. More angular cheekbones, the youthful roundness she'd had when she was a student having morphed into a more mature beauty. Eyes more guarded, expression less open. But essentially she was still the same Nelly that he had loved and lost.

'No amendments?' she asked after a few moments.

Isaac was abruptly dragged back to the matter at hand, and he realised she was referring to the plans. She would have seen the basic set of drawings when she was quoting for the contract, but not these most recent ones.

'Only a small one – here.' He pointed to the addition of a window high up on the gable end. 'Fire regs,' he explained.

Nora nodded. 'That's fine.'

'Will that affect the quote?' Petra asked, her gaze on Nelly.

Nelly was drinking tea, not the coffee she'd favoured when he had known her, Isaac noticed. Wasn't it odd what the mind focused on when it had been blind-sided? He should have expected to bump into her at some point though, now that he was back on her turf, and he felt foolish not to have braced himself for it.

'Yes, but only by a marginal amount,' Nelly assured Petra, and Isaac snapped back into focus as he reminded himself that this wasn't a trip down memory lane – he had a job to do.

'I'll be honest with you,' Petra said to her. 'We need to keep the costs down. How much preparatory work can we effectively do ourselves before you need to step in?'

Nelly shrugged. 'You can do quite a bit, up to, but not including knocking walls down, unless you're confident about supporting the roof adequately. The shed needs to be emptied, obviously, the partitions need removing, the floor needs to be dug down half a metre. It depends on how soon you want me to start and how long it will take you to get it build-ready.'

Isaac tuned out as Harry and Nathan discussed the feasibility of doing the preparatory work themselves, with Amos and Petra chipping in with the occasional comment. Nelly, he noticed, was mostly silent. Outwardly she seemed to be focusing on her clients, but he had a feeling she was as aware of him as he was of her.

From the second he'd heard her voice he'd tingled from his head to his toes and his pulse had raced.

Sipping the coffee he hadn't thought he'd wanted, and now grateful for anything to help with the dryness in his mouth, he kept glancing at her over the rim of his mug. And each time he did so, her eyes flickered as though she'd been watching him, and had looked away before he'd caught her.

He wasn't sure how he felt about Nelly Newsome coming back into his life, but he did know one thing – he didn't intend to let her into his heart for a second time.

Not when she'd broken it once before.

Isaac kept glancing at her. Nelly could feel his gaze on her face, as real as a finger stroking her cheek.

He used to do that, she recalled suddenly...trace a finger down her face from the corner of her eye to her mouth; then he would run that same finger across her lips until she couldn't stand the delicious tickle of it. She'd catch it in her mouth, and her nibbling on his finger always led to—

Enough, she told herself. It was in the past and that's where it should stay. There was no point remembering what they had once meant to each other, and she certainly shouldn't be thinking about it right now. She needed to focus on her clients and the job at hand, not on how deeply she had once been in love with Isaac Richards. Anyway, it was a long time ago.

They had both moved on with their lives. It was just unfortunate that they now had to work together. It was also unfortunate that Petra hadn't mentioned her architect by name when she'd spoken to Nelly, so that Nelly could have prepared herself. But at least Isaac had looked as shocked as Nelly had felt when he'd seen her, so Petra hadn't mentioned her name to him either. It was a small consolation.

All she hoped was that no one had noticed her reaction to him. At least she'd had a tiny bit of warning when she'd seen him sitting at the table, and although he'd had his back to her she would have recognised him anywhere, even if he hadn't spoken. It was just enough warning to stamp down on the sudden lurch her heart had given. Thank goodness October had shown her into the house and had disappeared before Nelly had heard that so-familiar voice, because she'd slapped a hand to her chest and her knees had almost failed her. She'd had to take a deep breath to steady herself, and only then had she been able to walk into the room with a professional smile on her face and a quip on her lips.

Damn and blast, but he was still as attractive as ever. More so, if she was honest. He'd always been a handsome devil with his tall, rangy frame and broad shoulders, and that face – it had been to die for. He'd worn his hair longer then, probably because he preferred to spend his money in the pub rather than in the barbershop, and he'd had permanent stubble on his face because his razor was constantly blunt. She had rather liked the look, despite the rash she'd had on her cheek from it. His chin was smooth now and she wondered if his skin would feel as soft as it looked.

That was the only soft thing about him she saw, as she studied him out of the corner of her eye. His stomach appeared to be washboard hard underneath the white shirt he wore, and she could just see the tops of his thighs and how the material of his trousers stretched across the underlying muscles.

Oh, poo, he'd caught her looking, and she hastily dropped her eyes to the table and the plans lying on it.

There was another part of him that was soft for the briefest of moments, and that was the expression in his eyes. But when she risked shooting him another swift look (she didn't seem able to help herself – he drew her gaze like iron filings to a magnet) his expression was blank, and his eyes were hooded.

Her heart thudded uncomfortably as she realised that he'd worn the exact same guarded expression the last time she'd set eyes on him. He'd been distant and wary, with no hint of the pain she knew she'd caused him.

But what else was she supposed to have done? She'd been between a rock and a hard place, and she'd loved him too deeply to tether him when there was little to no chance of things working out between them.

The hardest thing she'd ever done had been to let him go. The next hardest had been to bury her father. And that alone spoke volumes of how much she'd once loved Isaac Richards.

The burning question, and one she wasn't sure she wanted to know the answer to, was did she still love him?

She had a horrible suspicion that she did.

'Did you see the sparks flying between those two?' Petra asked Harry, as soon as Isaac and Nelly left, Amos and Nathan hot on their heels – Amos had dinner to prepare, and Nathan muttered something about fetching the ponies in from the field. She got heavily to her feet and began to collect up the mugs.

'I'll do that.' Harry came up behind her and wrapped his arms around her, cradling her stomach.

Petra leant back into him, feeling his solid chest against her aching back. Thirty weeks pregnant meant she still had two long months to go before their baby put in an appearance.

'They've definitely got history,' she mused. 'I wonder what it is.'

'As long as it doesn't affect the build, I don't care,' Harry said.

'Where's your sense of romance?'

Harry snorted. 'I never thought I'd hear the word *romance* coming from you. Remember when we first met? I don't think you knew what it meant.'

Petra tilted her head to the side so he could nuzzle her neck. 'Mmm, that's nice.' The baby seemed to like it too because he kicked vigorously. 'Did you feel that?'

Harry's voice was full of wonder. 'I most certainly did. He's a strong little blighter, isn't he?'

'Tell me about it. You ought to try being on the receiving end.'

'I would if I could,' he said, and she twisted around in his arms to face him.

'I know,' she replied softly, her arms around his neck.

He wanted this baby so much and he loved her so completely, that it took her breath away every time she thought about it.

What a change a year had brought to her life, she mused, as she gazed into his eyes and saw her love reflected in their depths. When she'd first met Harry, never in a million years would she have believed she could have gone from mistrustful animosity to loving him with every cell in her body.

He bent his head and kissed her gently, and the baby kicked again.

'Ow! Someone's jealous,' she said, and Harry grinned down at her.

'Someone is going to have to get used to his daddy kissing his mummy, because I've no intention of stopping.'

'We'll just have to wait until he's asleep,' Petra said.

'No, we won't! I want him to know how much I love you. It'll be good for him to see that his parents adore each other.'

'Oh, so you think I adore you, do you?' she teased, her mouth on his.

'You'd better, Mrs Milton, because *I* adore *you*.'

'I'm not Mrs Milton yet.'

'You soon will be. Have you found a dress you like?'

Petra pulled back and looked at her stomach. 'How can I when this is expanding faster than the damned universe? I need a marquee, not a wedding dress. No, I'm going to wait until after the baby is born and see what I can fit into.'

'Are you sure you don't want to sneak off to the registry office? We could be married in as little as three weeks,' Harry suggested.

'Are you that keen to get hitched?'

'Yes.' He nodded emphatically.

'That's so sweet.'

'I'm not sweet. I'm rough and rugged,' he objected in mock indignation.

'You're a total softie…'

'Sorry to interrupt,' Amos said, from the doorway. 'But you've got a class in half an hour.'

'So I have,' Petra said. 'I'd better give Nathan a hand bringing the ponies up from the field.'

'Do you want any help?' Harry asked.

'I've got this, but if you could ask Timothy when he's free? We've got a cow shed to clear.'

Wedding dresses and cow sheds practically in the same sentence? Petra smiled as she walked down the lane a few moments later, a couple of lead ropes in her hands. Running a riding school was hardly glamorous!

Nathan was unbolting the gate to the field when he saw her approach, and he waited for her to catch up. 'I think something is going on between your architect and your builder,' he said, holding the gate open for her.

'You noticed, too?'

'It was hard not to.'

'I wonder if they've worked together before?'

'Maybe, but didn't you say she owns a local firm and he's come from away?' Nathan asked.

'Yeah, Nelly owns Ken Newsome Building Contractors. They've got a good reputation. Her father started the business and built it up. Nelly took over from him when he died.'

'Do you trust her to do a good job?'

Petra bristled. 'I hope you're not implying that a female builder isn't as good as a man?'

Nathan gave her a sideways look. 'I wouldn't dare. I was talking about the way she reacted to your architect when she saw him. And he looked just as... I'm not sure how you'd describe it.'

Petra grinned. 'Hungry? Isaac looked at her like he was starving and she was a three-course meal.'

'You've hit the nail on the head,' he said, moving further into the field, Petra accompanying him, her eyes picking out the ponies they needed to catch for this afternoon's lesson.

If Isaac and Nelly's first meeting was any indication, the next few months were going to be interesting.

CHAPTER TWO

There were two stages to every build that Nelly particularly enjoyed – the beginning where she worked out the intricacies of the project, and the end where everyone's efforts were finally realised. The in between bit was pure hard work and frequently littered with problems. In her experience, it was rare for a build to run smoothly, to run to time and to come in on budget.

As she stood inside the cow shed, an iPad in her hand, Nelly was in her element. Planning a project was a complex activity involving detailed notes, meticulous attention to detail and a task sheet as long as her arm, but she loved it.

This morning she was on site trying to estimate how long each stage of the build would take so she could calendar in when she needed sub-contractors, such as the electricians, to do their bit. In her experience, each phase overlapped and often needed a certain degree of fluidity. It was challenging and demanding work, but that's why she enjoyed it so much. It might be difficult to envisage the finished product when standing in the middle of a dark and dirty stone-built barn that still smelt faintly of cow poo, but as she wandered around using a digital copy of the plans that Isaac had supplied, she could see the transformation taking place in her mind.

That massive stone trough? That was where one of the kitchens would be located. That wall over there would have three holes punched through it for windows. The corrugated iron sheeting on the roof? Replaced with new rafters and smooth grey slate, with solar panels to generate at least 50 per cent of the electricity the cottages would use.

Nelly added another item to her ever-growing list – ask Petra who was sourcing the panels. The stables' owners weren't employing a separate project manager, but were going to oversee the build themselves, which was a mistake in Nelly's opinion. Unless clients had experience in that field, it was going to be a steep learning curve for them. Petra especially, because Nelly had the feeling that it would be Petra who was going to be the person most involved in the decision-making and in driving the project forward.

And the woman was about seven months pregnant!

Nelly had to admire her. It wasn't going to be easy.

As she scribbled on the tablet, Nelly thought back to yesterday, when she'd met their architect for the first time. But it hadn't been the first time, had it? Her heart gave a jolt as she thought about Isaac. It had been doing that a lot over the last twenty or so hours. She wished she didn't have to think about him, but it was going to be hard not to since she would be working closely with him.

A line from an old black and white film flitted through her mind… "of all the gin joints in all the towns in all the world…" he'd walked into hers. Was it fate that their paths had crossed again? Or simply an unfortunate set of circumstances?

Considering the line of work they were both in, it might seem inevitable that they would bump into each other at some point, except for one thing – Nelly lived in Picklewick, and Isaac didn't. The last she'd heard, he was in Wiltshire and she wondered what he was doing here.

'Hello?' The unexpected sound of Petra's voice made Nelly squeak in surprise and whirl around.

'Sorry, I didn't mean to startle you,' Petra said. 'I saw your van and thought I'd check that everything was okay.' She was silhouetted in one of the doorways, a dark figure against the bright May morning outside.

Nelly put a hand to her thudding heart. 'I was in a world of my own,' she explained.

Petra walked towards her. 'As you can see, we've not begun yet,' she said, almost apologetically.

'I've come to write a plan of action,' Nelly said. 'A tentative one,' she added. 'How soon I can implement it depends on when I can start.'

Petra grinned at her. 'We've got a clearing party arranged for this weekend. You're welcome to come along.'

Nelly hesitated, not sure how she should respond considering that her clients had informed her they wanted to do this part of the build themselves to try to keep costs down. Had they changed their minds, or were they expecting her to work for free?

Maybe Petra read her mind because she added, 'Amos is firing up the barbeque, so you're welcome to pop in for a burger and a beer. No obligation: we don't expect you to put your hard hat on and join in, especially since this bit isn't part of your contract.'

'Thanks, I might drop by. I'll have to see how it goes,' Nelly said, relieved that was cleared up. She hadn't wanted to be rude and ask for clarification, but some bad experiences with a couple of clients she'd worked with in the past had taught her to be wary. Nelly was running a business not a charity, and even though she always wanted to do as much as she could to help her clients, working for free wasn't a good business model: the bank wouldn't be pleased for one thing, and for another she had her staff's wages to pay.

Anyway, however kind Petra's offer was, Nelly had no intention of dropping in because she knew she wouldn't be able to resist getting her hands dirty and joining in.

Which reminded her... 'You need to wear a hard hat from now on when you're on site,' Nelly said. She tapped her own.

'I've got a riding helmet. Will that do?'

'Probably, but be prepared for it to get ruined. Knocking things down and building them back up is a dirty business.'

Petra laughed. 'These hats aren't the fancy sort that you see on The Horse of the Year Show,' she said. 'You're thinking of the ones covered in velvet. The helmet I wear is a bog-standard fibreglass one – no fabric of any description.'

'I see.' Nelly didn't know the first thing about riding hats; or about horses, for that matter.

'Do you ride?' Petra asked.

'Regretfully not.' Horse riding hadn't appealed to her, unlike some of her friends who had been mad about ponies.

'Have you ever ridden?'

'Does a donkey ride on the beach count?'

Petra chuckled. 'It's a start. Would you like to learn?'

Nelly wasn't sure. She tended to prefer mechanical rides such as diggers, rather than horsey ones, and she made a see-saw motion with her hand, not wanting to offend her newest client.

'You're going to be here for a couple of months, so let me show you around,' Petra offered.

Nelly raised her eyebrows. 'This build is going to take more than a couple of months. You'll be lucky if it's completed in four. Even six would be pushing it.'

'I'm sure you'll give it your best shot,' Petra said airily. 'Come on, I've got a donkey to show you, and a stubborn pregnant goat.'

Isaac leaned back in his chair and rolled his head, wincing at the crunch in his neck. His shoulders were tense and his eyes felt gritty, which wasn't surprising considering his lack of sleep last night.

He'd driven away from the stables on Muddypuddle Lane with his senses filled with Nelly – the sight of her, the sound of her voice, the scent of the perfume he'd caught wisps of and had recognised instantly as one she used to wear when she could afford it. He'd bought her a bottle once for her birthday. The smell of it had swept over and through him, affecting him even more than seeing her had done. Even his skin had tingled as he remembered how she had felt in his arms, how soft she'd been, how demanding.

Oh dear, best not to go there. Seeing her so unexpectedly was bad enough, but allowing memories of delicious nights spent in each other's student bed was a step too far. If he was going to work with her (which he had no choice about) he must put their past to the back of his mind and keep it there.

Isaac swivelled in his chair and peered out of the window. His office consisted of a small suite of rooms (three to be precise) in a block of similar suites, which he was currently renting until he found a more permanent base. Leaving Wiltshire hadn't been the easiest of decisions to make, especially since he'd made a bit of a name for himself there as a decent architect, but needs must, and the needs of his mum had called him back. Dad leaving had sent her into a tailspin and Isaac wanted to be there to support her. He had no idea what had happened between his parents to end their thirty-seven-year marriage because neither of them would say anything other than they'd grown apart, but clearly it must be something drastic because his mum was inconsolable and his father was tight-lipped and defensive.

All Isaac could do was to be there for them, his mum in particular because she appeared to be coping less well with the split.

It had been a wrench leaving Wiltshire, but he was self-employed and he could relocate his business to anywhere he wanted. He had a professional website, with an impressive array of testimonials which was easily transportable, and in the four months since he'd returned to the area he'd grown up in, he'd managed to land a decent number of clients.

When he thought about it logically, he was surprised he hadn't bumped into Nelly before now, considering they were both in the same line of work and Picklewick was only about nine miles away. However, in his defence, he'd deliberately *not* thought about her. He'd spent the last thirteen years *not* thinking about her.

During those first horrible months when he had been forced to come to terms with the fact that she hadn't loved him as much as he'd loved her, he'd obsessively searched for any and all mentions of her and her dad's business online, but there hadn't been a great deal to be found. From what Nelly had told him, Ken had been a word-of-mouth type of builder, listed on yell.com but that was about it – no website, no Facebook account, nothing, and Nelly had also disappeared into the void as though she'd never existed.

As the months had turned into years, Isaac had begun to wonder if he'd imagined her, to ask himself if she really had existed. If it hadn't been for the hole she'd left in his heart, he might have believed he'd dreamt her.

When the initial acute pain of her leaving had eventually subsided to an ache he could live with without it being so debilitating that it crushed him during every waking hour, he'd put her in a box in his head and had hidden it in the depths of his mind. And there it had stayed (more or less), until yesterday, when his personal Pandora's box had been well and truly opened.

Taking a glance at the drawings he was supposed to be working on, Isaac let out a heartfelt sigh. He should try to concentrate on his work, but his wayward thoughts kept leading him back to Nelly.

He honestly wasn't sure how he felt about her. The attraction was still very much in evidence – she had become a beautiful woman – but was that the only emotion he was feeling?

Isaac blew out his cheeks. No, he didn't think so. What he was feeling was an undeniable resurrection of the ache in his heart that he'd long since thought he'd cured. But was the ache a rekindling of his old feelings, or was it nostalgia for a time when life was less complicated and he didn't have to adult? On looking back, life had been so much simpler then, even though it hadn't felt like it at the time. It had also been monochrome, with things either black or white. Shades of grey hadn't entered his world at that point, and when Nelly had dropped out of the course, left uni and had gone home, he'd interpreted it as her not loving him any more. Now, though he understood that she probably *had* loved him – just not enough to stay with him when life had got in the way.

He rolled his head once more, the tension easing slightly.

Maybe what he'd felt had been the intense emotions of first love, and everyone had their hearts broken sooner or later – unless they married their first loves, of course.

Speaking of marriage, he hadn't seen a ring on her finger but that didn't mean to say she didn't have a partner. Or that she didn't remove it when she was working, because rings could get caught, and building work was tough and physical.

Telling himself it was mere curiosity and nothing more, Isaac turned back to his computer and opened a new tab in the search engine and typed in her name.

A half an hour later and he was still none the wiser, and although there didn't appear to be any evidence of a man in her life, Isaac couldn't definitely say there wasn't.

Cross with himself for wasting time when he should be working, he shut the tab down and told himself to focus on what was important.

But the thought kept niggling away at him that Nelly's relationship status was very important indeed, and a part of him began to harbour the smallest of hopes that he and Nelly might be able to get to know each other all over again. Because, for him, the spark was still there, whether he wanted it to be or not.

'Have you and Isaac worked together before?' Petra asked.

She and Nelly were standing in what Petra had called "the tack room" where the saddles and bridles were kept. It smelled strongly of horse and leather. Nelly didn't find it an unpleasant smell, but she preferred the aroma of cement, if she was honest. Each to their own…

The tour of the stables had been nice though, especially when she got to stroke the long soft ears of a donkey, and she never knew that ponies' noses were so soft and nibbley. There had been fluffy chicks too, which were simply the cutest things ever.

Nelly and Petra each had a mug of tea in their hands and there was an open packet of Ginger Nut biscuits on the shelf next to the kettle, which Petra was busily munching her way through.

'Not really. We were in university together,' Nelly replied.

'What did you study?'

'Architecture.'

'I didn't realise you were an architect as well as a builder?'

Nelly pulled a face. 'I'm not. I dropped out halfway through my second year. My dad was ill and he needed someone to run the business for a while. I always intended to go back and finish the course, but Dad didn't get better, so…'

'You ended up running the company permanently?' Petra finished.

Nelly nodded. It sounded way easier and more straightforward than it had actually been. She'd dropped out of the course, meaning to pick it up again the following year, but it hadn't happened.

She'd also dropped out of something else – her relationship with Isaac.

Picking that up again would have been nigh on impossible. Everyone knew long distance love didn't work. Besides, they were both students, for god's sake – it wasn't meant to have been serious. But it had been, for her at least; and she'd got the feeling that Isaac had been just as heart-broken when she'd called it off. She wished she hadn't had to, but she'd had no choice – and she'd loved him too deeply and too fiercely to try to hang onto him.

She had set him free to get on with his life, and although she'd been heartbroken it had been the right thing to do. No doubt he had soon got over her.

Nelly wondered how he'd lived that life. Was he married? Did he have kids? Did he ever think about her?

Forget that last bit – she hoped he didn't, because she'd thought about him constantly for months and it had hurt so much. She wouldn't wish that kind of pain on her greatest enemy, and certainly not on the man she'd loved with all her heart, the man who she'd once hoped was The One.

She had yet to find anyone she wanted to spend the rest of her life with, because she hadn't experienced love like that since.

'You've done a good job of running it,' Petra said, bringing Nelly back to the present. 'When Harry was asking around for recommendations for local builders, Ken Newsome's name kept coming up, along with "don't be put off because Ken isn't a bloke". Your company has got a damned good reputation.'

'Glad to hear it,' Nelly said mildly.

Petra was giving her an assessing look. 'It couldn't have been easy.'

Nelly's gaze was level. 'It wasn't.'

There was silence for a few moments, then Petra said, 'You'll do.'

'Thanks!' Nelly chuckled.

'I bet you've had to work twice as hard and be twice as good as any bloke.'

'You've got that right.' Nelly had lost count of the number of times she'd answered the phone to a potential customer, only for the person on the other end to assume she was the office girl, especially in the early days when she had been so young.

It used to gall her that people equated youth with inexperience. She'd grown up with a father who used to take her with him when he went on a job. She'd been able to lay a course of house bricks before she'd been able to tie her shoelaces. Concrete blocks had come later, when she'd had the strength to lift them. Her dad had taught her about self-levelling concrete, lintels, the safest way to knock down a wall, the right sort of sand to use.

He'd taught her everything she knew, and he'd never been as proud as when she'd told him she wanted to be an architect. The plan had been for her to design it and for him to build it. They would have made a great team. But then he developed a pain in his back which he put down to a strain, and he had a cough that he'd ignored for far too long.

Now here she was, running one of the best firms of building contractors for miles around. Her dad had been proud of her right to the end.

CHAPTER THREE

'Timothy!' Harry cried, slapping his younger brother on the back and almost sending him flying. 'It's about time you did some manual labour.' Timothy and his girlfriend Charity were the first to arrive for the "clearing weekend". It was fortuitous that Timothy wasn't on call today because clearing the cow shed was going to be a mammoth job, Harry realised.

Timothy rose to his full height and bristled. 'I'll have you know that being a vet involves a great deal of manual labour.'

Harry winked at Charity, who said, 'Stand down, Timmo, he's having you on.'

'*Timmo?*' Harry chuckled. 'Is that your pet name for him?'

Charity smirked. 'Only when he's being a prat.'

'Being a prat, am I?' Timothy made to leave, shaking his head. 'And here I was, about to give up my valuable free time to help you guys out.'

'Did you have anything else lined up?' Petra asked.

'Yeah, sleeping,' was Timothy's reply, as he bent to give her a kiss on the cheek.

'You can sleep later,' she told him. 'Harry needs you.'

'After the comment he just made, Harry can go boil his head,' Timothy joked. 'I'm here for *you*, not for him. Have you managed to rope any other idiots in, or is it just me and Harry who will be doing all the hard work?'

'See, I told you he was scared of a bit of hard graft,' Harry said, dodging out of the way as Timothy aimed a playful punch at him.

'What am I? Decoration?' Charity demanded. 'I'm perfectly capable of hauling stuff around.' She looked positively put out at the implication.

'Don't let our builder hear you say that,' Petra said to Timothy. 'Just to give you a heads-up, she's female and she won't take kindly to you implying that she's not as capable as a man.'

Timothy looked horrified. 'I wouldn't dream of it.'

Harry thought it best to step in before his brother had both Petra and Charity on his back. 'I'd quit now, while you're still upright,' he advised. 'Have you *seen* Charity lift a bale of hay? *You're* more likely to be the decoration around here.'

'I can't help it if I'm pretty,' Timothy quipped, earning himself a round of rolled eyes and groans.

Harry grinned. Today might very well be hard work, but it also promised to be fun, especially with Amos manning the barbeque from lunchtime onwards and the promise of cold beers and a gorgeously sunny day. All he hoped was that he could keep Petra in check, because he knew she'd be wanting to get stuck in and do her bit. He'd have to box clever so that she didn't get on her high horse and give him the "I'm pregnant, not ill" speech. His fiancée was as bossy as they came, so he'd appeal to that side of her nature and try to persuade her to do the supervising. They still had to work out where all the stuff they were taking out of the cow shed was going to go, for a start.

He was still mulling the problem over when Nathan arrived with Megan, quickly followed by October's mum, Lena, who had been driven to the stables by Luca, October's boyfriend.

Harry had expected to see Nathan, but not his partner Megan, and he greeted them both with enthusiasm and gratitude.

'I thought Amos could do with a hand keeping the troops fed and watered,' Megan said.

Lena was also a surprise. 'I might not be able to do any heavy lifting, but I'm pretty good at clearing up,' she announced. 'Besides, I can always help out with the catering side of things too, and I know October won't be around all day as she's taking a hack out, so I thought you could do with all the help you can get.'

'That's very kind of you,' he said, touched, and when he glanced at Petra he could see that she was equally moved.

'I'm here all day,' Luca said. 'Just tell me what you want me to do.'

Harry was about to round everyone up and head over to the cow shed where Amos had already rolled out the barbeque, when another car trundled up the lane.

When it came to a halt and William Reid got out, Harry's eyes widened. He hadn't expected the manager of Picklewick's care home to pay them a visit this morning, and he wondered what the man wanted.

William saw Harry looking and he shouted over, 'Come and give me a hand with this, will you?'

"This" turned out to be a large silver-coloured urn, which would make several hundred cups of tea by the look of it.

'I thought it would come in handy, rather than boiling a kettle every five minutes,' William said, and Harry saw Megan's eyes light up. It would certainly make providing hot drinks easier.

'Thank you so much!' Harry exclaimed, feeling a lump in his throat at everyone's thoughtfulness and willingness to help. Petra turned away blinking furiously, and he guessed she was just as affected as he.

Back in January, when he'd had the idea to transform the cow shed into holiday lets, it had been a pie-in-the-sky dream, and he hadn't truly believed it would happen. There had been so many obstacles – the main one being the cost – that he hadn't thought it had a hope in hell of becoming a reality, despite him offering to plough the capital he'd received as his half of the sale of his parents' house (Timothy was in the process of using his share to buy the cottage he and Charity were living in). If it wasn't for Petra agreeing to be his wife and his insistence that once they were married what was his would also become hers, Harry didn't think Petra would have considered the venture. He just hoped that once the renovations were done and once the cow shed had been magically transformed into three holiday cottages, the stables would be able to turn a profit without his wife-to-be having to work all the hours God sends.

He was looking forward to spending as much time as possible with his wife and child, and it would be tough to run two businesses with a newborn to look after, although he might consider dropping his farrier business down to part-time in order to help Petra more. So he was hoping that the additional income from the holiday lets would allow her to employ someone else, enabling her to take a step back.

With so many people turning up to help with the preparatory work on the cow shed, the building work could start soon. It might be unrealistic of him, but he was hoping the bulk of it would be over by Petra's due date.

He had so much to look forward to over the next few months – a complete renovation project, a new baby and a wedding. Talk about not doing things by halves!

Amos wasn't ready to fire up the barbeque yet, but at least it was in position: Harry had helped drag it over from their enclosed garden at the rear of the house and position it near the shed. Actually, Harry had done most of the dragging and lifting where necessary, with Amos supervising.

Amos was busy checking the charcoal situation, while also keeping a beady eye on the weather, when he heard a gaggle of voices.

What on earth…? Putting the bag of woodchips down, which he'd planned on adding to the coals once they were lit, Amos stood with his hands on his hips and waited.

Within a few seconds, a group of eight people came around the corner, closely followed by Harry and William Reid from the care home in the village who were carrying what looked like a large urn between them.

Amos blinked. 'Is that an urn?'

'Yep. Have you got a power source?' William asked, puffing slightly as they shuffled it around and stood it on top of one of the tables which had been set up.

'Er, yes. There's an extension cable over there.' Amos pointed. He was running a lead from the barn in order to boil the kettle, but an urn was a much better idea.

'Got any jugs?' Megan asked, flexing her arms.

'Hi, Megan, I didn't expect to see you. Or you, Lena. How's your mum?' Amos enquired.

'So, so. But thanks for asking.'

'Are you all here to help?' he asked, confused.

'We most certainly are,' Megan said. 'More hands make light work. Now, have you got any jugs?' she repeated. 'The sooner we fill this urn, the sooner we can all have a brew.'

Amos watched Megan and Lena get to work with calm efficiency and he shook his head, bemused and more than a little grateful.

He knew Megan fairly well, even though she'd only been coming to the stables for about six months and had been with Nathan for less than that. She and Nathan had got together while Megan had been working her way through a series of letters that her deceased husband had left her. His last one had informed her he'd booked horse-riding lessons for her. It had been his final gift, a gift designed to set her free of her mourning and give her a chance to live again. It had worked – Nathan had fallen in love with her and she with him, and now they were practically inseparable.

She'd also brought cake. Lots and lots of cake. Megan had recently set up a cake-decorating business and Amos's mouth watered in anticipation at the sweet treats.

Lena, on the other hand, was a total surprise. He'd known Lena for years, but hadn't had a great deal to do with her. She'd moved to Picklewick about ten years ago when her mother, Olive, who'd recently had to go into a care home, needed help. He often saw Olive when he visited the care home, and he sometimes bumped into Lena too, but he hadn't expected to see her at the stables. He didn't think she particularly liked horses, for one thing, despite her daughter, October, being a first-class rider and a very competent groom.

While he was fetching mugs from the kitchen and digging out the paper plates he'd bought especially for today, Amos kept glancing over at her. For some reason she reminded him of Mags, his wife. Lord, how he missed her. She'd been gone a fair few years, but her loss wasn't any easier to handle now than it had been in those awful weeks and months after she'd died. The one saving grace to come out of his wife's passing was that he'd got to know his niece much better than he otherwise might have done. So well, that he'd asked Petra to move in with him and help run the stables. It had been a dream come true for her and a godsend for him, because he didn't know how he would have managed without her, especially after his angina diagnosis.

His gaze drifted to her, and he noted with satisfaction that she wasn't attempting to lift or move anything herself, but was busy directing everyone else. They might call it being bossy, but they took it in good cheer, and someone had even rigged up some speakers to their phone and dance music accompanied the laughter and the chatter.

This is a good day, Amos thought, and these were good

people. He was lucky to have so many friends who were willing to help, and a family who loved him. Of the people helping with this new and exciting phase in the life of the stables, he might technically only be related to Petra, but he viewed both Harry and Nathan as surrogate sons, and soon there would be a baby to love and cherish.

With a deep feeling of gratitude, Amos set about firing up the barbeque. Very soon he'd have hungry mouths to feed.

Isaac hadn't intended to go anywhere near the stables on Muddypuddle Lane today, but for some reason he found himself driving up the rutted track this afternoon, his car bumping over the potholes, before his brain had caught up with what the rest of his body was doing.

Telling himself that as he was here now, he may as well show his face, he parked his car in the carpark (which was nearly as pitted and potholed as the lane) and got out, inhaling the unmistakable aroma of horse, overlaid by a mouth-watering smell of charcoaled meat and frying onions.

He'd stay long enough to make sure they weren't knocking down a wall they shouldn't, he'd have a burger if there was one on offer, then he'd skedaddle. He didn't want to risk being asked to shift or lift anything. That job was down to the clients and the builder.

The builder…Isaac wondered if Nelly would be here, and he scanned the parked vehicles but none of them had Ken Newsome's name emblazoned on the side.

He wasn't sure whether to be relieved or disappointed.

After changing into the steel toecap work boots that he always kept in the car and grabbing his hard hat, he followed the sounds of music, laughter and the clang of metal.

As soon as he rounded the side of the barn he came face-to-face with Petra.

'Isaac! Nice to see you!' Petra was filthy, covered from head to foot in a coating of fine dust. Incongruously, she was wearing a pair of dungarees that stretched across her rounded belly, a riding hat, and a pair of bright pink wellies with navy flowers on them. At least, he thought they were pink – it was difficult to tell through all the grime.

'How are you getting on?' he asked.

'Come and see for yourself.'

Praying that they hadn't demolished something they shouldn't have, he walked slowly towards the shed, plonking his hard hat on his head.

'Have you come to give us a hand?' Harry called when he saw him, and Isaac shook his head and laughed.

'I've come for a beer and a burger,' he called back.

Harry gave him a thumbs-up. Harry and three other men were trying to manoeuvre the massive stone trough onto the tines of a tractor. Nathan was at the tractor's helm, and Isaac watched in fascination as Nathan delicately inserted the tines underneath the trough, and the stone edifice began to rise.

'Everyone move back!' Harry shouted, as the tractor trundled slowly out of the shed. He dusted his hands off and came to join Isaac and Petra, who were standing a safe distance away. The farrier was as grimy as his fiancée, but he had a huge grin on his face.

'The shed is almost clear, I see,' Isaac said. 'I can't believe you've done so much in such a short space of time.'

The cow shed had little else in it now, apart from the partitions which would have to come down at some point, but even with them still in place, he was finally able to fully appreciate how big the area was. The building would make three airy and spacious cottages.

'It's all Petra's doing – she's a real slave driver,' Harry chuckled, turning to the three men who'd been helping with the trough. 'Sorry, I haven't introduced you. This is Timothy, my brother. He's one of the local vets. This is Luca, October's other half – he's got a horse stabled here. And last but not least is William, who manages Picklewick's care home.'

With the introductions made, everyone headed outside and made their way over to the barbeque area, stopping off at an outside tap to wash their hands. Isaac got in line and rinsed his hands. It was as he turned to where Amos had set up the food that he spotted Nelly.

His stomach flipped and his heart stuttered. Appetite suddenly vanished, he wondered whether he should say his goodbyes and leave. He'd been half-expecting her (that *was* why you're here, a treacherous little voice in his mind pointed out) but faced with the reality of her, Isaac suddenly wanted to run. Or scoop her up in his arms and kiss her soundly. He couldn't quite decide which.

It didn't help that she was looking absolutely delectable. When he'd seen her the other day in Amos's dining room she'd been wearing jeans and a sweatshirt, with chunky work boots on her feet. Today though…oh, my goodness. Her pale blue dress clung to her waist and flared out over her hips, she was wearing sandals that revealed pink-painted toes, and her legs were bare. Her hair curled on her shoulders, and she had sunglasses perched on the top of her head.

Nelly Newsome hadn't come to the stables to lend a hand, that much was clear.

And she wasn't dressed for entering a building site either.

So why *was* she here? To offer moral support? Because she fancied some charred meat on a skewer? Or was she here because she hoped he might be?

It was a heady thought, and one he dismissed as soon as it occurred to him. *Of course* her presence had nothing to do with him. Why would it?

She might even be here with someone – a significant other.

Surreptitiously Isaac glanced around, coming to the conclusion that if she was here with a man, the only one it could possibly be was William. It set his teeth on edge to think they might be a couple and an unexpected bolt of pure, unadulterated jealously struck him in the chest.

Dry-mouthed and reluctant, he caught her eye and nodded.

Nelly nodded back, her expression giving nothing away. He couldn't tell whether she was pleased to see him, annoyed, or completely uninterested.

To his dismay he was extraordinarily pleased to see her – and that wasn't good. Not good at all.

Nelly's pulse hammered in her throat and she put a hand to her chest, trying to ease the sudden clamouring of her heart. She could feel a blush spreading across her cheeks and she willed it away. Seeing Isaac at the build wasn't unexpected, so why was she reacting like this?

Undoubtedly he was here for the same reason she was – to make sure the clients weren't too over enthusiastic in their clearing of the site. From the way he was dressed, he didn't appear to want to take part in the event either. His jeans were newish, and he was wearing a white tee shirt and trainers. His only concession to being on a building site was the hard hat he was holding. Nelly had hers in her voluminous handbag. She didn't intend putting it on until she went inside the shed because, let's face it, summer dresses and sandals didn't go with hard hats and work boots. She'd brought a pair of those with her too, and they were currently sitting next to one of the chairs that had been appropriated from the arena's viewing gallery and set up near the food.

By wearing a pretty dress and sandals, she wanted to make it clear to her clients that she wasn't here to work, but to give them some support.

Yeah, right… Ignoring her suspicion that the dress was purely for Isaac's benefit (as was the make-up and the freshly washed hair), and also refusing to acknowledge that she was here more in the hope of bumping into Isaac than for customer relations, Nelly accepted a burger from Amos, grabbed a bottle of non-alcoholic beer and took a seat.

Petra quickly joined her. 'I hate this,' she said, holding up a non-alcoholic beer of her own and giving Harry an evil stare. He was drinking the real stuff, Nelly noticed.

'You've got a little one to think of,' Nelly said. 'How long do you have to go?'

'Eight weeks.' Petra's tone of voice made Nelly laugh.

'Come and talk to me when *you're* seven months pregnant,' Petra moaned. 'I bet you won't be laughing about it then.' She pulled a face. 'I feel as though I'm carting a small horse around in here.' She brightened. 'And I'm not the only one expecting to hear the patter of tiny feet. Remember Princess the goat? She's due to give birth any day now.'

'Crumbs, it's all go, isn't it?'

'I love spring,' Petra said, taking a swig of her beer and grimacing. 'All the new growth and the new life. It's my favourite time of the year.'

'And a new build,' Nelly said. 'Here's to it going well. Which it will,' she added, clinking bottles with Petra. 'Do you mind if I take a look inside?'

'Want to make sure we haven't demolished anything vital?' Petra quipped. 'It's okay, Isaac has already checked, but you're welcome to see for yourself. Anyway, you're soon going to be spending more time in there than anyone else, so you might as well make yourself at home.'

Nelly slipped her feet into her work boots, her toes feeling naked without socks, and popped her hard hat on.

Petra tilted her head to one side. 'Can I just say that neither the boots nor the hat go with the dress.' She paused, then added, 'Would you like me to ask Isaac to go inside with you? I'm assuming you are usually in close contact with the architect on a build like this?' She looked innocent and wide-eyed, but Nelly frowned.

Had Petra realised that she had feelings for Isaac? Nelly hoped not. It was bad enough that she had them at all, without other people being aware of it.

Oh, hell! An unpleasant thought occurred to her. If Petra had noticed, might Isaac have noticed, too?

Embarrassment made her ears burn and she was glad her hat covered them. Bright red ear-tips had always been a sign that she was discomforted, and although Isaac had probably forgotten that little quirk of hers, she didn't want to take any chances that he might realise she was disconcerted.

'I'm fine on my own,' she said, noticing that he was occupied with a burger. Feeling reasonably certain she was safe to go into the shed without bumping into him, she put her food down on the table, took a swig of her beer and wandered casually off in the direction of the cow shed.

Wow, they'd done a fantastic amount of work, she saw. The place was empty apart from the dust motes swirling in the air, making her sneeze.

'I believe they are tackling the floor tomorrow,' Isaac said from behind, and Nelly jumped.

'I didn't expect to see you here,' she replied, without turning around.

'I didn't expect to see you, either. I thought you'd have had enough of building sites, without visiting one on your day off.'

'I only came for the free food. It'll save me cooking later.'

Nelly heard Isaac move closer and suddenly he was standing beside her, so close she could smell him. Mmm... She swallowed: her mouth was dry and her lips felt wooden. She knew that smell so well, and it set her heart thudding and the blood rushing through her veins.

Damn him! He could at least smell different. It was bad enough seeing him and hearing him, without the familiar and evocative scent of him wafting up her nose. All she needed to complete the hat trick was to kiss him, so she could taste him and feel him as well.

Woah there, girlie, she said to herself. Had the thought of kissing him really slipped into her mind? What a wally. She needed to get ideas like that out of her head, pronto. He was here to do a job, and so was she. The last thing she needed (or her clients needed, for that matter) was for her to drool over their architect. Isaac probably wouldn't be too pleased, either. For all she knew, he had a wife or a girlfriend who wouldn't appreciate an ex showing an interest.

Not only that, thirteen years was a long time. She should be over him by now.

Hell, she'd thought she was, until she'd seen him in her client's dining room, as large as life and twice as handsome.

Gosh, he really *was* handsome. The years had taken his boyish good looks and turned them into something more mature, and she felt the force of his presence like a hammer to her soul.

Briefly she closed her eyes, wishing that things had been different. If only her dad—

No! She refused to think like that. What had happened, had happened. She'd do it again in a heartbeat. Her coming back home and taking up the reins of the family business had made her dad's passing easier for him. She could no more wish that away than she could wish that Isaac still loved her.

And it was then that she knew without a shadow of a doubt that she still loved him. She always had, and she suspected she always would. More's the pity, because she now faced several months of working with him.

Stifling a cry, Nelly whirled on her heel. 'Sorry, there's somewhere I need to be,' she said abruptly. Then she fled.

She might have to work with him, but the ordeal didn't have to start now. All she wanted to do was to go home and try to forget Isaac Richards existed.

CHAPTER FOUR

Amos sighed theatrically and reached for a towel to wipe his hands. Why was it that whenever he had his hands in a bowl of water, the phone rang? He'd been about to wash the kitchen cupboards down because they hadn't been done for ages and he didn't want Petra to look at them and get the idea that she should give them a clean – his niece had more than enough to be going on with. The least he could do was uphold his part of the bargain and keep the house in order, so that she didn't feel she had to.

Expecting it to be a parent wanting to book, amend, or cancel their child's riding lesson, he hurried to answer it.

'Amos? It's Sandra from the HRC. I don't know if you remember me? We met at the agricultural show last year.'

Amos thought for a moment, racking his brains. Got her! She ran a horse charity which rescued and rehomed abused, abandoned and neglected horses.

'I remember,' he said, hoping she wasn't calling to tap him up for a donation. With the cow shed conversion going ahead, the stables needed every penny they could lay their hands on, despite Harry's very generous insertion of funds. Harry might soon be Petra's husband and had argued that what was his was hers, but Amos was keenly aware that it was the money Harry had got from the sale of his deceased parents' house that was paying for the project.

'What can I do for you?' he asked, warily.

'A huge favour, I hope.'

Amos's heart sank.

He was about to say that they weren't in a position to donate, when Sandra continued, 'Can you take a horse? I wouldn't normally ask, but she's in a bit of a state and is heavily pregnant. She's about to drop any day now and I can't risk moving her too far. We're full to bursting and can't take another animal, and the next nearest centre is over fifty miles away. I'm scared she'll go into labour on route.'

Amos hesitated. They had enough to go on with themselves, what with the clearing party on the weekend and the building work starting shortly after. The stables on Muddypuddle Lane was hardly going to be a haven of tranquillity over the coming weeks, and not only that, it sounded as though the mare might need a great deal of care and attention.

But then Sandra said something that made him sit up and take notice. 'She's producing colostrum.'

That changed everything. If the mare's teats had started secreting colostrum it meant that labour was imminent.

'How soon can you get her to us?' he asked.

'Within the hour.'

'We'll have a stall ready for her.'

'I can't thank you enough,' Sandra said, the relief in her voice evident.

As soon as she rang off, Amos hastened to find Nathan. It looked like the stables would soon hear the patter of tiny horsey hooves and, despite the amount of extra work it would cause, he found he was incredibly excited at the prospect of having a newborn foal to care for.

'All right, love?' Nelly's mum greeted her as she opened the front door and led her into the lounge. Jayne had been reading one of the crime novels she loved and enjoying a glass of wine.

'Where's Reggie?' Nelly asked. Reggie was her step-dad, and although Nelly was pleased that her mum had found love again after Dad died, it had taken her a while to accept him. Thankfully, Jayne had moved in with Reggie and not the other way around, so Nelly was spared the sight of another man residing over the table her dad used to sit at, or bumping into him on the landing. Nelly still lived in the house her parents had owned, and it would have been unbearable for her if Reggie had come to live with them. He had a lovely house of his own on the edge of the village and her mum seemed happy there, so the arrangement suited all three of them.

'It's Sunday – where do you think he is?' Jayne said with a fond smile.

'Golf?' Nelly hazarded a guess.

'You got it. Fancy a glass?' She picked up her wine. It was her mother's one indulgence – a glass of Pinot Grigio on a lazy weekend afternoon after the traditional roast had been consumed.

'I'd better not. If I start, I mightn't stop at one.' The way she was feeling, Nelly worried that she might just drink the whole bottle in one go.

'Tough week?' Jayne had half-shares in the business, and although she was for the most part a sleeping partner, she had a vested interest and she also did the accounts, so it wasn't unusual for the two of them to talk shop.

'You could say that,' Nelly sighed, as she sank into one of the squishy armchairs.

'Do you want to tell me about it?'

'I bumped into Isaac Richards.' Working with him could hardly be classed as "bumped" but it would do.

'Is he a new client?' Jayne was frowning.

'No, he's the architect at the stables on Muddypuddle Lane.'

'The cow shed conversion? What's he done? Or not done?' It wasn't unheard of for building contractors and architects to butt heads.

'Nothing – he's drawn up a decent set of plans. It's just…' Nelly took a deep breath. She had to get this off her chest or she might explode. 'I once knew him really well, Mum.'

Her mother's eyes widened. 'And seeing him again is a problem because…?'

'I was in love with him.'

'*When?* I haven't heard you mention him.' Her mother wore a shocked expression.

'In university.'

Jayne slowly closed her eyes and opened them again. 'I see. I knew you were upset, but I assumed it was because you dropped out of the course and because you were worried about your dad.'

'That was mostly it, but it wasn't the only reason.'

'I can see that now. Oh, love, I wish you'd stayed on to get your degree. Your dad and I begged you not to drop out.'

'And where would that have left him? He was worried sick about the business, and I wanted to take some of the burden.' Nelly couldn't have stayed in uni; her conscience wouldn't have allowed her.

'We'd have managed. You had your own life to lead, Nell. Neither me nor your father wanted you to sacrifice it for him.'

'*I* wanted to. I had to, Mum.'

Jayne's smile was soft and sad. 'You always were a daddy's girl. He couldn't take a step without you hot on his heels. He used to call you his little shadow.'

'I remember.'

'It used to scare me to death the way he took you onto building sites when you were small. I think you could hold a trowel before you could hold a crayon.'

'I loved every minute of it.' Nelly had tears in her eyes and she blinked them away.

'I wanted you to wear pretty dresses and curl your hair into ringlets, and you wanted to wear dungarees and have your hair in a ponytail to keep it out of the way.'

Nelly uttered a choked laugh. 'I still do.'

There was a pause for a while as they remembered the man who had played such a huge part in their lives, then her mum said, 'Do you still have feelings for this man?'

Nelly pulled a face. She didn't know what she was feeling, if she was honest. Confused didn't begin to explain it.

'Has seeing him again made you think about finishing your degree? Is that it?' her mum persisted.

'No, but even if I wanted to, it would be too late now.'

'It wouldn't,' Jayne insisted. 'You can do whatever you put your mind to.'

'What about Dad's business?'

'It's *your* business, and if you want to ask Gavin to manage it for you, or if you want to bring someone else in, or if you decide to sell it, that's up to you.'

Nelly supposed she *could* ask Gavin, her very capable and utterly loyal foreman, to run it for her, but she hesitated.

'I can't sell it.' She was adamant. Her dad had built the business from scratch, and over the years she'd fought fiercely to keep it going. She wasn't about to throw away all her hard work. Besides, she loved being in construction, she loved being her own boss, and she loved living in Picklewick.

'I'm sure the year and a half of the course that you've already done would count for something,' her mum was saying. 'So maybe you wouldn't have to repeat the whole thing?'

'I think I probably would, but I don't want to return to full-time education.'

Jayne was studying her shrewdly. 'If it's not giving up your degree that's got you all worked up, then it must be Isaac himself.'

When Nelly didn't say anything, her mum clambered out of her chair and put her arm around her shoulder.

'You didn't answer my question, but I don't think you need to. It's clear you *do* still have feelings for him. Did he love you?'

'I believe he did.'

'How does *he* feel about seeing you again?'

'No idea. Not much, I would have thought. It was a long time ago. He's moved on. So have I.'

Once again, her mum gave her a shrewd look. '*Have* you?'

Nelly couldn't answer her.

'Take my advice,' Jayne said, giving her a squeeze. 'Life is short. If you still care for him, do something about it.'

'He might be married or in a relationship.'

'If he is, then you walk away.'

'Even if he isn't, he mightn't feel the same way about me. It was such a long time ago,' Nelly repeated.

'If he doesn't, he doesn't. At least you'll know and can move on.'

Her mum's advice was sage, but Nelly wasn't convinced. It might be better to let sleeping dogs lie and not try to resurrect the past.

'You've been stagnating, Nell,' Jayne continued. 'I've often wondered why you haven't found love, and now I know. It's because you haven't been looking, have you?'

Her mum hit the nail on the head. Nelly *hadn't* been looking, and any boyfriends she'd had since Isaac had all been compared to him and found wanting. Her mum was wrong in one respect, though – Nelly *had* found love, but she'd walked away from it, and it had hurt so much that she wasn't sure she'd want to put herself through that ever again.

Anyway, Isaac no longer thought of her in that way. Whatever he'd felt about her in the past was long gone, so she'd only be making a fool of herself. Heck, he'd probably forgotten she existed and had only remembered when he'd seen her at the stables. Nothing he had done or said had given her any reason to think otherwise.

Nelly, she said to herself, *you're just going to have to get over it.*

But words were easy to say – doing it was a different matter entirely.

'I'll get these – what are you having?' Isaac's mate Frank leaned against the bar and eyed the pumps. 'They've got Stella on tap. You used to love a pint of Stella. Or six.'

Isaac chuckled. It was many years since he'd drunk lager, and even more years since he'd managed to sink more than a couple of pints. He must be getting old. 'A pint of Old Peculiar, please.' These days he preferred real ale, or wine, or even the occasional cocktail as long as it wasn't too sweet or fruity.

Frank caught the barman's attention and as he gave the man their drinks order, Isaac studied him. He hadn't seen Frank in years, not since he'd moved to Wiltshire.

He had met up with some of his other old school friends a couple of times since his return, but he hadn't done a great deal in the way of socialising, probably because nearly all of them had spouses or partners and several of them had children. Take Frank, for instance… Isaac hadn't seen him at all until this evening because he and his wife had four-month-old twins. Apparently, this was the first time he'd been out for ages, the poor bloke.

Even as he thought it, Isaac wasn't convinced there was anything "poor" about Frank. The man was glowing, despite the bags under his eyes, and the first thing he'd done when he'd spotted Isaac was to whip out his wallet and show him a photo of the babies.

Isaac felt a slap on his shoulder, and he turned around to see another old friend.

'Wotcha,' Chris said, easing his way between the two of them. For a Sunday evening the bar was crowded. 'She let you out then, Frank?' Chris teased. He turned to Isaac. 'His missus keeps a tight rein on him.'

Frank drew himself up to his full height. 'I'll have you know I like being at home. Do you realise I'm missing bath time to be out with you lot?'

'Yeah,' Chris conceded, 'I know what you mean, but you've got to let your hair down now and again, or the only thing you'll find yourself talking about is feeds and poo.'

'Poo?' Isaac raised his eyebrows.

'Believe me, it's a thing. When you've got kids, you become fascinated by the contents of their nappies.' Frank handed him his pint.

'Good grief!' Isaac took a deep draught, not wanting to think too closely about poo and nappies.

'I'd say you were lucky being single and kid-free, but I wouldn't mean it,' Chris said. 'I love my three to bits. Did I tell you that Levi is on the football team? He's only nine, but he's got a mean left kick on him. And Nenah is walking already and she's only ten months.'

The pride on Chris's face sent a bolt of envy right through Isaac and he bit his lip. It was strange seeing his old friends grown up and married, with kids of their own. The last time they'd had a proper get together, they'd still been kids themselves.

'Anyone on your horizon?' Frank asked him.

'Nah, as I said, he's single and fancy-free, aren't you, fella?' Chris gave him another slap on the back.

'Don't go telling my missis that – she'll be setting him up with one of her friends before you can say "mine's a pint".' Chris chuckled and raised his glass. 'Cheers.'

Isaac dutifully muttered 'Cheers,' and took a mouthful of the robust ale, wishing they'd change the subject. He didn't want to talk about his love life, or lack of it, and he definitely didn't want to talk about blind dates or being set up. He had enough to be going on with for the moment without romance.

Nelly's face flashed across his inner eye, and he shoved it away. Now was not the time to be thinking about lost love.

'What are you doing, workwise?' Frank asked a while later, after the conversation had moved on to football, cars and gaming, none of which Isaac was overly interested in. 'I hear you did the plans for that new house at the end of Trinity Street. They reckon it's going to be huge.'

'It will be fairly big,' Isaac said.

'And I've heard you did the plans for the cottages at the stables on Muddypuddle Lane,' Chris said.

'You heard right.'

'Nelly Newsome is doing the building work, isn't she?' Chris asked.

Frank said, 'She did the extension on my next-door neighbour's house. If we have any more kids, we might have to build one ourselves. We're bursting at the seams as it is. You could do the plans for us.'

'It would be my pleasure,' Isaac said. 'Just let me know when you're ready.'

'And I'd think about getting Nelly Newsome to build it,' Frank continued. 'Keep us posted and let us know how she gets on with those cottages. Tell me if you think she's any good.'

'She's good,' Isaac confirmed. He didn't want to discuss Nelly, but on the other hand he wanted to make sure people knew that her firm was one of the top ones in the area.

'Have you come across her before?'

'Once or twice,' Isaac admitted, but he didn't mean in a professional capacity.

'I'm not sure I'd want a woman building my extension,' Chris said, and Isaac inhaled sharply.

'You do realise that's extremely sexist,' he said. 'Anyway, I don't think she wields a hammer and chisel herself – she's got employees to do that for her. Although she *is* capable of building a house all by herself, if she

166

wanted to.'

'You like her, don't you?' Chris was grinning.

'She's nice enough.'

'Look at him, he's gone all red.'

Isaac was aware of the heat in his face, and he took another swig of his pint to cover his embarrassment. 'I know her in a professional capacity,' he said, sounding incredibly pompous. 'I have no interest in her other than that.'

'Yeah, right,' Chris teased. 'I know a lost cause when I see one, and you look like you've got it bad.'

Isaac frowned. 'I'm not interested,' he repeated. 'I'm perfectly happy being single.' If he told himself that often enough maybe he'd believe it. Because at the moment he was consumed with envy and regret. Abruptly, Isaac realised he didn't want to be on his own, that he did want to be in a loving relationship. The problem was that the only woman he could imagine being in one with was Nelly. Even after all this time and the way she'd dumped him, he still loved her, and in all those years no other woman had ever come close.

Petra gave Harry the gentlest of kisses on his nose. He stirred but didn't wake, so she crept out of the room as lightly as she could considering she was seven months pregnant, determined to check on the stables' newest arrival.

She felt absolutely shattered but she'd been unable to settle, not without checking on Star. Before she poked her head into the mare's stall, though, Petra couldn't resist taking a quick detour to have a look at the cow shed, so she grabbed a torch, crept out of the house and made her way down the track.

Flicking the torch on when she got to the cow shed,

she shone the beam around the inside of the building and marvelled at how much had been achieved in such a small amount of time.

The shed had been completely cleared and they'd even made a start on removing the ancient concrete base. The men had got to work with sledgehammers and crowbars, then Nathan had come in with the tractor and had levered most of the rest of it up, and carried the rubble off to be dumped in the pasture behind the cow shed, which was due to become a garden for the cottages and would now sport a rather large rockery. That had been Isaac's idea, and it would save them from having to try to get rid of the rubble. A rockery would be an ideal solution, and Lena had already offered to supply some plants from her own garden.

The generosity of people had taken Petra by surprise and she could feel her eyes welling up. Cross with herself, she blamed it on the pregnancy hormones. She wasn't usually such a cry baby, but lately she'd been bursting into tears at the drop of a hat.

She stood back, her hands on her hips, the darkness settling around her like a comforting blanket, and thought of how completely her life had changed over the past year. Not only was she soon to be a wife and a mother – which was mind-boggling in itself – but she was also about to expand the business in a way she never would have imagined.

Harry's vision of the cow shed becoming three cottages was inspired. She was still apprehensive about allowing him to sink his savings into the venture though; but apprehensive or not, it was too late to pull out now. The ball was well and truly in motion, so they had to see it through to the end.

Petra realised that some of her misgivings stemmed from a deep-rooted fear of something going wrong. What if things didn't work out in the long run between Harry and her? Where would that leave him? Or the stables?

Feeling rather foolish to be having such thoughts, especially considering they were about to get married and had a baby on the way, she gave herself a stern talking to. Nothing was going to go wrong. They had their whole lives ahead of them, and so much to be grateful for and to look forward to. It was just the baby hormones making her fretful.

Shaking her head at her silliness, she walked back to the stables and crossed the yard to the mare's stall. As soon as Amos had told her they were about to give a home to a pregnant mare in dire need of some TLC, Petra had moved Hercules out of his loosebox. It was the biggest and the one nearest the house, so she had given it to the mare for the duration, and that was where she was headed now.

The horse was skinnier than she should be and headshy. Petra guessed she'd been roughly treated, if not actually struck, and when she'd been led out of the horsebox, Petra's heart had gone out to her.

Her name was Star, on account of her having a white blob on her forehead, slightly off-centre. The rest of her was dark brown. Her coat ought to have been glossy with health, but it was dull and scruffy. She could do with a good grooming, but it would be a while before she had one; Petra wanted to let her settle in first and have her foal. There'd be time enough to make her pretty. Actually, she was quite pretty already, with a small head, neat ears, and a dish-shaped face. She was shy and nervous, but she'd allowed herself to be handled. Petra had almost sensed the relief in the animal when she'd been taken into a stall and the humans had retreated.

Star was indeed close to foaling, but a horse's gestation wasn't an exact science and she could give birth tonight, tomorrow, or tomorrow night. All Petra knew was that she wanted to be nearby when it happened to make sure everything went smoothly.

Quietly she opened the top door as unobtrusively as she could. The night lights around the yard threw some illumination, enough to make out the horse standing in the corner.

It also showed her something else – balancing on four ungainly legs was the most gorgeous little foal Petra had ever seen.

And not only that, October was sitting on a sleeping bag on top of a pile of straw, and when she met Petra's astounded gaze she smiled, before her attention reverted back to the newest addition to the stables.

Petra stood there for a moment and studied the woman, a feeling of gratitude sweeping over her. She would never dream of asking anyone to spend the night in a stable with a vulnerable or sick horse – that was something she'd do herself – but Harry had made it clear that a night on a stable floor was no place for a pregnant woman, so she'd given in to his pleas to go to bed. But Petra knew she wouldn't be able to sleep until she'd checked on Star.

It looked like October must have had the same idea, but rather than leave the horse on her own, she'd decided to bunk down with her instead.

What an absolute gem she was!

Satisfied that Star was in good hands and that October would fetch her if anything was amiss, Petra whispered a soft, 'Thank you,' then quietly closed the top door and padded off.

Not quite ready to return to bed yet, she made a beeline for Hercules. The stallion was an ex-racehorse and was her pride and joy. Generally no one rode him but her, although that situation had changed since October had started working at the stables at the beginning of the year, because October was an extremely competent rider. With Petra being pregnant and unable to ride (she *was* able, but Harry had made her promise not to) someone had to exercise the horse.

'Hello, boy,' she murmured, and Hercules gave her a soft whicker in response and huffed out a sigh of greeting.

He wandered over to the stable door and hung his head over it, allowing her to scratch his nose and tickle him under the chin. He suffered the attention for a short while, then he jerked his head up and retreated into his stall.

'I know, time for bed, right?' With a final pat on his haunches Petra left Hercules in peace and went for a stroll around the rest of the yard and the outbuildings.

May was one of her favourite months and in the stillness of the night air she could smell the honeysuckle that had draped itself over the fence, and the sound of lambs bleating for their mothers carried from the hillside opposite.

She could hear the chickens moving restlessly in their coop, and she called out softly to let them know that it was their friendly human corn-giver outside, and not a predatory fox. She would have liked to have a quick look at the chicks, but they were safely tucked up for the night and she didn't want to disturb them. She'd quickly check on Princess though, because she was another creature at the stables that was about to give birth any day, and Petra was looking forward to having a kid around. Baby goats were so funny and inquisitive, and so full of the joys of life.

When she crept into the barn expecting to see the goat asleep, Princess also had a surprise for her. Curled in the straw at her feet lay a tiny baby, the mother standing guard over the new arrival.

'Oh, aren't you clever!' Petra exclaimed, pulling the moveable fence to one side so she could slip through and take a closer look at the kid.

Princess eyed her warily, but she allowed Petra to pick the little creature up and check it over.

'You've got a little girl,' she said to her, 'and she's perfect.' The tiny baby smelled of the straw she'd been lying in, milk, and a not-unpleasant goaty scent. And she was so soft and cuddly, despite being over 50 per cent knobbly, wobbly legs.

Petra put her down and the kid immediately staggered over to her mother and searched for a teat, her little tail waggling furiously when she found it. Princess made a low grumbling sound in her throat that Petra knew was contentment, so she left the pair alone to continue to bond.

As she retraced her steps, she paused for a moment, seeing quick scudding movements in the field beyond. Rabbits! Loads of them, lolloping and hopping around, and amongst the tufts of grass she could see baby rabbits darting to and fro. It made her heart sing to see them.

As if sensing her joy, the baby kicked inside her, and Petra's hands automatically went to her stomach. 'It'll be your turn before you know it,' she whispered, but even that small noise was picked up by the rabbits, and en masse they scurried for cover.

'You've scared them off,' she said to her son. 'Never mind, as soon as we've gone, they'll come back out again. I can't wait for you to see them. Although, by the time you put in an appearance, they'll be nearly full grown.' She continued to stroke her tummy, convinced that her baby could hear and understand every word she said, but eventually she began to feel tired.

Satisfied that everything was as it should be, and feeling incredibly content and lucky, Petra returned to her bed and the arms of her husband-to-be.

CHAPTER FIVE

Nelly breathed deeply, got a noseful of horse aroma, and coughed, lamenting her stupidity. She'd lived in and around Picklewick for long enough to know that fresh air, when it came to rural locations, wasn't always as fresh as one hoped.

She took another hesitant breath, and a gust of wind brought the more appealing scent of the ferns on the hillside above and the crab apple blossom in the hedgerows. A faint hint of sheep was also in the air, adding to the mix of smells.

As she strolled across the yard, she spied Petra shooing several brown hens out of a stable, and she made her way over to her.

'Hi,' she called. 'How did the clearing go? Sorry I had to dash off,' she added as she grew closer. The chickens darted past, and Nelly froze, worried she might step on one of them or they might peck her. She tended to prefer her chicken on a plate in a sauce, rather than strutting around her feet.

'The blasted things get everywhere,' Petra grumbled. 'I was just about to jab my pitchfork into the straw when three of them fluttered out and gave me the fright of my life. Why don't you take a look for yourself?'

Without waiting for an answer, Petra walked away, leaving Nelly no option other than to follow her. Thankfully, she hadn't seen Isaac's car in the stables' car park, so she was as certain as she could be that he wasn't on site. However, she didn't fully relax until she rounded the corner of the shed and could see inside.

Harry and Nathan were there, but they were on their own, she noticed with relief. She was also pleased to see how much work had been accomplished in just twenty-four hours. The shed was empty, and the concrete floor had been removed and dug down to a depth of about a metre. Harry and Nathan were in the middle of clearing away the last of the rubble.

'That's great,' she said. 'I was hoping my men could get started soon. They're just finishing up a job and should be here on Wednesday, if that's all right with you?'

Petra nodded. 'Definitely! The sooner you start, the sooner you'll finish. Ideally, I'd like most of the work done by the time this one puts in an appearance.' She rubbed her tummy.

Nelly pulled a face. 'Two months is a bit optimistic,' she warned. 'I've prepared a schedule of works that I can email over to you, if you'd like to have a look at it. But I warn you, there is some flexibility built into it – very few jobs run to plan. I reckon, assuming all the subcontractors stick to the schedule that it will take five months from start to completion.'

'That long?' Petra sounded dismayed.

'I did tell Harry this,' Nelly said, and winced when Petra shot Harry a cross look.

Oh dear, Nelly thought, hoping that this wasn't an indication of the way things were going to be on this build. That was the problem when clients didn't employ a project manager, and wanted to do it themselves, and it was even more of an issue when the clients failed to discuss things with each other. Luckily, Nelly was fully capable of managing the project, if only they'd let her get on with it.

'Have you ordered the windows yet?' Nelly asked, trying to draw Petra's attention away from her hapless fiancé.

'Not yet. Should I have done?'

'Sooner is better than later,' Nelly advised. 'Isaac hasn't planned for anything out of the ordinary, but I'd still get the ball rolling if I were you. Some companies can take a while to manufacture them.'

'I think I do need that schedule of works,' Petra said, with a frown.

Nelly took pity on her. 'The schedule is for me and my men to refer to, but what if I add in all the things you need to be doing, and when you need to do them? Would that help?' So much for her rule of not doing more than she was contracted to do, Nelly thought with a sigh.

'That would be marvellous! Thank you. Although I don't know when I'm going to find the time to go shopping for windows.'

'You'll have to, if you want this project completed,' Nelly warned. There wasn't any point in beating around the bush, and she wasn't afraid of telling her clients the truth, no matter how much they didn't want to hear it.

'I suppose.' Petra made a face. 'You must think I'm a right pain in the arse.'

'Not at all. You're just inexperienced in this kind of stuff.' Taking pity on her once again, Nelly added, 'Pick the materials you want to use for the frames, pick the patterned glass you'll need for the bathroom windows, and pick the style of door and window handles, then give them a copy of the plans and let the company work from those. It shouldn't take more than a couple of hours to get them ordered. But don't pay more than a 20 per cent deposit until the windows are in and you're happy with them.'

'Thanks, that's a great help. Now all I've got to do is to decide on the boilers, the radiators, the flooring, the bathrooms, the kitchens…' Petra trailed off.

Nelly stared at her for a second, then the two of them burst out laughing at the same time.

Harry wandered over, dusting his hands off against the backside of his jeans. 'Glad to see you're having fun while me and Nathan are working our socks off,' he teased, giving Petra a kiss on the cheek. 'Come to check on us?' This was directed at Nelly.

'Yep. I want to know when I can send my men in. I told Petra Wednesday, if that's okay with everyone?' Nelly wasn't sure who she was supposed to be reporting to – Petra, Harry, Amos, or all three of them.

'Wednesday is fine,' Harry said, as Nathan, who'd finished scooping up the final load of concrete, joined them. 'I've been thinking that it might be a good idea to get some hardcore and chippings delivered to put on the track leading to the cowshed. I expect you'll have some trucks and lorries going up and down, and I'm worried the surface won't be able to cope with it.' He looked at Nathan for confirmation, and Nathan nodded. 'We'll need to tarmac it eventually, but I didn't want to do it just yet.'

'Good thinking,' Nelly said. 'There'll be a caravan here tomorrow, and that's only the start of it.'

'A caravan? You don't live in it, do you?' Petra looked shocked and Nelly hastened to reassure her.

'Not at all. No one lives in it, but there's a loo inside and cooking facilities, so the guys can take their breaks in comfort.'

'Wow, I didn't expect that,' Harry said.

'Neither did they! I used to arrange for a portaloo and they ate their sandwiches sitting in the van if it was wet, as did I. But I hated it, and as I'm on site almost as much as they are, I came up with the idea of a caravan. It's more comfortable and in the long run it's worked out cheaper than hiring a portaloo,' she added.

Nathan gave Petra a meaningful look.

'Don't start getting any ideas,' Petra warned. 'You can come into the house whenever you want.'

'I wouldn't mind a caravan down on the bottom field,' he joked, and Petra rolled her eyes.

'Now look what you've started,' she complained to Nelly.

Nelly grinned. This was one of the reasons why her workmen were so loyal – because she looked after them. Her dad always used to say that one good worker was worth three average ones, and she'd built her business's reputation by being able to attract and hang on to the best brickies, plasterers, general labourers, and roofers for miles around. Not all of them worked exclusively for her, but because she was fair with them, the ones who weren't on the books were always happy to help her out if she had a rush job on.

She was about to leave, when Petra said, 'Would you like to see a baby goat? She was only born last night and she's so damned cute.'

How could Nelly resist? 'Yes, please!'

'Follow me.' Petra began walking up the track, Nelly falling into step alongside her. 'We had a mare give birth last night too, but I'm trying to keep her as quiet as possible so I won't show you the foal today.'

When Petra went on to explain how badly Star had been treated, Nelly was appalled. 'Thank goodness you were on hand to take her in,' she said, glad that she'd gone the extra mile to help Petra out. Good people like her, Harry and Amos deserved all the help they could get.

'Oh, my goodness! Look how cute that is!' Nelly exclaimed when she saw the little kid. 'I want one! I've got nowhere to keep it, and no idea how to look after it, but I want one.'

'You won't when you see what they grow into,' Petra laughed. 'Princess, her mum, is a nightmare. She's an escape artist, and she eats anything she can get hold of.'

Nelly spent a few minutes gazing at the little animal, then she said goodbye to Petra and made her way into Picklewick. It was coming up for lunchtime, so she thought she'd pop into the village and pick up a sandwich before she went to the job her men were currently finishing.

As she drove down the lane, her thoughts refused to stay on work: they kept straying towards Isaac and the chat she'd had with her mum. Did she have the courage to take her mum's advice, or should she hunker down and try to pretend she didn't still have feelings for him?

One thing she did know – she fervently wished he hadn't come back into her life, because she had been doing just fine. Now though, she wondered whether she'd ever be fine again.

'I'm going to have to get off in a minute,' Harry said to Nathan after Nathan had taken the last load of earth and stones that had been lying under the concrete base of the cow shed and dumped it on what was shortly going to become a rockery.

It didn't look particularly attractive at the moment, but Harry had every faith in Amos's green fingers. 'Will you be okay sorting out the water and the electrics? I've got a couple of ponies to shoe,' he added.

Harry and Nathan had planned to hook up a previously disused tap that had supplied mains water to the shed in the past, and run an extension cable from the barn. The shed did have its own electricity supply, but it was old and would need rewiring.

'I can manage,' Nathan assured him.

'I want to thank you for all your help this weekend. I know it's not in your job description.'

Nathan chortled. 'You do know I haven't got a job description? Megan keeps teasing me about that. Seriously, I'm happy to help.'

Harry was touched. In the year since he'd known Nathan, they'd become friends and he knew that both Petra and Amos regarded him as a member of the family, rather than an employee.

'Can you do me a favour?' he asked.

'Anything,' Nathan said, without hesitation.

'Can you keep an eye on Petra when I'm not around? I know she's anxious about trying to get as much done as possible before the baby comes, and I'm worried about her overdoing it.'

Nathan looked affronted. 'You don't need to ask. I'm doing that anyway.'

'Good – between us maybe we can get her to slow down. Guess what she was doing last night when she should have been in bed?'

'Checking on Star. I know, October told me.'

'I know October spent the night in Star's stable. Did the pair of you cook that up between you?'

Nathan grinned. 'We did. It was supposed to be my turn tonight if the mare hadn't had her foal by then. I'm gutted I missed it.'

'Yeah, so's Petra,' Harry chuckled. 'She thought she'd got away with sneaking out, but she made the mistake of putting her cold feet on me when she came back to bed. See what I mean about her overdoing it?'

'You'll not change her,' Nathan warned. 'She's as stubborn as Princess and just as cantankerous.'

'Tell me about it!' was Harry's heartfelt reply. Then he softened. 'I wouldn't want to. She's perfect as she is.'

Nathan clapped him on the shoulder. 'Not as perfect as my Megan.'

'I think we'll have to agree to disagree,' Harry joked. 'Seriously, let me know if you think she's doing too much. I can scale back my farrier commitments and help around the stables more. I'm planning on doing that anyway, once the baby arrives. I can't wait! And neither can Petra but for a different reason – I don't think she's too keen on being pregnant. She's complaining of backache, being unable to sleep, the baby using her as a punching bag, Braxton Hicks…'

'Who is he?'

Harry stared at Nathan for a second, before he understood what he was asking. 'Braxton Hicks are what they call it when the uterus contracts and relaxes. It's a kind of practice for labour.'

'I see.' Nathan grimaced.

'Sorry, mate. You don't need to hear all this. But if you see her wince and rub her stomach, she's either being pummelled from the inside out, or she's—'

'I get the picture,' Nathan said hurriedly. 'Please don't tell me anything else.'

Harry laughed. 'Yet you'd have happily stayed with Star when she foaled.'

'That's different.' Nathan lifted his chin and refused to look at him. 'Star isn't my boss.'

'That horse was having a good go at bossing you around when you fed her this morning,' Harry pointed out. 'I saw her trying to stick her nose in your pocket, looking for a treat. She's only been here five minutes and she's got you wrapped around her hoof.'

'I feel sorry for her,' Nathan said. 'She deserves a bit of love and attention.'

'She certainly does. I have to confess to trying to give her a handful of pony nuts earlier, but she wouldn't come anywhere near me.'

'You've either got it, or you haven't,' Nathan replied with a smirk. 'She'll take a while to trust people again, but she'll get there. She's settled in well and she's got her baby to keep her occupied.' He paused. 'Don't worry about Petra – I'll do my best to keep her out of mischief. It'll be hard, mind you, because she's never been one to sit down and put her feet up, and the nearer it gets to your baby's arrival the more nesty she's becoming. She's like a bitch about to whelp. I'll be expecting her to make a den under the stairs soon.'

'I've noticed that – Amos caught her cleaning the boot room the other day. He had to threaten her with no supper if she didn't behave herself. No wonder she says she's exhausted.' Harry sighed. Pregnancy was a whole new experience for the two of them, but as he'd said to her the other night, they'd know more when they had the next one.

He'd had to duck when she threw Queenie's chew at him.

Isaac's head was swimming with ideas as he strode away from what he was hoping would be his next client.

The house was in Picklewick and the ladies who owned it wanted an extension leading out from the kitchen, and the whole of the downstairs turned into one large, airy space, with open plan kitchen, dining and living areas. In addition, there would be an attic conversion and a roof terrace above the new extension, with skylights. But what they wanted was something unusual – the "wow" factor – and it was down to him to deliver it.

He was intending to return to his office to sketch out a few options to show them, but first he wanted some lunch, so he decided to take a walk down Picklewick's high street and pop into a café. If he ate a substantial meal now, he could work into the evening without his stomach protesting too much.

It was while he was strolling along, wondering which of the two cafes he wanted to eat in, that he spotted Nelly. He'd been glancing in through the window of the first one he'd come to, and when he took a step towards the entrance, she was right there in front of him.

He came to a sudden halt, his heart hammering.

It was silly of him not to anticipate seeing her here. After all, this was where she lived, he was on her turf, in her neck of the woods. Half of him wondered if that was what had driven him to walk down the high street in the first place. He could so easily have chosen somewhere near the office. There had been absolutely no need for him to come into Picklewick, but he had done so anyway, and it occurred to him that his subconscious knew more about what he wanted than he did.

Nelly was staring at him, her eyes wide, her lips set in a line. He wondered what she was thinking. She didn't seem pleased to see him at all.

'Hi,' he said uncertainly.

She shrugged. 'Hi.'

'What are you doing here?' he asked, then immediately realised it was a stupid question.

'I live here. What's your excuse?'

'I've just been to see a client – a big extension, attic conversion…' He trailed off.

She studied him for a moment. 'I've been to the stables on Muddypuddle Lane. They've done most of the clearing. In fact, they've probably done it all by now. I told them I'll start work on Wednesday. Is that okay with you?'

'Of course it is. I've done my bit, it's all down to you now. I'm here if you need me, though.'

'Glad to hear it.'

From her tone he realised that she'd probably had issues with architects in the past. He knew it happened occasionally, especially when clients changed their minds halfway through a build and wanted additional features, or something removed. Sometimes, if the change was substantial enough, it might even mean a re-submission to the planning department, which could hold up a build indefinitely.

Suddenly, and without any conscious decision on his part, he found himself saying, 'I was just about to grab some lunch. Would you care to join me?'

He could almost see the cogs whirring in her brain as she considered his suggestion.

Okay,' she agreed slowly. 'That's what I came into the village to do anyway.' She sounded incredibly reluctant and he almost wished he hadn't asked her, but he had done and she'd agreed, so he couldn't go back on it now.

'Will this do?' He glanced at the cafe, and when she nodded, he held his arm out, inviting her to go ahead of him.

Following her inside, he couldn't help studying her. She still had the most incredible figure and he was so intent on watching the sway of her hips as she walked in front of him, that he almost bumped into her when she stopped.

'If you tell me what you want,' he said, 'I'll order and you can grab a table.'

'I'll order for myself, thank you.' She sounded prickly and defensive, and he wondered what he had said to upset her. Then he got it – she didn't want to feel indebted to him. She wanted to pay her own way.

'Okay,' he acquiesced airily, not wanting to make a big deal out of it. It was only a sandwich and a coffee, for goodness sake. 'You go first.'

Nelly narrowed her eyes at him, then ordered, and when she'd finished she found a table and sat down. He quickly joined her and as they waited for their lunches to arrive, he scrabbled around for something to say. Work seemed to be the safest option, so he started with that.

'Have you got another job on at the moment?' he asked.

She leaned back in her seat and folded her hands on the table. 'Two, although one of them will be done by tomorrow, except for the snagging.'

He nodded. Snagging made the difference between a customer being delighted with a job or complaining for weeks. He suspected that any issues at the end of one of Nelly's builds would only be minor and easily solvable.

'Which is why I can pull most of them off this job and get them started up at the stables,' she continued.

'Did you know Petra or Harry before this?' he asked.

'Not really. I knew of the stables, and I've seen Petra and Amos around, but I didn't much care for horses or riding, so the first time I went there was when they asked me to give them a quote. Harry is new to the village – or newish; he's been here about a year, I think.'

'They seem like nice people,' Isaac said.

'They are.'

An awkward silence descended, and Isaac's heart constricted. He was finding it hard to believe that the woman he'd once known so intimately and who he'd been able to share his innermost thoughts with, was now a total stranger. But then again, what had he expected? Nelly had become a stranger the second she'd dumped him, so perhaps he hadn't known her as well as he thought he had.

He glanced at her, caught her eye, and looked away, but when he looked back she was still gazing at him. Was there a softness in her that hadn't been there a minute ago, or was he imagining it?

'Is it strange being back?' she asked, and he took a moment to answer.

'Yes and no. In some respects, I feel as though I've never been away.' He thought back to last night – some of the banter he'd shared with his friends had been remarkably similar to the rubbish they'd spouted when they were teenagers. 'But in others, things are very different. I've got my own place for a start, and I run my own business. And everyone has changed around me. In my head they should still be the same age as when I last saw them, and places should still look the same. Did you know that the old cinema has closed down and they've built a multi-screen one?'

'I did know – it's near the supermarket.'

He shook his head, partly in wonderment and partly in despair. 'It feels weird,' he admitted. 'Picklewick hasn't changed much though.' He'd only visited the village a couple of times in his youth, despite it being just nine or so miles away from his hometown.

'That's both a blessing and a curse,' Nelly said. Abruptly, she looked beyond him, over his shoulder towards the door, and a smile transformed her face.

Isaac twisted in his seat, wondering who it was that she was so pleased to see, and wishing she'd smile at him like that. To his dismay, he saw William – the guy who managed Picklewick's care home – and his heart sank.

His instincts had been right, after all. She'd gone to the stables on Saturday because William had been there, and not to see how things were going with the clearing party or to have a beer and a burger, and certainly not because she'd thought Isaac might be there. She'd been all dressed up for William.

Blast, the man was coming over, and his focus was on Nelly.

Isaac squirmed uncomfortably as William asked, 'May I?' and pointed to an empty chair.

'Of course,' Nelly said.

Isaac wanted to tell him to get lost, but instead he smiled and nodded a greeting, dismay flooding through him. At least her interest in this guy might explain why she'd dashed off on Saturday. She clearly hadn't wanted to be alone with *him*, however briefly.

Suddenly Isaac couldn't face sitting there with the two lovebirds, and he leapt to his feet. 'Sorry, I've just remembered something,' he garbled, and he whirled on his heel and shot out of the door, leaving a bemused server staring after him.

As he hurried to his car, he wrestled with the knowledge that he'd probably made the wrong decision in returning to the area. He might live several miles away from Picklewick, but it was inevitable he and Nelly would continue to bump into each other.

But he couldn't consider relocating again – not when his mum needed him and his business was just becoming established. Workwise there would be a long way to go before he was in the same position as he had been in Wiltshire, but he was getting there.

So he was stuck here, whether he liked it or not, and he rued his rash decision to move nearer to his mum. Why couldn't he have simply visited her every weekend until she was back on her feet?

Yeah, and when would that be, he asked himself? It had already been seven months since his mum and dad had split up, and she was only marginally better now than she had been when it had first happened. If Isaac didn't know better, he would have thought his dad had died, not walked out.

But then, hadn't he felt the same way himself when Nelly had walked out of his life? So he could understand how his mum was feeling. He'd been in a dark place for months too, and his and Nelly's relationship had only lasted for a fraction of the time that his mum and dad had been married. No wonder it was taking her ages to get over it, and he was beginning to fear she never would.

Gah, he was sorely tempted to give his dad a piece of his mind, and he would have done so if he thought it would do any good. Funnily enough though, he didn't get the feeling that his father had left his mum because of another woman. The place his dad was renting was devoid of any feminine touches whatsoever, Isaac had observed during the twice he'd been there, so he wondered if it was an affair that had split his parents up (and the other woman was no longer on the scene) or whether it was because of something else entirely.

Sighing to himself as he drove out of Picklewick and made his way back to his office, Isaac was aware that he'd made his bed and he had to lie in it. Nelly had moved on with her life – he hadn't expected anything less. As far as he'd been concerned, she'd moved on the minute she'd told him she was dropping out of the course and going home. So, in effect, nothing had changed as far as that situation went.

But what *had* changed was the realisation that he still felt the same way about her as he'd felt all those years ago. He still loved her, and there wasn't a damned thing he could do about it.

What the hell was wrong with the man? Nelly asked herself as she watched Isaac dash out of the café and stomp up the road.

Was it something she'd said, or not said? Had he taken a dislike to William? Though how he could do such a thing was beyond her. As far as she knew, the two men had only met on Saturday, and William was such a lovely guy she didn't know how anyone could possibly dislike him.

Which brought her full circle to thinking that it must be because of her. Her mum's advice to do something about it if she still loved him was all well and good, because she *had* done something about it – she'd agreed to have lunch with him – and look where that had got her.

Oh, well, at least she knew where she stood; he'd made it clear he wasn't interested in her. But the other part of her mum's advice (to move on) simply wasn't going to happen, either.

Nelly hadn't imagined ever seeing Isaac again after she'd dumped him, therefore she'd had thirteen years in which to move on. But she hadn't done so, because she'd never stopped loving him. And if she hadn't found love again in all that time, she was unlikely to find it now.

'Is everything all right?' William asked.

Nelly jerked herself out of her thoughts. 'Eh?'

'You were miles away.' He was looking at her with concern.

'Yes, sorry, everything's fine.'

Poor William, despite him sitting right next to her, she'd forgotten he was there. She'd been so focused on Isaac and the way he'd walked out without any warning, that William had faded into the background.

He must think her really rude – and goodness knows what he must think of Isaac. He'd only just sat down when…

Nelly froze as a thought struck her.

Isaac hadn't left because he had suddenly remembered that he had to be somewhere or do something. That hadn't been a "damn it, I've forgotten something" expression on his face. Isaac had been *upset*. She'd known his every expression, his every gesture, so intimately – *something* had upset him.

One minute he'd been sitting there, chatting – okay, it might have been a little awkward, but that was to be expected considering they were just getting to know one another again, plus there was the elephant in the room of the way things had ended between them – and the next, he'd jumped to his feet and dashed off.

As far as Nelly could see the only thing to have changed was William's arrival, and as she'd already considered and dismissed the possibility that Isaac might have taken a dislike to inoffensive, kind, considerate William, she was left with another scenario.

Had Isaac shot off because he was under the impression that she and William were an item?

Surely not? William was—

'Here you go, love,' the waitress said, putting two plates of sandwiches on the table. She turned to William. 'Your toastie will just be a tick. Is the other gentleman coming back?' Curiosity filled her face.

'I don't think so, but leave them here anyway,' Nelly said.

William was gazing quizzically at her. 'He didn't say where he was going, did he? I could always ask for them to be wrapped up and I could pop them into him on the way to work.'

'That's kind of you,' she said, 'but I don't think you need to bother. He'll be miles away by now.'

See, William *was* a nice guy. A very nice guy. But even so, Isaac had nothing to worry about in that regard. If, in fact, he was worried at all. Which he probably wasn't.

Flipping heck! She wished she knew what Isaac was thinking, but she had no intention of making a fool of herself by asking him.

CHAPTER SIX

Even for the beginning of June, the weather was unseasonably warm and Isaac felt a trickle of sweat run down his back as he walked across the yard, heading for the former cow shed. He called it "former" because in the space of a couple of weeks it had been transformed. Nelly and her team were doing a fantastic job.

Not that he'd seen much of her – he'd managed to miss her so far whenever he'd paid the site a visit. The avoidance was deliberate on his part.

But today her van was here, and he wondered whether the heat he was suddenly feeling had more to do with seeing her again than the temperature. He'd not set eyes on her since the café incident a couple of weeks ago, and that was the way he wanted it to stay. But it was unrealistic of him to think he could avoid her forever, and if he drove off now, someone was bound to notice and wonder what the problem was. The last thing he wanted was for people to speculate, or for his clients to think there was something wrong. Therefore, he straightened his shoulders, lifted his chin, and prepared himself to meet his nemesis once more.

'Back again?' Gavin joked as he rounded the corner. 'I've never known such a hands-on architect.'

Isaac shrugged. 'I like to make sure my plans are being followed,' he said, then wished he hadn't as he saw Gavin prickle at the unmeant insinuation that Isaac didn't trust the builders to do a good job.

'Oi, Nell! This man is saying we can't follow a set of drawings,' Gavin called, and Isaac winced.

Nelly was standing in the open doorway of the caravan

that Nelly had put on the site for the comfort of her workforce.

'I didn't—' he began, then he noticed Gavin smirking and he realised he'd been set up. Maybe he hadn't disguised his feelings for her as well as he'd hoped.

'Tea?' Her voice was curt, but at least she was speaking to him.

Without waiting for an answer, Nelly went inside the caravan and, after a brief hesitation during which he wondered whether it was such a good idea to get so close to her knowing how he still felt, he followed her inside.

To his surprise the interior of the van was as clean as a new pin, and his astonishment must have registered on his face because Nelly said, 'If they don't keep it clean and tidy, they don't get to use it on the next job. I'm not their nursemaid and I'm not cleaning up after them.'

She didn't say anything further about it, but he guessed that in the early days one or two of her men might have been under the impression that because Nelly was a woman, it might be down to her to keep the place clean. Isaac would have loved to have been a fly on the wall when that particular issue was aired. He bet she would have put them in their place in no uncertain terms.

Abruptly he wondered just how hard it must have been for her – a female in a predominantly masculine world. In the beginning her dad would have still been on the scene in the background to give her guidance and advice, but after Ken had passed, Isaac couldn't begin to imagine what her life must have been like. In her early twenties and trying to run a construction business… it must have been tough.

Nelly handed him a mug of dark brown liquid. 'Sorry, I make builder's tea as a force of habit. Would you like more milk?'

'It's fine.' He didn't care how strong the tea was – his focus was on Nelly. He placed the mug on the side without tasting its contents. 'You're doing sterling work on the shed,' he said.

Her lips twitched. 'I thought you were worried about my men's ability to follow plans?'

'Nope, not me. I have every faith in you.'

'Pleased to hear it.'

'I always did have.'

Nelly looked down, her gaze on the mug she held. 'I didn't,' she replied quietly.

'It must have been hard.'

'It was.'

'And now?'

'Only when a client expects a fifty-something bloke to turn up, and he or she gets me.'

'Are the men worse or the women?'

'It's an even split.' She looked up at him. 'But let's not talk about gender bias in the workplace.'

'Okay. What *do* you want to talk about?'

Her eyebrows rose and she tilted her head to the side. 'The build, of course.'

'Of course.' Isaac didn't know what he'd been hoping for – her telling him that she and William were no longer an item, maybe? He said, 'It appears to be ahead of schedule.'

'It is. I'm hoping to have it watertight by the end of July.'

'You won't need me after that, unless there's a problem,' he observed.

'I don't need you now.'

'Right…' That put him in his place. It was hardly surprising that he wasn't needed. This job wasn't particularly technical, or large. It was a straightforward barn conversion that required a decent set of technical drawings (which he'd supplied) so any further consultation with the architect would usually only take place if something was unclear, or the build hit an unforeseen problem. Yet, here he was, still buzzing around and as welcome as a wasp at a picnic.

Nelly barked out a laugh. 'That came out wrong. I only meant that your drawings are good. Excellent, in fact.'

'Thanks.' His reply was dry. He sipped his virtually undrinkable tea and hunted around for something to say.

She beat him to it. 'You left in a hurry the other day. Was there a problem?'

Yeah, your boyfriend, he nearly said. 'Er, my mum. I suddenly remembered I said I'd call in to see her before my next appointment. Sorry.'

Nelly shrugged. 'These things happen. How is she?'

'Mum and Dad split up last year and she hasn't coped with it too well. That's the reason I came back here to live.'

'I'm sorry to hear that. How are you feeling about it?'

Isaac blinked. Nelly was the first person to ask how *he* felt. Everyone else had been (quite rightly) more concerned with how his mum was coping. But Isaac was hurting, too. Although he was still in contact with his father, the parental home that he thought was a permanent and steadfast feature in his life, was in tatters. Never in a million years would he have imagined that they would split up. Their love had been so strong, so sure... Isaac simply couldn't think what had gone wrong.

'I'm okay,' he replied, slowly.

Nelly scrutinised him. 'I don't believe you are.'

Isaac paused. They had known each other inside-out once, to the extent that they'd been able to tell what the other was thinking. Until one day she'd told him they were over, and he realised that he hadn't known what she was thinking at all.

Obviously it hadn't happened as abruptly or as cleanly as that. When Nelly's mum had shared the news that her dad was unwell, no one realised the extent of his illness. Nelly had travelled back and forth between uni and home for a while, struggling to keep up with the course, Isaac doing all he could to help, both of them believing it was only for the short term.

Then one day Nelly had slipped into his room in the house he shared with three other students, her eyes red, her expression anguished, and he'd held her as she cried.

He'd continued to hold her until she'd told him it was over between them, that she was dropping out of uni and going back home to live for the rest of the academic year.

Even then, he hadn't truly believed that had been the end of their relationship, of their love. He fully expected her to return to university, to resume the second year of her course and for the two of them to pick up where they'd left off.

It hadn't happened. Nelly had left for good and cut off all contact with him.

It had broken his heart. And now here she was, thinking she knew him, thinking she knew how he was feeling…

How dare she!

'You don't know me,' he said, his voice quiet, his temper rising.

Nelly flushed and looked away. 'I deserved that.'

Isaac didn't respond.

'I'm sorry if I hurt you,' she continued, a hitch in her voice.

'There is no *if* about it.'

Was she really going to do this now? Did he want to do this at all? Briefly he debated walking away: after all, she'd already told him that his presence on site wasn't needed. *But*, they were living in roughly the same area – him in town, her here in Picklewick – and they would unquestionably meet again, if not on this job, then on another. It was better they cleared the air now, so if they had to work together in the future they could do so as old friends rather than former lovers.

Yeah, right… his heart said – as if *that* was going to happen, not when he still felt the same way about her as he had all those years ago. He had no intention of letting her know that, of course. So he stayed, and prayed he could walk out of the caravan with his pride intact. It was far too late to hope his heart would be – that particular part of him had been shattered a long time ago. Even now he could feel the jagged shards of it grinding together. Damn – would this pain *never* go away? It had been thirteen flipping years!

'It hurt me just as much,' she said.

Isaac's laugh was harsh and bitter. 'Really?'

Nelly's eyes suddenly filled with tears, and he relented. He had to remember that she'd felt she had no choice, and her father had passed away, presumably as a result of the illness that had driven Nelly to leave university, the course, and him. Maybe she'd felt she hadn't had any choice, but – damn it! – she should have spoken to him about it. They could have worked something out.

'Sorry,' he said. 'You must have had your reasons.' Yeah, the reason was that she hadn't loved him enough to try to make it work. She hadn't loved him as much as he'd loved her.

'Do you want to hear them?' she asked.

'Bit late, isn't it? Thirteen years too late.'

'I didn't expect to ever see you again.'

'And now that you have, you feel the need to unburden yourself? Are you feeling guilty by any chance?'

Nelly got to her feet. 'Sorry, this is a bad idea. I'm going now. I need to check how they're getting on with the roof joists.' She brushed past him, heading for the door.

The scent of her invaded his nose and his heart constricted in pain.

Without thinking, Isaac grabbed hold of her arm, bringing her up short, and she let out a squeak.

Mortified, he released her. 'Sorry, I had no right to do that.'

Nelly's gaze bored into him. 'No, you didn't.'

'Did I hurt you?'

Mutely, she shook her head, but her hand went to her arm and she rubbed the area where his fingers had been.

He hadn't intended to touch her, and the shock of it reverberated through his whole body.

She hadn't moved, and her face was so close to his that he could feel her breath on his lips. Her eyes were huge and luminous, her pupils dark depths that a man could lose his soul in.

Isaac had already lost his to her. He'd lost it thirteen years ago…

With an anguished groan he gathered her to him. His lips found hers and they staggered back until she was up against the door, then he was kissing her with a passion he'd forgotten he'd possessed. Nelly kissed him back, her body moulding against him, an intoxicating blend of the familiar and the new. Her mouth opened, inviting him in, and his tongue found hers, to tease and tantalise.

Her whimper of desire struck him deep in the solar plexus and his arousal, immediate and intense, threatened to sweep him away with the force of his desire. He wanted her so badly that his very soul ached with longing.

Nelly squirmed against him, pressing herself into him, and he panted against her lips as he struggled to maintain control of himself.

He was going to claim her, here, now, against the door, and with her answering breathy sigh, he knew she was as eager for this as he.

His hand slid down her back, cupping her buttock and—

The door to the caravan rattled and he froze. So did Nelly.

'Hello? Nelly? Are you in there?' a man's voice called.

Isaac dragged his mouth from hers and Nelly pushed him away. He took a step back as she darted around him to stand in the middle of the caravan's tiny living space, her expression stricken.

Abruptly, Isaac came to his senses. What was he doing? What were *they* doing?

Her eyes were dark with passion, her cheeks flushed with desire, and her lips swollen from his kisses. Never had she looked so beautiful, and never had he desired her as much as he did right then. But that way madness lay, and heartache, and she'd already caused him enough of that for one lifetime.

'I'm sorry,' he muttered, his voice hoarse and his breathing ragged. 'I can't do this. I *won't* do this.'

Then he was gone, yanking the door open and stumbling down the steps as though the very hounds of hell were after him. And as he ran, his eyes filled with tears and his heart filled with pain, and he cursed himself for being a fool for a second time.

Nelly watched him go. That was the second time he'd fled from her in as many weeks. But this time her heart was splintering into a thousand little pieces.

What an idiot she'd been. She'd practically thrown herself at him.

For the briefest of moments she'd thought he was as willing as she, that he'd wanted it as much as she had, but then he'd abruptly come to his senses. Then he'd made it clear that he didn't want her at all.

She didn't blame him for going along with it – shared history and all that. But as soon as his head had gained control of his body, he'd rejected her.

Swallowing convulsively, she sat down, balancing on the edge of one of the benches, and she forced herself not to cry.

'Nelly, are you okay? Did he…? Do you want me to…?' One of the brickies, Alan, was staring at her. 'I'll fetch Gavin, he'll know what to do.'

'Don't!' she barked, and Alan's eyebrows shot up, alarm on his face. Lowering her voice and softening her tone, she said, 'There's no need. Nothing happened. We were just catching up.'

Alan's gaze came to rest on her swollen mouth, then rose to her eyes. 'Right.'

She could sense his doubt, and she could also see the slight twitch of his lips. It didn't take a genius to work out what had been going on, and she stifled a groan. Everyone would know about it by knocking off time – before then, probably.

Despite her regret, she couldn't help thinking how good it had been to be held by Isaac. How it had felt like she was coming home, that in his arms were where she belonged.

His kiss had been so sweet, so familiar, so damned *good*. She hadn't felt passion or desire like that since the last time he had made love to her, and her reaction to him shocked her to the bone.

Dimly she heard Alan leave, no doubt to spread the rumour that he'd caught the boss getting jiggy with the architect, but she didn't care.

All she could think about was Isaac. All the love she felt for him had come flooding back, engulfing her like a tidal wave, threatening to drown her. She'd never felt a fraction of what she felt for Isaac for any other man, and she knew now that she never would. She was a one-man woman, and unfortunately for her that man was Isaac: a man who had loved her once, but didn't love her any more.

How could she move on when she would never have anything as good to move on to?

With a cry of despair, she buried her head in her hands and tried not to weep. There would be plenty of time for crying in the lonely years ahead. But as she battled to keep her tears in check, she mourned his loss, and the loss of what they might have had together, of the love they might have shared, the memories they might have made, the babies they might have given life to.

And with that, Nelly gave in to her misery and cried for all the things that had been and all the things that weren't to be, and for the endless, loveless life ahead without the only man she would ever love.

Petra was in the feed room as she straightened up to watch Nelly trudge across the yard to the car park. The woman looked as though she had the weight of the world on her shoulders. Less than half an hour ago, Petra had spied Isaac doing the exact same thing, and she wondered if something was wrong. She didn't think it was anything to do with the build, because one or the other of them would have told her. So if it wasn't a work problem, she wondered if it was anything to do with the sparks that she'd noticed flying between them during the meeting in the dining room a few weeks ago.

She placed her hands in the small of her back and rubbed absently, wincing. Although she loved the concept of having a baby, Petra wasn't too keen on the reality of being pregnant.

Everything south of her neck was either sore or ached. Starting with her boobs, which had swollen to twice their normal size and hurt if she so much as sneezed. She'd found herself holding on to them when she came down the stairs the other day because the movement had caused them to bounce painfully. Then there was her back, which for the past few weeks had ached like hell, and had ached more these past few days, if that was at all possible. Then there was her stomach, which looked as though she was carrying a whole litter of small humans inside it, and not just the one. There had only been a single baby on the scans, hadn't there? Surely two different sonographers couldn't have got that wrong, no matter how many babies she feared might be in there.

Besides being the size of a small moon, her tummy was as tight as a drum, and if she had any more Braxton Hicks, Petra thought she might scream. They flippin' hurt and were getting worse. She could have sworn they weren't as painful or as frequent this morning.

Then there was her waterworks. She didn't believe it was possible to need to go to the loo as often as she did. Three times a night was getting to be the norm. Maybe she'd be more accepting of her need to wee, if her ankles weren't so swollen. Kankles, that's what she had: she was clearly hanging onto more fluid than she was getting rid of. And her fingers had also expanded, forcing her to take her engagement ring off. She didn't want to think about what state she was going to be in by the time this baby arrived!

Petra had come to the conclusion that she was a mess, and the sooner this baby was born the better, as far as she was concer—

'What the hell?!' A kind of popping sensation came from down below, a sudden gush of wee behind it, followed by one of the worst Braxton Hicks contractions she'd experienced so far.

Contractions…?

Wee…? *That wasn't urine.*

Oh, no. No, no, no. This can't be happening. It was too soon, too early. The baby wasn't due for another five weeks.

Petra clutched her stomach, her hand cradling its weight. Reaching out to hold onto the wall for support, she staggered a couple of steps, then a couple more. She had to get to the house and find Amos to take her to the hospital. But first she had to phone Harry.

She couldn't cope with this without him.

CHAPTER SEVEN

Harry ran his hand down the hind leg of the horse he was about to shoe and lifted its hoof. The animal shifted its weight to compensate for having to stand on three feet, and flicked him in the face with its tail.

He'd shod this horse in the past, and another one belonging to the same owner. The gelding was a gentle old thing, well used to the procedure, and as Harry checked his hoof, he felt a soft nose nuzzling at one of his back pockets.

'Not yet, boy,' he chided. 'You know how this works – you get your treat *after* you've got new shoes on, not before.'

Harry let go of the hoof and, one hand on the horse's rump to let him know he was still there, he moved around the back of him to the other side.

He was just about to lift the other hind foot when his phone rang. 'Excuse me a sec,' he said to the horse's owner, and pulled his mobile out of the pocket the horse had been nosing at.

'Amos, what do you need me to get?' It wasn't unheard of for Amos to ask him to pick up a loaf of bread, or a four-pinter of milk, or something he'd forgotten which was needed for their dinner.

'Harry…?' Amos sounded odd, and a prickle of concern nibbled at the edge of Harry's mind.

'What is it, what's wrong?'

'It's Petra, she's gone into labour.'

'What do you mean? She can't have. It's too soon. It'll be those practice contractions – the Braxton Hicks things.'

'Her waters have broken and she's having proper contractions. Harry, Petra is *definitely* in labour.'

Oh, god! This couldn't be happening. The baby wasn't due for another five weeks.

'I'll be there in half an hour.' Harry had already started walking. He caught the horse owner's eye and shook his head. 'Sorry, I've… my fiancée, the baby,' he blurted, then he was running to his van, his heart beating madly, his stomach churning.

He heard Amos yelling down the phone as he ran. 'Harry! Don't come to the stables. Are you still there? I said, don't come to the stables. I'm taking her to the hospital.'

'Call an ambulance,' Harry instructed.

'I've spoken to her midwife – she's told me to take her to the maternity wing myself. No need for an ambulance. And, Harry?'

'What?' He yanked the van door open and threw himself inside.

'There's no need to drive like a maniac. They said it'll be ages yet before the baby's born.'

'He's going to be all right, isn't he?' Harry had never felt fear like this.

'He'll be fine,' Amos said. 'They both will.'

Harry believed him – to think otherwise would surely tear him apart.

Harry didn't remember a thing about his mad dash to the hospital. Despite Amos telling him there was no hurry, Harry couldn't help but get there as fast as he could, and he almost took the sharp corner into the hospital's main car park on two wheels, earning himself a glare from a driver on the opposite side of the road.

It took him ages to find a parking space, and at one point he seriously considered abandoning the van in front of a row of parked cars.

He was about to do just that, when he saw a car inch out of the space it was in. Another vehicle indicated its intention to park there, but Harry ignored it and he shot into the space, narrowly missing the waiting car.

'What the hell do you think you're playing at?' the irate driver yelled at him as Harry leapt out. 'Oi! Come back, that's my parking space!'

Harry ignored him, and sprinted across the car park at full pelt, almost falling in through the door leading to the maternity suite.

'Can I help you?' A receptionist sat behind a desk, and he skidded to a halt.

'Petra Kelly. In labour. Just brought in,' he panted. 'I'm the father. The baby's father. Not *her* father.'

The woman, clearly used to panicking expectant dads, smiled politely and checked the computer screen, as Harry bent forward, put his hands on his knees and panted.

'Ah, yes. She's in room 7. Down this corridor, turn left, then right.'

Harry was on his way before she'd finished speaking, calling a thank you over his shoulder. Now that he'd arrived, his heart rate slowed a little, but he still felt jittery from the adrenalin and his stomach continued to churn.

Sick and anxious, he paused for a moment to compose himself. The last thing Petra needed was for him to burst into the room in the state he was in. She'd be worried enough already, without him adding to it. He wanted to appear calm and steady, even though his emotions were all over the place.

Slowly, the smells and sounds of the hospital's maternity wing seeped under the panic he was feeling and brought him up short. Like all hospitals, the smell of antiseptic was paramount, but unlike any other hospital visits he'd made in the past, the noises emanating from various rooms made his hair stand on end. If he didn't know better, he'd think people were being tortured inside them.

Until now, he hadn't given much thought to the stark reality of the birthing process, but these women sounded as though they were in agony, and he shuddered at the realisation that Petra would be going through the same thing.

Suddenly it seemed very real.

He was about to become a father. *Today*. Him, Harry Milton, would be someone's dad before the day was out.

Tentatively, he knocked on the half-ajar door of room 7, and with a considerable degree of wariness, he stuck his head around the door.

As soon as Amos saw him, he heaved himself to his feet and ushered him back into the corridor. 'Thank god you're here,' Amos said croakily. 'They reckon she'll have it in the next few minutes. You'd better go in. I'll stay out here.' Amos was pale and his hands were shaking.

'Is she okay?' His heart was in his mouth as he waited for Amos's answer.

'In pain, as you'd expect, and scared. I think she just wants to get it over with and get the baby out. Go.' Amos pushed him towards the door. 'It's you she wants, not me.'

A guttural moan came from inside the labour suite, and Harry's eyes widened.

'Harreeeey!' Petra yelled. 'Get in here!! Ohhhh, bugger! It hurts!'

Harry took a deep breath and dived through the door.

He only had time for the words, 'Baby's head is crowning' to register, before someone grabbed his arm and propelled him to Petra's side. Three people were gathered at the business end and two more hovered around the room, and Harry had no idea what was going on and was too frightened to ask.

Petra had a sheet draped over her swollen stomach, and her hands were gripping the sides of the bed she was lying on. Her face was a screwed-up mask of effort and determination.

'The head is out. Stop pushing,' one of the gowned midwives instructed, and Petra slumped back, her cheeks red, her eyes brimming with unshed tears. She reached for Harry's hand and clutched it, and he winced as the small bones were crushed together, feeling helpless.

Bending to kiss her on the forehead, he stroked a strand of hair away from her damp face.

'It's okay, everything is okay,' he murmured, praying it was true. She was in the best place and in capable hands, as was the little scrap who was fighting to be born.

'Wait, wait…' the midwife urged as she knelt between Petra's legs. Petra let out a whimper of pain. 'Okay, when you feel your next contraction building, I want you to take a deep breath, then push as hard as you can for as long as you can.'

'It's coming,' Petra panted, and she inhaled sharply, then curled her chin into her chest and pushed.

Harry wasn't quite sure what happened next, but there was a flurry of activity, a scream of triumph from Petra, and suddenly there was a baby. A real baby. *His* baby.

Tears streaming down his face, he gulped back a sob.

The squirming, wriggling infant let out a choked gurgle, followed by an outraged cry, then he was quickly wrapped in a blanket and handed to a waiting nurse.

'We're just going to check him over, then you can hold him,' one of the midwives said. 'As I explained to Petra, Baby is a little early, so we want to make doubly sure he's okay.'

'Give him to me,' Petra demanded.

'In a minute, love. They're just going to check him over,' Harry told her.

'He's all right, isn't he?' She turned her worried gaze up at him.

'Apgar score six,' he heard someone say.

'What's that? Is it serious?' Panic flared in his chest.

A midwife was busy cleaning Petra up and Harry looked away, his attention on his son. She said, 'An Apgar test is given to all newborns immediately after birth to check heart rate, muscle tone, and so on. The score tells us whether Baby might need some additional help. Six suggests he may need a tiny bit of help.' She glanced up. 'Don't worry.'

Easier said than done, Harry thought.

He watched anxiously as his son was checked, weighed, then wrapped in a blanket, and he didn't take his eyes off the baby until he was placed in Petra's waiting arms.

Suddenly the tension drained out of him as Petra unwrapped the little boy to examine him.

The baby was perfect. Ten tiny fingers, ten tiny toes, a button nose, two little ears, a mop of hair plastered to his little head, and the most disgruntled expression Harry had ever seen on another human being.

One of the nurses said, 'Dad, would you like to hold him? Then we're going to take him to the Special Care Baby Unit.'

'Why?' Petra wailed, holding the baby closer. She looked as panicked as Harry felt.

'It's just a precaution,' the midwife soothed. 'Baby is five weeks and two days early, and he's a little on the small side, so he'll be kept in for a few days for monitoring.'

Desperate to hold his son but not wanting to take him away from Petra, Harry knelt by her side and wrapped his arms around the two of them. And as he did so, an overwhelming feeling of love swept through him. Their baby would be okay – he knew it. He *had* to be, because anything else was simply unthinkable.

Isaac didn't think Nelly could hurt him again, but she had, and this time it wasn't her fault. He could have left when he'd seen her van in the stables' car park. He could have refused her offer of tea. He could have walked out of the caravan when she'd started talking about the past. He could have let her leave, instead of grabbing her arm.

Could have, should have, would have... He was a grown man, responsible for his own actions and his own mistakes. And this mistake had been a biggie.

Isaac had gone from having an aching heart, to having it shattered again in the space of a few moments, and now he had to live with the consequences.

Maybe if she hadn't kissed him back with such ardour—?

Bah, don't go blaming her, he told himself. He should be adult enough to accept that the fault was his. Whether she was in a relationship with William or not, or whether she was merely hoping she could be, was neither here nor there. *Isaac* had kissed *her*, not the other way around. She'd not given him the slightest encouragement, so this current heartbreak was all his own fault this time.

He'd known he was playing with fire, but he'd stuck his hand in the flames and had got burnt.

Unable to face going back to the office, he detoured to his mum's house in the hope that she'd be in. He wouldn't burden her with his misery, but he just needed to be with someone who loved him, someone who was on his side and would fight his corner (if only she knew that a fight was needed).

It would be a fight indeed to keep a hold on his despair and not let it show.

He was about to tell himself that his heart had healed once before and it could do so again, but he was forced to admit that it hadn't, had it? It hadn't healed at all – he'd just slapped a ruddy great big bandage on it to hold its shattered pieces together and had pretended everything was all right. It had taken seeing Nelly again to understand that he'd never got over her. And it had taken one kiss to understand that he never would.

'Hiya, love, I didn't expect you to call in today,' his mum said, when she saw him. She narrowed her eyes and tilted her head to the side. 'Is something wrong?'

'Not at all. I can pop in to see my mum if I want, can't I?' He gave her a customary kiss on the cheek.

She was looking brighter than the last time he'd seen her, less sorrowful somehow. But he'd seen her like this before, and he realised her grief over his dad leaving wasn't a constant thing – some days it was worse than others and she found it harder to cope. Today appeared to be one of her better days.

Isaac wished he knew why his parents' marriage had fallen apart. It wouldn't make any difference to the situation as such, but he wanted to understand. He could certainly empathise with his mum, because he felt Nelly's loss as keenly now as he had done back then. More so, after what had happened earlier. He wanted to tell his mum that things would get better, that she'd get over it eventually and move on. But it hadn't got any better for *him*, had it, and he didn't want to lie to her.

'Isaac!' Julie's voice was sharp.

'What?'

'You were miles away. Now, I know you say you're fine, but I'm your mother. You can't fool me: I can tell when you're upset. What's wrong? And don't say 'nothing', because I won't believe you.'

He hesitated. His mum had enough to be going on with, without adding his burden to the pile. She'd only worry, and he'd come back home to help her, not to cause her any more distress.

'You may as well tell me,' she insisted. 'If you don't, I'll only worry.

Once again, he cursed his impulsiveness. He should have gone back to work, not indulged in his need for comfort.

She sensed there was something wrong, so he may as well tell her, because she'd only keep on if he didn't, or think the worst. But where to start?

'Are you ill?' she demanded, concern creasing her brow.

'What? No! I'm as healthy as a horse.'

'Have you got money worries?'

'No more than anyone else.'

'The business is doing okay?'

'It's fine, Mum, honest.'

'That leaves one thing – a woman.'

His expression must have given him away because Julie cried. 'I'm right, aren't I? Tell me about it, Isaac. I might be able to help.'

'I doubt that very much.' He saw her face and sighed. 'Her name is Nelly and I met her in university, although she's originally from Picklewick and she still lives there.' He and Nelly had often marvelled that they only lived nine miles apart, yet it had taken a course in architecture in a university thirty-five miles away, to bring them together. Right now, Isaac wished he'd studied somewhere, *anywhere,* else.

'Picklewick. I see. Did you know her well?'

'I was in love with her.'

His mum blinked. 'Was she in love with you?'

'I thought so at the time, but I changed my mind when she dumped me and dropped out of the course.'

His mum nodded, and he saw understanding flit across her face. 'Your dad and I guessed something had happened, and we wondered whether it might be to do with a girl. But you didn't say anything and we didn't like to pry. It was in the middle of your second year, wasn't it? You seemed pretty upset.'

'I was.'

'This barn conversion that you're doing in Picklewick? Is it for her?'

'No, but I have bumped into her again.' He inhaled slowly, then let the breath out in a long sigh. 'The firm she owns is doing the renovations on the barn. It was because of that firm that she left uni. Her dad owned it and he became ill. Seriously ill, as it turned out. She left the course to run the company, but not before she ended our relationship. It broke my heart.'

'Oh, Isaac, I'm so sorry.' His mum's eyes filled with tears. 'First love can be so hard to get over.'

He put his arm around her and gave her a hug. 'I'm sorry, I shouldn't have said anything. I don't want to upset you.' At times like this Isaac wanted to take a swing at his father.

'I want you to feel you can share things with me. And I'm glad you told me. How do you feel about seeing her again?'

'I still love her.'

'Is that why you've never settled down? Your dad and I assumed it was because you hadn't found the right woman, or because you're only thirty-two and you didn't want to settle down yet.'

'The problem is that I *did* find the right woman, but she didn't want me,' he admitted, fresh pain coursing through him.

'Do you think she used the fact that her dad was ill as an excuse to end your relationship?'

'Good lord, no!'

'Then why did she?'

'I assumed it was because she never really loved me in the first place.'

'Have you looked at it from her point of view?'

'Not then. I was too young and too wrapped up in my own misery to look at it sensibly. I didn't appreciate how ill her father was, nor the extent of her sense of duty.'

'But you do now? Duty is why you moved from Wiltshire,' she reminded him.

'You needed me, Mum. After what Dad did—'

209

His mum closed her eyes slowly, and when she opened them again, he saw they were filled with anguish. 'Your father didn't do anything. It was me – I'm the one to blame.'

'For what?' Isaac was puzzled.

'For your dad and I splitting up.'

'Why? I don't understand.'

'I had an affair,' his mum said starkly.

'Pardon?' Isaac couldn't imagine his staid, sensible mother having an affair. He must have misheard.

'It's true,' she assured him. 'This isn't your dad's fault.'

'Who did you have an affair with? Why?'

'You don't know him. It was before you were born. He was the love of my life, but I was married to your father and no matter how much it hurt, I put duty to your dad before love. Don't get me wrong, I loved your father deeply – I still do. But I loved Emrys more.'

'But if this happened before I was born…?'

'He died last year, and when I found out I fell apart. Your dad quite rightly didn't understand why I was in such a state, so I had to tell him.'

'*That's* why he left?'

His mum nodded. 'It might have been a long time ago, but I betrayed your dad, and he can't forgive me. I don't blame your father. I haven't forgiven myself, either. The reason I'm telling you this is twofold. The first is that I don't want you to go blaming your dad or jumping to conclusions – I know you were thinking that he might have been unfaithful.'

Isaac shrugged. It had crossed his mind. 'And the other reason?'

'If you still love Nelly, you should tell her. I know how it feels to think you have to do the right and moral thing, and I suspect so does she. I also suspect she was setting you free because she loved you too much to tie you down. You see, I couldn't commit to Emrys in the end, so I ended the affair. I did it out of love for him.'

'And you regret it now?' He pulled a face. 'I'm kind of glad you did, or I wouldn't be here.'

'That's where you're wrong. I ended it when I found out I was pregnant.'

'What!?'

'Take that look off your face, Isaac – Emrys isn't your father. But I couldn't deny your dad the chance to be a full-time father to you. If I'd left him for Emrys, he would hardly have seen you. You see, Emrys was about to emigrate to New Zealand, and he wanted me to go with him. As much as I wanted to, and as much as it broke my heart to end it with him, I couldn't do that to your dad. I told Emrys it was over and that it had been just a fling. I told him it was your father who I truly loved, and I sent him away.'

'Oh, Mum.'

'I had to, because if Emrys had had any idea of my true feelings he would never have emigrated. So I set him free. I don't know Nelly and I don't know her side of the story, just the part you've shared with me, but from what you've told me, I think she might have been setting you free, too. Not because she didn't love you enough, but because she loved you too much.'

Isaac was lost for words. He was stunned and in a state of disbelief. Who knew his mother had such hidden depths? He'd taken his parents' love for each other at face value and had never thought to question it.

'Is there any chance of you and Dad getting back together?' he asked.

'Probably not. There's been too much water under the bridge, too much has happened, so much bitterness, so much heartache. It might be too late for me and your dad, but it might not be too late for you and Nelly. If you still care for her, then you've got to find out if she cares for you, too.'

At night the ward was quiet. The occasional soft squeak of a nurse's shoe, the murmur of a new mother and the occasional cry of a tiny baby were the backdrop to Petra's wakefulness.

She was in a side room off the main ward, which she was grateful for. The thought of seeing mothers with their new babies when hers was in the special care unit would have been difficult. Just thinking about him made her heart constrict with longing and her arms ache to hold him. She felt empty and bereft, and tears were perilously close to the surface. Petra didn't cry often, but since the surprise arrival of her baby earlier today, that was all she seemed to have done.

Sore, shocked, scared, vulnerable... Petra had never felt so weepy in her life, and she wished Harry was by her side to give her strength.

Even as a tear or two trickled down her cheek, she knew she should be grateful. Her baby was healthy, and throughout her pregnancy that was all she'd prayed for.

'All right, my love?' A nurse popped her head around the door.

'Fine,' Petra whispered back, then a sob escaped her, giving lie to what she'd just said.

The nurse slipped inside and automatically reached for Petra's wrist, checking her pulse. 'Do you want me to take you to the special care unit?'

'Now?' Petra's heart leapt.

'Yes. You can see your baby whenever you want. There's no restriction on mums visiting their babies. The only thing I'd say is that you make sure you get enough rest. Spend some time with your baby, then come back to bed and try to sleep.' She smiled gently at her. 'You'll soon wish you'd taken my advice when you get him home.'

Petra nodded, but she knew she wouldn't be able to sleep. She was too emotional, too strung out, and worry had settled in her chest like a stone. She'd been told that her baby was doing well, that him being in the unit was merely a precaution, and that she'd probably be able to take him home in the next few days, but it didn't stop her fretting.

'Have you decided on a name?' the nurse asked her, as they travelled down in the lift. Amos, bless him, had waited until he knew that she and the baby were okay, then as soon as he knew she was being kept in overnight, he'd dashed back to the stables to fetch her some pyjamas, a dressing gown and a pair of slippers. Petra secured that dressing gown more firmly around her middle, and thought for a moment.

She and Harry had batted a few ideas around, but nothing had seemed quite right, so they'd decided to wait until the baby was born, in the hope that something would leap out at them. They had considered naming him Gregory, after Harry's father, but although Harry had been touched by Petra's suggestion, he'd pointed out that her dad might feel a bit put out.

Petra hadn't given a hoot. They might be her parents, but she wasn't as close to them as she might have been. Since she'd come to live at the stables, she'd only seen them once or twice a year, and phone calls were also infrequent. Amos had played a much larger part in her life since she turned eighteen so, if anything, she'd prefer to name the baby after him instead. Now, that was an idea…

Gregory Amos Milton, Amos Gregory Milton: both combinations sounded good, but Petra felt that neither of them were quite right.

'Here we are,' the nurse said as the lift came to a halt and the doors pinged open. 'Do you remember the way from here?'

Petra did. She and Harry had been shown to the unit not long after their son had been taken there, and she'd never forget the sight of him, wrapped up like a burrito, his little face scrunched and red, as he lay in a plastic cot.

As she approached, she saw his delicate blue-veined eyelids fluttering as he slept.

What was he dreaming about, she wondered. What dreams did a newborn have? She wished she knew, and she wished Harry was here by her side so she could share her thoughts with him.

Her baby's cheek was softer than a cherry blossom petal, and she stroked his skin, her heart so full with love for this tiny human that she thought it might burst. He was perfect, and he looked so peaceful that she simply knew everything was going to be okay.

Petra smiled with sudden joy: she *knew* her baby's name and it was a wonderful blend of the names of the two men who had shaped her and Harry.

Amory.

CHAPTER EIGHT

'What time is it?' Harry asked

Amos glanced at him as he stumbled, haunted-eyed and tousled-haired, into the kitchen, and said, 'Five-thirty.' He flipped the switch on the kettle. Amos had been up for at least an hour, so he could do with another cup of tea.

'Oh, god.' Harry sank into a chair, put his elbows on the table and rested his head in his hands. 'I think I managed to sleep for about three-quarters of an hour. How about you?'

Amos had been dog-tired after he'd returned from the hospital, his emotions all over the place, but he'd not been able to sleep until he heard Harry come in some time after eleven, and even then his sleep had been fitful and restless. Yesterday had taken a toll on everyone, Petra most of all.

'So, so,' he replied. He had a feeling his sleep would be interrupted for a few months to come. He'd heard that babies liked to wake in the middle of the night, and they didn't care who else they disturbed in the process. He didn't mind, though – the thought of having a baby in the house was exciting. He just wished Mags was alive to see it – she would have doted on the little mite. So much so, that Petra probably wouldn't have got a look in. It was one of the major regrets in his life, that he and Mags hadn't been blessed with children. God knows they'd tried, but it wasn't meant to be.

He was intensely grateful for the opportunity to be a grandfather. As far as he was concerned Petra was his daughter, so any children of hers would be his grandkids. She was actually his great-niece, but whatever the physical relationship, the emotional one was the one that mattered.

'Petra thinks she'll be coming home this morning,' Harry said, taking his head out of his hands and curling his fingers around the steaming mug that Amos placed on the table in front of him.

'You've spoken to her already?'

'We've been messaging back and forth all night, off and on. I don't think she's slept much either.'

Amos hesitated to ask the next question. 'Will…erm…the baby be coming home today, too?'

Harry pulled a face, his eyes hooded. 'I don't think so. I'd be surprised if he did.' He brightened. 'You haven't seen him yet – shall I ask if you can visit?'

Harry had shown him a photo when Amos had dashed back to the hospital with stuff for Petra, but Amos longed to see the child in the flesh. 'That would be wonderful. I'm desperate to give the little fella cuddle. Has Petra told her parents yet? Or do you want me to do it?'

Petra wasn't as close to her parents as she could have been, and it didn't help that they lived so far away. Norwich – which was where Faith, Charity's twin, now also lived – wasn't exactly at the other end of the earth, but Petra never seemed to find the time to make the journey, and she'd only seen them once in the past year, when she'd introduced them to Harry. It was sad, but Amos got the impression that Harry and Petra's dad hadn't hit it off. And Petra wanting Amos to give her away, and not her own father, spoke volumes, in Amos's opinion.

'I don't think she has told them,' Harry said, breaking into Amos's thoughts. 'What with everything that happened yesterday…'

'She'd better call them. They'll want to see her, and the baby.'

Harry rubbed a hand over his face. 'I'll remind her, if she hasn't already done it. I'll give it a couple of hours, then go to the hospital. Is there anything you need me to do here before I go?'

'Nothing. Nathan and October will have it covered. I've told both of them what's going on. Just concentrate on Petra and the baby. And tell Petra not to worry: I know what she's like when it comes to the stables. We can manage perfectly well without her.'

'Make sure you don't do too much,' Harry warned. 'The last thing we need is for you to be ill.'

Amos wrinkled his nose. His angina was a source of ongoing irritation, but he just had to put up with it. He knew his limitations, and there was no way he was going to add to Petra and Harry's burden by doing something that might bring on an attack.

Harry told him that he and Petra would probably spend the day at the hospital, so after Harry left (with a change of clothes for Petra and strict instructions from Amos that they had to eat a proper meal at lunchtime) Amos updated the list of things that needed to be done today on the whiteboard, and left a note to ask if October could take the jumping class that was scheduled for later. He didn't want to cancel classes unless he had to, because every pound was vital. Despite Harry investing a significant amount in the holiday cottages project, Amos was determined not to let him pay for all of it, so it was imperative that any scheduled classes or hacks went ahead.

He'd just finished writing the last item on the whiteboard and was turning his mind to what needed doing inside the house when October appeared, and she wasn't alone. Lena was with him.

'Hello,' he said in surprise. 'What are you doing here? Has October persuaded you to take up riding?'

'I'll have you know, I used to ride quite a lot when I was younger. And so did my mum. She taught October to ride.'

'Well, I never! I hadn't realised Olive used to ride.' Amos squinted at Lena, as an idea occurred to him. 'Do you think she'd like to pay a visit to the stables?'

'I'm sure she'd love to. That's very kind of you. But not

for a bit, eh? You'll have enough to be going on with for a while. How is Petra and the baby?'

'Harry thinks she'll be home later today, but the baby won't be allowed home for a few more days. Anyway, what can I do for you?'

'I think it's more a case of what *I* can do for *you*. October was telling me that Petra and Harry haven't set up the nursery yet.'

'No, they haven't,' Amos confirmed, wondering where the conversation was heading.

'Shall we get started?' Lena rolled up her sleeves. 'There's lots to do to get ready for the little one's arrival, and I suspect the proud parents won't be spending a great deal of time at the stables while the baby is in hospital. Have they decided on a name for him?'

'Er, no, not as far as I know.' Bemused Amos wondered what it was that she wanted to get started on.

'Show me which room is going to be the nursery, and I'll fetch the cleaning stuff from the car.'

'We've got cleaning stuff here,' he protested. 'And I can do that myself.'

'I like using what I like using,' Lena stated firmly. 'Now, don't argue. You're going to need all the help you can get. And once you've shown me where to go, you can put the kettle on. Oh, and we've had a whip round in the village and I've brought a load of stuff that Petra and Harry might need for the baby. If she already has some of it, I can take what she doesn't want to the charity shop. It won't go to waste. There are some of the dinkiest clothes you've ever seen, perfect for premature babies. How much did he weigh?'

Amos stood there with his mouth open, his eyes wide, and his heart full. If he'd been awed by people's generosity when they'd come to help clear the cow shed, he was positively overcome with gratitude now. He felt tears gathering behind his eyes and when he tried to stutter out his thanks, his voice was croaky with emotion.

'Chop, chop!' Lena said. 'That cot isn't going to put itself together. And the more we get done today, the less we'll have to do tomorrow. Before you know it, that little baby will be home and then your troubles will start.'

Amos smiled widely. Despite her no-nonsense attitude, Lena's voice was filled with warmth and positivity, and Amos knew she was right. His life, and the life of everyone at the stables would never be the same again, and he relished the thought.

Isaac rose earlier than usual, having hardly slept a wink all night. He hadn't been able to stop thinking about what his mum had told him.

That she'd managed to keep it a secret for so many years shocked him, until he remembered that he'd kept his love for Nelly under wraps and he'd also managed to hide his broken heart.

It had taken finding out that the love of her life was dead, for his mum's secret to come out. Her grief had been too profound to conceal from his father, Isaac realised. Then he wondered whether his own heartbreak had led to him moving so far away from his hometown. He was aware that the risk of running into Nelly had played a part, but had he also had a subconscious urge to hide his pain from his parents? He'd tried to bury it so deep that he'd convinced himself that he was over her, that she was his past.

It had taken meeting her again to understand that neither thing was true. He was as in love with her now as he had been then, and she would never be his past, not when he carried her with him constantly.

He could fully appreciate the pain his mum felt and was still feeling, but he also wished his mum and dad would try to work through this. They'd been happy before and maybe they could be happy again. Isaac had never once had the feeling that his parents didn't love each other. In fact, as far as he'd been able to tell, even with the benefit of hindsight he still thought the love they'd had for each other had been immense, and love like that didn't simply disappear like dawn mist on a summer morning. It was still there, somewhere, if only he could tap into it and remind them of it.

It might be too late for him and Nelly, but it wasn't too late for his parents. So, with that in mind, he set off to his father's house. It was about time the two of them had a proper talk.

'I know what happened between you and Mum,' was the first thing he said when his dad answered the door.

Stephen stared at him in silence for a heartbeat or two, then nodded slowly. 'I see. You'd better come in. Tea? Coffee? I haven't had my morning cuppa, yet.'

'Coffee, please. Have you got time to talk?'

'I've always got time for my son. Work can wait.' His dad was a teacher, and an inspiring one, at that. He hesitated, then said over his shoulder as he walked down the hall and into the kitchen, Isaac following, 'She told you about Emrys?' He sounded resigned, his voice flat. There wasn't a hint of emotion when he said Emrys's name.

'She did, but only because she was trying to put something into perspective, something about me, not you guys.'

'Oh?' His dad lifted two mugs off the mug tree and placed them on the countertop. He looked tired and worn. The months since the split hadn't been easy on him, and he was showing every one of his sixty-one years.

Isaac said abruptly, 'I thought you were going to retire when you got to sixty. Wasn't that the plan?'

'It was. Things change.'

Isaac heard the unspoken reason. Emrys had died and his mum had fallen apart. He wondered whether his dad had decided to keep working for financial reasons or for emotional ones. Looking at him, he guessed it might be the latter.

'What was she trying to put into perspective?' his dad asked.

Isaac swallowed. 'I met a girl when I was in university. She dropped out because her dad was ill.' He paused. 'I was in love with her. I still am.' Then he told his father all about her.

When he'd finished, his dad said, 'I knew Ken. It was a shame he was taken so young. From what I've heard, his daughter has done a brilliant job of keeping the business going.' His lips quirked. 'Your mum and I thought there was something up and we guessed it might be to do with a girl, but you didn't say anything and we didn't like to pry. You should have told us; a trouble shared is a trouble halved, so they say.'

'What was the point? She'd made her decision.'

'Like your mum said, we might have been able to put it into perspective.' Stephen gave him a dry look. 'You were too close.'

'Like you are, you mean?'

'Fair point. But your mum and I are married – that's the difference. She was unfaithful, and I'm not sure I can forgive that.'

'The hurt is the same. Dad, Nelly was The One, and I let her walk away. Mum is your One. Are you going to let something that happened nearly forty years ago wreck everything?'

'She still loves Emrys.'

'He's dead. You're not. And I believe she's grieving for you just as much as she's grieving for him.'

'Are you grieving too?'

Isaac dropped his head and nodded.

'How about you follow your own advice?' his dad suggested.

'It's too late. She's seeing the guy who manages the care home.'

'William Reid?' Stephen started to laugh.

'What's so funny?'

'William is gay.'

'He is?' Isaac blinked in astonishment. He could have sworn he'd seen a spark between them, or if not on William's part, then certainly on Nelly's. How wrong could he have been?

His dad nodded. 'Believe me, there's nothing going on between William and your girl.'

'She's not my girl.'

'She could be – if you asked her. Did she kiss you back?'

'Dad!'

'Did she?'

Isaac shrugged, feeling like a teenager who'd been caught snogging in the park. 'I suppose.'

'There you go, then. Look Isaac, you can either go for it – what have you got to lose? – or you can mope about and be forever wondering *what if*.'

'What about you and mum? I could say the same about you, because the pair of you are miserable without the other.'

'We'll see.' His dad sighed and his shoulders drooped, but not before Isaac saw a glimmer of hope in his father's eyes.

With a sigh, Isaac realised he had done as much as he could; the rest was up to his parents. What he needed to do now was to concentrate on his own happiness – and he strongly suspected that it was inextricably linked to a certain female builder.

Had she done the right thing in dropping out of university and ending her relationship with Isaac? It was a question Nelly had been asking herself, and it had kept her awake

222

for the second night in a row. She was exhausted, physically and emotionally, and wished she could stop thinking about him, but Isaac invaded her thoughts as thoroughly as weeds invaded a garden if left unchecked. The problem was she couldn't control her thoughts: there was no equivalent of weed killer for the mind, and whatever she tried to occupy herself with, they kept returning to Isaac.

The kiss was the predominant thing dominating her thoughts, closely followed by the look on Isaac's face when he'd left: dismay, shock, and had she seen a hint of revulsion?

She wasn't sure, but whatever expression she thought she might have seen, one thing was abundantly clear – Isaac didn't want anything to do with her. The love he'd once felt had well and truly died, and her heart was breaking all over again.

Not that it had actually mended: for thirteen years it had been held together with sticking plaster and string.

She pottered around her kitchen, making herself a breakfast she wasn't able to face and psyching herself up to go to the stables, something else she couldn't face but knew she must. Gavin knew what he was doing and she had total faith in him, but she always, always performed daily checks on whatever jobs they had on. Sometimes it was just the one site, sometimes it was two, but she never failed to show her face, and if they were a man down or additional hands were needed, she'd get stuck in.

The only thing she wanted to get stuck into today was her duvet. The idea of going back to bed, pulling the covers over her head and sinking back into the oblivion of sleep was tempting, but if she put so much as one step on that slippery slope, she feared she might slide into a black hole of despair, never to emerge.

Had she been wrong to drop the course and drop Isaac?

'Stop it!' she cried, clapping her hands to her head. If she asked herself that question one more time she might scream. What was done, was done. There was no going back, no pressing rewind. Hindsight is a wonderful thing, because if she'd known back then that she would still be in love with him and that her heart would be just as broken thirteen years later, maybe she wouldn't have given up her dreams. But then again, how could she have done anything less and still be able to live with herself? She hadn't dropped everything on a whim – she'd done it for her *dad*.

Anyway, who was to say that their love would have stood the test of time? They may well have got to the end of their third year and have split up anyway. The relationship might have run its course and they would have gone their separate ways. Perhaps she was only feeling so bad simply because there was unfinished business between them, and no other reason.

That kiss hadn't felt like unfinished business, though.

'Stop thinking about it,' she commanded, then snorted. It was like trying to hold back the tide, and she was also starting to talk to herself. 'Nelly Newsome, you're falling apart.'

It took Nelly a second to realise that someone was ringing her doorbell, and with a sigh she threw her uneaten toast out of the window for the birds to feast on, and went to answer it.

Expecting it to be the postman (although if it was, he was early) she almost fainted when she saw Isaac standing on her step. Dizzily she put a hand on the frame to steady herself, and willed her racing heart to slow down.

God help her if she continued to react in this manner every time she clapped eyes on him.

'Can we talk?' he asked.

She tried to gauge his mood but failed. Was he here to apologise? To remonstrate with her? With her heart in her mouth, she stood to the side. 'You'd better come in.'

He stepped past and she caught his scent, her nostrils flaring as she inhaled. Her tummy turned over and she tottered after him on unsteady legs. Abruptly she wished she'd washed her hair and put some make-up on. She was keenly aware that she looked as bad as felt, and she didn't want him to think he was the cause.

'How do you know where I live?' she blurted, as he came to a halt at the end of the hall wondering whether he should go on into her lounge. She waved him inside. Is that the best you can do, she asked herself? There were much more important things going on here, and all she could think of was how he'd got hold of her address?

'Amos told me, but if he hadn't, I would have gone to your Mum's house. Although, she mightn't have taken kindly to a strange man turning up on her doorstep and asking for her daughter's address.' He turned to face her, and she saw that he didn't look much better than she did.

'She would have sent you away with a flea in your ear,' Nelly confirmed.

'I take it you never told her about me?'

'Not really, but even if I had, I doubt she would have remembered. She had other things going on at the time.' Nelly didn't see the point in telling him that her mum knew about him now.

'Of course she did.' He shuffled awkwardly from foot to foot. 'I'm sorry I kissed you.'

'Gee, thanks.' Her voice dripped with sarcasm and a flutter of annoyance replaced some of the pain she was feeling. It was better than the heartache, even though her ire wouldn't last.

'I didn't mean it like that. What I meant, was… Oh, hell, I don't know what I meant, except that I still love you.' He stopped, an anguished expression spreading across his face. He rubbed the back of his neck and swallowed convulsively.

Nelly was frozen. Even her churning thoughts had come to a halt. 'What?' she squeaked.

'Sorry, I shouldn't have come here. I knew it was a mistake, but my mum had Emrys and she didn't want me to be like her, and Dad…' He trailed off.

'What?' she asked again, confused. Has she heard him correctly? Or was she having some kind of an episode?

'Forget it. I'd better go.' He took a step towards the door, but Nelly was blocking his way and her feet refused to move.

She was frozen to the spot. 'Did you say—' she cleared her throat '—that you love me?'

'Forget it. I shouldn't have said anything. You clearly don't feel the same.'

'I do.'

'Erm… what?' His eyes bored into her.

'I love you, too.'

'You do?'

'Yes.' Her voice was stronger. This was crunch time – if she didn't tell him how she felt now, she never would. His declaration had taken her by surprise, but she realised he meant what he said. His love for her was written all over his face. It was a look she knew well, but one she didn't think she'd ever see again, and it made her soul sing.

His eyes softened. 'My mum explained why you ended things between us.'

'Your mum?' What did she know about this? Nelly had never met his mum.

'It's a long story, but we've got the rest of our lives for me to tell it.' His certainty took her breath away.

'We have?'

'If you want me.'

'Oh, I want you, all right,' she replied throatily, her tummy fizzing, her chest aching from sheer joy, and her heart threatening to leap out of her ribcage. 'I always have.'

'Thirteen years,' he began, then laughed quietly. 'It doesn't matter. I've found you again – that's what's important.'

He enfolded her in his arms, and his mouth came down on hers. Eagerly she kissed him back, melting into his embrace.

His fingers tangled in her hair, holding her close, and she had the feeling he didn't intend to let her go. Ever.

Finally though, she tore her lips away from his, feeling thoroughly kissed, her body and her mind in total disarray. She wanted to drag him off to bed and make love to him for the rest of the day, week, month, but she wasn't going to. As he'd pointed out, they had the rest of their lives together: she wanted to get to know him all over again, to thoroughly understand the man he'd become, to know him inside and out before she reacquainted herself with his body.

It was going to be fun, this exploration of hers, but she had a feeling she wouldn't hold out for long. She was as eager for him as he was for her, but a short wait would do them both good.

Anyway, she wanted to hear those three little words again. And again, and again…

CHAPTER NINE

'Now what?' Harry asked.

Petra wrinkled her nose. They were standing in their son's gorgeous nursery, staring down into his cot. They'd only brought him home this morning, and the little boy had been cuddled constantly since they'd lifted him out of his car seat.

It was now early evening. Amory had been fed, he'd been winded, he'd been topped and tailed, and he'd had a fresh nappy on. Then he'd been placed carefully in his brand new cot, with the soft white sheet and the colourful mobile hanging over it. A night light glowed in the corner and the soothing sounds of a human heartbeat emanated from an iPod on top of the brand new chest of drawers.

It was a perfect room for a baby.

Unfortunately, Amory didn't think so. From the second his little bottom had touched the mattress, he'd howled. His cheeks had reddened, and he'd screwed up his face, opened his mouth, and bawled. Petra had immediately scooped him back out again and cuddled him close. Amory had immediately stopped crying.

Reassured that nothing was seriously wrong, she'd checked his nappy again, Harry looking on anxiously, then she'd tried him with some milk, but the baby had only taken a few desultory sucks and had then fallen asleep with her nipple in his mouth.

So she and Harry had tried to put him down again.

Slowly, careful not to disturb Amory, she'd placed him back in his cot, and the pair of them had tiptoed out of the room, holding their breath.

They'd made it as far as the top of the stairs before their son let out a squawk of indignation, quickly followed by a full-throated bellow.

In resignation, she and Harry had returned to the nursery, to find Amory with a screwed-up face and angrily waving arms. His tiny hands were curled into fists and his legs kicked and jerked.

He clearly wasn't happy.

'What do you think is wrong with him?' Petra asked, anxiously.

'I don't know.' Harry was equally as worried.

'Shall I pick him up again?' she wondered.

'Better had. We can't let him cry like this.'

'Do you think we should phone the out-of-hours doctor?'

'If he doesn't stop crying…' Harry agreed.

Petra picked her baby up and held him against her chest. Amory stopped crying so abruptly it was as though a switch had been turned off.

Petra looked at Harry. Harry gazed solemnly back at her.

Wordlessly, she put the baby back in his cot.

The switch was immediately reactivated, and Amory began to cry once more.

'At least we know what's wrong with him,' Harry said, raising his voice so he could be heard over the sounds his furious son was making.

'What do we do?' she asked. 'Do we leave him to cry?'

'I don't think I can stand it,' Harry said. 'It breaks my heart seeing him so upset.' This time it was Harry who plucked the irate infant from his cot.

Once again the noise ceased, but Amory didn't drop back off to sleep straight away. Instead, he lay there in the crook of his father's arm and gazed up at him with mistrustful eyes.

'He's waiting for me to put him back down,' Harry said in wonderment. 'Look at his little face.'

Petra didn't need to be told. She'd hardly taken her gaze off her baby since he'd been born, and only then it had been because she'd had to leave the hospital to go home to sleep. Now that he was home, she hadn't been able to tear her gaze away from him.

She turned in a slow circle, scanning the nursery. It was a warm and tranquil place. Lena and Amos had worked wonders, and she would be eternally grateful for their help and for the generosity of everyone in Picklewick. But she had a feeling the room wasn't going to be used as much as she'd assumed it would be. Not unless she and Harry moved their double bed into it and they slept in there until he was ready to sleep on his own. Which might be a good few years away.

'I wish babies came with an instruction manual,' she groaned. 'A definitive one. Because all those baby books Lena brought give different advice. No two say the same thing.'

'What should we do?' Harry asked. He was still staring into his baby's eyes and the baby was staring back at him. 'He knows we're talking about him.'

'Of course he does. He's a bright little boy, aren't you, poppet? He's also got us wrapped around his little finger.'

'He's only been home five minutes, and he's already calling the shots,' Harry agreed. 'What's he going to be like in a month's time?'

'I've no idea.' Petra wound her arms around Harry's waist and rested her head on his shoulder. 'But I can't wait to find out.'

'Neither can I, my love, neither can I.'

'This is better than the student union,' Isaac said to Nelly. They were having their first proper date in thirteen years. Nelly had made him wait until Friday, although they'd seen each other every day since they'd declared their love. They were currently in the Black Horse, perusing the menu. Nelly had insisted he wined and dined her, but she hadn't been bothered about going anywhere posh, because tonight was the night she intended making love to him, and she didn't have much of an appetite.

'We had some fun though, didn't we?' he was saying. 'Remember when that girl with the green and pink hair came on to me? You were furious.' He chuckled.

'I had every right to be,' Nelly replied loftily. 'She soon scarpered when I told her to get lost.'

'Yeah, you were quite scary when you were cross.'

'It's because I've been giving as good as I get with chippies and brickies ever since I was small. I wonder what she's doing now?'

'She's got a husband, four kids and a hairdressing salon.'

'Really? Good for her. I don't think I can remember seeing her with the same hair colour or style twice.' Nelly sipped at her wine. 'Do you keep in touch with many of the people we knew?'

'A few. There's a Facebook group where some of the students in our year hang out.' He inclined his head to the side and regarded her thoughtfully. 'Would you ever consider going back to uni and finishing your degree?'

'I don't think so. My mum asked me the same thing, but I'm happy doing what I'm doing.' She giggled. 'We could always join forces – you plan it and I'll build it.'

'Isn't that what we're doing now at the stables on Muddypuddle Lane?' he asked, staring at her.

'I suppose it is. It's what my dad and I intended to do.' She was wistful for a moment, but only for a moment. This was the start of a whole new life. It was time she looked forward, not back – she'd done enough of that over the years. If it came about that she and Isaac joined forces workwise, it would be the icing on the cake.

But first of all, there was something else she wanted to do. How hungry are you?' she asked, catching her bottom lip with her teeth and looking at him from beneath her lashes.

The flare of desire in his eyes made her heart thump erratically. 'Oh, I'm starving,' he replied huskily, 'but I think you know it's not food I want. It's *you*.' And with that he stood up, grabbed her hand, and they raced outside.

They had thirteen years of catching up to do…

Despite Amos being out in the yard, he could hear the baby's furious crying, and he chuckled to himself.

'Listen to that,' he said to Star. 'Be thankful your little one doesn't make such a racket.' If anyone was listening, it might sound as though he was complaining, but he wasn't. He was proud – the little boy had a sterling set of lungs on him, and despite only being home for less than a day, he was already making his presence felt.

The mare flicked her ears and continued to munch on the hay net. Her foal mouthed at it, but Amos knew it was more out of curiosity than any desire to eat the dried stalks, although that would soon come. He was happy enough to nibble at the sweet grass when he and his mum were in the small paddock behind the house, but he'd yet to discover the delights of fresh hay.

Amos clicked his tongue and held out his hand. Cautiously the colt stepped towards him, his neck stretched, his nostrils wide. Suppressing a laugh, Amos felt the foal's soft nose tickle his palm. The little horse was growing in confidence every day, and so was his mum. She was now happy to be handled and groomed, although everyone was still careful around her. Since she'd arrived at the stables, she'd been shown nothing but love, and Amos was confident that she would eventually settle enough to be ridden. Not yet, though; she had a foal at foot, and that was enough for her to be going on with.

One thing Amos was determined about, was that neither Star nor her foal would be leaving the stables on Muddypuddle Lane. He'd been in touch with Sandra from the horse charity and had offered them a permanent home. The mare would probably never be suitable for the riding school, but maybe Megan would like to take her under her wing?

And as for the little colt, who they'd called Breeze for no other reason than October had liked the name, Amos had plans for him. The animal would be Amory's horse, and he and the baby could grow up together.

Amos sighed contentedly, his heart full of love and gratitude. His family was growing, as was the stables, and he couldn't wait to hear the patter of tiny feet (and hooves) as Amory and the foal enjoyed a whole world of wonderful adventures.

Nelly's bedroom was dark and silent, apart from the muted gleam of a streetlight outside, and Isaac's soft breathing. She could tell he wasn't asleep, but she didn't feel the need to say anything. Their bodies and their passion had been words enough, and they were happy to simply lie together in the afterglow, cocooned in the certainty of their love for each other.

Content for the moment to lay her head on his chest and to have his strong arms holding her close, Nelly couldn't remember ever feeling as blissful as she did right now.

This rediscovered love of theirs was deeper and more profound, a more mature version of the heat and excitement of those early years. This, she knew, was going to last. She felt the conviction deep in her heart and it brought her to soft tears.

Isaac must have sensed them, because he gently extricated his arm and propped himself up on his elbow, his face close to hers as he stared into her eyes, searching, worrying.

'I love you,' she said.

'Why are you crying?' Isaac touched a finger to the trickle of moisture.

'Because I'm happy. I didn't realise how unhappy I had been until now.'

'I love you, too,' he said. 'More than you will ever know.' He took a breath and let it out slowly. She felt the warmth of it on her cheek. 'I don't know how I lived without you,' he whispered. 'Promise you won't leave me again.'

'I promise. I can't.' Another tear escaped. 'You are part of me – how could I leave?'

Isaac continued to look into her eyes and Nelly felt as though she was drowning in the love she saw in them.

No, not drowning – she was floating, buoyed up by his adoration and his naked longing and hunger for her. He was her "The One", and she was his, and now that she'd found him again, Nelly Newsome had no intention of ever letting him go.

WEDDING BELLS

CHAPTER ONE

Julie Richards took a hankie out of her bag and wiped the tears from her cheeks. She really should stop being so self-indulgent, she thought. This constant crying wasn't doing anyone any good, least of all her. She knew that Isaac was starting to despair that she'd ever get over her grief.

To be honest, she was beginning to fear the same thing.

But there was no expiry date on mourning someone, was there? You didn't get to a certain point after losing a loved one and suddenly wake up the next day with the grief magically lifted. If she'd discovered one thing since she'd learnt of Emrys's death, it was that grief was a tricky thing to get a grip of. Some days she wasn't so bad and she'd think she'd turned the corner, but there were others where she didn't want to get out of bed.

Today was particularly difficult, because today was the first anniversary of his passing, and the only way she could feel close to him was to visit the one place that she and Emrys had returned to again and again – their special place.

Julie sank down onto the grass and stared across the valley. She was sitting some way above the same lonely layby where they used to come all those years ago. Sometimes they would sit in his car and kiss, other times they would take a walk up the hill and make out in the long grass, with the wind sighing around them as they whispered their love for each other.

It was the only place she felt vaguely close to him. She would have visited his grave if she could, but he'd been buried far away in New Zealand and she couldn't face travelling all that way on her own to say a final goodbye. So she'd come here instead, to a hillside not far from the quaint village of Picklewick, to mark the day that Emrys had died.

Out of necessity, they'd had to meet out of town, away from prying eyes, because she and Emrys hadn't been able to have a normal relationship – her marriage to Stephen had made sure of that. Even now, all these years later, she felt incredibly disgusted and ashamed of her behaviour. But she'd been pulled towards Emrys as strongly and as irrevocably as a star was sucked into a black hole, and there hadn't been a damned thing she had been able to do about it. Despite having been married to Stephen (patient, kind, loving Stephen) for three years, she had fallen desperately in love with Emrys.

He had been her deepest love, although not her only love, because after she'd finally found the strength to drive him away, she had tried so very hard to be the wife that Stephen deserved.

It wasn't as though she didn't love her husband. She did – she would never have married him if she hadn't. But she had also never experienced a passion like she had for Emrys. He had consumed her, heart, body and soul, like a wildfire raging through her life, out of control, burning hot and savage, and she had been helpless in the face of those ravenous flames.

Then she had discovered she was pregnant, and everything changed.

From out of depths that she hadn't known she'd possessed, she'd found the strength to tell Emrys she didn't love him – at least, not enough to emigrate to New Zealand with him. He'd begged and pleaded, scalding her with his hot, raw pain, but she hadn't relented. It was the only thing in the whole affair that she didn't hate herself for, because how could she have left Stephen when she had his baby growing inside her?

She might have been prepared to deprive him of his wife, but she couldn't, in all conscience, deprive him of his son.

She'd lied through her teeth to push Emrys away, and she had stayed in the UK and stayed in her marriage, and vowed to be the best wife that she could possibly be to make up for her failings. She had buried her love for Emrys as deeply as she could, and had concentrated on her marriage and all that was good about it. She'd been happy and so had Stephen, and she'd kept her vow for all this time – until she'd learned that Emrys was dead and her world had fallen apart.

Until that point, the thought of Emrys dying hadn't entered her mind. Whenever she thought of him (which hadn't been as often as she used to as the years sped by), he was still the handsome, witty, passionate man she had fallen in love with. In her mind he'd not aged, although she imagined that he would have moved on – wife, family, new career – but the details of his new life in a far-off country were hazy.

Never once had she been tempted to look him up or track him down. In the early days the internet had been non-existent so the option wouldn't have been available to her anyway, and as time went on and social media exploded, she'd still not gone looking for him for fear of what she might find. She didn't want to see photos of him with a wife, or with his children, or looking old. She wanted the image of him that she held in her mind to stay pristine and unsullied by the passage of time.

So it was a terrible shock when his daughter had contacted her at the end of last year. Julie could have kicked herself for making it so easy to be found. But then again, maybe a part of her hadn't wanted to move out of the house she'd been living in since she and Stephen had got married or change the phone number they'd always had, just in case Emrys had wanted to…

That was a silly notion. She'd broken Emrys's heart

when she'd told him that it was Stephen she truly loved, and he'd left for the other side of the world believing he'd been nothing more to her than a brief affair. Why would he ever have wanted to get in touch with her again?

He never did – but his daughter had, delivering the awful and incomprehensible news that Emrys had passed away. She'd found Julie's details hidden amongst some of his personal papers, with the instruction that Julie should be informed when he died. But his daughter hadn't found it until a few months after his death, and Julie couldn't help feeling desolate that she'd gone about her normal everyday life for all those weeks without the slightest hint that Emrys was no longer in this world. Surely she should have known? Surely some sixth sense should have told her that the man she'd loved so comprehensively had left this mortal coil?

It had been her lack of awareness, plus the message that Emrys had wanted her to know that he'd never stopped loving her, that had been her undoing. As grief had sunk its claws deeper into her heart, her life and the lives of her husband and son had unravelled. Stephen had left her, and Isaac had moved halfway across the country to be closer to her, giving up his home and his business because he was so concerned about her.

Julie dabbed her eyes again, marvelling how she still had so many tears left. She'd thought she'd done all her crying for Emrys when she had told him it was over. In the days, weeks, and months afterwards, she'd wept in secret. Whenever Stephen asked her what was wrong, she had blamed it on the pregnancy hormones making her weepy.

Since Emrys's daughter had phoned, Julie felt as though it was only yesterday that she'd pushed him away, that the intervening years had been a dream. And grief had risen up and swamped her. It was only a slim consolation that Emrys's daughter had reassured her he'd had a good life and had been happy, and he'd gone on to love again and had been loved in return.

Julie had been happy herself; she would be lying if she said she hadn't. Over the years her love for her husband had deepened, and eventually it had come to rival and even exceed the love she'd felt for Emrys. Stephen had been happy too, and it was this knowledge which convinced her that she had done the right thing in not choosing Emrys. Stephen loved being a father and had been a caring and involved dad. Whenever she saw him and Isaac together, she knew she couldn't have taken that away from him.

It was a pity everything had fallen apart now, when things were so good between them. Stephen had planned to retire when he reached sixty and they were going to take the opportunity (before grandchildren came along) to travel. They'd been so looking forward to spending their twilight years together.

Now, it seemed, they were going to spend them apart.

Desperately sad, Julie got up from the patch of grass she'd been sitting on, feeling lonelier than she'd ever felt in her life. She missed Emrys, goddamit.

But what was worse was that she missed Stephen *more*.

'What do you think?' Petra asked, moving a vase of flowers that was sitting on the dining table a few centimetres to the left, and standing back to eye it critically.

'It looks fabulous,' Nelly said, and Isaac nodded.

'It does look good,' he agreed. 'Just make sure you turn all the lights on when you take your photos – no matter how bright it is outside, you'll need some help to ensure the images do the place justice.'

'Have you found much that needs doing?' Petra wanted to know. Now that the work had been more or less completed on the barn conversion, she, Nelly and Isaac were checking the three cottages to make sure there weren't any issues which needed addressing. Nelly called it snagging – Petra called it doing the job properly. Luckily, the stables on Muddypuddle Lane had an excellent architect in Isaac, and Nelly and her firm of builders had proved to be thorough, efficient and extremely competent.

'Not a great deal,' Nelly said. 'I'll email the list over to you, and I'll copy you in, Isaac, for your records.'

'Like what?' he asked.

'A tap in the downstairs cloakroom of cottage number three isn't quite square on, and the door in one of the bedrooms in the second cottage will catch once the rug is down if a bit isn't shaved off the bottom. I can't see anything that needs attention in this one, though.'

They were standing in the living-cum-dining room of the first cottage, the one that Petra was scrambling to furnish in order to take photos to upload to the various holiday rental websites. She didn't intend to officially open until after her wedding in three weeks' time, but she wanted to get as much done as she possibly could beforehand. Then she could turn her attention to her nuptials, because she hadn't even bought a dress yet. She had suggested to Amos that she wore what she was happiest in – jodhpurs and Wellington boots – but her uncle had thrown a fit, and her groom hadn't been too enamoured with the idea either.

'I want to see you in a wedding dress,' Harry had said, taking her in his arms and kissing her. 'I don't care if you think I'm old-fashioned.'

'White doesn't suit me,' she'd retorted, only to be informed that he didn't care what colour it was, as long as it was a dress fit for the occasion of celebrating their marriage. Although he did have one caveat – he didn't want her to wear black.

Even Petra wouldn't have dreamt of wearing black to her own wedding! She didn't want people to think they were attending a funeral.

Nelly popped her iPad in the bag. 'I think that's it for today,' she said. 'I'll send a couple of guys around tomorrow to finish the snagging, then you're good to go.'

Petra wasn't so sure. She knew what she was doing when it came to horses and running the stables, but operating holiday rentals wasn't her area of expertise and she was worried she'd missed something or that she wasn't pitching it right.

Take the welcome basket she'd planned on providing, for instance…Was it okay to pop a bottle of wine in? How about the complementary chocolates? Was she overdoing it? Or not doing enough?

'You wouldn't like to test run this cottage for me, would you?' she asked, as an idea occurred to her. 'I could do with someone staying for a night or two to give me an honest opinion. I'd hate for our first guests to give us a bad review because we didn't provide a salad spinner, or something.'

'A salad spinner?' Isaac looked baffled.

'Amos was wittering on about one the other day. It shakes off all the water from your salad leaves after you've washed them.' Petra pulled a face. She honestly didn't give a hoot about salad spinners, but then again she wasn't the one who did the cooking, so perhaps she was being unfair.

'Is that really a thing?' Nelly asked.

'Apparently so.'

'Gosh. What happened to dabbing them dry with a clean tea towel?'

Petra shrugged. 'My thoughts exactly! So, what do you say about a trial run?'

'I think it's a marvellous idea to take a cottage for a spin, but we're probably not the best ones to do it,' Nelly said. 'We're too close to the project, don't you think so, Isaac?'

'Definitely! You need fresh eyes, and preferably from someone with no preconceptions,' Isaac advised.

'That's not going to be easy – everyone I could possibly ask has been involved with the conversion in one way or another.' Petra thought back to the barn clearing that had taken place earlier in the year. Loads of people had turned up to help them empty the old cow shed and get it ready for Nelly's builders to move in and do their bit.

Petra had been pregnant at the time and had been sternly warned by both Harry and Amos not to do too much. Gosh, she couldn't believe that little Amory was already nearly three months old. And neither could she believe that Nelly and her crew had managed to complete the job in such a short amount of time. Nelly had warned her that it might take as long as six months to convert a cow shed into three holiday cottages, but she'd pulled out all the stops and it had taken fourteen weeks from start to finish.

Petra gazed around in awe. She still found it hard to believe that the gorgeous living room she was currently standing in, with the stunning view across the valley, had once housed cattle. The transformation was unbelievable.

She was particularly pleased with *this* cottage because it was furnished. It had been a bit of a rush to get it done, with Petra having to do a great deal of something she wasn't terribly keen on – shopping. She loved buying horsey stuff and the last time she'd gone to The Horse of the Year Show she'd spent a fortune, but shopping for furniture and cushions? Meh, not so much.

Still, she'd done it, and now that everything was in place all she needed to do was to duplicate it for the other two cottages. October, who was her Girl Friday around the stables, was trying to persuade her to furnish each one in a different style, even if it was something as simple as changing the colour scheme, but Petra wasn't sure she could be bothered, although she had to admit that it would look better on the website to have each cottage with a different theme.

'I've got an idea,' Isaac said. 'How would you feel about my mum and dad staying for a weekend? I'm sure they'll give you their honest opinion, even if it was their son who designed the build.'

Petra noticed that Nelly was giving him an odd look.

'Er, won't that be a bit difficult?' Nelly said. 'They're not…um…together, in case you've forgotten.'

Isaac was grinning from ear to ear. 'That's the point. Are you game for a spot of matchmaking?' he asked Petra.

Petra grinned at him. He already knew she was. Before she'd met Harry love and romance hadn't been on her radar; now however, she couldn't get enough of it.

'Am I ever,' she declared rubbing her hands together. She was looking forward to this. She wasn't aware of the details, but she knew that Isaac's parents had split up a while ago. If Isaac wanted help in getting them back together, she was in.

She was just about to ask him what he was planning, when she heard a baby's cross wail. 'Oh dear, I think someone might be ready for a feed,' she said, as Amos appeared holding a grizzling infant in his arms.

Petra reached for her son, and he immediately began to cry louder. 'He's hungry, aren't you, baby?'

'I think that's our cue to leave,' Nelly said. 'Anyway, I quite fancy some lunch myself.' Turning to Isaac, she said, 'Do you have to rush off?'

'Definitely not. Lunch sounds good. Bye Petra, bye Amos, and I'm not going to leave you out, little man,' Isaac said to Amory, chucking the baby under the chin.

Amory blarted his indignation and Petra laughed. 'Come on, poppet, let's get you fed, shall we?' She headed outside to the bench next to the living room window and sat down.

Amos joined her.

'They make a lovely couple, don't they?' she said to her uncle as she undid her shirt and shifted the baby into position. Very soon, contented slurps filled the air.

'They do,' Amos agreed, watching Nelly and Isaac walk along the path, heading for their respective vehicles. 'How did the snagging go?'

It was amazing how quickly both she, Harry and Amos had picked up building jargon, Petra mused. Six months ago, she wouldn't have had a clue what that meant.

'There's not much, and nothing to be done in the first cottage, so after I've fed Mr Greedy here, I can go ahead and take the photos for the website.'

'Luca's getting on okay with it, is he?'

'I think so. It was looking really professional last time I saw it. It's so kind of him to help – I wouldn't know where to begin.'

'What does he do for a living exactly?' Amos asked.

'No idea.' Petra shifted the baby to the other breast and when he was settled, she said, 'Whatever it is, he's successful at it.' Luca had begun stabling his horse, Midnight, with them shortly before Petra had taken October on, and she'd got to know him fairly well over the course of this year, and especially since he and October had become an item.

'Do you think they'll get married?' Amos asked.

'October and Lucas? Possibly. You've got weddings on the brain,' Petra teased.

'Someone has to, because if it was left to you, you'd nip into the church on Sunday while still wearing your riding gear and expect the vicar to fit the ceremony in between the sermon and lunch.'

Petra stuck her tongue out at him.

'Be careful the wind doesn't change and your face will be stuck like that,' he warned. 'Right, when you've finished feeding the baby, you need to have something to eat yourself before you start taking photos. I've made some chicken and vegetable soup, and we've got some freshly baked rolls to go with it.'

Petra gently bumped his shoulder with hers. 'What would I do without you?' she said fondly, as he got to his feet.

'I'll go up to the house and begin warming it,' he said. 'Don't be long.'

'We won't.'

Petra waited for him to leave, then she leaned her head against the wall, closed her eyes and breathed deeply, enjoying the peace. A light breeze blew gently across her face, lifting the hairs that had escaped from her ponytail so they tickled her cheek, and she brushed them away. Aside from her son's contented suckling, the only other noises were the distant bleating of sheep on the hillside above and the chirping of birds in the hedgerow.

Feeling so happy she could burst, Petra thought how incredibly lucky she was. She was about to marry the love of her life, she had the most gorgeous baby in the world, and an uncle who was like a father; the stables was doing well and she had a brand new venture to look forward to.

For Petra, life was wonderful, and she was truly blessed.

'Dad, I've been thinking,' Isaac said as soon as Stephen answered the phone, and Stephen winced. In his experience, when someone says that they've been thinking, the person who said it usually had some hare-brained idea in mind.

'What about?' he asked cautiously, hoping it didn't involve him. He loved his son to the moon and back, but he didn't want to be roped into anything. He was quite happy as he was.

Actually, that was a lie – Stephen wasn't happy at all, and he hadn't been since Julie had announced that she'd been unfaithful and that her lover was dead. Admittedly, the affair had taken place before Isaac was born, but considering Stephen had only found out about it relatively recently, to him it felt as though it had just happened.

When he'd demanded times, dates, places (he'd wanted to know every sordid detail), and she'd informed him that she'd only ended it because she'd been pregnant, it had briefly entered his head that he wasn't Isaac's father and that this Emrys fella was. But Julie had quickly disavowed him of the notion, in a not particularly nice way. She'd informed him that if Isaac *had* been Emrys's child she would have gone to New Zealand with Emrys, because the only thing which had prevented her from leaving was that she hadn't wanted to deprive Stephen of his son.

Words had failed him.

He'd been so hurt it had taken his breath away. Even after nine months, the pain hadn't lessened. In fact, he believed it had grown worse. With every passing day he missed Julie more and more, and some days he wondered how he could go on without her.

In the beginning, his hurt had been overlain with bitterness and betrayal, and anger, too. But as the weeks had turned into months the anger had faded, as had the bitterness, until all he'd been left with was a deep and abiding sorrow and a persistent ache in his heart.

God, how he missed her. He missed talking to her about his day, snuggling up to her at night, her ready smile, her calm and gentle manner.

Stephen had come to realise that he was grieving for her as though she were dead, and in a way maybe that was true, because the woman he'd known and loved for all these years hadn't been the woman he'd thought she was. He was grieving for her, and for the life they'd had together. He was also mourning the loss of their future, which he was now having to face alone.

'Dad, did you hear what I said?'

'Huh? Sorry Isaac, you cut out for a moment,' Stephen lied. 'Run that past me again?'

'I was saying that Petra at the stables on Muddypuddle Lane wants someone who isn't connected with the barn conversion to stay in one of the cottages for a couple of nights to road test it, so to speak. You know, make sure everything works, that she hasn't forgotten anything…You get the drift.'

'I do indeed.'

'I've got to warn you, one of the selling points of the cottage is that it's a complete getaway from it all – there's no wifi and the phone signal can be a bit hit and miss. There is a TV though, and Petra has stocked the place with books and board games, so hopefully you'll manage to keep yourself amused for the duration. What do you say?'

'I suppose I could.'

'Don't sound so enthusiastic,' Isaac said. 'You could do with a break, and it's not as though it's going to cost you anything. Plus, you'll be doing me a favour: I trust your opinion and I know you'll be honest and fair.'

Despite his initial impulse to refuse because he didn't fancy going on holiday by himself, Stephen felt flattered that his son valued his opinion. Maybe if he looked on it as a job and not a weekend break, he'd be more inclined to go.

He tried the idea out for size and decided he could cope. He'd be methodical about it and check that everything worked, even if it was something he wouldn't normally use, such as a trouser press – did they still have those? He'd even try out the microwave if there was one, although that was another thing he wouldn't normally use on holiday; on those occasions where he and Julie had rented an apartment or a cottage, neither of them had wanted to do much in the way of cooking, preferring to eat out.

Stephen sighed and pushed thoughts of Julie and past holidays to the back of his mind. He had to look forward, not back; dwelling on the past never did anyone any good.

'Did you say it was in Picklewick?' he asked.

'A couple of miles outside.'

'That's right, I remember now. You've done a few more jobs since then.'

Isaac chuckled. 'I have, thank goodness. But I was back there this morning with Nelly, to do some snagging.'

'How is Nelly?' Stephen asked.

Isaac had fallen in love with Nelly at university when she was on the same course as him, but her father's illness had forced her to drop out and she'd subsequently taken over her dad's construction business and they'd lost touch. Isaac had bumped into her again when he'd drawn up the architectural plans for the barn conversion and Nelly's firm had been employed as the builder. Their love had reignited, and they'd been inseparable ever since. Stephen had a lot of time for Nelly – she was a lovely girl and he could tell she was head-over-heels in love with his son.

'She's good,' Isaac said. 'We're going out for a meal tonight.'

'Somewhere nice?'

'The Black Horse in Picklewick. You should have a meal there when you stay at the cottage. The food is pretty good and so is the atmosphere.'

'I might just do that,' Stephen said, warming to the idea.

Picklewick was only nine miles away, but he remembered Isaac telling him that the stables were halfway up the side of a hill, surrounded by farmland and with moorland above, so it would feel like he was in the middle of nowhere.

'Okay, you're on – I'll give the cottage a go if you think it'll help your clients. And who can say no to a freebie?' he added.

'Petra was hoping you could do this weekend,' his son said, sounding so delighted that it made him wonder if Isaac had been worried about him.

Stephen had to admit that he hadn't exactly been the life and soul of the party lately, so this break might do him good. Since last November he'd been stuck in a rut, not wanting to do anything apart from go to work. Even during the six weeks of the school summer holidays, which was finally coming to an end, he'd not felt like going away. The furthest he'd gone had been to the DIY store on the outskirts of town, and he'd only done that because he wanted a bookshelf to store all his school stuff on.

He had even gone into work once or twice, so that showed how the time had dragged. Oh, well, at least his classroom looked good and the displays on the wall were top-notch, ready for the start of the new term in September. He'd also caught up on all the paperwork, which was usually a slog he tried to avoid until the last minute, and he had to rush to complete it.

When he'd stayed so long at school the other day that the caretaker had kicked him out, Stephen had been forced to admit that he was lonely. Maybe he should get back out there into the world of meeting people and dating, but he didn't have the energy or the inclination.

In some ways, he regretted his knee-jerk reaction in leaving Julie, but he'd felt so hurt and betrayed, and he still did.

Silently, he shook his head. What was done, was done, and there was no going back. In fact, it might be time to consider getting a divorce. End it once and for all. There was no point in hanging onto a marriage that was dead in the water, so they may as well formalise the end of their union. After all, he could foresee him and Julie only having to spend time together in the future, if Isaac and Nelly got married or gave them grandchildren.

Seeing his son so happy made Stephen's heart ache. He vividly remembered what he and Julie had been like in the early days, how in love they'd been. How they hadn't been able to keep their hands off each other.

Things had calmed down somewhat once they'd got married, but that was only to be expected. The first flush of passion had mellowed into a different kind of love as they had learned to live together. They'd had their ups and downs, of course – every married couple did – but they'd worked through them and had come out the other side.

They had been happy, hadn't they? He hadn't imagined it. Julie couldn't have been that good an actress; she'd told him time and time again that she loved him and he'd believed her – he'd had no reason not to. Until recently. And even now, he found it hard to believe that she hadn't meant it. They had been together for nearly forty years, and he could have sworn those years had been happy ones.

Or, so he had believed.

He snorted bitterly. It was all a lie. It had to have been, otherwise Julie wouldn't have fallen into the arms of another man.

Suddenly Stephen felt weary and worn down, and the thought of living the rest of his life on his own sent a wave of depression through him. He had nothing to get up for in the morning – apart from his job – and it was incredibly sad to think that the only reason he was looking forward to the start of the new term was because it meant he wouldn't be alone all day. What kind of a life was that?

Even the brief spark of interest that the mention of a couple of days away had caused, didn't last. He wasn't sure that spending a long weekend in the middle of nowhere on his own would do much to help his mood, but he'd agreed to it now. Going back on his word for no real reason might ring an alarm bell in Isaac's head and the last thing Stephen wanted was for his son to worry about him.

He would just have to make the best of it. With scant enthusiasm he went to the cupboard under the stairs to root out his hiking boots. At least he could get a bit of exercise in the fresh air, and he guessed anything was better than sitting at home staring at the four walls.

CHAPTER TWO

'Tea, coffee, sugar, wine, chocolates, a loaf of bread, cake...' Petra was standing in the kitchen of one of the recently converted cottages, staring critically at the welcome pack. 'And there's milk in the fridge, both cow and soya, and butter. Have we forgotten anything?' She patted the little bundle of cosily-wrapped baby who was snuggled against her chest in his sling, and swayed gently from side to side. If only he'd stay asleep for another half an hour.

'I think it's more than generous,' Amos said. 'Home-made cake and freshly baked bread... hmph!'

Her uncle was grizzling because he was the one who'd whisked up the cake and had baked the loaf, but she could tell he didn't mean it. He was as keen to get this right as she was, and there was only one opportunity to make a good impression, as he kept telling her. Besides, he loved a spot of baking, did Amos, and he was good at it. Petra was certain that their guests would appreciate the homely touch.

Fresh flowers picked from the garden behind the farmhouse, with greenery gathered from the hedgerows while she was out on her early morning ride, made the living room look welcoming and cheerful, and she'd also remembered to leave a small booklet on the sideboard with information about things to do and local attractions. As an added bonus, she was offering a half price ride too, so that might appeal to some people.

'Eggs!' she cried, suddenly remembering. The stables had a resident flock of chickens looked after by a noisy cockerel called Fred. As the hens laid on a regular basis there were always eggs to spare, and she'd planned to include half a dozen in the welcome basket. If the guests wanted any more, they could always buy them from her.

'I've boxed them up ready,' Amos said. 'They're in the kitchen up at the house. I'll fetch them in a minute, and I've also swapped half a dozen for some of Walter York's pears. I thought we'd have poached pears after dinner this evening.'

'How is Walter?' Petra asked. Although he lived in Lilac Tree Farm further along Muddypuddle Lane, she hardly ever saw the old man himself. Just his sheep.

'Not good,' Amos said. 'He's struggling a bit. I get the impression he's not well.'

'Is there anything we can do to help?'

Amos shook his head. 'I did offer, but you know how stubborn and independent he can be.'

Petra had heard, but she didn't know Walter particularly well. In all the years she'd lived at the stables, she'd only spoken to him a dozen or so times. He tended to keep himself to himself. She knew he'd lost his wife years ago, and that he had a grown-up son who was a chef in London, but that was about it. The poor chap didn't have much in the way of family, and she'd also heard that a long-lost brother of his had died last year, so she felt rather sorry for him. But Walter was a stubborn old fellow from what Amos had told her and didn't; take kindly to offers of help. Often, the only reason she knew he was still around was because his sheep would be moved from one field to another. Occasionally she'd hear his Land Rover in the lane, and once or twice she'd catch a glimpse of him which, considering they were neighbours, wasn't much.

'We really should plant a pear tree of our own,' Amos said. 'How about if we plant one down here?' He pointed to the far end of the sloping lawn.

'We could, I suppose,' Petra said.

She didn't usually take much notice of the gardening

254

side of things, leaving that to Amos, who had a thriving veggie patch outside the back door. But she had taken an interest in the landscaping around the newly converted cottages, wanting everything to be just right. It was early days yet, as the area around the former cow shed was still rather bare, although Amos, with the help of October's mum Lena, had turned a tump of rubble that had been excavated from the floor of the barn into a rockery, and it now sported a variety of small alpine plants which were gradually establishing themselves. By next spring it should look wonderful.

None of the cottages had much of a garden, but they all had their own private seating areas out the back, which consisted of a patio surrounded by flowering shrubs, and there was a lawned area to the front where the planting had been kept deliberately low-key so as to take advantage of the wonderful views across the valley.

'Next month I'll pop some spring bulbs in,' Amos said, gazing out of the window. 'And Lena said she's going to separate some of her perennials, so I can have those as well. It should look lovely.'

Petra moved closer to her uncle and slipped an arm through his. 'It looks lovely already,' she said. 'You've done a wonderful job.'

'*We*,' he amended. '*We've* done a wonderful job. It's taken all of us to get this project up and running – you, Harry, me, Nathan, October, Luca, Timothy, Charity, Lena...'

Petra knew he was right. They'd come a long way from Harry's vague idea of turning an unused and semi-derelict outbuilding into holiday homes, and everyone had helped to make the dream become a reality.

They stood in companiable silence for a few more minutes, then Amos checked his watch.

'When are Isaac's parents arriving?' he asked. 'If there's anything left to do, we'd better get a move on.'

'Ah, this is where things might be a bit tricky,' Petra

said with a grimace. 'They're not arriving at the same time. Isaac's mum will be arriving first – Isaac is bringing her because she hasn't got a car – then his dad should hopefully turn up.'

Amos stepped back and shot her a look. 'Why do I get the feeling there's something going on?'

Petra smiled sheepishly. 'Because there is?'

Her uncle inhaled deeply then let the breath out in a sigh. 'You'd better tell me.'

'Isaac's mum and dad aren't exactly together,' she began.

'In what way?'

'They are separated and have been for about nine months.'

'They must still get along,' Amos pointed out, 'for them to be having a weekend break together.'

'Er, not exactly. The split wasn't amicable.'

'Then why would they—? Oh, *I see*, this is a reconciliation? I hope it works out for them.'

Petra shook her head. 'It's not a reconciliation. They don't know the other is going to be here. You see, Isaac thinks they still love each other, but things have gone too far for either of them to make the first move – so he's doing it for them.'

'Is that wise?'

'Maybe not, but considering they're not speaking anyway, I doubt if it'll make things any worse.'

'Don't be too sure,' Amos warned. 'Meddling in other people's relationships is never a good idea.'

'I'm not meddling – Isaac is.'

'You're helping him.'

'I'll deny all knowledge,' Petra said. 'As far as I'm concerned, Isaac suggested that his parents give one of the cottages a trial run, and that's the end of my involvement.'

'I bet it won't be,' Amos said. 'You've become a right little matchmaker recently. Mark my words, not everyone appreciates it. I certainly wouldn't.'

'It's lucky that there isn't anyone for me to matchmake you with then, isn't it?' she replied with a smirk.

But when a faint hint of colour spread across Amos's whiskery face, Petra began to wonder…

Dear god! Julie was seriously tempted to demand that Isaac turned the car around and take her straight back home, but the only thing preventing her was that she'd have to explain the reason why. And she didn't fancy telling her son that the road they were driving along was the very road where she and Emrys used to meet. Only the other day she'd walked up the same road, having caught the bus to Picklewick, and had climbed over the stile near the layby and scrambled up the hill to sit in the long grass and have a good weep.

She should have put two and two together and realised that the barn conversion that Isaac had drawn up the plans for was just down the road from *their* favourite meeting place.

The irony and the coincidence might have made her smile, if it wasn't for the fact that she felt like bawling.

How on earth was she supposed to spend three nights here?

She'd lose her mind.

But she didn't have a great deal of choice, did she?

However, as Isaac turned the car off the road and onto Muddypuddle Lane to drive up a rutted track, she began to have second thoughts. Maybe it wouldn't be so bad, after all; the layby was some distance up ahead and it wasn't as though she'd be going that way, because if she wanted a meal out or to mooch around some shops, Picklewick village was in the other direction.

'Is that the cottage?' she asked, seeing an old stone building just off the road. It didn't look all that big from this angle, and it appeared to be rather ramshackle, but…

'No, the stables are up there. See?' Isaac pointed to a group of buildings halfway up the side of the hill. 'The cottages are to the right, but you can't really see them from here.'

Even better, Julie thought. If they were hidden from the road, then the road would be hidden from them, and hopefully her memories would be too.

Shortly they were pulling off the lane and trundling down a narrow, tarmacked track which bypassed the stables and ended in a small parking area just big enough for three vehicles. Ahead, she could see a path leading to a row of cottages through a gap in a hedge.

Even from this distance they looked lovely, and Julie was surprised to find that she couldn't wait to see inside. She hadn't shown this much interest in anything for a long time.

Isaac lifted her case and a box containing foodstuff out of the boot and slammed it shut. 'Crumbs! What have you got in here?' he cried, hefting the box. 'It weighs a ton.'

'Gin.' She'd packed some food for appearance's sake, but she suspected she wouldn't bother to eat a great deal of it – she hadn't had much of an appetite since Stephen had walked out.

'Do you think you're going to need it?' Isaac joked, setting the case down on its wheels and lengthening the handle.

'Probably.' She gazed around, her eyes scanning the valley. 'It's so peaceful,' she said, changing the subject as the silence washed over her.

On second thoughts, maybe it would be *too* quiet she mused apprehensively, as she realised there wouldn't be anyone in the other cottages yet and she'd be here on her own. She wasn't used to such isolation and the thought worried her. If Stephen had been with her, she wouldn't have given a hoot about being so far from civilisation, but he wasn't, so it was a genuine concern.

'Er, I think I might be a bit lonely,' she said. 'It's incredibly quiet. And I'm not too happy about not being able to use my phone.'

'I didn't say you *couldn't* use it, Mum,' Isaac said, giving her that sideways look of his that made her feel like a little old lady – which she most definitely was not! 'All I said was, that the reception around here could be a bit dodgy. You might have to wave your phone out of the bedroom window or walk up to the house to get a decent signal, for instance.'

'That's no good if there's a prowler outside, is it?' Against her better judgement, Julie allowed her son to lead her along the path towards the cottages.

He gave her another sideways look, this time accompanied by a sigh. 'There's hardly likely to be a prowler, although you might find a goat wandering about. She's not supposed to, but she's a right little escape artist.'

'A goat,' Julie repeated flatly. She didn't know how she felt about goats. The closest she'd ever come to one was when she'd eaten a goat's cheese salad. And she suspected that the lamb dish she'd once had in a restaurant in Cyprus might have actually been goat.

'Princess is harmless enough,' Isaac told her.

'Back to my prowler problem,' Julie continued, as they came to a halt outside the front door.

'You haven't got a prowler problem.' He glanced at his watch, and she guessed he was eager to get her settled in so he could be off.

The door to the cottage was unlocked and he shouldered his way inside.

Julie frowned and followed him. 'Is the door always kept unlocked?'

'No, Mum, it isn't. Petra said she'd leave it open, and could we come up to the house to collect the keys? I told you she's not long had a baby, didn't I? She's up to her eyes at the moment trying to get everything ready, so before you start thinking that the cottages won't be secure, don't worry – she's got a system in place for when paying guests arrive.'

Julie was relieved, because that was the first thing she would have mentioned in her report.

'I'll leave your case here, and we can go on up to the house,' Isaac said.

'Do you mind if I have a quick look round first?' Julie asked. She had to admit that it all looked very nice.

The front door opened up into a small hallway with the stairs leading off and a cloak room to the side, and another door led into a bright and airy living room with a picture window to the front. There was a small television, and two squashy sofas, a bookcase laden with both fiction and non-fiction, and a shelf underneath holding an assortment of board games. The other end of the room held a dining table and four chairs, with French doors opening out onto a compact paved area with further seating and a hammock. The hammock was a sweet touch, but she knew she wouldn't try it.

To the left of the dining area was a small but well-equipped and perfectly modern kitchen, and its window also looked out into the little private garden.

'There are two bedrooms upstairs, both with their own bathrooms,' Isaac informed her as he propped her case at the bottom of the stairs, and she heard the pride in his voice.

'It's lovely,' she said. 'You've done a good job.'

'It wasn't a difficult design. Pretty straightforward really, but I must admit I am pleased with it.'

'So you should be.' She reached up to grasp his face and plonked a kiss on his cheek.

'Muuum,' he whined, rubbing at the lipstick mark she'd left on his skin.

Julie chuckled. He'd always hated her doing that – which was why she did it. He was fun to wind up. She rarely bothered with lipstick anymore, but she'd worn some today to make Isaac believe she was getting her life back together. She'd fallen apart when Stephen had walked out and Isaac had been so worried about her that he'd left his house and his business in Wiltshire and had moved to be nearer to her, even though she'd protested that she didn't need him to keep an eye on her.

It was yet another thing to feel guilty about – never in a million years had she wanted to disrupt his life – but at least his business was picking up now and he'd reconnected with Nelly, so Julie didn't feel as bad as she might have done.

She saw Isaac glance at his watch again and she sighed. No doubt he had somewhere much more exciting to be, and she was just about to suggest that they get the key-collection over with when she noticed the contents of the welcome basket.

'Ooh, that's nice!' She picked up the bottle of wine and looked at the label. 'I'm going to enjoy that,' she said, opening the fridge and popping it inside. 'Is Petra planning on doing this for every rental, or is this a one off?'

'For every one,' he assured her. 'Come on, let's go. I'm meeting a client in an hour. A chap is thinking about building an eco-house, and I'd like to get the contract to draw up the plans.'

'Lead the way,' she said to him, hooking her coat over the newel post on the way out, and securing her bag more firmly on her shoulder. She might be okay with leaving her case in an unlocked house, but she certainly wasn't prepared to leave her handbag unattended. Anyone could walk in!

'I'm still a bit concerned about being stuck out here with no transport,' she said, as they walked towards the stables. She could see horses grazing in the fields, and sheep on the hillside above. It really was very rural.

A chicken scurried out from under a fence, making her jump, and she tightened her grip on her bag. If the creature tried to peck her, she'd swing her bag at it.

'I don't understand why you haven't bought yourself a little run-around.' Isaac flapped a hand at the hen to shoo it away.

The hen ignored him.

'It's on my to-do list,' she said, with a sigh. It was only fair that Stephen had the car when he left because he had to travel to work and often had loads of books to cart back and forth. She'd already taken early retirement and everything she needed, such as shops, the dentist and the doctor's surgery were within walking distance or a short bus-ride away if she was feeling lazy.

She'd been meaning to look for a little car, but she simply couldn't summon up the energy.

'You won't be stuck here,' Isaac said. 'Picklewick is two miles in that direction.' He pointed to the south. 'And there's a public right of way through the fields that will take you into the village. The forecast for the weekend is good, so it'll be a nice walk. You can have lunch there – I can heartily recommend the Black Horse, or there are a couple of cafes you could try. If you don't fancy that there are plenty of other walks you can go on, or you can just enjoy the peace and quiet and read. You could even have a riding lesson.'

'I don't think so!' The very idea made her shudder. She didn't mind horses – they were magnificent to look at – but she preferred to do that from a safe distance, not from the back of one of them.

As they neared the house, a wonderful smell of cooking assaulted her nostrils and Julie sniffed appreciatively.

'That smells good,' Isaac said. 'I wonder what Amos is cooking. Look, there's Petra, and she's got the baby with her.'

Julie saw a woman around the same age as Isaac, who was standing in the open doorway of an old farmhouse. She held a small baby in her arms, and the infant gazed around with wide curious eyes.

Her heart clenched when a memory of her younger self holding Isaac when he was a baby popped into her mind, and it was then Julie realised that her worries about staying in the cottage had nothing to do with prowlers or a lack of transport. The real reason was that she knew she was going to be lonely.

Ha! Who was she kidding? She was already lonely and had been since Stephen had left her. At least this was a change of scenery, and being away from the house she'd lived in with Stephen might give her a chance to clear her head and decide what she was going to do with herself for the rest of her life.

'Hello,' the woman said, holding out a hand. 'I'm Petra and this is Amory. You must be Julie. Nice to meet you. I hope you enjoy your stay, but please let me know if there's anything you think we're not doing right.'

'Nice to meet you, too. And you, little one.' Julie gently stroked the baby's cheek. 'Don't worry, if I find anything I'll let you know, but I like what I've seen so far. The cottage is gorgeous and it's so welcoming.'

'Phew, that's a relief. You're the first person who hasn't been involved in the build to have seen it.'

'You've done a good job,' Julie said. 'I'm sure I won't find anything major.'

'I hope not. Come inside and I'll make a pot of tea. Amos, my uncle, has also made a cake – not the same one as in your welcome basket, so would you like a slice of that? Oh, and Isaac told us you don't have a car, so Amos has also made you a casserole for this evening, in case you didn't feel like venturing out.'

Julie was astonished. 'I don't know what to say – that's so kind of you.'

An older gentleman was taking the lid off a casserole dish, a wooden spoon in his hand, and she craned her neck to see what was in it.

Whatever it was smelled delicious.

'Hang on, let me give this a quick stir,' Amos said. 'I hope you like lamb. We have an abundance of them around here.'

'Not goat?' she chuckled, and Amos looked horrified. 'Sorry, it was a joke,' she added hastily. 'I love lamb and that smells divine.'

'Please don't feel obliged to eat it,' he said, and he looked so concerned that Julie felt for him.

'Do you mind if I have a taste?' she asked.

'While you do that, I'll put the kettle on,' Petra said.

Julie said to Isaac, 'Do you have to get off?'

'I've got time to join you for a quick cuppa and see you settled into the cottage,' her son said, with a glance at Petra, who nodded.

She had nothing to do, apart from unpack her small case, and she had nowhere she needed to be, and Petra seemed lovely and so did Amos, so she was more than happy to stay for a little while, although she didn't want to impose.

Feeling better about the weekend already, she was suddenly glad that she'd agreed to this little break.

The stables on Muddypuddle Lane was easy enough to find. Just off the main road, up a narrow lane that was pitted with potholes which Stephen guessed would be full of muddy water when it rained, and there it was on the right.

Remembering Isaac's instructions, he drove past the little carpark that said "parking for riders only", and aimed for a single track which he'd been informed led to a parking area for the cottages.

It looks pretty enough, he thought, as he parked the car and got out. The cottages were in a row of three, identical apart from different coloured benches outside each one.

Everything was spick and span, and as neat as a pin. He could tell that the landscaping around the building had only recently been done because the plants were small and not yet established, but it still looked lovely.

So far, first impressions were good. The only thing he could comment on was that the distance from the parking area to the cottages was about fifty metres, but he could see why the owners hadn't wanted people to park their vehicles directly in front of the houses, because…just look at that view!

It was rather impressive. From here Stephen could see right across the valley to the hills on the other side and everything in between. And if he craned his neck, he could just make out the turret of Picklewick's church in the distance.

He turned around to gaze up at the hillside above, seeing swathes of bracken and heather, and the occasional white blob of a sheep, and he realised he was really looking forward to exploring. Although he only lived ten or so miles away from Picklewick, he'd never really paid the village or the surrounding area much attention. Maybe after he'd unpacked and had a bite to eat, he'd put his hiking boots on and go for a walk. The views would be even more impressive from up there he thought, as he scanned the hillside, his eyes coming to rest on the swathes of bracken and heather on the open moorland above.

The door to the first cottage was unlocked, as expected, and Stephen carried his holdall inside. Then he hesitated.

A case was sitting at the foot of the stairs and a jacket was hanging on the bannister.

Was he in the correct cottage, he wondered?

Perplexed, he went back outside and tried the doors to the other two houses. Both were firmly locked.

He returned to the first cottage, and after dithering for a moment he ventured inside once more. This *must* be the right one.

Stephen bit his lip, then took his phone out of his pocket. Damn it, he'd forgotten Isaac had told him that he mightn't get any signal.

Slipping his mobile back into his pocket, he realised that the scene was probably staged. Isaac had explained that the owners were in the process of setting up a website and taking photos, so the case was probably to do with that.

Feeling somewhat happier, he went into the living room and came to another halt. This time it was because he liked what he saw, and after he'd taken it all in, he moved over to the table on which sat an old-fashioned wicker shopping basket. It contained a box of tea bags, a jar of coffee, and other things, and there was also a box beside it containing a bottle of gin: Isaac must have told Petra that he was partial to a G&T. It also held pasta and fresh veg, and when he went into the kitchen and saw a bottle of wine in the fridge, plus milk, butter and eggs, he was extremely impressed.

He hadn't got as far as thinking about dinner this evening, except for a vague idea that he might pop into Picklewick, but on seeing what the welcome pack entailed, he might not bother going out. He wasn't brilliant in the kitchen but he could rustle up a decent enough meal if he had to, and he could certainly do something with the pasta.

He couldn't see a set of keys anywhere, which was a bit troubling, but he decided to unpack first, then have a good look for them. And if he still couldn't see them, he'd go up to the main house and ask.

The upstairs of the cottage was just as nice as the downstairs he saw, as he stepped onto the landing. There were two good-sized bedrooms and both had en suites which consisted of a bath with a shower, and a loo.

Experimentally, Stephen turned on all the taps to check they worked, then tried the shower to make sure there was decent water pressure. After that, he flushed both loos and declared himself happy with the state of the plumbing.

Deciding he liked the front bedroom best with its sweeping views over the valley, he sat on the bed and gave the mattress an experimental bounce. Neither too firm nor too soft, and he was pleased to find that it didn't squeak. Not that it mattered to him, but a squeaky bed might be an issue for others.

Suddenly Stephen was acutely aware that he was here on his own. No significant other to share the bed with, no one to enjoy a meal with, or to enthuse with over the view.

But then again, he should be used to that by now. He hadn't had any of those things since Julie had confessed to having an affair, and it would probably be a long time before he had them again. Maybe never, because at the moment, despite telling himself that he should buck his ideas up, press on with getting a divorce and start enjoying life again, he simply couldn't bring himself to.

The only woman he'd ever wanted was Julie, and he couldn't see that changing anytime soon.

His heart feeling suddenly heavier, he trotted back downstairs to make himself a cup of tea and have a slice of cake. He'd feel better after a nice cuppa. He hoped.

Removing his jacket, he popped his car keys, wallet and mobile phone on the worktop, then set about making himself at home.

He swilled the kettle out, then filled it and plugged it in, and while he waited for it to boil, he opened the cupboards and peered inside. The kitchen was very well appointed, he admitted, taking a mug with a picture of a goat on it out of one of them and putting it next to the kettle.

It was while he was getting the milk out of the fridge that he heard the front door open, and he frowned. The owners must have guessed he was here because his car was in the parking space, so he wasn't happy about them walking in unannounced. Stephen was sure that was against the law or something. Surely, Petra, or whatever her name was, should have at least knocked first?

Stephen heard footsteps in the hall and turned to have a word with her. This wasn't a good start and he intended to——

Julie!' He blinked in astonishment at the sight of his estranged wife standing in the doorway to the kitchen. Her mouth was open and she looked as shocked as he felt. She seemed to be holding a casserole dish with a tea towel wrapped around it, and for a second Stephen fixated on that, as he tried to work out what she was doing here.

When he eventually looked at her face, it was as white as the linen on the bed upstairs and her eyes were wide with shock.

She glanced behind her, and said, 'Isaac?'

'Hi, Dad.' Isaac waved at him from the doorway.

'What are you doing here?' Stephen looked at Julie, then back at his son. 'Isaac? What's going on?' He didn't need to ask – he'd already guessed, and he wasn't happy.

'Take me home, Isaac,' Julie demanded. 'I don't know what you're playing at, but it's not funny.'

'No,' Isaac said. 'I won't.'

'Fine, *I'll* go.' Stephen put the bottle of milk down on the worktop. He hadn't wanted to come here in the first place. Julie was welcome to it. He reached for his keys, irritation washing over him.

Isaac said, 'I don't think so,' and before Stephen realised what his son was doing, Isaac had scooped them up and was heading out of the door.

'Give those back!' he demanded, hurrying after him. 'Isaac! Give me my keys.'

Isaac ignored him and hotfooted it out of the house. By the time Stephen reached the door, Isaac was running up the path as though the hounds of hell were after him.

Isaac!' Stephen yelled furiously. How dare he! He began to chase after him, but only managed a few steps before realising he didn't stand a hope in hell of catching him. 'Come back here this instant!' he shouted, using his best teacher voice.

It seemed to do the trick, because Isaac slowed down and turned around, but he didn't stop. Instead, he danced backwards, dangling Stephen's car keys, and called, 'You can thank me later.'

'Isaac!' Stephen thundered. 'Get back here *now*!'

'Enjoy your weekend,' Isaac shouted back. He had a huge grin on his face, which infuriated Stephen even more.

'I'll do no such thing!' he yelled. What on earth was Isaac thinking? Just wait until he got his hands on the boy!

'At least try.' Isaac was almost at the end of the path. 'It's an ideal opportunity for you and Mum to sort yourselves out. Bye!'

Then he was gone, leaving Stephen staring balefully after him.

'We'll see about that,' he muttered, and turned around, intending to go back inside to ring for a taxi.

It seemed that Julie had the same idea, because she was standing in the doorway, her mobile in her hand, frowning at it.

He watched as she held it above her head, moving it this way and that, and he guessed she was trying to get a signal. Damn and blast, he'd forgotten about the patchy reception.

'I'm going to go back up to the house,' she said, not looking at him. 'I can't get a signal here. Petra can call a taxi for me.'

'You needn't go – I will,' he said crossly. He intended to give this Petra-woman a piece of his mind: she must be in on this outrageous plan of Isaac's, and he wasn't happy at all. How dare their son play such a stupid prank! What the hell did he think he was going to achieve?

Wordlessly, Julie shrugged, then plonked herself down on the bench outside the cottage. At least she was as shocked as he, Stephen thought. If she'd been in on it too, he'd have been even more annoyed.

He fetched his phone, and muttering darkly he headed up the path, giving his car a stern glare as he walked past.

He'd go to the stables, where hopefully he'd find the owner.

However, the yard was deserted apart from a couple of chickens scratching about, and there was no answer to his shouted 'Hello.' He dithered for a moment then decided to try the house, but there was no answer to his insistent knocking, either. He debated whether to try the handle to see whether the door was unlocked, but thought better of it. As desperate as he was to get away from this place, he couldn't bring himself to enter a house without permission.

Sullenly, he backed away and peered through the nearest window, but he didn't see any sign of life. And he didn't have any more luck when he stuck his head into a barn, although he did have a bit of a shock when a goat bleated. The creature got up on its hind legs, it's front ones on the bars of its pen, and stared curiously. Another, smaller goat was in the pen with it, and it also stared at him. He'd never realised how odd looking their eyes were, and he shuddered.

'Shoo,' he said to them as he retreated, wincing as the goat's bleating followed him outside.

He scanned the yard once more and listened hard for signs of human activity, before giving in and returning to the cottage.

'I hope you ordered two taxis,' Julie said.

'I didn't order any,' he admitted. 'I couldn't find anyone.'

'Strange. Petra and Amos were there a few minutes ago.'

'We've been setup and the owners are in on it,' Stephen told her. Disbelief rode him hard. That Isaac should do such a thing when he knew what his mother had done and how Stephen felt about it, was inexcusable.

'What do we do now?' she asked.

Julie seemed far less annoyed than he was.

She was subdued and not in the least bit like her

normal sparky self, and a worm of worry unfurled in his chest.

Stephen was struck by how wan she looked, and how drawn her face was. His wife had lost weight since he'd seen her last, and it didn't suit her. She'd never been robust and had always been slender, but now she looked positively gaunt, and he wondered whether she was eating properly.

An awful thought struck him.

Might she be ill?

She certainly didn't look well, so maybe she *was* unwell. He'd have thought Isaac would have mentioned it though, so he was probably overthinking it. Still, that worm of worry was now squirming around and making its presence felt.

'We've got a couple of options,' he said, thinking hard. 'We can wait until someone shows up and demand they phone a taxi for us. Or if we don't want to wait, I can take a stroll and find somewhere I can get a signal, or I can walk into Picklewick – I'll be sure to get one there. This isn't Timbuktu, for goodness' sake!' He stopped. There was a third option, one that he would never have considered if he hadn't seen her. 'Or we can make the best of it,' he said.

'Make the best of it?' Julie repeated woodenly.

'I don't know about you, but I could do with a few days away,' he found himself saying. 'Before the start of a new term…' He trailed off.

Her expression was unreadable. 'I thought you were going to retire?'

'Yes, well, things change.' What was the point of retiring when he didn't have anyone to enjoy all that free time with? Over the past few months his job had been the only thing to have got him out of bed some mornings.

Julie dropped her gaze and stared at the ground in front of her feet.

'We're two civilized people,' he carried on hurriedly, not wanting to rake everything up again. They'd said more than enough already. 'I'm sure we can co-exist in the same house for a few nights. It's not as though we'll have to share a bedroom.' As soon as the words left his mouth, he winced. He hadn't meant to sound so harsh.

She shot him a glance, and he saw two spots a colour bloom on her cheeks.

'That would be unthinkable,' she said, and he could have sworn there was a hint of sarcasm in her voice.

He let it slide. 'We can still be friends, can't we? After all, we have a son in common.'

Even as he said it, Stephen wasn't sure *friends* was the right word. They'd hardly spoken since he'd walked out after she'd dropped her bombshell, but the son part was right. If Isaac and Nelly carried on the way they were going, there could be wedding bells on the horizon and grandchildren. It would be good if he and Julie made an effort to get on. They could start the process here. And if they were at each other's throats come the morning, then one or the other could go home.

'You want us to stay here? Me and you, on our own?' Julie said.

Now that she put it that way, he wasn't so sure it was a good idea.

But before he could say anything else, she said, 'Okay, I'm game if you are. I wasn't looking forward to sleeping here on my own.' She blushed suddenly, the spots on her cheeks flaring into life to suffuse her face and neck with colour. 'That's not what I—'

Stephen leapt in. 'I know what you meant.' Good lord, this was going to be awkward. They were behaving like strangers, not like a couple who had been married for decades and who knew each other inside out.

Ha! But he *hadn't* known her as well as he'd thought he had, so maybe she *was* a stranger, after all.

Feeling that he'd made a mistake in suggesting they spend the weekend together but not wanting to back out now and look a pratt, Stephen did the only thing he could think of – he made a cup of tea.

CHAPTER THREE

Julie slowly unpacked her overnight case with trembling fingers. Stephen had carried it upstairs for her while the kettle boiled, putting it in the bedroom at the back of the cottage. His holdall already sat on the floor of the front bedroom, and she guessed he'd bagged that one for himself.

She hadn't brought much with her – a couple of changes of clothes, sturdy shoes for walking, her night things – so she was soon done, and was placing her toiletries bag in the en suite and feeling thankful that they didn't have to share a bathroom, when Stephen's voice floated up the stairs.

'Tea's ready.'

Gosh, this situation was totally unreal, and she wasn't sure how to deal with it. Never in a million years would she have thought she'd be spending a weekend with her husband. She'd assumed that he wanted nothing more to do with her – and he hadn't, not for many months. She'd not set eyes on him since he'd walked out, and she'd only had the briefest of conversations with him when he'd phoned to arrange to collect his things. He'd requested that she be out when he did, to avoid any awkwardness, and she'd obliged, not wanting to witness his grief first hand. Or his anger.

Stephen had been very angry and she didn't blame him. If she had discovered that *he'd* had an affair, she'd have been furious too, no matter how long ago it had taken place.

The olive branch he was now holding out was bittersweet.

She didn't know if she would be able to cope with them being friends, or whether it would be too much to bear. Still, she'd give it a go, for Isaac's sake if nothing else. Isaac…Hmm…She'd have a few choice words to say to her son the next time she saw him.

'Coming,' she called, rinsing her hands and wiping them on a large fluffy towel.

She checked her appearance in the mirror above the wash hand basin, and didn't particularly like what she saw. So in a vain attempt to look less ghoul-like, she pinched her cheeks to try to bring some colour into them.

Oh well, she reasoned, giving up on her appearance, Stephen had seen her in far worse states than this. Yet, as she went downstairs, she wished she'd made more of an effort. If she'd known she was going to see him, she'd have—

What? Had her hair done? Painted her toenails?

She found Stephen on the patio, a tray on the table. He was pouring tea from a proper teapot. It was in the shape of a horse and it brought a smile to her lips, as did the mugs which had pictures of various farm animals on them. His was a goat, hers was a sheep.

'Cake?' he asked, handing her a mug as she sat down.

'Yes, please.' She wasn't hungry, but she guessed she could do with the sugar because she was feeling decidedly shaky. 'Mmm,' she said, taking a bite. Amos was a good baker, which gave her hope for their dinner later. 'Amos has made us a casserole,' she told him, brushing cake crumbs off her lap. 'He's Petra's uncle. Isaac says he owns the place. He made this cake, too.'

'It's nice, but it's not a patch on yours. Do you do much baking these days?'

'Not really.' She didn't do any baking at all. There seemed little point since she'd be the only one to eat it.

In fact, she didn't do much in the way of cooking either, for the same reason.

Anyway, her appetite wasn't what it had been. If she did cook herself a meal, she found she'd only eat a few mouthfuls, then she'd lose interest. And she hated eating on her own, so she had resorted to taking a tray into the sitting room and eating in front of the TV. It was company of sorts, and by having the telly on she didn't feel so alone.

Unless Isaac was joining her – then she'd make a show of cooking a decent meal, so he didn't worry. However, now that he had Nelly, Julie was seeing less of him at mealtimes, and as a consequence her food intake had taken a hit as she tended to snack only when she was hungry and didn't bother with three square meals a day.

'I used to love your upside-down cake,' Stephen said. 'And your scones. You used to make a mean cream tea.'

'I suppose I still could if I put my mind to it.'

'You mentioned a casserole?'

'Yes. Amos made it, in case I didn't want to venture out. I assumed it was because they knew I wouldn't have any transport.' She gave him a meaningful look.

'Anyone would think this had been planned all along,' Stephen said. He was staring at the hillside above the cottage, so she took the opportunity to stare at him. He'd lost some weight, she noticed, and she wondered whether he wasn't eating properly either. He was a decent enough cook, and when she'd been working full-time they'd shared kitchen duties. He looked well though, so maybe he'd been on a health-kick.

A thought stopped her in her tracks. Maybe he'd been working out, getting himself all thin and ship-shape for another woman?

Isaac hadn't mentioned that his father was dating, but perhaps that was what this subterfuge was about – a last-ditch attempt by Isaac at a reconciliation between his parents before Stephen fell in love with someone else.

Julie was surprised that Stephen hadn't told her he wanted a divorce. She'd been expecting it ever since he'd left, and every time a letter landed on the mat her heart had been in her mouth.

It was the next step. She knew they couldn't continue in this limbo for ever. Sooner or later, they'd have to sever this last tie.

Her gaze dropped to his left hand, and she noticed with a twinge that he no longer wore his wedding ring. She still wore hers. She'd removed her engagement ring and her diamond eternity ring, but she hadn't been able to bring herself to take her wedding ring off.

Stephen let out a sigh. 'So, here we are.' He sounded as nonplussed about the situation as she felt.

'Yes, here we are,' she agreed. She tried to smile, but she guessed it was more of a grimace.

'I think I'll go for a walk,' he said. 'Explore a bit.'

'Good idea.' A couple of hours of not being in his company might go some way to settle her ragged nerves. On the other hand, she might spend them fretting about his return.

This wasn't going to work, was it? They'd not spoken in months and now Isaac expected them to spend the weekend together.

'Would you like to join me?' he asked.

'Pardon?'

'I was thinking we could go for a walk, but if you don't—'

'I'd like that.' She'd spoken without thinking, her heart leaping at the chance before her brain could protest. 'I'll just change my shoes,' she said, getting to her feet and collecting up the tea things.

'I'll do that,' Stephen said. 'You go and get ready.'

Julie was glad of a few moments alone. What on earth had possessed her to agree to go for a walk with him? She'd already concluded that this weekend wouldn't work, yet here she was, shoving her feet into a pair of trainers, her heart hammering with anticipation at the thought of being in his company. She must be mad to put herself through such torture. He was clearly only trying to make the best of it for Isaac's sake. If she wasn't careful she'd have her already broken heart shattered into a million pieces, and she had a feeling that if she suffered any more heartache, she wouldn't ever recover from it.

'Psst, Harry, come here.' Petra beckoned him over to the window. She was peering out of it, feeling quite smug.

Harry had only just returned to the stables after a day of blacksmithing and the first thing he'd done was to pick Amory up and give him a cuddle. 'What is it?' he asked, lumbering to his feet, the baby in his arms.

'Look.' She pointed to the middle-aged couple walking down the path towards the cottages. 'That's Isaac's parents. They've been out for a walk. I watched them leave.'

'And now they've returned.' Harry's voice was dry. 'What's for supper?'

'Um, lamb casserole. Amos made two, one for us and one for them. They're talking to each other, see?'

'So?'

Petra sighed, irritated at his lack of interest in what she thought was an absorbing topic. He hadn't appeared too interested when she'd initially told him about Isaac's plan either. 'Isaac's dad, Stephen, came up to the house earlier. Isaac warned me he might do that. He didn't look happy and kept staring at his phone. So we hid upstairs.'

'We?'

'Me, Amos and the baby.'

Harry shook his head. 'I'm glad I wasn't here. What if he comes back?'

'I doubt if he will.' Petra sounded more confident than she felt, but at least the pair were talking to each other, so that was a start. 'If he wanted to leave, he could have walked into Picklewick, or got a signal while they were on their walk,' she added.

'He could have got a signal in the yard,' Harry pointed out.

Petra was glad Stephen hadn't realised. 'I hope Isaac's plan works, and they get back together.'

'I hope they give us a good report on the cottage,' Harry retorted, giving her a meaningful look. The couple were now out of sight, and he drew away from the window. 'Are you still going dress shopping tomorrow?' he asked.

Petra pulled a face. 'I suppose.'

'You don't have to,' Harry told her. He juggled the baby onto his shoulder, holding Amory firmly with one hand, and put the other around Petra's waist.

In a teasing voice she said, 'Now that you come to mention it, I have seen a pair of white wellies with a ribbon on them. I could wear them with white jodhpurs.' Actually, that did sound rather fetching.

'If you want to wear jodhpurs, wear them,' he said. 'You'll look beautiful regardless. Besides, what you wear isn't important; what's important is that we're getting married.'

'Aw, do you know how much I love you?'

'Enough to ask Amos when supper will be ready? I'm starving.'

'You're such a romantic,' she said, kissing him on the cheek. She was so lucky to have found him, and although she wasn't too keen on all the weddingy fuss, she couldn't wait to be his wife.

As she leant into him, she smiled to herself, remembering the first time she'd set eyes on him. Never would she have guessed that she'd fall in love with him and they would create such a gorgeous child together!

'I'll warm the casserole up in the oven,' Julie said to Stephen as he took it out of the fridge. 'It'll be nicer than in the microwave.'

She held her hands out and he passed the dish to her, but as he did so his fingers brushed against hers and he almost leapt out of his skin.

'Careful,' she said, as he fumbled the hand-over. 'It would be a shame to drop it. It looks delicious.'

Stephen couldn't care less about their dinner. He was too busy thinking about his reaction to that fleeting contact. He'd felt such a surge of desire, it had taken his breath away.

Heart thudding, he turned back to the fridge and reached for the bottle of gin. He could seriously do with a drink or two, after the day he'd had.

Without asking whether Julie wanted one, he poured the drinks, being careful to place her glass on the worktop. He didn't want to risk touching her again in case he did something silly.

The problem was, this afternoon had been like old times and it had stirred up too many memories and emotions.

He'd known that he wasn't over her and he guessed he probably never would be, although for these past few months he'd managed to bury his feelings deep enough to be able to function without falling apart. But this afternoon had brought all of the love and the heartache rushing back to the surface, until he was barely holding himself together.

The initial awkwardness as they had begun their walk had gradually given way to a more comfortable atmosphere, and by the time they'd hiked onto the moorland above the fields neither of them had much breath to spare for talking, having to use all their energy to climb ever upwards. And on reaching the top the view had taken whatever breath they had left.

All the while though, he'd been acutely aware of Julie by his side, of every step she took and every sound she made, and he'd longed to take her in his arms and beg her to tell him that she loved him.

His heart ached as he remembered how easily she'd spoken those three little words in the past, and it bled as he wondered whether she had ever meant them.

Taking a gulp of gin and tonic, he wandered onto the terrace and slumped into a chair.

This was such a mistake. He should have left while he had the chance, before the walls that he'd so carefully built around his heart were destroyed. He could already feel them crumbling and if they fell he didn't know how he'd be able to carry on. Because the short amount of time that he'd spent with his wife this afternoon confirmed what he'd already feared – he still loved her, totally and utterly, and the thought of spending the rest of his life without her filled him with despair.

Thankfully Julie had turned the radio on in the kitchen, so at least there was some noise to alleviate the tension. He didn't know whether she could feel it too, or whether it was his imagination, but he could have sworn it filled the very air, as real as the song that was blaring cheerfully from the speakers.

He snorted to himself – Petra really had thought of everything. He'd make sure to add to his notes that the radio was a nice touch.

'Sit yourself down, it's almost ready,' Julie said, appearing on the patio, and he felt a pang of guilt that he hadn't helped her prepare the meal.

Not that there had been a lot of preparation to be done, but at least he could have helped lay the table or something. After all, she was here to have a break just like he was. She wasn't here to wait on him and neither would he want her to. It would be far too reminiscent of when they used to live together. He hadn't expected to be waited on then, but after she'd taken early retirement and he was still working, she'd insisted on doing everything around the house. Which he'd appreciated, because teaching wasn't an 8:30 to 3:30 profession. Just because school ended mid-afternoon, didn't mean he was free to leave at that time. He often ran after school clubs, mainly aimed at the examination classes, and there were always meetings to attend and training sessions to be sat through. Not only that, there was all the paperwork that teachers were expected to complete, as well as the necessary lesson preparation and marking.

But right now, he didn't want to feel beholden to her, even for something as simple as reheating a casserole. Sharing a meal with her felt even more intimate than that brief touch of fingers earlier. He vividly remembered the last time they had sat down to eat together, because that had been the day Julie had blown his world apart.

He'd known there was something wrong the second he'd walked in from work, but he hadn't been able to put his finger on it.

She'd looked as though she'd been crying and her face had been flushed, but when he'd asked her if she was okay, she'd blamed it on the menopause, and he knew she still suffered from it so he took it at face value. Although he distinctly remembered feeling a frizzle of unease as he'd taken the pile of books he had been carrying up to the spare room which he'd turned into an office. It wasn't until her face had crumbled over her bowl of chicken noodles had he realised something was very wrong indeed.

It had all come out. How could it not when she had been in so much distress? She'd been distraught: he couldn't ever remember seeing her as grief stricken. Not even when her mum had passed on, had she broken down like that.

His own grief was swift to follow when he'd realised what she was telling him. She had loved someone else.

Loved them enough to consider leaving him, and it was only because she had been pregnant that she hadn't.

He'd shouted, he'd cried, there had been recriminations and accusations, but at least he'd never doubted that Isaac was his, because if the boy hadn't been, Julie would have walked out of their marriage.

Stephen supposed he should be thankful that she *hadn't* left him, that she had allowed him the joy of seeing his son grow up, and had allowed him to be a father to Isaac. She could so very easily have lied to both him and Emrys, and claimed that Isaac was Emrys's son. If she had done, she could have followed her heart. But she hadn't. She'd stayed with him, and all this time he'd been oblivious to the pain she was hiding. He'd also been oblivious to the fact that she hadn't loved him as much as he'd loved her.

Although he might be thankful that she hadn't left, he couldn't bring himself to forgive her for her betrayal. No matter how deeply he still loved her, how much he missed her, or how little his life was worth living without her, forgiveness was beyond him.

So why was he here?

He'd been asking himself that very question ever since he'd suggested they spend the weekend together. He tried to justify it by claiming it was for Isaac's sake, but he was lying. It was for his own sake. He so desperately wanted to be with her because he wanted, however briefly, to remember what it was like being married to her.

Then he snorted to himself as he thought how ridiculous he was being. He was *still married* to her, despite feeling that they should get a divorce.

He honestly didn't think he could bring himself to start the ball rolling. What was the point?

It might sever their ties completely, but that didn't mean to say he was going to move on. His half-baked idea about putting himself back out there, back on the dating scene, was a ridiculous notion.

He knew he wouldn't, no matter how lonely he felt. He simply couldn't face having any other woman in his life.

Julie put a plate laden with food in front of him and he looked up. 'Thanks,' he said, giving her a small smile. 'It smells divine.'

'It does, doesn't it?' she agreed, slipping into the seat opposite with her own plate in her hands. He noticed that she had about half of the amount of food on hers that he had on his.

'Are you trying to fatten me up?' he asked.

'Not at all, although you have lost some weight. You're looking good.'

It was more than he could say for her. She was still beautiful, but her beauty now had an ethereal quality. Her skin was like porcelain, and he worried that she might break.

'You know what it's like,' he said. 'I'm too busy to eat some days.'

Stephen was making excuses. He wasn't too busy at all: he just couldn't be bothered. Cooking for himself wasn't something that appealed to him, and neither was eating a meal alone, so during term time he usually ate in the school canteen, surrounded by hundreds of shouting children and the pained faces of his colleagues as they tried to ignore the noise. The food wasn't exactly gourmet and he did try to choose a healthy option, but despite the Healthy Schools Initiative, the food tended to be full of stodge. The only thing that counteracted the excessive amount of carbs, was the fact that the portions were small.

Very often when he got in from work, he didn't bother with a meal, he just snacked. He knew he'd lost weight over the course of the summer holidays, because he hadn't had a school cafeteria to visit and neither had he wanted to go anywhere such as a pub or cafe to eat. The thought of sitting there on his own filled him with despair, so over the past five weeks he'd been living on a selection of sandwiches, tins of soup and the occasional frozen meal. It probably hadn't helped that he didn't have much of an appetite.

'How about you? You seem to have lost weight, too,' he pointed out.

'Well, you know what it's like,' she echoed, then trailed off and smiled at him.

The smile was sad and uncertain, and he saw the despair behind it. She was still grieving for Emrys, and despite his own misery his heart went out to her.

They ate the meal without speaking, allowing the music to flow over them and the chatter of the radio presenter to fill the dead spaces between them. Stephen ate without tasting, although he did acknowledge that the casserole really was rather delicious, but after the first forkful he was on automatic pilot, simply chewing each mouthful with grim determination.

He was surprised, however, when he saw that he had cleared his plate, and he pushed it away feeling replete. Julie, he noticed, had hardly touched hers.

'What's wrong with your dinner?' he asked.

'I'm not hungry,' she replied, putting her knife and fork down neatly.

He blurted, 'Would you have eaten more if I hadn't been here?'

Her smile was still sad. 'I doubt it.'

It was none of his business – *she* was none of his business – but he found himself saying, 'You can't go on like this, you'll fade away.'

She didn't say anything for a moment, then she muttered, 'What do you care?'

Stephen frowned. 'It might surprise you to know that I do still care about you. I worry about you.'

'Do you?' She stared at him expressionlessly.

He pursed his lips. 'You can't be married to someone for as long as we were married, without still caring about them.'

She looked up and away, blinking furiously, as her eyes filled with tears.

Dear god, please don't let her cry, he pleaded silently. It would be his undoing. Julie had never been a crier. Over the years he'd seen her cry maybe less than a dozen times. And one of those times had been the day she'd informed him that she'd been unfaithful. She'd cried some more a day later, when he'd walked out on his marriage.

He couldn't stand to see her cry, even if the tears weren't for him.

'You've got a funny way of showing it,' she said with a gulp.

He shrugged and took a deep breath, then let it out slowly. What could he say to that?

She fanned her face. 'I miss you,' she said quietly.

The admission took him by surprise. 'Is that why you're crying?' He knew he was being sarcastic but he couldn't help himself.

'Actually, it is.'

Stephen hadn't been expecting that. He'd assumed the tears were for Emrys.

'I miss you too,' he said, and her eyes shot to his and he saw a flicker of...was that *hope*, in her face? 'But it's too late,' he continued, and the flicker dimmed.

'I know.' She stared at the table. Then abruptly she shoved her chair away and scrambled to her feet. 'I think I'll turn in,' she said, and he watched her dash out of the room and heard her feet on the stairs and then on the floorboards overhead, and he let out a deep sigh.

'Isaac,' he muttered, 'What the hell were you thinking?

Stephen couldn't blame the boy for trying, but neither could he thank him for it. This weekend was doing neither him nor Julie any good, and they hadn't even been here a day yet.

With another sigh, he rose and collected the plates. It was early, not quite eight o'clock, and he wasn't ready for bed. If the truth be known, he wasn't sleeping too well these days, and he didn't fancy going upstairs just to lie awake for hour after hour, especially with his wife in the room next door, only a short landing separating the two bedrooms.

Instead, after he washed up, he put his hiking boots back on and went out for another walk.

If nothing else the exercise would do him good and he might be able to clear his head. Anything was better than lying there, wishing that things were different.

CHAPTER FOUR

Julie woke with a start, and it took her a moment to realise where she was. Abruptly she sat up and listened for any signs of life, but she heard nothing apart from the birds tweeting outside her window this morning, so she sank back down onto the pillows.

After she'd gone upstairs she'd heard the front door close, and she'd sneaked into the front bedroom and peeped through the curtains to see Stephen striding off in the same direction they had taken this afternoon. She couldn't be entirely certain, but she didn't think he was leaving. He didn't have his holdall with him for one thing, and neither was he going in the direction of Picklewick. However, he might well be searching for a place where he could get a phone signal so he could ring for a taxi.

Julie hadn't gone to bed to sleep last night: she'd gone to bed early to escape from Stephen. However, she hadn't been able to escape her feelings, and she'd lain there with tears trickling down her cheeks for quite some time, until she'd managed to pull herself together and the sobbing had turned to sniffling. At some point she must have drifted off to sleep, long after it had grown dark, but she still hadn't heard him come in, so this morning she was none the wiser as to whether he'd spent the night in the cottage or not.

A noise from downstairs made her sit up again, and she listened intently. There was a tinkle of what she thought might be cutlery, and she wondered whether Stephen was downstairs making himself breakfast.

She eased out of bed as quietly as she could and padded to the bathroom, where she stared grimly at herself in the mirror, not liking what she saw. She had bags under her eyes bigger than the suitcase she'd brought with her, and her face was worryingly pale. She really must get out in the sunshine and the fresh air more, so at least she wouldn't look as though she was about to pop her clogs. No wonder Isaac worried about her.

After splashing her face with cold water and brushing her teeth, she dragged a comb through her hair and attempted to put on some makeup. A little blusher wouldn't go amiss, and neither would a sweep of mascara. She didn't bother with lipstick, because she needed a cup of tea and she'd only end up licking it all off, so instead she bit her lips, nibbling at them to try to make them look a little more pink. Satisfied that this was the best she could do for the time being, she got dressed and went downstairs.

Stephen was out on the terrace, which seemed to be his favourite place in the cottage, and when he heard her come into the living room he got to his feet.

'Would you like a cup of tea?' he asked.

'I'd love one, please.'

'How about some breakfast?'

'No, thanks, not just yet. I'll have tea first and see what I feel like later.'

'You must eat something,' her husband insisted. 'There's nothing left of you.'

'I eat when I'm hungry,' she said, eliciting a snort from him.

'Clearly you need to be hungry a little more often,' he shot back at her.

She took a seat and tilted her face up to the sun. Five minutes basking in its rays wasn't going to bring much colour to her face, but every little bit helped, she reasoned.

'Thanks,' she said, when he placed a cup of tea in front of her on the table.

'How did you sleep?' He was gazing at her with concern, and once more she felt tears perilously close to the surface.

'It took me a while to get off,' she admitted, 'but when I did I slept like the dead—' She stopped suddenly, and he made a face. 'How about you?' she asked.

'After you went to bed I went for a walk,' he said. 'I didn't get back until after dark.'

'Where did you go?'

'Back up onto the hill. I needed some time to think.'

'What about?'

'Us.'

'And?' Good grief this was worse than pulling teeth.

'We can't go on like this,' he began.

'I know,' she said softly. 'What do you suggest?'

'I don't honestly know.'

Her voice was even quieter when she said, 'Do you want to get a divorce?' and she was gratified when he shot her a horrified look.

'No, I don't. I have thought about it,' he admitted, 'but is there any point?'

'You said yourself that we can't go on like this,' she replied.

He said, 'Divorce or not, we'll still be in the same situation, won't we? Living in separate houses, leading separate lives.'

'We don't have to make any decisions right now,' she pointed out. 'In the scheme of things, it's still early days.'

'It feels like forever,' Stephen said. He also had bags under his eyes, and didn't look as though he'd slept very well. He looked better than she did though, she conceded.

'Yes, it does,' she agreed quietly. It felt like they'd been apart for years, not months.

They sat in silence for a while, Stephen staring into the distance, Julie sipping her tea and watching him out of the corner of her eye.

'I'm going to make some sandwiches,' he announced, getting to his feet.

'Isn't it early for a sandwich'? she asked.

'I think we should go exploring and take a picnic with us.'

'More walking? Didn't you do enough yesterday?'

'You don't have to come if you don't want to,' he told her.

'I'd like to come. Where were you thinking of going?' Even as she asked the question, she knew deep down what his reply would be and her heart sank.

'How about if we head over that way?' He pointed to a track running parallel to the road. A little way long that track she knew she'd be able to see a certain layby.

She briefly thought about suggesting another direction, then she realised it was futile; she couldn't run away from Emrys, because he was in her heart. She had carried him there for all this time and she couldn't dislodge him now, and neither did she want to. He was as much a part of her as Stephen, so did it matter if they took the path above the road where she used to meet him?

'That sounds lovely,' she said, meaning it. In fact, it seemed fitting that she, Stephen and Emrys would all be in the same place. Emrys might not be there in body, but he'd be there in spirit. It was time to reconcile the three parts of herself, and maybe, just maybe she might begin to feel whole once more.

'Come on, Petra, there must be something you like,' Charity said. 'How about this one?' She held up a blush pink dress that looked more like a ball gown than a wedding dress. Petra thought it was too low cut and a bit flouncy, all chiffon and layers. She'd look like a silly doll in it.

Crossly, she shook her head. She was seriously getting to the end of her tether. She had never liked shopping, unless it was for horsey stuff. Thankfully Amos did all the food shopping, so she was spared that weekly chore, and she'd had her fill of shopping lately, when she'd kitted out the three cottages. She was all shopped out. Even if she hadn't been, she hated shopping for clothes. She had no idea what suited her, but it certainly wasn't any of the dresses she'd seen on the rails today.

She could tell that Charity, October and Megan were starting to become a little exasperated. They weren't the only ones – she was exasperated, too. She supposed it served her right to leave buying a wedding dress until the last minute.

To her shock, the staff in the first bridal shop they'd tried had been rather sniffy with her. Apparently they only stocked sample dresses that were just meant to be tried on and not bought there and then. She had been informed that if she liked one of the dresses then they would order it in in her size and she could have it altered if necessary. When Petra explained that she needed it for two weeks today, she was met with a horrified gasp and a hushed exclamation of how that time scale simply wasn't feasible. The standard lead time was eight to ten *months*.

Petra wasn't too bothered, because she hadn't seen anything she really liked anyway. Nothing was *her*. Although she wasn't actually sure what was *her*, when it came to dresses. She couldn't remember the last time she'd worn one. Possibly when she went to the prom when she finished school? Hang on, no, she hadn't worn a dress then, either. She'd worn what was commonly referred to as a playsuit, an all-in-one outfit with wide pant legs and a fitted bodice with little straps. She'd been sixteen and able to get away with wearing that kind of thing. She'd look ridiculous if she attempted to wear something similar these days.

Petra and her entourage were met with the same reaction by the staff in the next shop they went into, and by this time October and Charity were holding hushed conversations about how important it was to plan weddings well in advance. After the third shop, they retreated to a rather large department store, and were now rooting around in the ballgown section.

Blush pink indeed! Petra snorted. She wasn't a blush pink woman. Anyway, although Harry had said he didn't mind what colour dress she wore, she guessed he'd be disappointed if it wasn't white, or at least cream. White didn't suit her complexion, but she could possibly manage ivory or cream. Unfortunately, there weren't a great many dresses in this shop that were even remotely suitable in that colour.

Megan held up a sheath dress with a diamante effect around the waist. 'How about this?'

Petra wrinkled her nose. It was plain enough, apart from that silly bit of decoration, but she wasn't sure about the style. Pre-baby she would probably have got away with it, but not post-Amory. Even though she hadn't put on a great deal of weight when she was pregnant and it had now come off thanks to all the riding she did plus breastfeeding, her figure had changed nevertheless and she didn't think it was for the better.

At least this marathon dress-hunt was showing her what she did and didn't like, so there was that. But unfortunately, she had to buy something today or be forced to return again next weekend when she would be under even more pressure to buy something.

'Right,' Megan said, taking charge. 'You sit there.' She put her hands on Petra's shoulders and forced her into a chair. Petra wasn't sure the chair was meant for sitting on and was just for decoration, but she obediently sat anyway, wondering what was going to happen.

'The three of us…' Megan pointed to herself and the other two bridesmaids, 'are going to get you a selection of dresses and you're going to try them on.'

Petra stared at them. She didn't like the sound of that. So far she'd actually managed to avoid trying anything on at all.

'You won't know until you try something,' October urged, and Charity nodded vigorously.

'You'd be surprised,' Charity added. 'You might think something doesn't suit you or you don't like it, but when you get it on you realise that it's actually perfect.'

Petra didn't think that was likely to happen, but she decided to go along with it anyway. What choice did she have? And as she hadn't seen anything she liked yet, she might as well give this a go.

She waited impatiently for her maid-of-honour and her bridesmaids to return, and as she sat there she fretted that Nathan was okay. He'd taken a hack out this morning, to free her up to come shopping, and although he'd mellowed since he and Megan had got together, he was still a taciturn man who much preferred horses and tractors to people, so wasn't the best front-man for the stables.

Petra smiled to herself, thinking that neither was she, if she was honest. She was well aware that she didn't suffer fools gladly, but her regular clients knew that and accepted her anyway. All that mattered to them was that she was a good riding instructor, although some of the mums of her young pupils would probably appreciate it if she had a more client-focused approach.

Petra tapped her foot, wondering how much longer this was going to take. They'd arrived in town at nine o'clock on the dot, ready for the shops to open, and it was now eleven-thirty. Amory would need feeding soon, and she had to get back for a lesson at four. She was getting hungry too, and could really do with a cup of coffee. Or maybe something stronger?

'Ta da!' The three would-be stylists leapt out from behind a rail and held up an assortment of dresses.

Petra stared at them in dismay before slowly closing her eyes and opening them again. God help her, but she just might wear jodhpurs and wellies after all.

'There's something very endearing about a donkey,' his wife said, as Stephen reached over the half-door of the stall to scratch between the animal's long ears. He thought she was right – donkeys were rather sweet.

They were on their way back from their walk, having been out all day, and had heard braying coming from the stable block, and Julie had insisted they investigate.

'Stay there,' she instructed. 'I want to take a photo.' She took her phone out of her jeans pocket and aimed it at him. 'Guess what?' she said, after she'd taken the photo. 'I've got a signal.'

Stephen's mouth twisted into a wry grin. 'It's lucky I didn't know I could get a signal here yesterday,' he said, 'otherwise I'd have phoned for that taxi.' He sobered. 'I've enjoyed today.'

'Me, too. I've got an awful feeling I'll ache like the devil tomorrow though. I can't remember the last time I did so much walking.'

It had been rather lovely. For whole stretches of time Stephen had forgotten they weren't together anymore, and they'd fallen into the easy way that they used to have.

Then he'd remember and would feel awkward for a while, but it soon passed as his attention was taken by the wonderful scenery.

At the start of their walk, they'd headed across county, along a path well used by horses from the look of all the hoof prints. It ran parallel to the road below, separated from it by lush green fields on which several horses grazed, one of whom had a foal.

Stephen had pointed it out to Julie, but she'd seemed lost in thought, and he'd begun to wonder whether it was a good idea to spend all day in her company if she was going to be morose. After a while she'd cheered up though, and he'd even go as far as to say she'd blossomed, and by the time they'd sat down beside a babbling stream to eat their picnic, Stephen was suddenly glad Isaac had forced them to come on this weekend away.

If their son's plan was for him and Julie to get back together, it wasn't going to work. But if Isaac's intent was for them to be able to be in the same room without awkwardness and tension, then he'd done a good job. Stephen felt confident that should Isaac and Nelly's relationship progress, he and Julie could play their parts as parents of the groom very amicably indeed.

However, every now and again Stephen had caught his wife's eye and he'd had to hastily look away, because he'd had a sudden urge to take her in his arms and kiss her. Or he'd brush against her, or she him, and a bolt of desire would shoot through him.

Along with the attraction he still felt for her (to him she would always be beautiful and incredibly sexy), were other emotions – love, longing and regret. He hadn't stopped loving her, and he longed for things to return to the way they'd been this time last year, when he'd been blissfully ignorant of the bombshell she would shortly drop on him. But he knew they never could.

A clatter of hooves brought him out of his thoughts, and he looked towards the noise. Several ponies were being led out of a barn and were heading their way.

'Hi,' a young woman in her early thirties said. She handed over the reins of the pony she was leading to a girl of about eight or nine. 'Heidi, can you pop Parsnip into his usual stall and give him a brush down? You can put Tango in with him if you want. I'll be along in a minute.' The woman turned back to him and Julie. 'I see you've found Gerald. He'll let you do that all day.'

Stephen was still scratching between the animal's ears, and the donkey's eyes were almost closed in bliss.

'How are you finding the cottage?' she asked. 'I'm Petra, by the way.' This last bit was addressed to him, as Julie had met her yesterday.

'Nice to meet you,' he said, wondering how much of a part she'd played in setting him and Julie up. He didn't think she was entirely innocent.

'It's lovely,' Julie gushed. 'I honestly can't find fault with it.'

'Wifi might be a good idea,' he said, tongue-in-cheek, and Petra chuckled.

'Not having wifi is one of the selling points,' she told him, 'so you can get away from it all. What have you been up to today?'

'We went for a really long walk. The scenery around here is stunning, isn't it? Lots of little valleys with streams running through them – we had a picnic by one – and the open moorland with all that heather and bracken, and those glorious views,' Julie said.

'We found an old building right on the top. Did someone used to live there?' Stephen asked.

'It's an old farmhouse,' Petra explained, then chuckled. 'Perhaps I ought to do it up – it would be the ultimate get-away-from-it-all holiday.'

'You can say that again! It took us a couple of hours to get there on foot, and I'm not sure I'd want to be that secluded,' Julie said, and Stephen agreed with her.

'Maybe not,' Petra laughed. 'Anyway, it doesn't belong to the stables. It's on common land, but I believe it's part of the farm at the top of Muddypuddle Lane. Right, I'd best get on. I'm so pleased you are enjoying your stay, but do let me know if you can think of anything we should or shouldn't be doing.' She was about to walk off when she stopped. 'Oh, if you're interested, there's a fete on in Picklewick tomorrow. It should be good fun. I can drive you into the village, if you like?'

Ah ha! He thought. Gotcha! Petra was definitely in on this scheme of Isaac's. He narrowed his eyes at her, but before he could say anything, she added, 'It's probably best not to take your car, because parking will be a nightmare and there are so many lovely food and drink stalls, that you might want to indulge in a tipple or two.' Her smile was wide and innocent, and Stephen pursed his lips.

'It's okay, we can walk,' Julie said. 'But thanks for the offer.'

'I thought you said you didn't want to do anymore walking,' he said to her, once Petra was out of earshot.

'I don't,' his wife told him, 'but she's got a new baby, a business to run, and a wedding in a couple of weeks. I think she's got enough on her plate without taxiing us around.'

'I didn't realise. You're right, of course. Besides, the village isn't far.' He gave the donkey a final pat. 'Fancy pasta for dinner? I noticed you brought some with you. Then I thought we could have a quiet drink in the garden. Unless you've got other plans?'

'No, no plans. I'll cook; you made the picnic. But first, I need a long shower.'

'Good idea. I'll join you,' he said without thinking, and winced when she stared at him in shock. 'I mean,' he added hastily, 'that I'll also need to freshen up before we eat.'

'Yes, of course. I realised that…I didn't think you…I knew you meant…' She sighed, and changed the subject. 'Would you like tomato sauce, or creamy mushroom with the pasta?' And with that, the easy-going atmosphere was gone, and they were back to walking on eggshells again.

Stephen felt like kicking himself.

CHAPTER FIVE

'Did you get anything?' Amos asked, and Petra wrinkled her nose.

'Yes and no.'

'Nothing is ever straight forward with you, is it?' her uncle said fondly, as he grabbed the toast before the over-zealous toaster shot the bread halfway across the room.

Harry, who was nursing Amory whilst trying to eat a bowl of cereal, barked out a laugh. 'You should have seen her face when she showed it to me last night. Anyone would think she'd had to choose a dress to wear to the gallows, not for a wedding.'

Petra gave him the stink-eye. 'It's the best of a bad bunch,' she said. It was white, but that was about all the dress had going for it. It looked more like a nightie than a wedding gown, but at least it fitted and wasn't that awful shiny material that highlighted every bump and lump.

'What's wrong with it?' Amos wanted to know.

'What's right with it,' Petra muttered, buttering one of the pieces of toast and biting into it.

'Why did you buy it if you don't like it?' Amos's question was reasonable, but Petra wasn't in the mood to be reasonable.

'Because there are now only thirteen days to the wedding and everyone—' she shot Harry a filthy look so he was in no doubt that she was referring to him '— expects me to wear a dress.'

'I've told you, you can wear what you like,' Harry replied mildly.

'I thought it was bad luck for the groom to see the dress before the wedding?' Amos said.

'I wanted a second opinion.' Petra took another bite of her toast.

'Didn't you get one from Megan? And a third from October, and a fourth from Charity?' Amos raised his eyebrows.

'Ha, ha, very funny.' Petra scowled back.

'If you've shown it to Harry, you might as well show it to me,' Amos said.

'Can you take Amory?' Harry asked her. 'I've got stuff to do.'

'What stuff?' Petra wanted to know. 'It's Sunday, surely you aren't working today?'

'Oh, I, er, won't be long. I've got a Shire to look at. Split hoof.' Hurriedly he passed the baby to her and was gone before Petra had a chance to quiz him further.

She glared after him with narrowed eyes. He was up to something and she guessed it might be wedding related, and prayed he wasn't going to do anything outrageous. All she wanted was a quiet ceremony in the church, then return to the stables for a small glass of bubbly.

But the ceremony was growing – having a maid-of-honour and two bridesmaids ensured that – and she had a feeling that Harry and Amos were planning more than just a bite to eat and a bottle of plonk.

'What's he up to?' she asked, and when Amos shook his head in wide-eyed innocence and said, 'Nothing, why?' she knew he most definitely was.

'He'd better not be planning a fuss,' she warned.

'I'm sure he's not,' her uncle said.

Petra wasn't.

Amos said, 'Can you hold the ladder? I want to go up the attic.'

'Whatever for?'

'Just you wait and see.'

Petra followed him upstairs and put Amory in his cot, winding up the mobile hanging above it to try to keep the baby amused for a few minutes. Her son thought it was his right to be held constantly and was rather averse to being ignored.

Praying he wouldn't start bawling, she slipped out of his bedroom to find Amos opening the hatch to the attic and easing the folding ladder down. 'Would you like me to go up?' she offered.

'No.' His reply was clipped. 'I can manage.'

Petra pulled a face behind his back. Amos could be sensitive if he thought he was being fussed over, and he hated being reminded that he wasn't as young as he once was. The angina didn't help either, and Petra was always conscious that he might have an attack at any time. Besides, she was smaller than him, so it was easier to lever herself through the little square hatch.

She held her tongue though, not wanting to make him cross, and waited at the bottom of the ladder, listening to him clumping around up there and grizzling to himself.

Eventually he found what he was looking for, because he shouted, 'Watch out below!' and flung a box down through the hatch, nearly landing on Petra's head.

'Careful,' she cried as she dodged to the side.

'Sorry.'

He didn't sound sorry at all, and she narrowed her eyes. He'd done that on purpose.

While he slowly climbed down the ladder, Petra eyed the box, wondering what was in it.

She found out when he said, 'Go on then, what are you waiting for? Open it.'

Intrigued, Petra waited for him to reach the bottom of the ladder safely, then she bent down, picked up the box and walked into Amory's bedroom with it. Thankfully her son was still gurgling away, his eyes on the mobile which was gradually winding down. Hastily she wound it back up again, hoping for a few more minutes during which she could find out what was so important to make Amos decide to go up the attic at this very moment. Surely whatever it was could have waited? She was taking a hack out in an hour, and she had things to do.

She put the box on Amory's changing table and eased the lid off. Inside, underneath a layer of tissue paper, lay a mass of ivory lace.

Gently she lifted it out and gazed at the dress she was holding. 'Is this what I think it is?'

Amos grinned at her and nodded. 'Yep, your Aunt Mags wore it on her wedding day.'

Petra shot him an incredulous look. 'Do you honestly think I'm going to fit into this?' she asked. And it wasn't only the fit she was worried about – it looked so delicate she thought it might fall apart if she so much as sneezed.

'You won't know until you try it, will you?' Amos said. 'It might look tiny, but your Aunt Mags wasn't as slim as you.'

Petra studied it. Maybe her uncle was right. But even if he was, she wasn't sure she wanted to risk wearing it. 'It's beautiful, but—'

'I know what you're going to say.' Amos wagged his finger at her. 'I don't want any of that nonsense about it being too precious to wear. I'd prefer to see it get some action, rather than have it sit and rot in the attic, and I know your Aunt Mags would agree with me if she were alive.'

Petra still wasn't sure. She was honoured that he trusted her to wear it, but was it *her*? Compared to most of the other dresses she'd seen yesterday, it was quite old fashioned, almost Edwardian with its high neck and long sleeves. It was floor length, probably a little too long for her, but she could see that the length wouldn't matter as it would simply puddle around her feet. The lacy high neck was offset by long lace cuffs from mid-arm to wrists, and the same lace was repeated in the bodice. It had quite a wide band around the waist and flared out gently in a myriad of pleats and folds which cascaded to the floor, and the skirt of the dress had more lacework around the bottom. It was probably the most beautiful dress she'd ever seen, and something sparked inside her.

'Try it on,' Amos urged.

His eyes were suspiciously damp and she realised how emotional this was for him. Not only had he given Harry his wife's engagement ring for Harry to propose to her, which now sat on the third finger of her left hand, but he wanted her to wear Aunt Mag's wedding dress. The old photos didn't do it justice, because it was so much more beautiful in real life. She was surprised he still had it, but then again if she owned something this beautiful she wouldn't want to give it away or sell it either.

Petra left Amos with the baby, and took the dress into her bedroom. She was hesitant to try it. What if it didn't look right on her, or she didn't like it once it was on? It would be no good lying to him and saying it didn't fit because he'd expect to see her in it, so how could she tell him that she didn't want to wear it because she didn't think it suited her?

She slipped it over her head and wriggled her way into it. Then she looked in the mirror.

Oh, my!

Petra turned to one side then the other, examining herself from all angles. She wished it was full length, so she could see all of the dress, as she couldn't stand back far enough to be able to get it all in. But even from the bits she could see, she knew this was it. This was the dress. She hadn't managed to do it up by herself and she prayed that it would fit, because now that she'd seen it and tried it on, she couldn't imagine wearing anything else. If she couldn't do this up, then she'd go to her wedding wearing white jodhpurs and those white Wellington boots that she'd seen online with the ribbons on the side.

'Amos?' she called. 'Can you come in?'

Amos poked his head around the door and gasped, and when he stepped inside, tears were rolling down his face. 'You look…' He couldn't continue and hitched in an unsteady breath.

She turned and presented her back to him. 'Could you do me up? But don't force it: I don't want to risk tearing anything.'

She could feel his fingers trembling as he struggled to push the tiny seed-pearl buttons through the fabric loops, but eventually he got there and Petra was able to take a breath. She'd been trying to suck in her stomach and everything else, and had been scared to even breathe in case she ripped something.

'Turn around,' he said, his voice hoarse, and Petra turned slowly to face him.

Niece and uncle regarded each other solemnly.

'Well?' he said after a few moments, when he'd managed to compose himself.

'Thank you.' Petra was tongue-tied. She didn't have the words to describe how she was feeling – honoured, overwhelmed, beautiful. She never would have guessed that an item of clothing could make her feel as special as she did right now, and she couldn't wait to see Harry's face when she walked down the aisle of Picklewick's little church wearing it. She hoped he'd be impressed.

'I think we'd better sort a car out,' she said, unable to take her eyes off her reflection. 'I did think me and you could go to the church in the Land Rover, and the bridesmaids could meet us there, but now…'

'Over my dead body!' Amos exclaimed. 'If you think I'm going to let you travel to your wedding in a dirty old Land Rover, you can think again. I've already sorted out alternative transport.'

'What alternative transport?'

'Don't you worry your head about it,' he said. 'It's all in hand, and it will most definitely be better than the Land Rover.'

'I hope you haven't wasted money on a wedding car?' Petra said. What with all the money they'd invested in the cottages – which hadn't started bringing in any income yet – they couldn't afford fripperies like expensive wedding cars. When Petra had said she thought she'd better sort a car out, she'd been thinking of asking Luca to drive her and Amos to the church in his Range Rover.

'I haven't,' Amos assured her, and she heaved a sigh of relief at having yet another expense spared. She could also return the dress she'd bought to the department store, so that was an added bonus.

'I'd better take this off,' she said, on hearing an indignant squawk from her son. 'Can you keep it in your room? I don't want Harry to see it – I want it to be a surprise. I hope he'll like it.'

'He'll love it. I loved it when I saw Mags wearing it. I was standing in the front pew when the Wedding March started playing – in the same place that Harry will be waiting for you to walk down the aisle – and I turned around, and there she was. I had never seen anything so lovely in my life, and Harry will look at you and think the same.' He paused and Petra could see he wanted to say something else but was hesitating.

'What is it?' she asked.

'Are you sure about me walking you down the aisle? It should be your dad.'

'Amos, we've talked about this. Dad doesn't mind, honestly. You're like a father to me, and after all you've done for me—'

Amos leapt in. 'That's not the point,' he said, as she offered him her back so he could undo the buttons. His hands were more sure this time, although he continued to be very careful. 'Your father is still your father.'

'I know, and I do feel awful, but I am closer to you than I am to him.'

'That's sad,' he said. 'You only have one father—'

It was Petra's turn to interrupt. 'Not true,' she said. 'I've got my dad and I've got you.'

'How would you feel if…?' Amos cleared his throat before he carried on speaking. 'If both me and your dad walked you down the aisle? Would that be silly?'

Petra could have kissed him! 'What a brilliant solution,' she said. 'I should have thought of that.'

Amos chuckled.' You haven't really been thinking about the wedding at all, have you?'

'Is it that obvious?'

'Um…yeah?'

'Oh, dear. I hope Harry doesn't think that it's because I don't want to marry him, because I do, very much. I can't wait to be his wife.'

'He knows that – he knows what you're like. But now that the cottages are finished, you can spend next two weeks concentrating on your forthcoming nuptials.'

'I don't think there's a lot of concentrating left to be done,' Petra said. She'd got her dress and the bridesmaids had theirs, Amos was sorting out a car, the church had been booked, and her parents would be arriving on the Friday, and she was going to put them up in one of the cottages. Everyone knew she was getting married, so there was an open invitation for them to attend the church if they wanted. Not that she expected many people to turn up, and she was anticipating a small ceremony, but one thing she hadn't considered, which she supposed she should do, was the reception.

Amos was adamant that there was going to be some kind of celebration, but she didn't know what he was planning. Anyway, she decided to leave it up to him – he knew that she didn't want a big fuss, and if he decided to put on a bit of a buffet and invite a few people round for a glass of champagne, she wasn't going to object.

'It's a figure of speech,' Amos said. 'Anyway, everything is in hand, so there's no need for you to worry.'

Petra wasn't worried in the slightest. The only thing that mattered was that the church was booked, and that she and Harry turned up on time and said their vows. Anything else was window dressing. Anyway, aside from the church burning down or the vicar having a bout of dysentery, there wasn't much that could go wrong.

It was a beautiful day for a fete, Stephen thought, as he peered out of the living room window. The sky was brilliant blue and there wasn't a cloud in it, and when he opened the patio door and stepped outside he discovered it was already quite warm.

He inserted one of those little pods into the coffee machine and pressed the button, then leaned against the work top while he waited for it to brew. He knew that Julia was awake because he could hear the water running in her room and guessed she was in the shower.

Reflecting on yesterday he decided that all-in-all it had been a pretty good day. They'd managed to come to an understanding of sorts, despite one or two awkward moments, the first being when they'd discussed getting a divorce. There was still no resolution on that problem, but he didn't feel they needed to hurry.

Neither of them wanted to move on when it came to their love lives, and they'd already sorted out and separated their finances, so there wasn't much else to do apart from sign on the dotted line. He knew it was the sensible thing to do to formalise their separation, but he just couldn't bring himself to do it.

It seemed so final somehow, so he decided that unless Julie wanted to start divorce proceedings, he'd leave well alone for the time being. If he met someone else (ha! that was very unlikely) he'd revisit the subject and make a decision then.

The other really awkward moment had been when he'd said he would join her in the shower. He hadn't meant it like that, and he knew that Julie hadn't taken it like that, but for a split second the thought of his wife with water cascading over her shoulders, her hair wet, and her smooth skin fragrant from the shower gel she used, had made him feel weak with longing. Right at that very moment if she'd had said, 'Yes, join me,' he would have done. He had no doubt about that.

But he'd stumbled out an apology, and she'd stumbled out an acceptance, and they'd both hurried off to their respective bedrooms, Julie probably thinking what an idiot he was for even thinking that she might take it the wrong way, and Stephen feeling a right prat.

After that, the rest of the evening had been a bit like walking on eggshells, with Stephen very conscious of thinking before he spoke, in case he said the wrong thing again. He'd also been excruciatingly aware of her, of the expressions flitting across her face, of the sound of her voice, the way she delicately crossed her legs at the ankle, her smile...

He was reminded of when they'd first got together and he hadn't been able to take his eyes off her, soaking in every look, every curve, every expression, to savour during those times when they were apart.

How quickly had the awareness fled. He guessed all marriages were the same, familiarity wearing away at it like water eroding rock. He supposed they'd both taken each other for granted. It was one of the reasons he'd been looking forward to retiring, so they could reconnect as a couple without the distractions of work. He'd been thinking about telling her that he'd like them to travel, to discover new places together.

He snorted. He certainly didn't feel like travelling anymore. The idea didn't appeal to him at all now that he would be doing it alone.

'Can I smell coffee?' Julie asked, coming into the kitchen.

It was just about ready, so he handed her a cup, careful not to touch her. She was looking less ethereal this morning, her skin having absorbed some sun yesterday, which had given her more colour. She was still too thin, but she no longer looked as though she would shatter. It probably helped that she'd eaten better yesterday too: the exercise must have given her an appetite, because she'd polished off all of her portion of the picnic and she'd cleared her plate at dinner, which he was pleased to see.

She lifted the cup to her lips and closed her eyes briefly. 'Mmm, the first cup of coffee in the morning is always special,' she said, adding, 'Thank you. What time do you think we should leave?'

'I reckon a gentle stroll will take about half an hour, so what if we leave in an hour's time?'

'Perfect,' she said.

'Shall I do us some breakfast?'

'That would be lovely.'

As he pottered around in the kitchen, it almost felt like the last few months hadn't happened. If he ignored the ache in his chest, he could almost believe that they were still together and that they were enjoying a lovely weekend away.

Actually, he realised he *was* enjoying it. He'd enjoyed himself yesterday more than he'd enjoyed himself in a while. Since she'd told him she had been unfaithful, in fact.

The insight was a worry. Would he only ever be happy again if Julie was by his side? He guessed that he was also going through a form of mourning, and he was stricken with grief over the death of their marriage, but what if he never emerged from it? What if he was destined to spend the rest of his life yearning for Julie, but never allowing himself to forgive her?

He'd end up a lonely, miserable old git, that's what – and the thought wasn't a pleasant one.

Yesterday had brought what he was missing into sharp focus and now he didn't know what to do for the best.

'Toast and marmalade?' he suggested, pushing his troubled thoughts to the back of his mind and concentrating on getting some food inside her.

'Brilliant,' she said.

She smiled but it didn't reach her eyes and he hurriedly looked away. Sadness surrounded her like breath on a freezing day, and he wished he could do something to alleviate it. Not only did he dislike seeing her so unhappy, but her melancholy also served as a constant reminder and if he was honest he was sick of thinking about it. He wanted to forget it had ever happened. And today he intended to pretend that it hadn't; he wanted them to be a normal couple, doing normal things, despite knowing that he might be setting himself up for even more heartbreak.

The pain would be worth it.

CHAPTER SIX

'Oh, my word, I haven't seen a helter skelter in years!' Julie cried. 'Fancy a go?' She didn't mean it – she just wanted to see Stephen's face, and she burst out laughing at his horrified expression. 'No? How about the big wheel instead?' She widened her eyes hopefully.

'Not a chance. And neither am I going on the teacups, the dodgems or the pirate ship.'

'Spoilsport.'

'Tell you what, how about I find a bench to sit on and you can have a go?'

'Erm, that's okay,' she said.

'Chicken.'

Julie made clucking noises, earning herself an indulgent smile from a woman pushing a pram.

'People are staring.' Stephen nudged her, but he was grinning as he said it.

The contact was only fleeting, but she bit her lip at the surge of emotion it generated in her.

He edged away a little and a wash of colour spread up his neck, and she wondered whether he'd felt it too. She'd noticed that he'd been studiously avoiding touching her, and she guessed he must still be disgusted with her. He'd told her as much that awful day when she'd broken down and confessed her adultery. She would never forget the pain on his face, or the things he'd said to her. The worst thing he'd said was that he'd told her he still loved her. Then he'd walked out.

Pushing the memories away, she said, 'How about some lunch instead?'

'Good idea. Do you want to find a table in one of the cafes? Or the pub? Isaac said that the Black Horse does decent food.'

'Shall we save that for later? If you want to, that is.'

'Are you suggesting we go there for dinner tonight? It's a long trek to the cottage and back,' he warned.

'I thought we could stay in Picklewick for a few more hours, then have an early supper. Even if we don't leave until eight it should still be light enough to walk back, and if it isn't, we can get a taxi.'

'It's a plan,' he agreed.

It wasn't that Julie wanted to linger around the fair or watch the dog agility display which was on in an hour or so. Neither did she want to admire any woodcarving skills, or see which sheep won best of breed. Not going back to the cottage for several hours meant that Stephen's presence was diluted by the crowds of people, the noise, the activity. Being in such close proximity to him was difficult enough, without it being on a one-to-one basis. And if they stayed in the village until early evening, it might be late enough by the time they got back to the cottage to just have a quick nightcap and then slope off to bed, where she could weep in peace.

She really did feel like crying, but her tears were no longer for Emrys. They were for her and Stephen, and for what she'd destroyed. If only she had been able to hold herself together, she could have grieved for Emrys in private and Stephen would have been none the wiser. What good had knowing done him?

With a bright smile she nodded towards a group of pop-up eateries. 'Fancy taking a look at those?'

The smells drifting in the warm late-summer air were mouth-watering and Julie was surprised to discover she had an appetite. She'd gone from pushing Amos's casserole around on her plate on Friday evening, to scoffing everything put in front of her yesterday.

She assumed it was because of the unaccustomed exercise. After hardly leaving the house for months, apart from a few necessary visits to the shops, she'd gone for two long walks in the countryside in as many days. Three, if she counted the walk into Picklewick earlier today. When she returned home she decided it might be a good idea to incorporate a walk into her daily routine. But even as she considered it, she knew she wouldn't – going for a walk on her own didn't appeal in the slightest.

They came to a halt at the first of the food vans, which was selling pulled pork baguettes made from wild boar with caramelised onions and a quince chutney, and Julie inhaled the delicious aroma.

'Want one?' Stephen asked.

'I don't think I can manage a whole one,' she said. Despite her new-found appetite, the baguettes were the length of her forearm.

'We could share, and if we're still hungry we could try something else afterwards?' he suggested.

A lump came to Julie's throat. They used to do the very same thing whenever they went out, even if they only popped into a cafe for coffee and cake. She'd choose one thing and he'd choose another, and they would share.

Not trusting herself to speak, all she could do was nod.

Stephen ordered and bought a couple of chilled cans of lemonade to go with their food, and they strolled around the fete nibbling at their lunch and taking it all in.

'Look, there's Amos,' Julie said, spotting him talking to a woman of roughly the same age. He had Petra's baby with him, and looked every inch the proud grandad.

Amos waved when he saw them and Julie made her way over to him, Stephen following.

She cooed at the little boy and stroked his downy cheek, and the baby grinned back at her, his smile dribbly and gummy.

'How are you enjoying it so far?' Amos asked, before remembering to introduce himself to Stephen. 'Sorry, I'm

Amos, and this is Lena. A friend.'

Something about the way he said the word *friend* made Julie wonder if there was more than friendship going on.

Amos lowered his voice and glanced around. 'She's helping with the wedding arrangements, but don't tell Petra. She's got no idea we're having a big reception in the arena at the stables. It's all hush hush.'

'How lovely! It's not long now, is it?' Julie said, taking both Amos and Lena in with a smile.

'Thirteen days. And there's still so much to do.'

'Anything we can help with?' Julie said 'we' without thinking, and she glanced at Stephen apologetically. However, he was nodding, so she assumed he wasn't put out at being included in the offer.

'It's all in hand,' Amos said, 'but thank you anyway. The hardest part will be keeping Petra away from the arena and the stables on the morning, because that's when we'll be setting it up and decorating it. She's going to want to do her usual morning routine of checking on the horses.'

'But it's her wedding day!' Julie said.

'You don't know Petra,' Lena replied grimly. 'She lives and breathes horses. My daughter, October, is the same. She works at the stables, and between us we're trying to hatch a plan to get Petra away from the place for the night, but I don't think we'll be able to manage it.'

'Could you book her into a hotel somewhere?' Julie wondered.

Amos pulled a face. 'Not really; the only place in Picklewick is the Black Horse, and she's not going to see the point in staying there when she has a perfectly good bedroom at the stables. Then there's Amory to consider – he'll be better off at home on the night before the wedding, because Petra will have enough on her plate without worrying whether she remembered to pack the nappy cream.'

All four adults looked at the baby, who gazed serenely back at them.

'Oh, dear. I'm sure you'll work something out,' Julie said.

'I hope so.'

'Good luck,' Julie said, giving the baby another huge smile. Amory beamed back. 'Remember when Isaac was that age?' she asked Stephen as they walked away. 'He wasn't as happy as that little chap.'

'He was a bit of a misery, wasn't he?' Stephen agreed. 'He didn't stop crying for at least six months. I kept wondering what we were doing wrong!'

'He's turned out okay though, hasn't he?'

'He's more than okay. He's a credit to us, even if I do say so myself.'

'Do you think he and Nelly will get married?'

'I wouldn't be surprised. He's absolutely besotted with her.'

'And she him,' Julie said. 'A right pair of love birds, they are. It makes my heart melt just seeing them.'

'We used to—' Stephen stopped abruptly.

'Yes, we did.' She could see him looking at her out of the corner of his eye, and she guessed he was wondering whether it had all been an act on her part.

It hadn't. She had genuinely loved her husband. She still did.

But she had loved Emrys more.

For a while.

It had taken losing Stephen for her to realise that for all those years the love she'd had for her husband had grown and deepened, until he'd eventually become as necessary to her as the very air she breathed.

Emrys was her past, her youth, and her first love: Stephen had been her present, her future, and her enduring love.

Until she'd driven him away.

Three glasses of wine at dinner had gone to Julie's head, Stephen thought. To be fair, he'd had a pint before their meal at the Black Horse and he'd also had two glasses of wine with it, so he was faring only marginally better than she. They should have been sensible and called for a taxi to take them back to the cottage, but it was such a lovely evening that they'd decided to walk.

Stephen was starting to regret it now, because Julie wasn't as steady on her feet as him, and every so often he was forced to catch hold of her as she stumbled up the rough path leading from Picklewick to the stables. Going up the hill was harder than going down and was taking longer too, so the estimated half hour walk back was turning into an hour. And having to hold her hand as she picked her way up the path was excruciating.

Still, he'd enjoyed the day at the fete and he'd enjoyed the meal. He'd also enjoyed Julie's company – far more than he'd have thought possible prior to this weekend, and far more than was wise, considering the situation.

Gosh, he'd missed her so much, and he hadn't fully realised just how deeply until now. The thought of going back to his lonely rented house tomorrow filled him with dread.

As he put an arm around his wife's waist to steady her, he wondered how she felt about living alone in the house they'd shared for over thirty years. Was she as lonely as him, or was she glad she had the freedom to mourn Emrys without his disapproving presence?

His fingers tingled where he held her, and when she leant into him for support his heart gave a lurch. He'd been feeling this way since they'd left the pub – his heart thudding, his mouth dry, and he had been fighting an overwhelming longing to gather her to him and kiss her until she begged him to stop.

'Not far to go now,' he said, as they crested a small rise.

It was still light – just – and he could make out the stables in the deepening gloom, relieved to find that another ten minutes or so should bring them to the door of their cottage.

Knee-high grass lay to either side of the narrow path that they were trekking along and wavelike ripples danced across its golden surface. The sky held a fast-fading reminder of the day in the swathe of russet colours where the sun had dipped below the horizon, a harbinger of approaching autumn.

They were now walking in single file so as not to trample the grass, and when Julie came to a sudden halt, he bumped into her.

'Sorry,' he mumbled, a waft of her familiar perfume assaulting his nostrils once again.

'Look,' she breathed, her eyes scanning the valley. 'Isn't it beautiful?'

It was, but he didn't mean the view. He was gazing at his wife. Her face was serene, a gentle smile playing about her mouth. Her eyes shone in the gloaming, and the fading day lit her in soft focus.

'I'm glad you stayed,' she said. 'Being here wouldn't have been the same on my own.'

'It's been a good couple of days,' he agreed, his voice hoarse, and he cleared his throat.

'I'd say we should do this more often, but...' she tailed off sadly.

He wanted to suggest that they make this an annual thing, but he couldn't bring himself to contemplate another whole year without her. The bleakness of it sent shivers of despair through his very soul. He didn't want to think of getting to the end of another 365 days, and nothing having changed in his life. Something would have to give, but he didn't know what. What he did know was that he couldn't face another twelve months of his life the way it was.

As though she sensed his dark thoughts, Julie shivered.

He said, 'Come on, let's get inside. You're cold.'

'I'm fine; someone's just walked over my grave, that's all.'

Stephen gave her a sharp look. She had sensed his mood, and it sent a tremor down his own spine. He and Julie used to be so in-tune with one another that it was almost as though they'd read each other's minds. It appeared the connection was still there.

In a sudden burst of anger, he grunted at his stupidity. If he really had been so in-tune with his wife, surely he would have realised that she'd loved someone else for all these years?

Then he let out a slow breath and drove it away. Anger was such a fruitless and negative emotion, and holding on to it did no one any good. He supposed that intense emotions like the ones he'd been feeling since that fateful day last November were unlikely to disappear overnight, and he realised that the heartbreak probably wouldn't fully leave him, although he hoped it would fade with time.

'Here we are,' he said, sounding unnecessarily cheerful as they approached the cottage. He fished the keys out of his pocket and unlocked the door, pushing it open to allow her to step inside ahead of him.

She hesitated for a second, then went in.

He followed more slowly. He hadn't missed the tears in her eyes, and her sadness pricked him to the core.

'Drink?' she asked, her back to him.

She'd paused in the kitchen doorway, her shoulders up around her ears, her back rigid. He fought the urge to massage the tension away with his strong hands.

'Gin?' he suggested. 'You brought enough with you.' His tone was deliberately light as he tried to alleviate the tension.

He left her to it and went to stand by the patio doors. The garden was in darkness and his reflection stared back at him. The face gazing out belonged to a stranger. Where had all the years gone? When had he become this middle-aged man?

He closed his eyes, a flashback of Julie on their wedding night swooping through his mind and catching him unawares.

They had spent it in an airport hotel because they were flying to Paris for their honeymoon the following day. He'd been in the bathroom, having just cleaned his teeth, feeling unaccountably nervous even though he wasn't a stranger to her body. He knew it as well as he knew his own, but tonight – the first time they would make love as a married couple – held a deep significance for him.

Julie had come in behind him and he'd seen her reflection in the glass above the basin. She'd been naked…

He watched her approach now, a tumbler in each hand, a ghostly figure in the glass, and he pushed the memories away. Thinking those kinds of thoughts wouldn't do any good at all.

'Thanks.' He sipped at his drink, and their eyes met in the glass of the door.

She held his gaze, hers unwavering, and slowly, oh so slowly, he turned to face her.

Just as slowly he took her drink from her and placed both tumblers on the table, his eyes never leaving hers.

He couldn't say why he did it, why he kissed her. He just did.

And it felt like coming home.

CHAPTER SEVEN

Without opening her eyes, Julie knew that she was on her own in the bed, but just to make sure she opened them anyway and her hand slid across to the side Stephen usually slept on. The duvet was pushed back and there was a dent in the pillow where his head had rested. The sheet was cold. He hadn't just left; he'd been gone a while.

However, she could hear the shower in the other bedroom running, and she smiled to herself. He always did have a tendency to wake up earlier than her, and he would often sneak out of bed and go downstairs, ready to start his day long before she emerged from the land of Nod. She wondered how long he'd been up, and when she glanced at the clock she saw that it was already nine. She hadn't slept this well in a very long time, and her insides tingled as she thought of the reason why.

When Isaac had asked her if she'd like to spend a weekend in a cottage as a favour to him, the last thing she'd imagined was that Stephen would also be there. Even when she'd come back from the house up at the stables, clutching that casserole in her hands, and had spotted her estranged husband in the kitchen peering into the fridge, not in a million years did she think that they might end up in bed together.

But they had, and it had been wonderful.

Aside from them getting back together, for which she was profoundly thankful and grateful, the sex had been amazing. Like most couples, they'd had make-up sex after an argument, but it had been nothing like last night.

She had felt such a profound connexion to him, that it touched her soul.

Her heart was still singing this morning and a deep contentment spread through her bones, making her feel languid and satiated, and she would be quite happy to stay in bed for the rest of the day – as long as Stephen was under the covers with her, of course.

She'd get up in a few minutes, have a shower, and then she'd entice him back to bed. She wasn't entirely sure what time Isaac was coming – she thought he'd mentioned something about eleven o'clock, but that was two hours away. A great deal could happen in two hours.

Briefly she wondered why Stephen hadn't used the shower in her room, but then she realised how thoughtful he was being. The shower would have woken her up, and he'd probably wanted to let her sleep. Aw, how sweet. Also, it made sense for him to use that one, considering all his clothes were in the other bedroom. She wondered whether he would bother getting dressed, or whether he'd pad into her bedroom, naked and expectant, so they could continue where they'd left off last night.

The thought made her toes curl with delicious anticipation. He'd been tender at first, hesitant almost, then passion had taken over and she bit her lip at the memory. He'd been almost animalistic, focused and driven, yet her passion had matched his. She could still feel his hands on her body, here his groans of delight, feel his—

Whoa, girlie, she said to herself, recognising that she could probably do with a shower herself before she leapt on him again. She'd also like some tea. And maybe some breakfast. All that physical activity yesterday (she nearly giggled when she thought of precisely what that physical activity had entailed) had given her an appetite. As soon as her hunger for food was satisfied, she could think about satisfying a hunger of an entirely different kind.

Julie could feel the grin on her face, and she let out a

little squeak of happiness. After nine long months and all the despair and heartache, she and Stephen were back together. And she had finally exercised Emrys's ghost. She'd always have a special place in her heart for her first true love, but he no longer dominated it. Stephen had that honour and had done for a long time, had she been aware of it. It had taken the news of Emrys's death for her to fully appreciate how deep her love for Stephen was, and how right they were together. He brought out the best in her and complemented her perfectly. They were different sides of the same coin, neither of them complete without the other.

She pushed the duvet back and sat up. The shower in the other room was still going, so she decided to nip downstairs to put the kettle on and prepare some breakfast, so when Stephen came down she could simply put it in front of him. She thought about putting something else in front of him too, the innuendo making her giggle, but she'd wait until after they'd eaten.

Sliding her feet into her slippers, she put on the little wrap that was draped over a chair in the corner. There was no need to get dressed because she intended to get naked again very soon and the wrap would cover her modesty for the time being.

Scrambled eggs, that's what she fancied. Fluffy yellow egginess on hot buttered toast. Mmm...her mouth watered, and she realised her appetite had returned with a vengeance. It had been creeping back over the course of the weekend, and now she could feel hunger pangs clawing at her stomach despite the amount she ate yesterday. The meal in the Black Horse had been delicious, and she'd polished off every morsel on her plate and had even eaten pudding.

She found she was looking forward to getting back into the kitchen again and cooking proper meals for her and Stephen. The only time she'd really bothered cooking since he'd left had been when Isaac came for lunch or dinner, but she only cooked to stop their son from worrying about her.

Well, there was no need for him to worry anymore, was there. She was aware that she'd lost weight over the past few months, and she was also aware how quickly she would put it all back on again once she started eating more regularly. She would have to keep an eye on that. She quite liked the new slender her, although she didn't care much for the reason for the weight loss. She could afford to put on a few pounds, but not too many. Anyway, she'd probably get far more exercise when Stephen moved back in, she guessed, giggling to herself once more.

She couldn't wait. In fact, when Isaac returned with Stephen's car keys, she would tell him that there was no need for him to take her home. Stephen could do it. They could call around to the place he was renting on their way, and pick up a few things for his immediate needs, just to see him through the next few days. There was no rush for him to move everything out and back into the marital home, although she would prefer him to do it sooner rather than later. No doubt he'd have to give a month's notice on his lease, so that would give him plenty of time to clear out the place and decide what, if anything, he wanted to keep.

Of course, she had never set foot in it, although Isaac had, and he'd told her it was quite basic, so she couldn't imagine Stephen would want to bring much with him. She certainly didn't expect him to bring big things like his bed or sofa. If his landlord was willing, Stephen could leave those items there for the next person who moved in, or if that wasn't appropriate, he could arrange for someone from one of the local charities to pick up any large items he didn't want.

She got the eggs out of the fridge and cracked them one by one into a bowl, then whisked them up with a little salt and pepper and a tiny drop of milk. As she worked, she realised she was humming, and it made her smile. It had been a long time since she'd hummed, and a flame of pure happiness ignited in her chest. Last November she thought she'd never be happy again, but how wrong could she be. She was almost delirious with it right now, excitement flitting through her as she planned for their future.

Ever since he'd walked out, Julie had barely thought more than a day ahead. But now she was thinking that perhaps they could go on holiday at half term. Somewhere hot and exotic. Somewhere where they could be waited on and spoilt, and spend hours floating in the sea and kissing. She'd never kissed in the sea before and she quite fancied trying it.

A morning spent at the beach, a leisurely lunch, then an afternoon siesta, which she hoped would consist of very little sleeping, sounded idyllic. Okay, maybe a nap afterwards, because they weren't getting any younger.

Another giggle escaped her, lighthearted and girly.

She was so happy, she could cry.

The water trickling down Stephen's face wasn't just from the shower. He was leaning against the tiles, his eyes burning, his chest heaving with silent sobs, crying so hard it hurt.

What had he done?

How could he have been so stupid?

He'd made a complete hash of this weekend. Why, oh why, had he thought he could spend three days with Julie and not suffer the consequences?

Last night he'd given in to his loneliness, given into his love and his desire for her, and he'd ended up in her bed. It might have been indescribably perfect, but that didn't stop him from regretting what he'd done.

Even as he'd been making love to her, a little voice in his head had been telling him to stop, that he'd regret it, that it wasn't a good idea; but he'd ignored it. He hadn't been able to stop. He'd wanted her so badly, and from the way she clutched at him, the way her nails had scratched his back, and her soft whimpers of pleasure, she had wanted it as much as he. He'd so completely lost himself in the taste of her, in the feel of her skin, and her passion, that common sense had deserted him.

Why hadn't he listened to it? In ignoring it, he'd succeeded in heaping misery on top of heartache, because although he might have made peace with himself when it came to his feelings of betrayal over what she'd done, he could never forget.

He must have been out of his mind. There was no way they could go back to the way they were. And now he'd made things a hundred times worse.

He couldn't face the future without her, but neither did he feel able to let her back into his life and risk yet more pain. He didn't think he could cope with it. He'd been barely coping as it was.

Lifting his head, he let the water sluice down his cheeks to wash away the scalding tears. He couldn't let her see him like this, so he heaved in one final hitching breath and let it out slowly. He was done crying for now, although he guessed he'd do more of it before the day was out. As soon as Isaac appeared with his keys, he'd leave. He'd go back to his rented house, lock the door and wallow in misery. And he'd probably carry on wallowing until a week Thursday when the new term started and he'd have no choice other than to go to work and pretend everything was normal.

To be honest, he didn't want to go back to his sad, lonely house, and neither did he feel he could face his job. In fact, he didn't want to carry on living the life he'd been living for the past few months, but what else could he do?

Turning the shower off, he reached for the towel hanging on the rail outside the cubicle and wiped his face.

Suddenly he stopped towelling himself dry as a thought struck him.

He'd go travelling, that's what he'd do.

He'd let the school know he was taking early retirement and ask how soon they'd be able to release him. If he was lucky, he might be on the other side of the world by October half term.

The plan didn't fill him with as much excitement as it should have done. It didn't fill him with any excitement at all, but it was better than moping around, day in, day out. At least he wouldn't run the risk of bumping into Julie in a supermarket – or give Isaac another opportunity to set them up again.

With a heavy heart, Stephen finished drying himself off and pulled on some clothes, hastily stuffing everything else into his holdall so he'd be ready to leave as soon as Isaac showed up.

After a final look around to make sure he hadn't forgotten to pack anything, he made his way downstairs. He couldn't put it off seeing Julie any longer. He knew she was awake because he could hear her in the kitchen, and he wondered if she was also feeling bad about last night. No doubt she was regretting it as much as he. How could she not when she was in love with someone else? She might be married to him, but it was Emrys she really loved, Emrys who she'd been breaking her heart over.

These past few days it had been so easy to slip back into their old ways and the familiar lovemaking, that it must have taken her as much by surprise as it had him. He hoped she wasn't beating herself up over it, like he was, but he suspected she probably would be.

With these thoughts in his mind and fully expecting to find Julie in as much distress as he over the events of the previous night, he was shocked to see her cooking scrambled eggs, her body moving gently from side to side

326

as she chased the mixture around the pan to ensure it was thoroughly cooked. Not only that, but she was *humming*.

He swallowed, dread spearing him in the stomach. Oh, god, she *wasn't* regretting it. She was happy about it. And when she glanced up from the stove and saw him standing there, her smile tore his heart in two. She looked radiant, and more beautiful than he had ever seen her look before.

'I'm making us some scrambled eggs,' she said. 'The toast is about to pop any second – can you butter it?'

'Julie…?'

'Oh, and there's tea in the pot if you want to pour yourself a cup.'

'Julie.'

'What?' She stopped stirring the eggs and peered at them. 'I think these are just about done.'

'*Julie!* Please, just stop…We need to talk.'

The miserable expression on her face would stay with him for the rest of his life.

The sound of a car engine outside made Julie look out of the window, hoping it was Isaac coming to fetch her. She couldn't wait to get out of this place and away from Stephen. Since he'd informed her that last night had been a mistake and that he was sorry it had happened, she'd been hiding in her bedroom, watching the minutes tick slowly by and trying to stem the tears that flowed from her eyes in a steady stream.

Her relief when she saw her son sauntering towards the row of cottages almost had her sobbing out loud.

Hastily, she dabbed a tissue under her red and swollen eyes, then blew her nose. She knew she looked a mess and that Stephen and Isaac would realise she had been crying but there was nothing she could do about that. In fact, it would serve them both right to see the hurt they'd caused.

Isaac's actions in throwing her and Stephen together for the weekend might have been coming from a good place, but he'd done more harm than good. And Stephen must be extremely pleased with himself for executing such a fitting revenge: he'd made love to her so expertly and thoroughly that his passion and tenderness had led her to believe they had a second chance at love.

How wrong could she be.

He must have been laughing his socks off when he'd seen her playing happy families in the kitchen, knowing that she was thinking that they were back together and that everything could return to the way it had been.

More fool her. She should have known Stephen wouldn't find it easy to forgive and forget what she'd done. Although he had never been a vindictive man and he'd never been one to hold a grudge, he'd made it clear when he'd left her all those months ago that they were over. Isaac throwing them together must have seemed an ideal opportunity for Stephen to get his own back.

She doubted whether he'd started out with that intention, because he'd probably thought she was still grieving for Emrys, but over the last two days when they had appeared to reconnect, he must have decided to love her and leave her.

Or, even worse, had she merely been an opportunity to get his leg over?

The thought made her want to cry again, just when she'd managed to stem the flow, and she hurriedly blew her nose again and cleared her throat, before splashing some cold water on her face and checking her appearance.

She didn't like what she saw in the mirror but that couldn't be helped, so she grabbed her jacket, her bag and her case, and trundled downstairs.

She had just got to the bottom of the stairs when she heard voices, and she hurried to the front door to find Isaac and his father outside. Stephen's bag rested on the bench below the window, and she assumed that he had been waiting in eager anticipation for Isaac to arrive.

'Why, what's happened?' she heard Isaac ask.

'Nothing. Can I have my keys, there is somewhere I need to be.' Stephen's voice was short and clipped.

Nothing? She'd hardly describe what had happened last night as *nothing*. But perhaps that is exactly how her husband thought of her.

Julie bit her lip, holding back a sob, and busied herself with putting on her jacket and slinging her bag over her arm, so that neither her husband nor her son could see how upset she was.

Isaac was looking at his dad with a bewildered expression. 'Did you have a good time?'

'It was all right.' Stephen was gruff. He held his hand out for the keys and Isaac pulled them out of his pocket and placed them in his palm.

Stephen's fingers curled around them and he nodded once. 'Right then, I'll be off.' He picked up his bag and began to walk away.

Isaac said, 'Have you got any recommendations for Petra?'

'I'll email them to you.' Stephen waved a hand in the air and kept on walking.

'At least say goodbye to Mum,' Isaac called after him.

Stephen faltered for a second before carrying on up the path, and Julie realised that was all the acknowledgement she was going to get.

'What's up with Dad?' Isaac turned to her.

'You'd better ask him.'

'Have you been crying? Mum? Is everything okay?'

'No, it's not.'

'What happened?'

'You tricked me and your father into spending the weekend together. What do you think happened?'

Isaac stared at her, his expression bleak. 'Did you have a fight?'

'Worse. We slept together.' Julie gleaned a small amount of satisfaction when she saw her son wince. 'What did you expect would happen?'

'Erm…I *hoped* you'd kiss and make up.'

'You got the kissing part right,' she said. 'But we haven't made up.' Suddenly angry at Isaac for putting her in this position, she rounded on him. 'What did you expect, eh? We're not a pair of little kids who've had a squabble over a crayon.'

'But you just said you'd…er…'

'We did. Look, Isaac, I don't want to talk about it. Your father has made it perfectly clear that he's not going to forgive me and I don't blame him. I'm not sure I could forgive me, either. In fact, I don't. So please don't ask any more questions. Just take me home.'

'Oh Mum, I'm so sorry.'

Julie nodded, not trusting herself to speak.

Without another word, he picked up her case and closed the door, and they drove home in silence, the only noise being Julie's quiet snuffles as she tried to contain her heartache.

CHAPTER EIGHT

Julie studied the photo on her phone and smiled sadly, although it wasn't the photo itself that made her sad, it was the memories it evoked.

Isaac did look handsome though, and Nelly was gorgeous in a light blue dress and high heels. Her hair was a loose cloud about her shoulders and the pair of them appeared to be very much in love.

They were on their way to Petra and Harry's wedding, and it was the event itself that brought Julie's memories of the weekend she'd spent at the cottage the other week flooding back. She had been trying not to think about it, but it hadn't been easy. And when it came to crying, the slightest thing set her off.

Tears pricked at her eyes now, and she brushed them away with an impatient swipe of her hand. She was starting to get on her own nerves, so goodness knows how irritating she must be to Isaac. Bless him, he didn't show it. He'd been full of remorse and contrition these past two weeks, and had been going out of his way to pop in and see her most days.

Julie realised she must have worried him a fair bit on the drive back from the stables on Muddypuddle Lane, because she'd sobbed steadily the whole time.

She didn't know whether he'd spoken to his father about what had happened, or how Stephen was feeling about it. Smug maybe? Justified? Or maybe he didn't feel anything at all and hadn't given her a second thought. The latter was the more likely scenario. And the most hurtful.

She, on the other hand, hadn't been able to stop thinking about it and wishing she hadn't agreed to spend the weekend in the cottage in the first place. Or hadn't agreed when Stephen had suggested that they give it a go together. If she'd had even the smallest inkling of how badly it would end, she'd have walked into Picklewick on that Friday evening and would have arranged for a taxi to take her home. But hindsight is a wonderful thing, and she had stayed to suffer the consequences instead.

She sent Isaac a quick message back, telling him how lovely they looked and telling them to have a good time, and afterwards she couldn't help wondering how Amos had got on with setting up the reception, and whether Petra had found out about it ahead of time. Which brought the image of her and Stephen chatting to Amos at Picklewick's fete to mind. If only she hadn't suggested going to the Black Horse for a meal, she wouldn't have drunk three glasses of wine and she might have kept a tighter rein on her emotions.

Oh, well, what was done, was done. She couldn't change anything so there was no point in dwelling on it – but that was easier said than done, wasn't it?

'Keep still,' October urged, slapping Petra gently on the arm. 'I can't do these fiddly buttons up if you keep squirming around.'

Petra stopped fidgeting long enough for October to finish buttoning her into her wedding dress. She was already nervous but as the morning wore on she had been finding it increasingly difficult to sit still. Something was bothering her, but she didn't know what.

It wasn't anything to do with Harry because she'd spoken to him on the phone this morning. He'd spent the night at Timothy and Charity's cottage, and right at this moment she guessed he was going through the same process, although he'd be getting into a suit not a dress. Amos had picked some flowers from the garden and had dropped them down to Timothy's house, for buttonholes, so that wasn't what was niggling at her. And she knew Harry was planning on being at the church a good fifteen minutes before she was due to arrive, so that wasn't it, either. There was no car to worry about for him, because it was only a three-minute walk. And Luca was driving her, Amos and her dad to the church in his car.

Petra turned her attention to her son who was currently being entertained by Lena.

Knowing that Petra and Amos would be up to their eyes in it this morning, Lena had offered to pop up to the stables to look after Amory while they got ready. Petra's mum and dad, who were staying in one of the cottages, had also offered, but Amory had only seen them once since he'd been born, and as far as he was concerned they were total strangers, so Petra hadn't taken them up on it. Amory knew Lena and liked her, and she was very good with him, so Petra was happy for her to take care of him this morning while she was getting ready. Then she guessed he'd be passed around like a parcel until the ceremony was over, and after that she would rescue him. He'd probably be ready for a feed by then, anyway.

In anticipation at not being able to get in and out of her dress very easily, Petra had expressed some milk, and for the past couple of weeks she had gradually introduced him to the bottle, which he had taken to with some reluctance, but at least he drank it.

Petra listened intently, but all she could hear was Lena playing peekaboo, and Amory's endearing little giggles, so she knew there wasn't an issue there.

She'd checked and double checked that his changing bag contained everything he could possibly need, and she knew Lena would leave it until the last moment before swapping his babygro for the little outfit that Harry had bought him especially for the occasion. If they dressed him in it too soon, it was guaranteed Amory would be sick all over it, or worse.

Amos was fine, too. He was already dressed in his suit, and he kept poking his head around her bedroom door to check on progress. He'd seemed quite flummoxed when on the first occasion, expecting to see Petra fully dressed, he had found her wearing a tatty old dressing gown. October had been standing behind her with a comb clamped in her teeth and her curling tongs in hand, and Charity had been crouching down in front of her, staring intently at Petra's face, and wielding a small brush. Megan had been in the middle of popping a cork on something alcoholic and bubbly, and Amos had taken one look at the four of them and had beaten a hasty retreat.

So what was it that was putting her on edge?

'You look stunning,' Megan said, handing Petra another glass of champagne.

Petra hadn't touched the first one yet. She wanted to keep a clear head, and anyway she was still feeding Amory, so alcohol was out of bounds.

Petra looked in the mirror for the first time since the three women had descended on her with the express intention of turning her from a horse rider into a bride, and she didn't recognise herself. Gone was the make-up-free face, the messy ponytail and jodhpur-wearing reflection she was used to seeing. In its place was a vision in ivory silk and lace, with subtle makeup and artfully styled hair.

She turned to her three bridesmaids in horror. 'Harry's not going to recognise me!' she cried.

October chuckled. 'I think he will. He's going to think you look beautiful.'

Petra looked in the mirror again, then glanced back at October. 'Do you think?'

'Definitely. Now, are you ready?'

'I don't know,' Petra said, feeling a sudden attack of unwelcome and unexpected nerves.

When she got to the church all those people would be looking at her, and the thought was terrifying. Few people had actually been invited to the wedding but she had a feeling that half of Picklewick might turn up, and the thought of all those eyes trained on her made her feel sick. Which was silly really, considering she was happy enough to be the centre of attention when she was in the arena, conducting classes, or ensuring a gymkhana went smoothly. But she knew what she was doing when it came to horses. She was entirely out of her comfort zone when it came to weddings.

'Are you going to tell me what you've been up to?' she demanded. Perhaps that's what the problem was? Maybe the fact that she hadn't been allowed anywhere near the stable block or the arena this morning was making her nervous. Bless them, October, Charity and Nathan had insisted on seeing to the horses, even though she had been itching to get outside and do what she always did.

Amos had backed them up. 'It's your wedding day,' he'd told her firmly. 'Just take it easy and relax. Spend some time with Amory and pamper yourself.'

Petra wasn't sure what pampering herself entailed. She wasn't a pampering herself sort of person. She might shave her legs and armpits, but that's about as far as it went. Oh, and she did slather moisturiser on her skin every evening after her shower, but that was because she was outside a lot and the wind and the sun tended to be drying on any exposed areas, so it was more a case of damage control rather than a beauty regime. And she had never used a face mask or a bath bomb in her life and she didn't intend to start now, wedding day or not.

Instead, she'd moped around, peering out of the window now and again, and wondering what was going on – because clearly something was. Although she wasn't a hundred per cent certain, she was convinced she'd heard more than the usual stable noises earlier, and everyone seemed furtive and anxious to keep her in the house. Which made her itch to go outside even more.

'Well?' she demanded, when it didn't seem she was going to get an answer. 'I'm not going anywhere until you tell me.'

Her maid-of-honour and the two bridesmaids shared a look. October shrugged and Charity nodded. Megan pulled a face.

'Okay,' Megan said. 'But you've got to act surprised and if anyone asks you didn't get it from us.'

'What?'

'Amos and Harry have arranged a reception and a party in the arena,' Megan said in a rush. 'Harry has been up half the night, and Timothy too, decorating it, laying out tables, arranging flowers. Amos and Nathan helped, and so did quite a few others.'

Petra was stunned. She hadn't been expecting that. She had been thinking that there was something wrong with one of the horses and they were keeping it from her so as not to worry her.

'I didn't want a fuss,' she objected.

Megan narrowed her eyes. 'Tough, you're having one. Oh, and your mum and dad helped as well. They've sorted out the food.'

'What food?'

'You can't have a wedding reception without food. It was delivered to the cottages earlier. While you and Harry are having your photos taken outside the church, William has arranged for some of his staff at the care home to come up to the stables and set it all out ready.'

Petra felt faint. 'Why?' was all she managed to squeak.

'Because you deserve a special day with everyone who loves you,' Megan said.

Petra was astonished to feel a prickle of tears in the back of her eyes, and she blinked furiously.

'Don't you dare cry,' Charity warned. 'You'll spoil your makeup.'

'I never cry,' Petra said, then promptly burst into tears, evoking a flurry of activity as her bridesmaid's attempted to limit the damage.

She'd been overwhelmed with gratitude at the number of people who had turned out to help clear the old cow shed before the builders arrived to do their part. But this was even more amazing, and she was overcome with emotion.

Suddenly she was delighted that she and Harry weren't having a small ceremony – she wanted to proclaim her love for him from the rooftops and she wanted everyone there when she did. She never realised so many people cared, and her heart constricted with love and gratitude.

'There's one more thing,' October said. 'If you're ready, come outside and see.'

'We've got to leave in a minute,' Petra warned, clocking the time. She needed to be at the church in half an hour. 'Is Luca here?'

'He's here – he's been here for a while, helping decorate the arena.' October grinned. 'Come on, you've got to see this!'

October's excitement was catching, and Petra allowed herself to be led down the stairs, Megan following closely behind to hold the skirt of Petra's dress off the floor.

'Close your eyes,' Charity instructed, nodding to Amos who was waiting in the hall. The front door was shut, but he didn't open it until Petra closed her eyes.

With October and Amos guiding her, Petra was tentatively led outside and brought to a halt on the step. She felt the sun on her face and was grateful that the weather had held. It hadn't rained for several weeks, but it would have been just her luck for it to pour down today.

The breeze blowing gently across her face held the heady perfume of the flowers which were growing around the door, the unmistakable aroma of horses, and a faint but sharp tang of smoke, and she wondered if Amos was planning to serve barbeque food at the reception later.

'Open your eyes!' Amos cried.

Petra took a deep breath and slowly opened them.

In front of her was a white open-topped carriage, with two horses standing between the shafts. Their coats gleamed in the sunlight and the harnesses twinkled and jingled as they tossed their heads.

'That's Storm and Midnight!' she exclaimed. 'How? When—?' She glanced at the people gathered around – Amos, Megan, October, Charity, Luca, Nathan, Lena, her parents – and she felt like crying again.

'You can blame October,' Amos said. 'It was her idea. Harry happened to mention seeing an old carriage when he was shoeing a horse a couple of months ago, and she thought it might be a good idea to train Storm and Midnight to pull it, to take you to the church. So he bought it, and has spent the last few weeks doing it up. What do you think?'

'It's gorgeous,' she said. So that's what he'd been up to. She gazed at it an awe. It was perfect, absolutely perfect. Her attention settled on the horses, and one in particular. 'Will Midnight behave himself?' she asked worriedly. The gelding had a reputation for being naughty.

'Surprisingly, he's taken to it like a duck to water,' Nathan said. He was at the horses' heads, his hand on the reins as he held the animals steady, and she noticed he was wearing coattails and was carrying a top hat under his arm. 'Madam, your carriage awaits.' He bowed deeply and gestured to it.

'We'll meet you there,' Megan said, giving her a kiss. 'Let's get you and your fabulous dress settled, then we'll be off. Your dad can sit one side, and Amos the other. Lena will take Amory and your mum in her car. Is that okay?'

'It's perfect,' Petra said. She walked carefully towards the carriage, admiring its white woodwork, which had been freshly painted, and the large old-fashioned wheels.

Her dad opened the door for her and shoved a small set of steps in front of it. 'Petra, you look beautiful. I'm so incredibly proud of you,' he said, bringing fresh tears to her eyes. For years she'd thought she was a disappointment to him, having not gone to university and working in Amos's stables instead. To have him say he was proud of her nearly set her off crying again.

'I love you, my darling girl.' Her mum wrapped her arms around her carefully, so as to avoid crushing the dress or smudging her makeup. 'Promise me we'll see more of each other? Now that your dad is taking early retirement, we can visit more often, if that's all right with you?'

'Of course it's all right. I love you too, Mum. And you, Dad.'

Gosh, this wedding was turning out to be far more emotional than Petra had anticipated. She couldn't believe how weepy she felt, nor how her heart was filled with so much love that she thought it might burst.

'I'm getting married,' she said, beaming widely as she climbed into the carriage. In a little over an hour, she'd be Mrs Milton!

She settled herself in the middle of the seat, her bridesmaid's fussing around her, arranging her skirt so it didn't get trodden on, when Petra abruptly stiffened.

She suddenly knew what had been bothering her.

Slowly she raised her head and looked up at the fields above the stables.

Beyond them lay open moorland, where sheep grazed and skylarks nested. At this time of year, it was cloaked in gold and russet from the dried grass and the bracken, with the occasional hardy tree reaching for the sky.

Petra squinted, trying to see past Amos who was heaving himself up the little steps, and she peered around him.

Then she inhaled sharply and her stomach dropped to her boots.

That wasn't smoke from a barbeque that she could smell – it was smoke from a grass fire.

Even as she finally understood what it was, a whisp of grey crept over the horizon…And she knew without a shadow of a doubt that she wouldn't be getting married today.

Because the mountain above the stables was on fire.

Stephen took a cup of tea into the living room and glared at the TV. He wasn't in the mood to watch anything, so he turned the radio on instead. The house tended to be depressingly quiet if he didn't put something on. Besides, if left to his own devices he knew he'd dwell on the last time he'd seen Julie. She kept popping into his head at the most inopportune of moments, and once she was there he had a devil of a job shifting her.

Although he didn't particularly feel like marking the exercise books he'd brought home from school yesterday, it would give him something to do and it might even stop him thinking about his wife for a while, so he sat down at the table and started work.

'Dear lord,' he grumbled, as he opened the first book and noticed the state of it.

The pupil in question had only been given the book three days ago, yet the child had already managed to tear the first page, scribble out most of whatever he'd written on the second, and drawn a cross-section of an eyeball on the fourth (he'd skipped the third page for some reason). The drawing wasn't bad but it had nothing whatsoever to do with glaciation, which was the topic he'd introduced to this particular class last week. The child had only gone and done his Biology homework in his Geography exercise book.

Stephen snorted as he imagined Abbie Cole's expression when she was presented with a paragraph on how U-shaped valleys were formed. The young science teacher would not be amused.

Thinking of Abbie made him feel old. These days teaching was a fast-moving profession, with so many new initiatives and increasing number of boxes to tick and hoops to jump through that he was more than ready to throw in the towel. He'd been planning on doing precisely that when Julie had dropped her bombshell on him.

He'd needed the familiarity and stability of his job during the past academic year, but with his new resolution to go travelling, he'd already started the ball rolling and had announced that he'd be retiring at October half term. He should have been excited about this new chapter in his life, but the only emotion he was feeling at the moment was apprehension – he simply wasn't sure he felt up to travelling alone. He was supposed to have been doing this with his wife by his side, and he was worried that the experience would be empty without someone to share it with.

Stephen sat up straighter and his ears pricked up. Something on the radio had caught his attention, something about a wildfire and Picklewick?

He put his pen down, turned up the volume and listened intently.

"…fire fighters are on the scene and are tackling the blaze. A spokesman told us that the recent dry weather has led to a spate of grass fires across the region, and the stiff easterly breeze today will hinder attempts to extinguish this one. She assures the public that there is no immediate danger to life, but they are keeping a close eye on the situation. At present the blaze is confined to the hillsides to the north and east of the village, and fire fighters are confident they will be able to contain it. We'll keep you updated as events unfold, but there is no need to panic at this moment in time.'

As soon as Stephen heard the word "panic" that was exactly what he felt like doing, until common sense kicked in. The radio said the fire was nowhere near Picklewick and they had every confidence in being able to contain it, so there was no need for him to worry.

But contain it wasn't the same as extinguishing it, was it? And Stephen was aware that grass fires, if they penetrated the surface of the soil, could smoulder for days. Weeks, even.

He turned the radio's volume down and picked up his pen again, ready to do some more marking, but then he paused.

Gazing out of the window, his eyes lost their focus as his attention turned inward.

He thought about Picklewick's location.

Then he thought about it in relation to Muddypuddle Lane and the cottage he and Julie had stayed in.

He might be wrong but...

Stephen reached for his phone, noticing that Isaac had sent him a photo of him and Nelly dressed in their finest. They were off to Petra's wedding today, and that was why he was a little concerned. He wasn't overly worried, but he did have a prickle of unease in the back of his mind, and it was only marginally alleviated when Isaac answered his call.

'Hi, Dad? Did you see the photo? I think we scrub up well. Ow! Nelly just elbowed me. What?' Isaac mumbled something Stephen couldn't hear. 'She said that *I* scrub up well – *she* always looks this gorgeous.' Isaac laughed, and Stephen heard Nelly's giggle in the background.

He hated to dampen their spirits but...

'The two of you look lovely,' he said, 'but that's not why I called. The radio has just announced that there is a wildfire on the hillside above Picklewick. Have you heard anything?'

'No, not a thing.' Stephen heard the rumble of a car engine and he guessed they were on their way to the church, as Isaac continued, 'Now you mention it though, there is a smoky smell in the air. I assumed someone was burning their garden rubbish. Oh, shit!'

'What?' Stephen's heart sank.

'We are just coming into Picklewick now and there's smoke on the mountain. Nelly, are you thinking what I'm thinking?' Isaac paused, then said, 'It's above the stables on Muddypuddle Lane. Hang on a minute.' Another pause and Stephen heard voices, but he couldn't make out what they were saying. 'Dad? I've got to go. I've just seen Harry and he's heading up to the stables. Petra is worried about the horses, and Harry said that Amos thinks the old guy who owns the farm further up the lane might need a hand to get his sheep off the hillside.'

'Isaac? Isaac! What do you mean *need a hand*? You're not going up there, are you? You don't know the first thing about sheep.'

'It's all hands on deck, Dad. I'll keep you posted. Bye!'

Stephen slowly lowered the phone. The prickling worry had grown into a nagging stab. He knew that Isaac wouldn't be content to stand by and watch. He'd want to do what he could to help.

Pushing the marking to one side, Stephen reached for his phone again. He knew it was pointless to try to call Isaac back, but there was bound to be something about it on social media – there always was.

'At least get changed first,' Petra's mother told her. Everyone had piled into the kitchen and the room was packed.

'There's no time to spare.' Petra had kicked off her delicate sandals and was stuffing her feet into a pair of dirty wellies. She caught Megan's eye and sighed. Turning her back to her maid-of-honour she said, 'Undo me, will you? October, can you go upstairs and fetch me a pair of jodhpurs and a tee shirt?'

'Of course. I'll get changed as well.'

'Me, too.' Charity was already heading for the stairs and Petra sent them a grateful smile, thankful that they'd got ready for the wedding here, rather than in their own houses.

Amos toed off his shiny shoes and Petra glared at him. 'Don't even think it,' she warned. 'I need you to take care of Amory.'

'I can do that,' Lena said.

Petra widened her eyes at the woman, and Lena caught her meaning.

Lena said, 'But maybe it's best if Amos has him. The poor little mite is bound to pick up that something is wrong.' She handed the baby over to Amos, and Petra sent her a small smile of thanks.

The last thing Petra needed right now was Amos overdoing it and having an angina attack. She'd have enough on her plate in getting the horses down from the top field. She could already hear the occasional whinny of distress through the open window as the animals picked up the scent of the growing fire. If she didn't act soon, they might bolt and injure themselves.

'There,' Megan said, indicating that Petra could take the dress off, and Megan hurriedly helped her out of it.

Not in the slightest bit self-conscious as she stood there in her lacy underwear, she shouted up the stairs, 'Hurry up!' and when she heard October coming down them she held her arms out for October to fling her clothes down to her.

Petra knew they didn't have a moment to spare as she dragged the jodhpurs on and yanked the tee shirt over her head. She put the wellies back on and stuffed her phone into her pocket.

Nathan was already leading Storm and Midnight to the lower field where they'd be safe for the time being, having unharnessed them as soon as he'd become aware of the situation.

He'd thrown his top hat onto the seat of the carriage, his suit jacket following, and had started to unbuckle the horses, Luca helping. She knew the two men would catch up with her as soon as they were able.

'Let's go,' she urged, heading for the door.

'What can we do to help?' her dad called after her.

'Make tea, lots of tea. I've got a feeling we're going to need it.'

With October and Charity by her side, Petra raced into the tack room and grabbed an armful of lead ropes.

'Here.' She thrust them at her stable hands, and reached for some more.

If push came to shove, she'd ride one of the horses down and herd the others, but she'd prefer a more orderly descent. It all depended on how far and how fast the fire travelled, and on how successful the fire fighters were at blocking it. The smoke was already thicker, the breeze carrying it down the hillside to sweep across the valley below.

She shot out of the tack room and ran across the yard, skidding to a halt when she heard the sound of engines coming up the lane.

Harry was in the lead with Timothy (she was grateful for the vet's presence but prayed there would be no need for his professional services), but she was surprised to see Isaac and Nelly in the car behind. She gave them a quick smile, before turning her attention back to Harry.

'We're going to bring the horses down now,' she told him. 'Nathan and Luca have just taken Storm and Midnight to the bottom field.'

'I'll park the car and follow you up,' Harry said, and just as she was about to shoot off, he added, 'I love you.'

'I love you, too,' she called over her shoulder, wishing she had time to tell him how handsome he looked in his morning suit.

She was racing up the hill, breathless and anxious when her phone rang.

It was Amos. 'I've just spoken to Harry and he's on his way, but I've asked Timothy to check on Walter. I'm not sure how fast the fire is travelling, and he may have some injured sheep on his hands.'

Damn! Walter! The elderly gent would have trouble rounding the critters up, she knew.

'As soon as the horses are safe, we'll head back up and see what we can do to help with the sheep,' she said.

'Isaac and Nelly are here – as soon as they've got changed, I've suggested they go with Timothy. They can help hold gates open and whatnot.'

'Okay, let me know how they get on.'

'Will do. And Petra? Take care, eh?'

'I will,' she promised.

'Isaac? Isaac? Answer your goddamn phone, son.' Stephen left a message and glared at his mobile. He assumed that as he couldn't get through, Isaac must already be at the stables.

He didn't like to think of him up there, not with a grass fire bearing down. Although there weren't many trees and he didn't think the situation would be as bad as the wildfires in California and Australia that had been on the news in the past, he knew from when he and Julie were up on that very same hillside a couple of weeks ago, that the bracken was head height and tinder-dry. Flames could sweep through it and the dried grass at a rate of knots.

He bit his lip, worry coursing through him. Then he cursed himself for being silly.

It was unlikely that the stables themselves would be in any danger, and he hadn't seen much about it on social media, so it couldn't be that bad, so surely he was fretting over nothing. He doubted that the farm further up Muddypuddle Lane would be at risk, either

But he still couldn't prevent himself from fussing. No matter how old your kids were, you still worry about them, he thought, trying to convince himself that he was overreacting, and he sat down at the table again and eyed the pile of exercise books with dislike. Then sighing heavily, he got to his feet once more and began to pace, and every so often he'd look at his phone as though he expected it to magically burst into life.

Should he try Isaac again?

Stephen shook his head. It would be pointless. When Isaac got a signal he'd call. Until then, he'd simply have to wait.

But that was the problem – he *couldn't* wait.

He was worried, and no amount of telling himself he was being silly would stop him.

Amos! He'd answer, surely?

Hastily Stephen looked up the phone number for the stables and dialled it.

'Hello?' Amos sounded flustered.

'It's Stephen Richards, Isaac's dad. Sorry to bother you, but I wondered if everything was all right? I spoke to Isaac and he said he was on his way to help. Has he arrived yet?'

'He has. He and Nelly have gone up to the farm at the top of the lane to see if the bloke who owns it needs a hand.'

That's what Stephen was worried about. 'He's not answering his phone,' he said.

'I expect he will when he gets to Walter's farm. Parts of the lane can be a dead spot. Sorry, I've got to go, I can hear sirens.'

'Sirens?' Stephen asked, but Amos had already rung off and dread flared in his chest and caught in his throat.

He couldn't stay here and fret – he'd wear a hole in the carpet.

He dialled Julie's number, his heart leaping traitorously when she answered. 'Have you heard from Isaac?' he demanded without any preamble.

'No, why? What's happened?'

'There's a fire on the mountain above the stables,' he said. 'It's on the local radio.'

He heard Julie's exasperated sigh and winced. 'You had me worried for a minute,' she said. 'He's nowhere near the stables. The wedding is taking place in Picklewick. I do hope the stables will be okay though – but I'm sure it will be. These things usually burn themselves out, don't they?'

'Not always. The radio said the fire brigade are at the scene.'

'There you go, then. I don't know what you're worrying about.' She sounded cross.

Stephen sucked in a deep breath. 'I've just spoken to Amos. Isaac isn't in Picklewick; he's gone to the stables to help. And Amos had to ring off because he heard sirens.'

Julie was silent for a second. When she spoke, her voice was strained. 'Pick me up in five minutes.'

Another wave of unease swept over him.

Julie hadn't tried to convince him he was being silly: she was just as anxious as he.

'Timothy?' Harry yelled into his phone. 'Can you hear me?'

He and Petra were heading back up the lane after depositing the last of the ponies in the field. They'd had a bit of a to-do because two fire engines had come racing up the lane as they were coming down it, sirens blaring and blue lights flashing, and the four ponies she and Harry had been leading had spooked. They'd had a devil's own job to calm them down. Nathan was in the field now, checking them over.

Petra swiped a loose strand of hair from her face, and pursed her lips. Harry had been trying to call Timothy on and off for the past fifteen minutes without any luck.

Each time Timothy answered, the phone would go dead. Mostly, he failed to answer at all.

'I'm going up there,' Harry said.

'I'll go with you.'

'No.'

Petra blinked. 'You can't tell me what to do,' she objected. If Timothy was in trouble, she didn't intend to sit on her hands and do nothing.

'No,' Harry repeated. 'It's too dangerous.'

'If it's too dangerous for me, it's too dangerous for you,' she reasoned. Fire fighters were tackling the blaze on two fronts, and gusts of smoke-laden air poured down the hill, hot and acrid.

For the first time since she'd realised there was a problem, Petra began to fear for the stables. She was desperate to go up there to see the situation for herself, so she could decide whether all the other residents of the stables needed to be evacuated, human and animal.

At the moment they were safe enough, and Walter's farm was still standing, but seeing the fire engines race past had given her the heebie-jeebies.

'You need to stay with Amory,' Harry said, and fear stabbed her in the stomach as she heard the subtext behind his words – they couldn't risk something awful happening, and for Amory to be without both his parents.

'Don't go,' she said, catching hold of his arm. 'Please.'

'I have to. Timothy is up there.'

'It's not that dangerous, is it? I mean, they would have said. They would have evacuated Walter if it was.'

'It probably isn't,' Harry said. 'But I don't want to take any chances. Watch out!'

Harry yanked her to the side as three ewes careened past and charged off down the lane. 'Nathan!' he yelled, waving his arms.

Nathan was closing the gate, and he looked up when he heard his name being called.

'Sheep!' Harry shouted, cupping his hands around his mouth. He pointed vigorously, and Nathan nodded to show he understood.

Petra saw him open the gate as the sheep came into view, and she watched in relief as he shepherded them into the field. They'd be okay in there for now. If they'd had made it as far as the road, it could have been a disaster.

Harry's phone ringing made her jump, and her heart was in her mouth as he hastened to answer it.

'Timothy!' he cried. 'Are you all right?'

There was a crackle then, 'cut off... Isaac and Nell... shelter... valley... for now... fire...' That was all they heard before the line went dead.

Petra looked at Harry in horror. 'What do you think that meant?'

'That Isaac and Nelly have got cut off? With or without Timothy. God, if anything happens to him, I don't know what I'll do.'

'Go,' Petra urged, against every instinct she had. She wanted to drag him back to the house and force him to stay there until it was safe to go back outside, but she knew he had to find his brother.

'Nathan!' she cried, as her stable manager caught up with them. He was breathing hard and looked tired. 'Harry's going up the mountain,' she told him. 'Timothy tried to phone but the line was dreadful. We think he might have got cut off. Isaac and Nelly, too. Go with him?' She looked at Harry and Nathan followed her gaze. 'Keep him safe?' she pleaded.

Nathan gave her a keen look and nodded once.

Petra let out a breath. He knew what she meant.

Dear god, she prayed as she watched them walk away, please don't let anything happen to them.

'Any news?' Amos pounced on Petra as soon as she stepped through the door.

Julie stared at her, seeing the tightness around the woman's eyes and the tense set of her jaw. Petra was worried, which made Julie worry even more. She and Stephen had arrived about twenty minutes ago and she'd been on pins ever since.

Petra glanced at her then looked away, holding her hands out for the baby, and when he was safely in her arms she nuzzled the fine hair on the top of his fuzzy head.

That brief look made Julie's blood run cold. 'What is it?' she demanded, catching Stephen's eye and seeing her own fear reflected in their depths. He'd noticed it, too.

Ever since he'd phoned to tell her that their son might be in danger, she'd been scared out of her wits. She knew it was unlikely Isaac would come to any harm, but you heard such dreadful stories and after the things she'd seen on the news, she didn't want him anywhere near a wildfire, no matter how small it might be.

The sirens had set her heart racing until October and Charity had come in to say that the noise had been made by a couple more fire engines going up the hill. Julie had thought it might be an ambulance and dread had caked her heart in ice.

'Where's Luca?' Petra asked.

'He's at the farm, digging up the field above it,' October said.

Petra nodded. 'Good thinking. I didn't know he could drive a tractor?'

'Amos gave him a crash course.'

'Why is he digging up a field?' Julie demanded. What use was that? Luca, whoever he was, should be out there, trying to put this damned thing out.

Amos explained, 'Bare earth will create a firebreak, stop it in its tracks.'

'Walter wanted to use his ploughshare,' October said, 'but it was rusted to hell. I remembered we had one in the barn, so I suggested he used that. Anyway, he looked dreadful, really unwell, so it's better if Luca does it.'

'I'm going back out,' Petra announced, gently placing her son in Megan's arms. 'I can't stay here and—' She broke off and sent Charity the same look she'd given Julie a few moments ago.

'What is it?' Julie felt sick, her skin clammy, her heart pounding. 'What aren't you telling us?'

'Where's Timothy?' Charity was staring at Petra, her eyes wide with fear.

'He's…um…I don't know,' Petra admitted. 'Harry has gone to look for him. Timothy tried to phone, but we couldn't hear him properly. He kept breaking up. I…er…think they might have got cut off.'

A moan rose up in Julie's chest and into her throat. She turned to Amos. 'Didn't you say Isaac and Nelly were with Timothy?' And when he nodded, his eyes brimming with sympathy, the moan escaped her lips.

Suddenly she felt strong arms around her, holding her tight. 'They'll be all right,' Stephen crooned in her ear. 'They'll be all right, I promise.'

'You can't know that.' Julie twisted around to face him. 'Don't make promises you can't keep.'

His gaze was intense as he stared deep into her eyes. 'I never do.'

She looked away, blinking back tears. What a time to bring up the fact that she'd broken a fundamental one of hers.

As if reading her mind, he whispered. 'That's not what I meant.'

'Isn't it?'

Before he had a chance to reply, Petra's phone rang. She was half out of the door, but she stopped and took it out of her pocket.

The kitchen was totally silent as she said, 'Harry?'

Julie saw Petra's shoulders sag, and she bit back a sob.

'Thank the lord!' Petra cried. 'Where were they…? And you're sure they're all right? How about everyone else?' She stepped back into the room, her face wreathed in smiles, and gave them a thumbs up.

Julie slumped against Stephen, feeling weak with relief, and his arms tightened around her as he held her up. She was shaking and tears poured down her face.

Petra's eyes widened and her mouth dropped open. 'Are you serious? If you think we can… Oh, you have, have you?… I can't wait—' Abruptly Petra stopped talking and a blush spread across her face. 'I…erm…have an audience,' she said. 'I'll be ready… Of course they can – the more the merrier. But are they sure the fire is out?'

Julie was hanging on Petra's every word, and so were the others. Even the baby was staring intently at his mum, his little chin wet with dribble.

Petra pulled a face and dropped the phone in her pocket. 'That was Harry,' she told them.

'We gathered that.' Amos raised his bushy eyebrows. 'What's the news?'

'The news is that Timothy, Isaac and Nelly are fine. They got caught in the small valley not far from the old farmhouse, so they sheltered in there until the fire passed by. Harry said they got a bit hot and Isaac singed his eyebrows, but they're okay. It was starting to burn itself out at that point, because one of the appliances had saturated the vegetation. They're on the way back. Oh, and you'd all better get changed and clean yourselves up – I'm getting married in an hour!'

CHAPTER NINE

'Doesn't she look beautiful?' Julie whispered in Stephen's ear, her eyes on Petra as Amos helped her climb into the carriage.

'She certainly does,' Stephen agreed, although he secretly thought that Julie had actually been more beautiful on their wedding day, but maybe he was biased.

'I can't believe they've managed to pull it all together in an hour,' she said. 'Even with everyone pitching in, it took some doing.'

It certainly had. Stephen had watched in amazement as Petra had been whisked off upstairs by her bridesmaids. Amos had got on the phone to some chap called William and had arranged for the food for the reception to be sorted out. Nathan, the bloke who managed the stables, had grabbed hold of a guy called Luca as soon as the poor fella had stepped inside the door, and had marched him back out again, saying something about getting the horses hitched up to a carriage. And when Harry and Timothy arrived, it had only been to collect the car and dash off to Timothy's house to get cleaned up. Petra's parents had gone with them because according to Petra's mother, it was going to take a miracle to sort Harry's suit trousers out.

To be fair, most of the flurry of activity had gone over his and Julie's heads, because they only had eyes for their son and his girlfriend, and Julie had smothered Isaac in so many kisses that he'd joked he wouldn't need a wash to get rid of the soot and dirt.

'You look a right state,' Julie had said to Isaac when she'd calmed down a bit. Nelly didn't look much better, but at least the pair of them had been wearing borrowed clothes and not their wedding outfits. 'What happened exactly, and why were you anywhere near the fire in the first place?'

'Can we talk about it later?' Isaac suggested. 'We've got to get to the church.' He'd looked at his borrowed clothes and grimaced.

Julie had wrinkled her nose. 'You need a shower – you smell like a bonfire in an allotment.'

Amos said to Isaac, 'Why don't you and Nelly go and get cleaned up in the cottage next to the one Julie and Stephen stayed in? In fact, why don't you go with them?' he said to Julie. 'Come to the wedding – the more the merrier. I think half the fire department will be there too, although I suspect they'll be more interested in the food afterwards rather than the ceremony.'

So that's what they did. Julie confessed she felt a little self-conscious because she wasn't wearing a dress, but Stephen assured her it didn't matter.

He wasn't exactly dressed for the occasion either, with his faded jeans, old chambray shirt and scruffy trainers. But he didn't care. Isaac and Nelly were unhurt, no one had been injured (apart from a daft sheep who had tried to leap a fence and had got tangled up in some wire), the stables and the farm at the end of the lane were also safe, and the wedding was going ahead, although rather later than planned.

Did it matter what they wore?

'I suppose not,' Julie said after he'd said the same thing to her, 'not when you put it like that.'

'Come on, we'd better get going if we don't want to run the risk of arriving at the church *after* the bride,' he said, as the bridesmaids all piled into Luca's Range Rover.

'What a day!' she exclaimed as they hurried towards Stephen's car. 'I certainly never expected all this drama when I got up this morning. I've never been so scared in all my life.'

'Me, neither.' The thought of losing Isaac had been more than he could bear. The fear had been indescribable. He wanted to hug his son to him and never let him out of his sight again.

It came as no surprise to realise that he felt the same way about Julie.

He loved her – he always had done – and the weekend they'd spent at Petra's cottage had made him realise how utterly bereft he felt without her.

So why was he being so stubborn about things?

Julie had hurt him deeply, but he was no longer convinced that she was still pining over her lost love. She'd seemed so happy the morning after the fete, until he'd told her that making love to her had been a mistake. He'd seen how broken she was, and he'd turned his back on her.

Had he been a fool?

The thought that he might have had crept over him when he'd been standing in Amos's kitchen, his arms around her, as they waited to hear whether their son was safe. And he'd had a sudden vision of how he'd feel if he lost Julie too. What if something were to happen to her? What if she became ill? He was finding it hard enough to plod through each day as it was – he'd fall apart if Julie died.

It was a macabre way to view things, but neither of them was getting any younger and every day brought news about people their age passing away. Life was so damned short and could be very cruel, and it had taken Isaac being in danger to make him see that.

Stephen knew he could never forget the hurt Julie had caused, but he could – and did – forgive her. They had been so young and it had happened such a long time ago. Was he prepared to let the past sour his future?

He had to tell her how he felt, and maybe they could start over – this time without any secrets between them.

But now wasn't the time. It could wait until later. Right now they had a wedding to go to.

Petra swallowed nervously. This was really happening – she was getting married! After the events of earlier, she didn't imagine the wedding could possibly go ahead, but Harry – wonderful, handsome, thoughtful Harry – had asked the vicar to put the ceremony on hold, vowing it would take place today. He'd had such faith that everything would be okay, it had made her heart melt.

So here she was, standing outside the church, with her maid-of-honour handing her a bouquet of pale pink and white roses, and grinning madly at her. Amos took his place on her right, her dad on her left, and the bridesmaids behind, in the traditional manner.

Everyone else was already inside, including Nathan, who had handed the horses over to one of the vets who owned the practice where Timothy worked. Petra couldn't imagine getting married without stalwart, dependable Nathan being there to witness it.

The organ which had been playing holding music in the background, struck up the Wedding March, and Petra lifted her chin. She no longer cared whether all eyes were on her. She no longer minded being the centre of attention. All that mattered was that she was marrying the most wonderful man in the world, and she knew everyone was happy for her. Picklewick had come together to make sure her beloved stables was safe, and she was consumed with gratitude for the generosity and selflessness of the villagers.

'Ready?' Amos asked. He was beaming with pride, and she kissed him on the cheek. She gave her dad a kiss too, not wanting him to feel left out. She mightn't have had the best relationship with her parents in the past, but this was a new beginning, and she knew they were happy for her.

'Ready,' she said, and slowly and surely she walked into the church and into her future.

'I know this is a stables and that we're in the middle of an arena,' Julie said, 'but I didn't expect horses to be here.' When Lena had said that Petra lived and breathed horses, she hadn't been wrong.

The horse-drawn carriage that had driven the bride to the church and had brought her and Harry back to the stables had been a lovely touch. But Julie wasn't so sure about seeing a whole herd of the beasts being ridden around the arena by a load of children.

Petra though, was clearly thrilled.

The tables for the wedding guests had been laid out at one end of the large space, and Julie had assumed the other end was meant for dancing – although how anyone would be able to strut their stuff on a floor made of bits of rubber was beyond her.

But no...the area had been kept free for a parade of horses, all decked out with flowers in their bridles. They seemed to be doing some kind of a strange co-ordinated dance, to music no less!

'It's called dressage,' Lena said, seeing her confusion. 'October has been getting them to practice for weeks. It hasn't been easy, because she was only able to do it if Petra was out on a hack. A ride in the hills,' she explained, as Julie's confusion deepened.

'Aw, look, it's the donkey!' Julie cried. Gerald had a panier on his back and was being led to each table for the guests to take a favour out of the basket. 'You liked the donkey, didn't you, Stephen?' She remembered how Stephen had scratched the animal's ears. They'd just returned from a walk, on their first day in the cottage. Such a lot had happened since then – but nothing had actually changed.

She and Stephen were still estranged.

Julie felt a tear or two in her eye and she fanned a hand in front of her face, willing herself not to cry.

'Are you okay?' Stephen asked. He'd been remarkably attentive throughout the course of the ceremony and the reception, and she didn't know what she was supposed to feel or how she was supposed to react. Looking at them, anyone could be forgiven for thinking he doted on her, when the opposite was true.

'I'm fine,' she replied, adding, 'what is it about weddings that make people so emotional?' She didn't want him to think she was upset because of him.

'Perhaps it's because they remember their own, or they wish they were getting married to the love of their lives,' he said.

Julie knew what he was referring to, and even though she knew it wouldn't make the slightest bit of difference, she wanted to put the record straight once and for all.

The horses had been led away, and different music started up. It was a song she vaguely recognised, "Wild Horses" by Natasha Bedingfield, and she saw Harry hold out his hand to his bride. Petra had taken her shoes off and her feet were bare. She looked delirious with happiness and another lump came to Julie's throat.

'Emrys isn't the love of my life,' she said. 'You are.'

Stephen was staring at her with such intensity it scared her.

But when he didn't reply, her heart shattered all over again. He could at least acknowledge her.

Tears blurring her vision, she scrambled to her feet. Other people were rising to theirs as they took to the dance floor, and she dodged around them, desperate to escape. She had to get out of here, she had to get away from Stephen.

Before she had taken more than a few steps, a strong arm caught her around the waist and spun her on her heel. 'Let go,' she began, thinking it was Isaac.

It wasn't.

Stephen had hold of her, and there was such a look of love on his face that it stole her breath.

He said, 'You are the love of my life, too. I don't want to live another day without you in it. I love you, Julie, and I realise that you love me, that you always have.'

She opened her mouth to tell him how much she loved him but she didn't get to say the words, as his lips claimed hers and he kissed her with everything he had.

When he finally pulled away, his eyes dark pools of love and longing, and said, 'Let's get out of here. We've got a whole world to explore – together,' Julie felt the flames of hope reignite in her heart, and she knew she'd follow this man to the ends of the earth and back.

She'd finally laid her ghosts to rest, and she couldn't wait to spend the rest of her life with the man she'd married all those years ago.

CHRISTMAS

CHAPTER ONE

Amos walked slowly down the stairs, gripping the handrail and wincing at the ache in his right knee. It was playing up something rotten this morning, and he reminded himself to add some ibuprofen gel to the shopping list. He'd pop into Picklewick later and pick up a few bits and pieces, and he'd pay a visit to the care home whilst he was there. He liked to call in once or twice a month, knowing that the residents welcomed his visits. Actually, it wasn't so much they wanted to see *him* – they loved seeing Queenie, Petra's black Cocker spaniel.

The dog in question was curled up in her basket next to the fire, he noticed, as he entered the kitchen. Patch, the little Jack Russel terrier that belonged to Nathan, the stable's general manager, was also crammed in with her. Both dogs opened their eyes when they saw him and Queenie wagged her tail, but neither got out of bed and he didn't blame them. It might be seven-thirty in the morning, but it was pitch-black outside and freezing.

Amos pulled a face. He was late on parade again. Petra, Harry and baby Amory were already up and getting on with their day. Lately Amos was finding it hard to get out of bed in the mornings. He might blame it on the time of year, but he had a nagging suspicion that age was creeping up on him. Seventy-three wasn't old, not these days, not when pop icons who were older than him were still touring and actors in their seventies and eighties were still churning out block-buster films, but try telling that to his stiff joints and aching back.

As the day wore on and he moved around more, he would gradually loosen up, but right now he felt like a mechanical metal toy that had rusted up and needed a good dose of oil.

'Morning,' he muttered, smelling the mouth-watering aroma of frying sausages. 'If you'd have waited, I'd have cooked those.'

Harry was at the stove, a wooden spatula in his hand. 'It's okay. We were up, so I thought I'd make a start on breakfast. There's tea in the pot.'

Grumpily, Amos took a seat at the scarred wooden table and Petra smiled at him. She had little Amory on her lap and the baby's face lit up when he saw his great-great-uncle, and he held out his chubby arms.

Petra passed the baby over. 'He slept through again last night,' she said. 'I think we've cracked it.'

She still looked tired, but not as exhausted as previously. Mind you, Amos wasn't surprised that she was knackered: what with the stables to run, a six-month-old baby, and a new holiday let business to get off the ground, she'd had a busy few months. And she'd even managed to get married in the middle of it.

Harry hadn't been slacking, either. He'd done what he could around the stables whilst continuing to work as a farrier, and he also did his fair share of looking after the baby – which was why Amos felt guilty for sleeping late again. Because of his angina, Petra wouldn't let him do any physical work, so the least he could do was keep his little family fed. The kitchen had become his domain, and although he knew he was being silly, he resented anyone else cooking in it.

'Sausage sandwich?' Harry asked.

Amos wasn't resentful enough to turn down a sausage sandwich. 'Yes, please. Red sauce.'

'That's so wrong,' Harry joked. 'It has to be brown. Everyone knows that. Here you go.' He put a plate in front of him.

'Ta.' Amos picked up half of the sandwich, careful to keep it out of the reach of grabby starfish hands, and took a bite. Not bad, he conceded. If he wasn't careful, he'd be out of a job.

'I'm going into Picklewick this morning,' he said, between mouthfuls of the butcher's finest pork and beef sausages and his own bread, baked fresh this morning. His final task every evening was to fill the bread maker, so the family could wake up to a freshly baked loaf. 'Would you like me to take Amory?'

'It's okay,' Petra said. 'I'm planning on spending today in the office, so he can stay here with me.'

Amos didn't show it, but he felt a little aggrieved. Paperwork was his job, too.

'Oh?' was all he said.

'It's about time I got to grips with the accounts,' she explained. 'It's not fair leaving it all to you.'

'I honestly don't mind doing them,' Amos said, but even as the words left his mouth, he understood Petra's reasoning. He wasn't getting any younger and at some point she'd have to take over. It made sense for her to start now. If he suddenly popped his clogs, she wouldn't know where to begin.

'I know you don't,' she soothed. 'But I expect you've got other things to do today.'

Not much, he thought. Aside from a bit of shopping and cooking the evening meal, he was at a loose end. He supposed he could defrost the freezer, but it was currently full of festive food so it would probably be better to leave it until after Christmas. He could always clean the oven. However, there was one thing holding him back – it was a job he hated doing and invariably put off for as long as he could.

'I'll finish my breakfast,' he said, 'then I'll see to the chickens.'

They were let out of their coop every morning to roam free during the day, then rounded up again in the evening so the foxes didn't get them. He'd heard one barking last night when he'd woken up to go to the loo, but had then taken ages to get back to sleep. Gone were the days when he'd slept like the dead and woke refreshed in the morning. These days he was more like the walking dead!

Petra made faces at her son, who chortled back at her. 'It's okay, Nathan has already done it. One of the holidaymakers wanted to take a dozen home with them and they are leaving early, so I asked him to pop some down to them before they go.'

'Right.' Amos's voice sounded flat. Considering there was always something that needed doing when there were loads of animals to look after, there seemed to be surprisingly little for him to do. Or should he say, there was little that Petra *allowed* him to do.

Maybe 'allowed' was the wrong word – after all, the stables belonged to him, although it would go to Petra once he was gone – but she fussed over him so much if she thought he was over-exerting himself that it simply wasn't worth the hassle. Anyway, he knew she was right, and he didn't want to risk an angina attack. Gentle pottering was what he had been reduced to these days; and to think that when he was younger he never used to think twice about throwing bales of hay around or wrangling a stroppy horse.

Things had moved on since then, some for the better, such as Petra coming into his life and baby Amory, and others not so good. Top of the not-so-good list was losing his wife to cancer. Whoever had said that time was a great healer was a big liar, because Amos missed Mags as much now as when she'd first passed. More so, because he couldn't help wondering what she would have made of all these changes.

For years he and Petra had been on their own at the stables, apart from Nathan, but when Harry had taken over old Ted's farrier business a couple of years ago, their lives had been turned upside down. First, Harry had moved into the stables with them, then shortly after he had dreamt up a new business venture in the form of converting an old cow shed into holiday lets, and on top of that, Petra had discovered she was pregnant. Amory had arrived early, bless his little cotton socks, and then she and Harry had got married.

This past year had been all go, so Amos should be thankful that things were now on an even keel and they had a chance to draw breath. Instead though, he felt unsettled and out-of-sorts, and he had no idea why.

Oh, how he wished Mags was still alive.

But if wishes were gold, he'd be a rich man, so there was nothing for it but to get on with it. At least he'd be able to cheer up some old folk this morning.

The irony that he was probably only a few years younger than the residents themselves, wasn't lost on him.

'How is Mum today?' Lena Rees asked as she approached the reception desk in the foyer of Honeymead Care Home and glanced around at the glittering Christmas tree in the corner, decorated in gold, and at the fairy lights draped around the large mirror on the wall next to it. It all looked very festive, as was the smell of berries and cinnamon perfuming the air. But she wasn't in the mood for Christmas. Her mum hadn't been herself lately and Lena was worried.

Charity Jones was manning the desk this morning and she looked up from her computer screen and smiled. 'She's had a good night, I believe, and she's eaten some breakfast. A bit of porridge and some fruit.'

'Grapefruit?' Lena asked, hopefully. Half a grapefruit was her mum's favourite, even though it sometimes gave her heartburn.

'No, just a couple of raisins.' Charity's smile was sympathetic. She was as aware as Lena, that Olive's appetite had decreased steadily since the summer, and Lena felt like crying. Her mum was fading before her very eyes and there was nothing anyone could do about it. Old age, the doctor had said. His smile had been sympathetic, too.

'She's in the day room,' Charity informed her. 'I tried to persuade her to have her nails done because we've got a manicurist in today, but she wasn't keen.'

Her mum wasn't keen on anything these days, Lena thought. 'I'll make her a cup of tea, then go on in,' she said.

'I'll bring it through, if you like?' the girl offered. The care home had a cafe area, where residents and visitors alike could help themselves to hot drinks, cakes and biscuits.

'That's kind of you, but I can manage. You've probably got lots to be going on with.' Lena had a great deal of time for Charity. She was a lovely girl, and was only a few years younger than Lena's own daughter, October. October worked at the stables on Muddypuddle Lane as a groom, and Charity also helped out there in exchange for stabling her horse.

Charity was a favourite of her mother's too, and she and Olive had originally bonded over Charity's tales of the antics the animals at the stables got up to. Plus, Charity brought cat food in for Marmalade.

It had worried Lena to death when her mum had been caught sneaking food out of the dining room. She used to secrete roast potatoes, pieces of fish, and on one occasion even a dollop of trifle, in her pockets. Lena had been convinced that Olive must be suffering from dementia, until Charity discovered that her mum had been feeding a stray cat.

Lena had still been a little concerned about her mum's mental health, because Olive was quite savvy when it came to animals and she should have been aware that cats didn't like trifle. But Lena was wrong. The cat did indeed like trifle. It also liked mashed potato, cheese, cake (but only if it had buttercream icing on it) and blackberries. Lena had stood corrected, and was no longer concerned about the state of her mum's mind. If anything, the old lady was sharper than she was.

Lena was very worried about her mum's physical health though, because the old lady had been growing noticeably frailer over the past few months, and Lena had a horrible feeling that she mightn't be around for much longer.

The thought of being without her mum filled her with dread. Her mother had been such a rock over the years, especially when Lena had discovered she was pregnant all those years ago and the baby's father hadn't been interested. Olive had shored her up, in more ways than one, and had convinced her that she was totally capable of raising a child on her own.

They had always been close and they still were, and Lena simply couldn't imagine life without her mum in it.

But she knew there would come a time when she'd have to do more than imagine, because Olive was ninety-three, and was lately showing less and less interest in things. She seemed to be withdrawing into herself, and not even the excitement of putting the Christmas decorations up had lifted her out of it. She used to love Christmas so much, unlike some of the other residents who did nothing but grumble about the festive season, that it gave Lena even more reason to worry.

When she stuck her head around the day room door, Lena spotted her mum sitting in front of one of the large picture windows – her favourite spot of late – with a black spaniel at her feet. The old lady was bending forward to pet the dog's silky head. It was the most interest she'd shown in anything for weeks and Lena's spirits rose.

Her mum loved animals, and the highlight of her week was when Amos came to visit. Sometimes he brought

Petra's baby boy too, so Olive had a double dose of cuteness.

Amos would work his way around all of the residents who wanted to stroke the dog, but he always seemed to spend more time with Olive.

'Hi, Mum, how are you today?' Lena asked, putting the cups of tea down on a side table, and planting a gentle kiss on the wrinkled cheek.

'Not so bad,' her mum said, but Lena could tell she wasn't being entirely truthful.

Trying not to let her worry show, she turned to Amos. 'Hello, Amos, how are you? I've brought you both some tea,' she lied. She had a soft spot for Amos, and she would happily forgo a cup of tea so that he could have it instead.

'You're a gem,' Amos said to her, taking a sip. He looked tired, not his usual bubbly self, and a ripple of unease travelled down her spine.

'Where's the baby today?' she asked and saw his expression cloud over.

'He's with his mum. She's in the office this morning, so my services aren't required.' He looked crestfallen and she wondered why that should be an issue. She knew he loved the baby to bits and enjoyed looking after him, but surely this was only for one day? No doubt Petra would be back in the saddle tomorrow. Literally, because she would probably take one of the horses out for some exercise.

Lena's unease continued to linger. She knew all about Amos's angina and she prayed that his heart wasn't giving him any more trouble. She also knew that Petra, Harry, Nathan, and her own daughter, all made sure he didn't exert himself, and she vowed to give October a ring later to ask if she knew what was wrong.

'I'd better do the rounds,' he said, gesturing to an old gent who was staring intently at the dog.

Lena smiled. 'You better had. Brian adores Queenie.' Brian was a lovely old man who suffered with dementia. Prior to moving into the home, he'd had a dog, and Lena knew how badly he missed the animal. But he increasingly forgot that his dog had been rehomed, and when he remembered, the poor chap broke his heart all over again.

Her gaze followed Amos and Queenie, and she saw Brian's face light up as he ruffled the dog's ears.

In contrast, her mum's expression was blank. She was staring out of the window, her eyes distant.

'You love Queenie too, don't you, Mum?' Lena said in a jolly tone.

Her mother twitched a shoulder, which Lena took as a yes.

She bit her lip and tried again. 'What did Amos have to say for himself? Any funny stories about the animals?' Her mum loved hearing about what the horses and the other creatures who lived at the stables got up to.

Olive brought her attention back to Lena with a tangible effort. 'Amos was telling me about Princess.'

'What has that flippin' goat been up to now?' Lena sing-songed. She knew she sounded like an adult talking to a child, but she couldn't seem to help herself.

'She managed to get into the boot room and ate one of Amos's flat caps.'

Ah, that was better: her mum seemed to have perked up a bit.

Lena laughed. 'The little madam! I've never come across such a naughty animal. And she's teaching her kid bad habits too.'

'I want to go outside,' Olive said abruptly.

'Er, okay. If that's what you want, I'll get your coat. You'll need a hat and a scarf, as well. But are you sure? The garden doesn't look its best at this time of year, and it's not very nice out there. In fact, it's freezing. Brrr,' she added, theatrically.

'I don't want to go into the *garden*.'

Lena was confused. 'Where do you want to go?' she asked, before realising what her mum wanted. 'Oh, I see, do you want to go out to lunch?'

Until recently her mother had been able to shuffle around using a walker, but over the past few months her mobility had worsened. It would be difficult to load the wheelchair into the car, and get her mum in and out of the passenger seat, but Lena would manage somehow.

'I don't want to go out to lunch. Or shopping. I want to go *there*.'

When Lena followed her mother's gaze, she sucked in a sharp breath. Olive was staring at the view, which consisted of rolling hills leading up to the moorland. She could just make out the stables from here and Lilac Tree Farm above it.

'You can't!' she cried.

'Why not?' Olive's chin jutted out like a sulky child.

Lena floundered. Where should she begin? 'It's just not possible.'

'Amos could take me.'

'*Amos?*'

'He lives at the stables, doesn't he? He could drive me. I want to smell fresh air and heather, and I want to feel the wind in my face again before I die.'

'Mum! Don't say that!'

Her mother gave her a keen look. 'It happens to all of us – some sooner than others. I've had a good life and been blessed with a wonderful family, but I'd like to see horses again.'

'I've got some photos on my phone. October shared them with me—'

'That's not what I mean and you know it,' her mum interjected. 'I've not got long left, Lena. I just want to…' She ground to a halt, then waved her hand in the air and sighed. 'Ignore me, I'm just being silly. Tell me, what are you going to do with the rest of your day?'

Lena blinked as the abrupt change of topic caught her by surprise. 'Erm, I don't know.'

'Why don't you go have some fun?' Olive suggested.

'Fun?'

'Yes, you know…do something you enjoy, something that brings you happiness.' When Lena continued to gaze at her with a stricken expression, her mum tutted and rolled her eyes. 'I'm tired,' she said abruptly. 'You get off home. I think I'll have a nap.'

'You've not long got up,' Lena protested. It was only ten-fifteen.

'Yes, well…'

The animation in her mum's face had drained away and Lena felt like crying, because she knew in her heart that her mum was right – she *didn't* have long left.

The thought was unbearable.

'Excuse me,' Amos said to Brian, as he saw Lena hurry out of the day room. She looked upset and he couldn't let her leave without asking if there was anything he could do to help. 'Queenie, come,' he commanded. 'I'll be right back,' he promised the old chap.

Queenie leapt to her feet and followed obediently as Amos hastened after Lena.

He caught up with her just as she was about to step outside. 'Lena!' he called. 'Wait.'

Lena halted but she didn't turn around, and when he reached her, he realised why.

She was crying.

'Whatever is the matter?' he asked.

Lena blinked furiously. 'It's nothing.'

'It is clearly *something,*' Amos said, gently taking hold of her arm. 'Why don't we go over there, where it's nice and quiet and have a cup of tea?'

Lena sniffed and allowed him to lead her to a chair in a quiet corner of the cafe area. He fetched her a cup of tea and one for himself, and sat down opposite. 'Now, then,' he said. 'What's all this about?'

Lena looked up at the ceiling, blinking furiously, her chin wobbling. 'It's Mum. She says she doesn't think she's got long left.'

'Ah.' Amos pulled a face. He had also noticed that Olive had become more distant over the past few months, but he hadn't liked to say anything.

'She's right,' Lena added. 'I've been thinking the same thing myself, but it shocked me when she came right out and said it.'

'I expect it did.'

'The doctor says old age is catching up with her.'

'Is there anything I can do?' he asked, guessing the answer would be no, but offering anyway.

Lena gave him a small sniffling smile as she dabbed a tissue to her cheeks. 'Not unless you can turn back time.'

'If I could do that, I'd have done it already,' he said, his thoughts gravitating towards Mags.

'I suppose you would. I'm sorry, that was thoughtless of me,' Lena said, and Amos immediately felt awful.

'There's nothing to be sorry for,' he hastened to assure her.

'At least my mum has had a good long life,' she said, wiping away her tears and blowing her nose.

'October tells me she used to ride. As did you,' he said, turning the subject away from his wife. Although he usually loved talking about Mags as a general rule, for some reason it didn't feel right discussing her with Lena.

'She did,' Lena said, and Amos was relieved to see that she was no longer crying. 'Mum was a pretty good horsewoman in her day, if I remember rightly,' she added.

'What about you?' Amos had known Lena ever since she had moved to Picklewick about ten years ago to look after Olive. She had helped with clearing the cow shed prior to the builders coming in, and she had been there for him when Petra had gone into early labour. In fact, Lena had insisted on making sure that the nursery was ready for little Amory when the baby was eventually discharged from hospital. She had also helped organise the surprise reception for Petra and Harry's wedding, and she had stepped in to help when the wedding was delayed because of a grass fire.

But he didn't really know her as well as he should, and when the sudden thought that he would like to get to know her much better and in a way that wasn't at all platonic, popped into his head, his eyes widened and his breath caught in his throat.

Fancy him having thoughts like this at his age! After Mags died, he'd assumed that this kind of thing was behind him. Apparently not. Which was daft considering that only this morning he had felt every one of his seventy-three years and then some. He should be past all this nonsense at his age, but here he was fancying a woman nearly ten years younger than him and one who had so much life left to live. She would never give an old codger with a dicky heart a second glance.

'I haven't ridden for years,' Lena was saying. 'I used to love it, but life kind of got in the way.'

'So that's where October gets her love of horses from – you as well as Olive?' He hadn't known Lena could ride, although he knew that Olive used to. It had been a good few years since he'd been on the back of a horse himself.

Lena smiled. 'It's more than love with October, it's an obsession.'

Amos nodded his understanding. Lena's daughter had worked at some of the best show jumping yards in the country, but she had never quite made it in that highly competitive world. She had come to work at the stables on Muddypuddle Lane nearly a year ago, after having left her previous position under a bit of a cloud. Neither he nor Petra had expected her to stay long, but she'd fallen in love, and the rest, as they say, is history.

To Amos's consternation, Lena's eyes filled with tears again.

'This will be Mum's last Christmas,' she said. 'I can feel it!' She slapped a hand to her chest, above her heart. 'I wish I could do something to make it special for her. Maybe I could take her to a show, or something?' Lena pulled a face. 'Or maybe not – she was never one for musicals or the theatre. You'll never guess what she said just now: she told me she wants to smell the fresh air and feel the wind on her face, and she wants to see a horse again. As if that's going to happen.' She sniffed and dabbed at her eyes once more. 'Oh, well, never mind.'

Slowly Amos said, 'Maybe we can work something out? How about if I speak to William and ask if it's possible to bring Olive to the stables? Do you think that will be allowed?'

Lena frowned as she thought. 'I don't see why not. The residents are often taken out on trips if they're up to it. I believe some of them are going to the panto next week.'

'Oh, no, they aren't,' Amos chorused, earning himself a shake of the head from Lena at his pathetic panto-inspired joke.

'Are you sure about this?' she asked.

'Definitely! She can be wheeled into the yard to see the horses close up, if she doesn't mind the cobbles, and the views from there are stunning, as you know.' His eyes suddenly widened as a thought occurred to him. 'Do you think any of the others might enjoy a trip to the stables?'

'I've no idea. Brian might – he was quite taken with Gerald last year.'

'Most people were,' Amos said. 'It's not often a donkey rocks up at Honeymead.'

'I suppose not.' Her expression lightened. 'You looked very convincing in your Santa outfit. Will you dress up as Father Christmas again this year?'

'I'm not sure that's a compliment,' Amos chuckled. 'You're right, though – I *am* old and whiskery, but I'm not as cuddly as Santa.' He patted his stomach, pleased that he only had a small paunch and had had to shove a cushion inside the jacket of his Father Christmas outfit last year to make it look more authentic.

'I think you look very cuddly,' Lena declared, then blushed when she realised how it sounded. 'That didn't come out right. I'm not saying you're overweight. What I meant was... oh, dear!' She looked mortified.

'I do give rather nice cuddles,' Amos said, trying to make her feel better. 'Ask Amory.'

She shot him a grateful smile and changed the subject. 'Do you really think you can arrange for the residents to visit the stables? It's not the sort of place they normally get taken to, and I'm not sure how much they'll get out of it, apart from my mum. She'll love it.'

Lena had a point, Amos thought. It wasn't as though the stables had a tearoom or a cafe, and considering they couldn't wander around the yard, the only thing they'd be able to do would be to sit in the gallery and watch a lesson, or watch Petra lead a couple of ponies around the arena for them to take a gander at. Hardly riveting, was it?

Unless...?

He could always provide mince pies and hot chocolate, and what if Petra put on a mini show, like a kind of gymkhana?

'I've got an idea,' he said, abruptly. 'I'm not going to tell you what it is, because it mightn't get off the ground yet. But if it does...'

'No. Definitely not.' Petra was adamant. She looked horrified. 'What on earth are you thinking? Holding a nativity play at the stables for an audience of care home residents isn't going to work. Admittedly, we've put on nativity plays in the past, but they were just for the parents and were only a bit of fun. Anyway, I've got too much to do as it is, without putting on a damned play.'

'*You* don't have to do anything,' Amos told her. 'October and Charity are more than happy to organise it.' He winced as he said it. He was trying to present Petra with a fait accompli because he knew she wouldn't be keen on the idea, so he had already asked the girls to help, and they had seemed quite keen.

Petra lifted the saddle off Parsnip's back, and steam rose from the pony's coat where it had rested. Scooping up a handful of clean straw, she proceeded to rub his fur dry. At this time of year the pony was as fluffy as a teddy bear, and the exercise, plus his thick winter coat of long cream guard hairs, had made him sweat. Amos guessed that she would probably pop a rug on him before she turned him out into the field for the afternoon.

'*They* might be happy about it, but I'm not,' she said. 'Christmas is only three weeks away. There's not enough time. And even if there was, having a bunch of OAPs in a drafty arena catching their death of cold, isn't a good idea. The viewing gallery isn't at all suitable. And what about those poor souls who can't travel? It's not fair for them to miss out.'

Amos cleared his throat. 'Ah, now, I've thought about that. Luca says he can live stream it.'

Peta narrowed her eyes. 'Am I the last to know about this?'

He knew he was looking sheepish. 'Not quite. I haven't told Nathan yet.'

'Because you know that he'll tell you it's a silly idea, too,' Petra pointed out.

'I haven't spoken to him because he's repairing the dry stone wall at the top of the field by Walter's house, and it's too cold to walk all the way up to Lilac Tree Farm.' Amos blew on his hands as though to demonstrate just how cold it was, but Petra was right and she knew it. He added, 'Megan said she'll bake a cake or two.'

'You've spoken to *Megan*?' Petra's voice rose an octave. Oh, dear…

'I bumped into her in Picklewick.' Amos gave his niece an innocent smile, but he knew she wasn't fooled. The 'bumping' had been pre-planned.

'What does William think?' Petra had a triumphant look on her face, but if she thought she'd won this argument, she was sadly mistaken.

'He thinks it's a great idea.' Amos tried not to smirk. The care home manager had been all for it.

'Then he's even more of an idiot than you,' Petra snapped. In a softer voice, she added, 'It's a lovely idea and a wonderful thing to do, but it's simply not feasible.'

'I thought we could involve some of the children from the local primary school,' Amos continued as though she hadn't spoken. 'They could be the choir.'

Petra finished fastening Parsnip's rug and patted the pony on the neck. 'You've thought of everything, haven't you?'

'I've tried to.'

'Why are you so set on doing this? It's not as though the care home ignores Christmas. They put on lots of things, and you could always take Gerald to see them, like you did last year.'

Suddenly Amos didn't feel so sure of himself, and he shuffled his feet and his gaze dropped to the ground. He wanted to put on a nativity play for the residents of the care home out of the goodness of his heart, but there was another reason – he had a soft spot for Lena. A very soft spot indeed, and he hated to see her so upset.

'Er, it's because of Olive,' he said.

'Lena's mother?'

'Yes. Lena reckons this will be Olive's last Christmas and she wants to do something special for her. You see, Olive used to ride a lot when she was younger, and she loves hearing me talk about the stables, and Lena said…' He trailed off, heat creeping into his face, as he realised how enthusiastic he sounded.

Petra was scrutinising him intently, and he cleared his throat and scuffed the ground with his foot.

'I've not seen you this animated since the wedding,' she said. 'I was getting worried about you. You seemed to have fallen a little flat lately.'

'Aye, well, maybe I just needed something to get my teeth into,' he mumbled. 'A bit of a project. You know how I like to keep busy.'

He wasn't lying, but he wasn't being strictly truthful either. His enthusiasm was as much to do with Lena, as wanting to give himself something to do.

Petra placed a hand on his arm. 'Okay, if it means that much to you, we'll hold the damned nativity play. But just be careful, eh? I don't want you overdoing it.' She paused and a slow smile spread across her face. 'Say hi to Lena for me, next time you see her.'

Her expression left Amos wondering whether Petra had guessed that he had more than a friendly interest in the woman in question.

CHAPTER TWO

Amos was unaccountably nervous about speaking to Lena this morning.

He thought it might be because he'd had such trouble talking Petra round. Nathan, once he knew about the proposed nativity play, had also added his two-pence worth into the conversation. It had taken a while for Amos to convince the stable manager that it was a good idea, but he'd got there in the end and eventually Nathan had come around to his way of thinking, despite his initial grumpiness that he had enough work to be getting on with at the stables as it was, without adding a last-minute nativity play to his never-ending list of jobs.

Actually, Amos didn't want Nathan's involvement – apart from moving the odd chair and bale of hay – and neither did he want Petra's interference. He wanted to do this himself, with a little help from October and Charity who would sort the ponies out, and a lot of help from Lena. He was going to enjoy spending time with her. *If* she agreed to help, that is. Because he hadn't asked her yet, and there was the possibility that she might say no.

Tentatively, and with his heart in his mouth, he rang her doorbell.

When she opened the door and saw him on the step, she looked taken aback. 'Hello? I thought you were a delivery driver,' she said.

'I am in a way. I'm here to deliver some good news, I hope.'

'You'd better come in.' She stood to the side and held the door open.

Amos went inside and waited for her to close it behind him, then she led him down a small hall and into a living room.

It was alive with colour and lights, and for a moment he was taken aback. This lady certainly did like Christmas. There was a tree in the bay window, which he had noticed when he was dithering about knocking on her door, and a garland was draped around the mantlepiece, which also had twinkling lights threaded through it, illuminating acorns, berries and little felt-covered robins, and some knitted stockings hanging from it. Above the fireplace was a mirror, which was also adorned with a garland with yet more fairy lights, and there were Christmassy ornaments on the mantlepiece itself.

And that was just the start of it.

Through another doorway he saw a dining table which was nearly obliterated by a whole range of decorations and neatly wrapped presents, and he did a double-take.

Lena saw him staring. 'Excuse the mess. I was in the middle of putting the trimmings up.'

'Sorry. I can see you're busy. I'll call back another time.'

'Oh, no, you don't. I'll be on pins for the rest of the day wondering what you wanted. Anyway, I was about to break for some lunch. Would you care to join me?'

'Er...I...um. Yes, please,' he decided. 'I'd like that very much.'

'It's only soup,' she warned.

'I like soup. What kind?'

'Mushroom. I made it myself. And there's some cheesy bread to go with it.'

'Lovely!'

'Come through to the kitchen, and you can tell me why you're here while I heat it up.'

Thankfully the kitchen was devoid of anything Christmas-related, apart from a bowl of nuts with their shells still on them, a nutcracker in the shape of a reindeer, and a festive tea towel. The room was light, modern, and spotlessly clean, unlike the kitchen at the stables. It put him to shame when he thought of the open fireplace, the dogs and cat, the scruffy old armchair, and the clutter that he seemed to be constantly clearing away.

'This is nice,' he said, after Lena had indicated for him to take a seat at a small table in the corner. He sniffed appreciatively as the aroma of garlic and onions began to fill the air.

'It's too big for me now that October's moved in with Luca,' she said. 'It's got four bedrooms and two reception rooms, and I'm sick of cleaning them – although they might come in handy when I have grandchildren.'

'Is that on the cards?' October hadn't mentioned anything about being pregnant, and although he would be thrilled for her, Amos hoped the stables wasn't going to lose her just yet.

'I wouldn't be surprised. She and Luca have been together for nearly a year now, so it looks like it's serious. I'm expecting them to get engaged soon.'

'Doesn't time fly? I was only thinking the other day that it'll soon be a year since she started work at the stables.'

Lena ladled soup into a couple of bowls and placed one of them in front of him. She popped the cheesy bread between them on the table and sat down.

Spoon in hand, she said, 'Tuck in, and while you're eating you can share the good news.'

Amos ate a mouthful of soup and closed his eyes in delight. 'This is delicious. You must give me the recipe.'

'Not until you tell me why you're here!' she cried, laughing. 'You can't keep me in suspense like this.'

Amos reached for a slice of bread. 'You know that idea I had yesterday? The one I couldn't tell you about in case it fell through?'

She nodded, her eyes searching his face.

'The stables is going to put on a nativity play and all the residents of Honeymead are invited. William is on board with it, so all we've got to do now is make it happen.'

Lena put her spoon down, resting it on the edge of her bowl. 'When you say *we*…?'

'Me and you.' Amos was grinning so widely he thought his face might split in two. 'What do you think?'

'I don't know anything about putting on a play. Are you expecting me to act? I'm a bit old to be Mary, although I'm sure little Amory would make an adorable Baby Jesus, and you do have a donkey you can use.'

'I'm going to ask the kids who come for riding lessons if they would like to be in it. We've laid on nativity plays in the past, so I expect they'll be up for it. What do you think?' he repeated.

'I think it's a lovely idea…'

'But?'

'The arena is freezing. And what about those old folk who are not very mobile? How are they going to manage in the gallery?'

'I've thought about that,' Amos said, taking another mouthful of the delicious soup. 'Hot water bottles, patio heaters and blankets. Oh, and nicer chairs. Those hard plastic ones are so uncomfortable.'

'Where are you going to get nicer chairs from?'

'William estimates that we will need about twenty-five, and he's got seventeen old ones we can use, as long as we supply the transport – they're in storage in a shed at the moment. We have two up at the house, and we can borrow the rest from the cottages and from…er…you, or Nathan, or anyone who's willing to lend us one really. And some of the old people, like Olive for instance, will be in a wheelchair, so they'll sit in those.'

'You've really thought this through, haven't you?'

'I've tried to think of everything, but I expect I've missed something.'

Lena thought for a moment, then said, 'Let's eat this before it gets cold, then we'll have a chat about it. If we're going to do this, it has to be done properly.'

Amos grinned. She mightn't have said yes, but he simply knew she was going to agree to help. After all, this whole thing was for her mum's benefit.

But giving the folks in the home a nice afternoon was only part of it. The other part was the thought of having Lena with him every step of the way, and he couldn't wait to get stuck in.

When Amos had appeared at her door, telling her he had some news and looking very pleased with himself, Lena had been expecting him to say that he'd arranged to drive her mother up to the stables. Thinking back, she could simply have asked October to give her a hand in getting her mum in and out of the car, especially since she worked there. Lena felt certain there wouldn't have been an issue with having an old lady call in to see a horse or two, so there really wasn't any need to have involved Amos whatsoever.

But when he'd relayed the news that he was planning to put on a nativity play, she had been astonished. It was simultaneously a lovely idea and a worrying one. She had no doubt that the kids would have a wonderful time, but she was concerned about the elderly care home residents. Still, if William was fine with it, then maybe she should be too. He was far more qualified to assess the risks and the needs of the residents in his care, and he was blimmin' good at what he did. She had never heard a single complaint about the home or the way it was run. In fact, it had a reputation for being one of the best in the area, and Lena knew her mum was in excellent hands and was very well cared for.

'Okay,' she began, after she had cleared away the lunch things and Amos had wiped up whilst she'd washed the dishes.

They were sitting at the table with a slice of rich, aromatic Christmas cake in front of them. Lena considered having a mug of hot chocolate to go with it, but thought tea might be better for her waistline. At her age, it was far easier to put weight on, than to take it off.

'We should make a list of everything that needs to be done, the order in which it needs doing, and the timeline,' she began.

Amos blinked owlishly. 'It's all sorted, more or less.'

'It's the *less* bit that concerns me. If you want this to run smoothly, you can't leave anything to chance.'

'It's only a little nativity play.'

'You do realise that relatives may want to come too,' she said. 'Especially the parents of the children taking part.'

Amos blinked again. 'I never thought of that. But that's only a few more people to accommodate, surely?'

'Maybe, and maybe not.' Lena's mind was buzzing with possibilities. Not only did she want to make what was probably her mum's last Christmas extra-special, but she had an idea to help Amos and the stables.

'I was thinking bigger,' she said, and when she told him her idea and saw his face light up, she clapped her hands in delight.

Amos had been looking down in the dumps recently, and this seemed to have perked him up no end. She hadn't liked to admit it, but she had been worried about him. Ever since Petra and Harry's wedding he had seemed subdued, not his usual self, and she'd been concerned that his health might be deteriorating. Seeing him come up with the idea of putting on a nativity play and being so full of enthusiasm for it, warmed her heart. He appeared ten years younger, and she was struck, not for the first time, by how attractive he was for an older man.

He was in his early seventies, nine years older than her, but she supposed he could be described as a silver fox. However, it wasn't his weather-beaten features or upright bearing that was the most attractive thing about him – it was his kindness. He didn't *have* to call into the care home and sit with the old folks a couple of times a month, but he did it anyway out of the goodness of his heart. Neither did he have to put the wheels in motion for a nativity play – once again, it was pure altruism on his part. The stables had nothing to gain from it, apart from a lot of hassle, so when an idea had popped into Lena's head as a way of saying thank you, she leapt on it.

'Right,' she said, pulling a notepad out of a drawer and fetching a pen. 'Shall we work backwards from the event itself, make a list of what needs doing and when it needs doing by, then we can divvy them up.'

Amos was staring at her, concern on his face. 'Are you going to have time for this? I honestly don't mind doing it on my own.'

'Of course I've got time; far too much of it, as it happens.' Since her mum had gone to live in Honeymead, Lena had more time on her hands than she knew what to do with. Visiting Olive every day only took up a couple of hours, and she was often scratching around for things to do. She wished she enjoyed baking, like Megan, but every cake she made turned out flat, and although she pottered in the garden there was a limit to how much weeding, mowing or planting she could do. Besides, it was winter, and she really didn't want to work in the garden in this weather. It would be a welcome change to have something to get her teeth into, and she'd enjoy working with Amos. In fact, she couldn't wait to get stuck in.

'If you don't mind me saying,' Amos began, 'I get the impression you've done this kind of thing before.'

'You could say that,' she chuckled. 'I used to be a project manager for a rather large company. This stuff is second nature to me.'

'If I'd have known that, I would have just mentioned the idea, then let you get on with it. You can clearly do this on your own,' Amos grinned.

She could and she might have done, if not for one thing – she was looking forward to spending time with Amos. And she wasn't entirely sure why, although she did have her suspicions.

Amos was bubbling with excitement as he headed back to the stables. Lena's idea was grander than anything he could have dreamt up himself, and he marvelled that the little nativity play which had originally been meant for a few elderly folk, might become a village-wide affair. It was going to be hard work, and it might prove impossible to pull off in such a short amount of time, but they would give it their best shot.

He and Lena had been hard at it all afternoon, and he'd marvelled at her organisational skills. At one point he had seriously wondered whether he was surplus to requirements, a feeling of déjà vu creeping over him as he thought of how he'd felt yesterday morning when faced with Petra and Harry getting on with things without him, but he had soon changed his mind when she'd issued him with a variety of tasks.

It was too late to start on them today though: he needed to get back to the stables to prepare the evening meal. Briefly he wondered how Petra had managed without his help this afternoon. Had she stayed in the office, working on the accounts, or had she been forced to take the baby with her when she tacked up the ponies that were being used for this evening's lessons? Or did Harry not have any clients today?

Amos felt guilty for abandoning his niece, but he also felt a sense of freedom. He'd had the whole day to himself.

It was strange, but not unwelcome. Usually, he was only away for a couple of hours and then he would return, eager to do his bit, conscious that although Petra might run the stables, the business was ultimately his responsibility.

Maybe it was time to hand the reins over to her?

But then again, what would he do with himself all day? The stables was the only thing he'd known for all of his working life.

He hadn't set out to own horses, and he hadn't had any dealings with the creatures at all until he'd met Mags. He had lived in a small town on the east coast with his older brother and parents, and had only really been interested in having fun. But when he'd taken a trip into Great Yarmouth with a group of friends, he had met Margaret. She had been on holiday with her family, and he'd been captivated by her. So much so, that he had slept on the beach that night so he could meet her for breakfast the following morning. Talk about a whirlwind romance! He had followed her halfway across the country to a little village called Picklewick and had married her within six months.

He had been surprised to learn that she lived on a farm with her parents, and he'd been even more surprised to discover that he enjoyed working outside with the animals. But what he really loved (aside from Mags herself) was her horses.

She'd already started offering hacks onto the hills, and gradually the stables side of the farm became more important than the sheep-rearing side, until eventually the stables on Muddypuddle Lane was born. Amos had taken to it like a duck to water, and had been a swift learner, immersing himself in everything and anything to do with horses.

After a period of time Mags's parents passed away, leaving the house and the land to Mags, and she and Amos had run the stables together, a self-contained unit of two.

He wished they'd had children but it wasn't to be, and if he was honest, he had been perfectly content with his life as it was – just him and Mags.

Then Mags died and Petra had come into his life, and Amos didn't know what he'd have done without her. She was like a daughter to him even though she was his great-niece, his brother's son's child. The stables would pass to her when the time came, and he knew he would leave it in safe hands, because it already was.

'There you are!' Petra exclaimed, when he stomped into the boot room and shed his waxed cotton jacket and flat cap.

Queenie leant against his legs and politely nudged his hand with her nose, asking to be petted.

Amory wasn't as polite. As soon as he saw Amos he shrieked at the top of his voice and leant towards him, his pudgy little hands opening and closing.

'I think someone is pleased to see you,' Petra said, as she handed the baby over to him for a cuddle.

Amos nuzzled his nose into the infant's fuzzy hair and breathed in the lovely scent of talcum powder and freshly changed baby. He could also smell the aroma of roasting chicken, and he gave an exaggerated sniff and raised his eyebrows.

'What can I smell?' he asked.

'I've put a chicken in the oven,' Petra said. 'I saw it in the fridge and guessed that's what we're having for supper.'

Amos was put out. It was *his* job to do the cooking, not hers. That was the arrangement – Petra saw to all the outside stuff, with the help of Nathan, October and Charity, and he dealt with all the inside things, such as the household chores, the cooking and the paperwork. It seemed he was being usurped at every turn, and he didn't like it.

Abruptly his good mood evaporated.

Maybe he *was* past his sell-by-date, after all?

CHAPTER THREE

Amos studied the list of tasks and sighed. All yesterday evening and throughout most of the night he had been having second thoughts about the nativity play. It still wasn't too late to change his mind, although he knew he would be letting a few people down – Lena being the most important. Luckily, he hadn't approached any of the children who attended riding lessons at the stables to ask if they would like to be involved, and neither had he spoken to the headteacher of the local primary school. The other good thing was that none of the residents of the care home knew. William might be disappointed, but Amos was sure he wouldn't be too put out. After all, if the nativity play didn't go ahead, William wouldn't have to ferry thirty or so residents up to the stables and back, with all the headache that would entail.

He'd speak to Lena this morning, he vowed, and tell her it was off. He wasn't looking forward to the conversation because he'd seen how enthusiastic she had been, but he was sure she would be alright once he explained the reason why.

Actually, what reason *was* he going to give?

He didn't want to tell her that the reason he had lost heart was because he was starting to feel useless and a burden at the stables. That was hardly a valid reason, was it? But valid reason or not, that was how he felt.

Amos checked the time. It was eleven a.m. and he guessed that at this time in the morning Lena might very well be at the care home. He'd leave it until a little later to pop in and see her, he decided. He could just as easily call her on the phone and tell her, but he thought it would be better face-to-face.

'Have you got any plans for today?' Petra asked as she breezed into the house, bringing a blast of cold air with her. Amos was giving the boot room a bit of a tidy. It was amazing how quickly mess seemed to accumulate. The boot room was an area just off the kitchen where coats were hung, boots were left (hence the name), and where the dog and cat bowls were kept. But it didn't end there: anything and everything usually ended up in this room, from sacks of chicken feed to garden implements. No sooner had he cleared the place out, than new stuff appeared. He supposed it was better than having it migrate into the rest of the house, but still...

Petra had shucked off her coat and was toeing off her Wellington boots. Queenie and Patch, Nathan's small terrier, were already heading for their usual spot in front of the fire, where Tiddles was already sleeping. The cat opened one gimlet eye, gave the dogs a threatening glare which they ignored, and went back to sleep.

'Amos? I asked if you've got anything planned for today?' Petra repeated.

His thoughts flew to Lena. 'Not really. Why, did you have something particular in mind that you want me to do?'

'Yes and no. Nathan will be doing the heavy lifting, but I need you to decide where it's to go.'

'Where's what to go?'

'The Christmas tree,' Petra said. 'I've usually put it up by now, but I'm glad I didn't because we'll need to locate it with the nativity play in mind.'

'About that...' He ground to a halt.

Petra had finally got her wellies off, revealing three pairs of thick socks. She kicked the boots into the corner, spotted the stern expression on his face, retrieved them and placed them neatly side by side underneath the row of jackets and coats hanging on the wall.

'Sorry,' she said. 'Hello, sweetie.'

This was addressed to Amory, who was in his bouncy chair gurgling happily. The baby chortled when he saw his mum.

'I thought I'd see if he wanted a quick feed, and have a cup of tea while I was here. And then we could go into the arena and work out where you want to put the tree. I don't think where we had it last year would work, not if we're going to have loads of people in the gallery all at the same time, because it would spoil their view. I was thinking about the far corner. It would make a nice backdrop, but I'll leave it up to you to decide.'

Petra seemed quite on board with the idea of the nativity play and Amos pulled a face. How could he now tell her that it wasn't going ahead? Especially since she and Nathan had taken quite a bit of convincing. He neither did he want to share the real reason with her. He knew how he felt and that his feelings were valid, but he feared that by saying them aloud he would sound daft.

'Wherever you think is best,' he said.

'Oh no, you're not leaving this one with me,' Petra stated firmly. 'This is your idea, so you're going to have to sort everything out. I've got enough to be getting on with.' She was smiling as she said it, but he knew she was right. She really did have enough to be getting on with.

She could be doing without all this, he thought. Although she had told him that the nativity play was his responsibility, he suspected she would nevertheless fret and worry about it, even if it was from behind the scenes. His niece had always been a bit of a control freak, which was a good thing considering that she now had two businesses to juggle, plus a baby. Was it fair on him to add yet another burden? In fact, it would be the perfect excuse not to go ahead with it. Petra might argue a bit, but he suspected she'd be pleased.

He was about to tell her his decision, when the phone

rang. Petra had just picked the baby up and was unbuttoning her shirt ready to give the little boy a feed, so Amos hurried to answer it.

'Hello, you're through to the stables on Muddypuddle Lane. How can I help?' There was always a pad and a pen next to the phone, and he picked up the pen in readiness.

'Amos?' It was Lena on the other end.

'Hi, Lena, I was going to pop over to see you later,' he began, but her excited voice cut through what he was going to say.

'I've just been on the phone to The Picklewick Paper,' she said in a rush, 'and they're very keen on covering the nativity play. They think it's a great idea, and they reckon it's the sort of thing their readers love at Christmas.'

'I see,' Amos said, his thoughts whirling.

'And I've also spoken with the headteacher of Picklewick Primary and she said she'd love to bring some of her pupils to sing a few carols. They're already doing rehearsals for the carol service on Christmas Eve in the church, so she said it's not any trouble. She sounded delighted, and she agreed that loads of parents and grandparents would want to come. She also said she would ask the children to make some flyers to advertise it.'

'Advertise it?'

'Yes, you know –leaflets that the pupils can take home to show their parents. If we're going to ask for donations to charity on the day, we're going to want as many people as possible to come. Have you spoken to Megan yet?'

'Um, no, not yet.' One of his tasks was to have a chat with Megan about making a Christmas cake to raffle, although he had already sounded her out about making cakes and mince pies to eat on the day. He was also supposed to be tapping up a shopkeeper or two in the village for more raffle prizes. 'Er, Lena—?'

'Is that Lena on the phone? Tell her I said hi,' Petra called as she walked past on the way upstairs, Amory in her arms.

'Say hi back for me,' Lena said. 'Sorry, I've got to go, there's someone at the door. Speak later. Bye.'

Amos stood there, holding a dead phone and wondering what had just happened.

'How's her mum?' Petra asked from halfway up the stairs.

'What? Er, oh…still the same, I think.' The speed with which Lena had moved was breathtaking.

'What did she want?'

'Just to update me on a few things to do with the nativity play.' Bugger! He could hardly back out now, not when Lena had already got the ball rolling. It was more than rolling, it was bouncing down a hill at breakneck speed.

'She's helping you, is she?'

'Um, yeah. Didn't I say?'

Petra smirked. 'No, you didn't.'

Crossly Amos slapped the phone down on the hall table. He caught sight of himself in the mirror above it and rolled his eyes at his reflection. It looked like the nativity play was going ahead whether he wanted it to or not.

'I'm just going to pop Amory into his snowsuit, then we'll go to the arena, yeah?' she said, resuming her climb to the first floor. Then she paused again. 'How about inviting Lena to the stables for supper this evening, and the pair of you can fill me in on what's going on – because I have a feeling there's more to this little nativity play than meets the eye.'

If only she knew the half of it, he thought with a resigned sigh.

Amos reached for the phone again…Petra was going to do her nut!

395

At least organising the nativity play was helping take her mind off her mum, Lena thought, as she dashed home to get changed. She had spent the afternoon at the nursing home, spending some time with her mother and the rest of it with various members of staff, William especially.

The whole thing had grown from a simple visit to the stables for a mince pie and a hot chocolate whilst watching some of the young riders put on a little play, to an event of epic proportions. She knew she had hijacked Amos's idea and it had run away with her a bit, but she couldn't seem to help it. She kept telling herself that she was doing this for her mum, but she had a sneaking suspicion she was doing it more for her own benefit. Lena wanted her mother's last Christmas to be special for several reasons – the main one was because Lena wanted to treasure the memory, but she was realistic enough to know that by keeping busy she was also keeping her fear of not having her mother around for much longer at bay.

What was she going to do without her? Lena had moved to Picklewick a decade ago to care for Olive when it became clear that she was struggling to live on her own, and Lena had looked after her ever since. Even though Olive was living at Honeymead now, Lena still spent a proportion of each day with her, because what else was she going to do with her time?

That was something else she was scared of – being alone. She had October, but her daughter was getting on with her own life. She had a job she loved and a man she adored, and although she made time for Lena, her mother wasn't October's priority. Which meant that when Olive passed, Lena's days would be all the emptier. And incredibly lonely.

Lena had already started to feel the bite of loneliness since her mum had moved into the care home last year, but she guessed that was nothing compared to the loneliness she would feel when she no longer had her mum to visit.

'Stop being so maudlin,' she muttered to herself as she rounded the corner into her street and spotted the festive lights twinkling in the windows of her little house. She had finished trimming up and was pleased with the results, even if she was the only one who would get to appreciate them. They always served to cheer her up, and her spirits lifted at the sight of them.

They lifted even more once she was inside and saw the full effect. No wonder Amos had done a double-take when he'd entered her living room. It was quite something, even if she did say so herself.

The Christmas decorations weren't the only reason she was feeling a little more chipper than of late. She had been invited to supper at the stables. Amos had phoned her this morning, to ask if she'd like to join them for their evening meal to discuss how the plans were coming along. Lena knew the invitation was for purely functional reasons because there was a great deal to do in a rather short space of time, but it was so rare for her to go out in the evening these days that she was really looking forward to it. It was also a treat to have a meal cooked for her, because since her mum had moved out, Lena sometimes simply couldn't be bothered to cook for herself.

'What do you mean *sometimes*?' she mumbled aloud, as she trotted upstairs to have a wash and to put on fresh clothes. *Often*, was more accurate. The toaster had become a firm friend, as had the ready meal section in the supermarket. And, to her shame, even heating one of those had become a bit of a chore. However, she had made some soup recently she recalled, and she would have had enough for a couple of meals if Amos hadn't helped her eat it. It had been rather fortuitous that she had been in a cooking mood that day.

She knew that Amos did the majority of the cooking at the stables, and she also knew he was good at it. Barbeque food, at least – he'd fired up the barbie (as the Aussies say) when many of the villagers had got together earlier in the year to help Petra clear the old cow shed ready for the builders to move in and turn it into three lovely holiday cottages.

Now, should she wear a dress, Lena wondered, opening her wardrobe door and peering inside. Or would that be too formal? She didn't want to look as though she was going to a fancy restaurant. But neither did she want to look as though she'd not made an effort.

A sudden realisation made her pause.

Who was she making the effort for?

Lena tried to convince herself that it was for her, but she knew deep down that it wasn't. She wanted to make an effort for *Amos*.

Oh, my…where had that idea come from?

Lena edged backwards until she felt the back of her knees touch the mattress, then she plopped onto the bed, the springs bouncing under her weight.

Amos, she mused, her mind filled with images of him – playing Santa Claus at the care home last Christmas, waving a fork around as he cooked burgers and sausages at the cow shed clearing, the stricken look on his face when Petra had gone into labour early, the way he gave each resident at the care home his full attention when he spoke to them…

He was a lovely man. Very kind, extremely thoughtful. And, despite having his family around him, Lena suspected he might be lonely. His wife, Mags, had died before Lena had moved to Picklewick, but Lena had heard that the two of them had been inseparable and that Amos had been devastated at her loss. He must miss her dreadfully still.

There was something else that Lena had become aware of, and it had only just hit her, which was why she'd had to sit down.

Not only was Amos a thoroughly nice man, he was also a handsome one. A *very* handsome one. One that she would like to see more of.

Considering she had been man-free for so many years, Lena felt quite giddy at the unaccustomed attraction she was feeling, and she had absolutely no idea what she should do about it.

That was lovely, Lena thought, as she ate the last mouthful on her plate, and she wasn't just referring to the meal, which had been delicious and cooked by Amos's own fair hands. Actually his hands were large and strong-looking and she wondered how they would feel on her— Stop it!

'Everything alright, Lena?' Amos wore a concerned expression.

'Yes, why?'

'You made a kind of groaning noise.'

Lena felt heat rush into her cheeks. 'Did I? Sorry. I was just thinking how delightfully full I am. I don't think I could eat another morsel.'

'Thank goodness for that! I thought I'd poisoned you.' He grinned at her. 'Does that mean I can't tempt you with a portion of chocolate pavlova with spiced pears?'

'Oh, go on, then. I'm sure I can manage some. It sounds yummy.'

'It is,' Petra said. 'I can vouch for that. Amos is a darned good cook. He'll make someone a wonderful husband.'

Lena assumed Petra was joking until she noticed Amos colouring up, then she caught Petra's eye and saw that Petra was grinning at her.

Lena didn't know where to put herself. Was that comment aimed at her? Or was she reading too much into it?

If it hadn't been for her realisation earlier that she was starting to develop a crush on the stables' owner, Lena wouldn't have thought twice. But here she was, thinking that Petra was right – Amos *would* make some lucky woman a wonderful husband. However, she was fairly sure he wasn't in the market for a wife.

And neither did she want a husband. She'd come close to it with October's father but it hadn't happened, and she was far too old to consider sharing her life now.

A little voice inside her head muttered about ending up a lonely old maid, but she ignored it. She was already an old maid, and she'd just have to find something to occupy her to stop her from getting lonely, wouldn't she.

Dessert tasted as wonderful as it sounded, and by the time she had spooned up the last mouthful, Lena really did feel like groaning. She was fit to burst and wished she had worn a looser pair of trousers. Saying that though, the ones she was wearing had been loose enough when she'd put them on a couple of hours ago.

Amos got to his feet to collect the dirty dishes and when Petra tried to help, he waived her away. 'You and Harry go have a check around and make sure everything is bedded down for the night. I can manage.'

'With my help.' Lena added. 'You don't think I'm just going to sit here and watch you clean up!'

'You're a guest,' Amos protested.

'Nonsense! I'm an old friend.'

'That you are,' Amos agreed, beaming at her. 'Not as old as me though!'

'When you get to be as old as we are, age is just a number.'

'Hmm.' Amos didn't look convinced, so she hastened to reassure him.

'You don't look a day over sixty,' she said. 'It must be all the fresh air and good food. Petra is right, you are a good cook.'

'I've got to do something to earn my keep,' he said. His tone was light, but Lena sensed something was bothering him.

'I think you probably do plenty,' she said.

400

'Not enough,' he muttered as he ran a bowlful of hot water.

Lena moved the pile of stacked dishes closer to the sink and looked around for a tea towel. 'Want to talk about it?'

Amos sighed. 'It's nothing.'

'It must be something for you to look like a cat that's lost her kittens.'

Amos barked out a laugh then sobered. 'It's just...I think...Oh, forget it. I'm just being a daft old codger,' he said.

'You are not a codger, daft or otherwise. And neither are you old. Seventy... what is it? One, two?'

'Three. I'm seventy-three.'

'Seventy-three isn't old. Seventy is the new fifty, apparently.'

'I wish! I feel more like ninety, these days.'

'As I said, you don't look your age, and neither do you act it.'

'Thank you for saying so,' Amos said, but he still seemed down in the dumps.

Clearly he didn't want to talk about it, but if he knew that he wasn't alone, he might open up to her. The animation which he had displayed while they were talking about the nativity play and the progress made in such a short amount of time, had leaked away, and she couldn't help but wonder why.

Conscious that it was none of her business and that she shouldn't pry, Lena nevertheless wanted to do what she could to help, even if it was only offering a shoulder to cry on.

'It's me who should be thanking you,' she began.

'Nonsense, Olive and the others deserve to have a great Christmas. Anyway, you're doing most of the work.'

'That's not why I'm thanking you,' Lena said, amused. 'Or rather it is, but I also want to thank you on behalf of myself. I've...erm...been a little down lately, and not just because I know I'm going to lose my mum soon.' Lena blinked, trying not to cry. 'You see, I've been rather lonely and at a bit of a loose end since she went into Honeymead, and I think I might have lost my way. This nativity play has given me something to focus on.'

Amos had stopped scrubbing a particularly stubborn pot and was gazing at her sympathetically. 'What will happen when Christmas is over?'

'I've no idea,' she replied truthfully. At the moment she was struggling to see past the nativity play. Or maybe she simply didn't want to. 'You're lucky having Petra and Harry living with you, and little Amory of course. I'll just carry on being lonely, I suppose.'

Amos continued to gaze at her, his expression intense. 'Can I let you into a secret? I'm lonely, too. Oh, I know what you're thinking – how can I possibly be lonely with my family around me? But I can, and I am. I feel surplus to requirements some days.'

Lena gasped. 'Petra isn't trying to kick you out of your own home, is she?'

'Gracious me, no! Nothing like that.' He looked so shocked at the idea that Lena believed him.

'You know I've got angina?' he said, and when she nodded, he carried on. 'I'm doing okay, as long as I keep taking the tablets and don't overdo things.'

He turned his attention back to scrubbing the pot, Lena hanging on his every word.

'The deal is that I do all the indoor stuff, like taking care of the chores, doing the cooking, and seeing to the bookings and the accounts, plus the shopping, pottering in my veggie patch, and since Amory came along, doing a fair bit of babysitting during the day. All this frees up Petra to see to the horses, teach the lessons, and so on. But lately…' He trailed off, and Lena noticed that his eyes were suspiciously damp.

'She has been doing some of the things that you usually do?' Lena guessed.

When Amos shrugged, she knew she'd hit the nail on the head. 'Is that so bad?' she asked gently. 'She probably thinks she's saving you a job.'

'I expect she does, but it makes me feel useless.'

'Is that why you've not been your usual bouncy self lately?'

'I'm never bouncy,' Amos objected.

'But you have been a bit down,' she persisted. 'I thought you might be ill.'

'No more than usual. You haven't been your usual sunny self either, but then how can you be when you're worried about your mum?'

'We're a fine pair, aren't we?' she smiled, holding her hand out for the recently washed saucepan. 'Where does this live?'

'In that cupboard, there.'

Lena gave it a quick wipe and popped it inside.

'I miss my wife,' he said suddenly, and Lena froze. 'I thought time was supposed to be a great healer, but I miss her more with each passing day. Seeing how happy Petra and Harry are just makes it worse. Does that make me a bad person?'

'It makes you human,' Lena replied gently.

'I remember how we were together and…' He stopped again. 'I miss someone of my own to cuddle up to, someone with the same frames of reference as me.'

Lena stroked him on the arm, unable to think of anything to say that might make him feel even a tiny bit better. She couldn't begin to imagine what he was going through.

'Has there been a special someone in your life?' he asked, his voice low.

'There was once – October's father – but it never came to anything. I can barely remember what he looks like now. How awful is that!'

'I wonder sometimes if it's better to have loved and lost, than never to have loved at all.' She envied the love that Amos and Mags had shared, even if the price of that love was the pain he still suffered.

'So do I.' Her reply was heartfelt. 'When October was little and even after she'd grown up, I was so busy with work that I didn't have time for a relationship.'

'And now?'

'Now?' She drew in a slow breath. 'I believe it's far too late. That ship has sailed long ago.'

Anyway, there was no one she could even contemplate having any kind of a relationship with. Then her gaze was drawn to the man standing at the sink, up to his elbows in hot, soapy water, and she thought that maybe there was...

However, even after all this time, Amos still only had eyes for his wife.

'I miss you, Mags. You don't know how bad it can get. It hurts me here. 'Amos thumped himself on the chest. 'And I'm not talking about the angina either, so get that out of your pretty little head.'

He replaced her photo on the bedside cabinet and gently stroked his wife's cheek with his finger. It was his favourite snap of her, taken when she wasn't looking at the camera but staring at something off to her left (he couldn't remember what) and her face was alive with laughter.

They had been so young back then, so full of hopes and dreams, and although some of those had failed to materialise (children, for instance) they had been so very happy together.

Mags had been beautiful too, even to the very end, when she'd been—

Gah! He didn't want to think of her that way. He wanted to remember her when she was young and full of life. Just as he used to be. But now he was old, and life was carrying on without him.

Still, he had enjoyed himself this evening, he thought, as he changed into his pyjamas. But having Lena sitting at the table in the very chair where Mags used to sit, had brought memories of his wife sharply into focus. Especially since he'd been talking about her to Lena. Although he talked to Mags's photo every night, many weeks would go by when no one else spoke her name, and he sometimes wondered whether she had been nothing more than a figment of his imagination.

'I hope I haven't scared poor Lena off,' he said, his gaze shooting to the photo again. 'She must think I'm a miserable old git. She's nice, you'd like her.'

Mags and Lena would have got on like a house on fire, he knew. Although he didn't know Lena very well, he had a feeling she and his wife were similar in many respects, both of them with a no-nonsense, get-on-with-it attitude, hiding a soft heart.

'She told me that Petra just thinks she's saving me a job. I still feel like a spare wheel, though,' and he smiled, hearing Mag's voice in his head telling him not to be such a daft sod.

'Yeah, I know I'm putting on a nativity play, so I can't be that useless, but so far, it's Lena who has done the lion's share of the work.'

Amos thought back to the conversation he'd had with Lena whilst they were clearing up. Had she been telling the truth when she said that helping to organise the play was giving her something to focus on? He knew she was worried about her mum, and for good reason, but Lena had always seemed so capable and together.

'It just goes to show that you can't go by appearances,' he said sadly. 'I would never have guessed she is lonely.'

He had just clambered into bed and was about to put out the light when he could have sworn he heard Mags whisper, 'As are you, my love, as are you.'

CHAPTER FOUR

If Mags were here, what would she do? Amos was standing in one of the outbuildings, thinking. If the shoe was on the other foot and she was alive and he was dead, what would she do?

He'd had the most dreadful night's sleep last night because he'd lain awake for most of it thinking about his wife. He'd mourned her for over a decade, never once looked at another woman since he'd lost her. He'd not wanted to. But now…

His emotions were all over the place and he didn't know what to think or how to make sense of how he was feeling.

However, this morning his first and foremost worry was Petra.

It wasn't fair for her and Harry to have to tiptoe around him. They needed their own space to be a couple, and not falling over him every time they turned around.

Until recently Petra and Amos had rubbed along together quite nicely in the farmhouse, each of them with their distinct and separate roles. Okay, so things did overlap occasionally, namely when Amos couldn't help interfering. Which was why he was relegated to the house and the garden most of the time, because he couldn't be trusted not to do something strenuous, like lift a bale of hay for instance. He knew Petra worried about him, but sometimes he just had to prove to himself that he wasn't a total invalid.

However, he might have been naive to think that nothing would change once Petra married Harry.

Everything had changed. For the better, he hastened to add. Without Harry, there would be no Amory, and no holiday cottages. And Petra wouldn't be happier than Amos could ever remember her being. He was so thankful that Harry had taken over old Ted's farrier business, because if he hadn't, Petra would still be lonely and alone. Not that she had ever admitted it, but he'd been able to tell. She had been adamant that she was perfectly happy with her life the way things were. But when Amos compared the Petra of then to the Petra of now, there was such a marked difference that it made him want to weep. These days she was glowing, joy shining out of her.

Amos remembered when he used to feel like that. When Mags was alive, every day had been a blessing, and he was so thankful for the time he'd had with her. They had been a unit, him and her, self-contained and not needing anyone else.

And this was the reason he was worried about Petra. Neither she nor Harry deserved to have him skulking around like the ghost of Christmas Past. They needed their own space to be a proper family, and they weren't getting it with him in the way.

It was definitely time he seriously thought about moving out of the old farmhouse. It would be a wrench to leave it, because he had lived in it for most of his adult life. It was full of memories of Mags, but now it needed to be full of memories of Petra and her growing family. Amos could take his memories with him. They lived in his head and in his heart. He didn't have to be in the farmhouse to remember his wife. Flipping heck, all he needed to do was close his eyes and there she was.

The question was, where was he to go?

It was because he was pondering this very thing, that he was now standing in one of the old outbuildings, the one that was currently used to store all those bits and pieces that farmers everywhere seem to accumulate, from broken pieces of equipment to old water troughs, to bits of wood, and everything in between. One of the reasons farmers tended to hoard things was because they never knew when something would come in handy. Another reason was that it was such a pain to get rid of it. He remembered clearing out the rubbish from the old cowshed, and as he stood there scanning the interior of this particular outbuilding, he noticed that quite a number of the items from the cowshed had ended up in here.

The outbuilding had originally been a feed store, and was built from the same stone as the farmhouse and the cowshed. It was in pretty good nick actually. It probably needed repointing, and no doubt it would need a new roof, but it was sizable, and if he put a door there and a window here, and a few partition walls obviously, it would make a very nice dwelling. A bungalow, that's what he was thinking, because he wasn't getting any younger. At his age he had to be practical and plan for the future. How much longer would he be able to negotiate the steep stairs in the farmhouse? How much longer would he be able to lever himself in and out of the bath?

A bungalow with wide doors just in case he needed a walker, a generous bathroom with one of those wet room showers, and a bath that was more suited to his advanced years, would be the sort of things he should be thinking about.

He would still be able to potter up to the house if he was needed of course, although thinking back over the past week or so, it seemed that he would be needed less and less. He could continue to do the accounts, the ordering, and the bookings, but only if Petra and Harry wanted him to.

Petra wasn't aware that he had overheard her chatting to Harry, but he had, and their conversation had been playing on his mind. Harry was a farrier, but as this year progressed, he had been doing less and less blacksmithing, and more and more helping out at the stables. With two businesses to run, Petra had a lot to contend with, so Harry was talking about selling his farrier business.

Amos thought it was a brilliant idea. But he was realistic enough to know that with Harry on site all day, every day, his own role would likely to be even more reduced. And actually, he was okay with that now. Talking to Mags had helped. And so had talking to Lena.

To think that she felt as lonely as he! He never would have guessed. He was lucky: if he did move into the old feed shed, he would still be at the stables and he would still have company if he wanted it. Lena, bless her, no longer had anyone living at home now that her mum had gone into Honeymead, and October had moved in with Luca.

Thinking of Lena, brought him to his other worry.

Actually, it was not so much of a worry, as a revelation.

Mags was right, he *was* lonely.

'What should I do, my darling?' Amos paused as though listening, and stuffed his hands into the pockets of his trousers, hunching down into his jacket.

He knew what he would tell her, if their situations were reversed. He would tell her that she had to start living again. That he would hate to think of her mourning him day after day. That she had too much love to give, to keep it locked in her heart. And that was what she would say to him, he knew it. In fact, she had said those very words not long before she died.

'Promise me you won't grieve forever,' she had breathed, her voice weak and barely there. 'Promise me you will find someone else to love.'

They were almost the last words she had said to him, and it was the last promise he had made to her.

But he hadn't kept it, had he?

He had wrapped his heart in sadness and grief, and told himself that this was the way his life would be from now on.

But these past few days (longer than that, if he was honest) he had started seeing Lena in a different light, and he could slowly feel the frozen depths of his soul thawing as his feelings for her grew.

It scared the daylights out of him.

He wasn't ready to move on, no matter what his heart was telling him.

Anyway, Lena didn't think of him in that way, so he'd just have to be content with being friends.

Lena looked up as a figure walked into the day room, ad her face broke into a wide smile as she saw who it was.

'Look, Mum, October has popped in to see you. Isn't that nice?'

October closed the distance in two strides, and plonked a sloppy kiss on her grandmother's cheek. 'Hiya, Granny. Have you had your hair done?'

'You have, haven't you? Just this morning,' Lena said.

'I've got a voice in my head. I can speak for myself,' Olive snorted crossly.

October sent Lena a sympathetic smile. 'You certainly can, Granny,' she said, dropping down into the chair next to her.

Lena quelled a sigh. She had been trying to cheer her mother up all morning, but nothing was working, not even this unexpected visit from October.

'You'll never guess what Princess did,' October said. 'She only went and—'

I don't care,' Olive interrupted.

'Pardon?' October's eyebrows shot up.

'You heard.' Olive turned away and stared out of the window, her lips pursed.

October mouthed, 'What's up with her?' but all Lena could do was shake her head.

'Shall I fetch us all a nice cup of tea?' Lena suggested. 'October, will you help me carry them?'

'No problem – did you know they've got gingerbread men and mince pies in the cafe, and I spied a bowl of marshmallows to go on top of hot chocolate. Would you like a hot chocolate instead, Granny?'

Olive refused to answer, and the only sign that she had heard was a further tightening of her lips.

'Okay, then.' October made a face. 'A cup of tea coming up.'

As soon as they were out of the room, October said, 'I thought Granny would be pleased about the nativity play.'

'I haven't told her yet. None of the residents know. Amos and I wanted to make sure we had all our ducks in a row before William told them. I'd hate for the play to be announced and for something to go wrong, and it not to take place.'

'What could go wrong?'

'Bad weather, for one thing.'

'But nothing else, surely?'

'Hopefully not. Ooh, that hot chocolate does look nice.' Lena's eyes were drawn to a wizened old lady sitting at one of the tables with a giant mug of hot chocolate in front of her. It was oozing with whipped cream, marshmallows and tiny gold balls.

'Can I make you one?' Rose, the office manager asked. 'They're proving to be very popular.'

'I bet they are! Go on, then, I'd love one, please,' Lena said.

'October? And how about Olive? Would she like one?'

October grinned. 'How can I say no? But I think Granny would prefer tea. I'll fetch it, while you see to the hot chocolates.'

October wandered off in the direction of the hot water dispenser, leaving Lena with Rose.

'What are you doing for Christmas?' Rose asked. 'Apart from organising the event of the year!'

'I was hoping to have lunch here. The kitchen put on a lovely feast last year.'

'I'll put your name down, shall I?'

'Please.' Honeymead allowed visitors to share meals with the residents as long as the care home was given enough notice, which was a wonderful touch and meant a lot to the old folk and their families. Lena would have lunch with her mum, then go home and cook another meal for herself and October to enjoy later.

Oh, wait…

'October, what are you doing for Christmas lunch?' Lena called to her.

'Er…'

Lena saw the panicked expression on her daughter's face, and said, 'It's okay, I understand. You'll want to spend your first Christmas with Luca in your own home.'

'Do you mind? We'll pop over to see you in the morning.'

'That's fine. I'm having lunch here with Granny anyway, so it'll save me having to cook.'

Last year October had just moved back to Picklewick and was staying with Lena, so the two of them had eaten turkey with all the trimmings later in the day, after Lena had returned from the care home. She'd never felt so stuffed in all her life, having eaten two Christmas lunches, so in a way she was pleased that this year she'd only have to eat the one. Still, she knew she'd be lonely with the rest of the afternoon and evening ahead of her with only the telly for company.

There was no way she was going to let on though – she didn't want October to feel guilty. Her daughter had her own life to lead; Lena couldn't expect to be involved in everything, and at least she was seeing both October and her mum on Christmas day, which was more than could be said for some people, who might not see a single soul.

Her thoughts went to Amos who, despite having his family around him, would also be feeling lonely. It was depressing how one could be in a roomful of people and still be alone, she thought.

After she'd finished here, she'd give him a call to thank him for inviting her to supper last night.

'What are you doing right now?' Amos asked when Lena phoned to thank him for supper. It was a nice gesture and he appreciated it.

'Nothing. Why? Did you need me for something?'

'I was wondering if you'd like to meet me in The Black Horse for a bite to eat? I'm popping into the village, and I thought I'd treat myself to a pub lunch. Petra and Harry are having a takeaway this evening, and I'm not too keen on curry, so…What do you say?'

'I'd love to. What time?'

'About half an hour?'

'Great. I'll see you there.'

Amos rubbed his hands together with glee. This would be a rare treat indeed. Lunch out with a beautiful woman who he liked more than was good for him, wasn't to be sneezed at.

'Petra?' he called as he lifted the keys to the Land Rover off the peg in the kitchen. 'I'm just going into Picklewick for some bits and pieces. Will you be okay for a few hours?'

'Just how many bits and pieces are you planning on getting? Or are you going to the care home as well?'

'I'm popping into The Black Horse actually. I'm taking Lena out for lunch.'

Petra's eyebrows rose so far up her forehead that they almost disappeared into her hairline.

'Don't look at me like that,' he warned. 'It's just a quick bite to eat to discuss the play.'

413

'I thought we'd discussed everything last night?'

'Yes, well, Lena and I need to finalise some details.'

Petra smirked. 'You like her.'

'Don't start on me with your matchmaking tricks. It won't work. Lena and I are just friends.'

'But I reckon you'd like to be more.'

'You can reckon all you want. I don't need another woman in my life. Your Aunt Mags was the only woman for me.'

'Amos…' Petra began quietly. 'She's been gone a long time. Don't you think—?'

'No, I do not.' Amos felt heat flood into his face.

'I was just thinking—'

'You can jolly well stop thinking. If there's any thinking to be done, I can do it myself.'

'You don't fool me, Amos. I can tell you're not happy.'

'I haven't been happy for years. Not since I lost my Mags.'

'Isn't it about time you were?'

'And you think Lena Rees will make me happy, do you?'

'She might.'

Amos was bristling worse than a hedgehog facing a fox. How dare Petra try to tell him he should be happy. Just because she was all loved up, didn't give her any right to comment on his happiness or otherwise. And why did she think Lena could ever replace Mags in his heart?

As though Petra had read his mind, she said, 'There's room in your life for both of them – Lena and Mags. Do you think I'd stop loving Amory if I had another baby?'

'Don't be daft. Love doesn't work like that.'

'Exactly!'

'This is different.'

'How?'

'Because I don't *want* anyone else. I'm too old for all this romance nonsense.'

'You're never too old for love.'

'I don't love Lena and she sure as hell doesn't love me.'

'Yeah, I know…you're just friends.' Petra fell silent; her gaze locked with his, and he saw the concern and love in her eyes.

'Thank you,' he said, after a while.

'For what?'

'For not telling me that Mags wouldn't want me to be on my own forever.'

'I don't need to. You already know that.' She looked away and took a deep breath. 'I'd better go. Amory is in his chair in the living room watching the lights on the Christmas tree flash on and off. I'm surprised it's kept him entertained for this long.'

Amos said, 'I've left the Indian takeaway menu out. It's next to the fruit bowl. I thought you and Harry could have a curry tonight.'

'Good idea.' She stepped towards him and kissed his cheek. 'I just want you to be happy,' she said. 'It breaks my heart to know you're not.'

'Get away with you. I'm alright.'

'Before I go, do you remember when Harry first came into our lives, and you told me not to leave it too late?'

'I do. You took my advice, I'm delighted to say.'

'How about taking it yourself? You said that finding love is the only thing that truly matters. If you spend your life alone, you'll miss out on so much.'

'I did find love: I had your Aunt Mags,' he repeated.

'I know, but you and Lena could be good together, if you let yourself.'

'She doesn't think of me like that,' he insisted. 'We've known each other for years.'

'But you haven't known her that well, have you, not until these past couple of weeks. All I'm saying is, don't close your mind to the possibility. And don't leave it too late to tell her how you feel, eh?' She squeezed his shoulder. 'Enjoy your meal.'

Amos fervently hoped that he would – because all he could think about was Lena and his growing feelings for her. Petra was right, and Mags was right. He didn't want to live out his remaining years alone. He wanted someone of his own to love and cherish, who would love and cherish him back.

And he was beginning to hope that person might be Lena Rees.

CHAPTER FIVE

'You had better give these out,' Lena said, shoving a sheaf of papers into Amos's hand and standing back warily. It was a long time since she had been this close to a horse and being in the arena up at the stables with at least ten of the large creatures hemming her in, was a bit unnerving.

She never used to be this nervous around horses – heck, she used to ride regularly when she was young. Olive had taught her, and she'd also taught October. Lena used to blame her mother for October's obsession with anything equine. She still did, but at least her daughter was now living nearby and not on the other side of the country, as was the case when October had been chasing her dream of being a professional showjumper and living at whichever yard she happened to be employed by. Lena had lost count of the number of Christmas Days that she'd spent without seeing her daughter, so she was grateful that at least she'd get to see her on Christmas morning this year, even if she would have to spend the rest of the day on her own.

She caught October's eye and smiled warmly. Lena knew that she was luckier than many people, and she had spent last night counting her blessings and telling herself not to be so miserable.

Looking at the bright and expectant faces around her this afternoon, Lena definitely wasn't miserable, although she was apprehensive that this first rehearsal went well. It was going to be a rather novel and unusual take on the nativity play for there to be so many ponies around, but the main actors would be safely on the ground, in the more traditional manner.

Petra, bless her, had done the preliminary work of choosing who should play the key roles, such as Mary and Joseph, so Lena was spared that, and Harry and Nathan had borrowed a piano from the grandma of one of the young riders and had already carted it into the arena.

Conscious that they had less than two weeks to pull this off, Lena clapped her hands and called for silence.

'Right,' she said. 'This is the order in which things are going to happen. The manger and the stable will be set up over there,' she pointed, 'and the inn scene will take place here. Before that, Mary will be led into the arena on Gerald. Are you sure he can take her weight?' Lena asked Petra. She was concerned about the little donkey's back, especially since he was getting on a bit and hadn't been ridden for yonks.

Petra nodded. 'Heidi weighs less than a wet puppy.' She pointed to a pretty girl of around eight or nine, who was as thin as a whippet. 'She won't be on him long, ten minutes at the most. He'll be fine and it's about time the greedy creature earned his keep.'

'Okay,' Lena nodded. 'Joseph— Who's playing Joseph?'

A boy's hand shot up.

'What's your name? Actually, don't tell me, I'll only forget,' Lena said. 'I'll call you Joseph. So, Joseph, you'll lead Gerald with Mary on his back into the arena, after you hear the last bars of *O Little Town of Bethlehem*. You'll walk over to the innkeeper and ask for a room for the night. Who's playing the innkeeper?'

Another hand was raised, this time by a girl.

'We've got more girls than boys taking lessons,' Petra explained.

'No problem. Who said the innkeeper had to be male anyway? It could just as easily have been a woman. Anyway, where was I? Oh, yes, I remember…The innkeeper will tell Joseph that there are no rooms, and direct him and Mary to the stable.'

Lena soon got into her stride and started to enjoy herself, and by the end of the exuberant and chaotic first rehearsal, she was exhausted but happy.

'I thought that went well for a first attempt,' she said, as the riders led their horses out of the arena, leaving her and Amos to tidy up. There were a few pieces of paper that had been dropped, and some impromptu props to be put away, but that was about it. 'I think we'll need at least another two goes to get it right,' she added, 'and the final one will have to involve the choir. I thought you did ever so well on the piano.'

Amos pulled a face. 'I haven't played for years. Not since I was a nipper.' He flexed his hands. 'I don't think my fingers will forgive me. Thank goodness one of the teachers will be playing it on the day.'

'You were brilliant,' Lena said. She turned to him, looking him square in the face. 'I really want to thank you for doing this. And Petra, too.'

'Aw, give over. Today was fun.'

'It was, wasn't it?'

'Do you fancy coming up to the house for a glass of mulled wine and a slice of Christmas cake before you go?' he asked. 'And I want you to taste a new mulled wine recipe that I've been experimenting with. It's a kid-friendly version, although the adults are welcome to have some, especially if they are driving. I've made it with real blackberries and it's delicious, even if I do say so myself.'

'Ooh, yes please. I could do with warming up before I head off.' Lena rubbed her arms. 'It's a bit chilly in here.'

'I've been thinking about that,' Amos said, threading an arm through hers and leading her outside. 'Mind your step – I didn't realise it was so dark. It'll soon be the longest night.'

Lena shivered. Winter had never been her favourite season, for that very reason. It was only five in the afternoon, and it was already blacker than a witch's hat.

'I've spoken to Dave,' Amos continued, 'and he says that we're welcome to use his patio heaters for the duration. The Black Horse has no need of them at this time of year, and they are only sitting in the shed doing nothing. He suggests switching them on a good couple of hours before the play starts, so the gallery has a chance to warm up before our elderly guests arrive.' He snorted. 'Listen to me! I'm not that much younger than they are.'

'You're years younger!' Lena cried, cuddling into him to avoid the chill wind that was blowing across the yard.

Amos halted and Lena wondered what was wrong. She was keen to get out of the wind and wrap her cold hands around a glass of hot spiced wine. Hopefully, the fire would be lit too, and she could warm the rest of her.

'Hang on a minute,' he said.

They were walking across the yard and had almost reached the house. But instead of hurrying inside, Amos had come to a stop next to a shed door and was reaching inside.

Without warning, the yard was plunged into darkness.

'Oi!' Petra yelled from the depths of one of the stables. 'Switch those lights back on. Some of us can't see a hand in front of our faces!'

'In a minute. I want to show Lena something. Look at that,' he said. His head was tilted back and he was gazing up at the heavens.

Lena looked up and let out a gasp. The sky was inky black and dotted with thousands of stars. She didn't think she'd ever seen so many. And, as she watched, a streak of light travelled overhead, blazing briefly before it petered out. Then there was another, and another.

'It's the Geminid meteor shower,' Amos said in her ear. 'It appears at around this time every December.'

'It's beautiful,' she whispered.

They stood there, arm in arm, watching the flashes of light for a while longer, Lena forgetting about the cold as wonder swept over her. 'This is so humbling. I feel like a very insignificant speck, compared to the wonders of nature.'

'You're not insignificant to me.'

Something in Amos's tone gave her pause, and when she looked at him, he was no longer staring up at the heavens: he was looking at her, his warm breath wreathed around his head like smoke, and his eyes glittering.

The intensity of his gaze made her catch her breath, and she swallowed nervously. For some reason she was worried that he might be about to kiss her.

Then she feared that he wouldn't.

Petra's voice shattered the moment. 'Amos! If you've finished stargazing, please can you turn the ruddy lights on!'

'Lena, I…' He shook his head, reached around the door and switched them back on.

Lena blinked, her eyes adjusting to the glare as light flooded the yard, and she wondered what he had wanted to say. Had he been about to kiss her, or had she imagined it?

She shivered with sudden longing, but Amos misconstrued the tremor.

'You're freezing. Let's get you inside,' he said, taking the lead once more and guiding her towards the house.

Lena tottered along on legs that refused to do as they were told, her heart thudding so hard she feared he might hear it.

Mortification gripped her. What a silly thing to think. Of course he hadn't been about to kiss her. And she wouldn't have wanted him to.

But for hours later, long after the taste of the mulled wine had left her lips and long after she had snuggled down on the sofa in her living room, she could still feel his gaze on hers. And she was forced to admit that she did want him to kiss her after all, and if he ever did, she might never want him to stop.

'What was all that about?' Petra asked, when Amos returned to the kitchen after escorting Lena to her car.

'Pardon?'

'Switching the lights off. I was in the middle of unsaddling Parsnip.'

'I wanted Lena to see the meteor shower,' he mumbled.

He had no idea what had possessed him to do such a thing. He could simply have told her about it and suggested that she took a look at the sky later this evening. It wasn't as though it was a you-have-to-watch-it-now-or-miss-it event. She could have seen it when she got home, if she had wanted to. The forecast was for a clear night, so there was no risk of cloud cover obscuring the view, either.

But he had wanted to be there when she did. He vividly recalled the first time he'd set eyes on it, and how magical it had been. Mind you, he'd only been a young lad, and in those days everything had seemed magical.

It was odd though, because he'd not thought about that in years, and it was only by chance that he'd happened to glance up at the sky this evening and had spotted a streak of light shoot across it, and realised what he was looking at.

For a silly nonsensical second, he had imagined that Mags was sending him a message, because why else would he have seen a shooting star when the yard lights hid most of the night sky from view?

He'd known he was being daft, but...

And then he'd come a cat's whisker to kissing Lena.

Her face, as he'd captured and held her gaze, had given nothing away, so he had no idea whether she would have welcomed his kiss, or whether she would have given him a clip around the ear.

'Are you feeling okay? Is it your heart?' Petra's head was tilted to the side as she studied him, her expression one of concern. Amory was on her lap, sleepy and replete after a feed.

Actually, it *was* his heart that was the problem, but not in the way his niece imagined. 'I'm fine,' he said. 'Stop fussing. I thought we'd have spaghetti bolognese for supper. There's mince in the fridge that needs using.'

Petra made to get up. 'If you take Amory, I'll cook supper. You could probably do with a rest after all that hard work today.'

'I don't need a rest.'

'Let me make it anyway,' she insisted.

'Why? Do you think I'm getting past it?' he shot back crossly.

'Not at all! Whatever gave you that idea?' Petra appeared to be genuinely hurt, and Amos felt a heel.

She was only trying to look after him, and he was throwing it back in her face. Besides, he'd already had the conversation with himself where he had acknowledged that it might be time for her and Harry to start to get used to him not being around. The idea of turning the old feed shed into a bungalow was still bumbling around in his mind. He wouldn't say anything to Petra, yet though. Not until he was sure it was what he wanted to do. And even if he was sure, there was no guarantee the stables would get planning permission, or whether it was even doable. Maybe he should run the idea past Isaac and Nelly first? Isaac could draw up some rough plans and Nelly could give him a ballpark figure as to how much the building work would cost.

Only when he had all that information, could he decide whether his idea was feasible, and if it wasn't he'd have to have a serious rethink, because he was determined that Petra and Harry would have the farmhouse to themselves, without him cramping their style.

CHAPTER SIX

Ten days later saw Lena clapping as enthusiastically as though this final rehearsal was the real thing. Amos was standing by her side, and he was whooping and clapping too.

The headteacher had done them proud, and her pupils had been practising like mad, she'd told them. They had sung an array of traditional carols, some of which would be sung during the play itself, and some afterwards, as well as more modern upbeat songs.

The cast and choir took a bow, the children's faces glowing, bright smiles stretching from ear to ear. They knew they'd done a good job and they'd had fun, too.

'Bravo!' Lena called, earning herself some odd looks from the children, many of whom had probably never heard the expression before. 'You did brilliantly! I'm so proud of you, and I know Amos and Petra are too, as well as your teachers. Your parents are going to be so thrilled!'

The play was far from perfect – how could it be when there were children and animals involved, and they'd only had a couple of weeks to practice? – but she was so incredibly proud of them all.

Suddenly Lena felt herself being picked up and swung around, and she squealed with surprise and delight. But her squeal soon turned to a gasp when Amos landed a smacker on her lips before putting her down.

'Oh!' she cried, her fingers creeping towards her mouth.

Amos immediately looked contrite and took a step backwards. 'I'm sorry, I shouldn't have.'

'I don't mind,' she replied honestly. She hadn't minded one little bit. She had simply been taken aback because she'd not been expecting it. The kiss had been far too fleeting, and she abruptly hoped he would kiss her again. Properly, this time.

'Yes, well…' He was sheepish and uncomfortable, and Lena wondered whether he wished he hadn't done it, in case it gave her the wrong idea about their relationship.

Cheeks flaming, she turned to the cast again, who were milling around, preparing to leave, and she tried to put the kiss to the back of her mind. There would be time enough to mull it over later, when she was alone.

She tilted her head to Amos and hissed out of the side of her mouth, 'We must get the children a little something from Father Christmas.' She raised her eyebrows meaningfully, hoping he would understand what she was getting at.

Amos gave her a sideways look. 'Oh, no, not this year!'

'You *must*! You're the most perfect Santa Claus ever!'

'Because I'm old, plump and whiskery? You know how to flatter a fellow.'

'Because you're kind and you've got the most adorable crinkly eyes,' she countered. There was no way Amos could be described as plump (far from it), and he wasn't old, either. Not as far as she was concerned. 'Maybe you are a little on the whiskery side,' she conceded, 'but that's because you have a beard.'

He scratched his chin, and Lena's eyes were drawn to it. She had never kissed a man with a beard before, and although the contact just now had been fleeting, it hadn't been as scratchy as she might have thought.

She stamped down on the urge to kiss him.

'Do you really think I should dress up as Father Christmas again this year?' he asked, frowning.

'I do. The children will love it, and so will the oldies. Take my mum, for instance: she adores getting a present from Santa, even though she knows it's you under the costume.'

'She does? Drat! I didn't think anyone had realised.'

Lena was about to tell him that his disguise wasn't that good, when she realised he was teasing her.

'I'll do it,' he agreed, 'but on one condition. You have to dress up as an elf.'

Lena snorted. 'I'd make a terrible elf!'

'I think you'll make an adorable one.' Amos was gazing at her with an unreadable expression on his face.

Did he mean what he'd just said, or was he just being nice?

She caught her bottom lip between her teeth and worried at it for a moment before saying, 'I've not got an elf costume and it's a bit late to buy one. The play is only two days away, and there's still so much to do.'

'You're not getting out of it that easily,' he warned. 'I'm sure that between us we can cobble something together.'

'If I'm going to do this, I want a proper elf outfit, not a cobbled together one,' she replied haughtily, hoping that was the end of the matter.

Two of the teachers were still in the arena, waiting for parents to pick up their children, and Lena was mortified when Amos called to then, 'Have either of you got an elf outfit that Lena could wear?'

'I have,' one of them said. 'We'll be wearing our Christmas jumpers, so she can borrow mine. It's a bit short but it does have lovely thick stripey tights to go with it, and I bought a red cape with a white fluffy trim in case I got cold. You're welcome to borrow that, too.'

'Great,' Lena muttered under her breath. 'I can't wait.'

'Thanks,' Amos replied, then looped his arm through Lena's. 'I think me and you have some gift buying to do. If you've not got anything planned, how about we meet in Picklewick in the morning? I'll treat you to a coffee in the cafe before we start. And if necessary, we'll have a spot of lunch out, too.'

Lena readily agreed, despite knowing it wasn't wise to get too used to Amos's company, and she was already looking forward to spending the biggest part of the day with him tomorrow. Resolutely she pushed the uncomfortable worry away that once this play was done and dusted, she was going to miss him far more than was good for her.

'I'm going to have a slice of pumpkin spiced cake and a butterscotch latte to go with it,' Lena announced. She was examining the selection of festive cakes and drinks on offer in the cafe, while Amos contented himself with examining *her*.

He couldn't help marvelling at how lovely she was, especially when she smiled. And right now she was smiling a lot. He loved her pert nose, her generous mouth and her expressive eyes, and he was pleased to see that the sadness which usually lurked in their depths wasn't there today.

She looked cute – if he was allowed to call her that, considering neither of them were spring chickens. Bundled up in a brightly knitted hat, a matching scarf and thick woollen coat, she was also wearing tan-coloured boots with a cream faux fur trim, and she looked very festive and wintery.

'I'll have the same,' he said. 'Why don't you grab a table and I'll place our order?'

By the time he joined her on the squashy sofa next to the window, she had removed her hat, scarf and coat, to reveal a knitted cream dress, and he thought she looked incredibly elegant. It made him feel rather scruffy by comparison, with his brown cord trousers and a sweater that he'd had for years. At least he was wearing a flannel shirt underneath it, in a matching colour, so he didn't look a total mess. He wished he'd made a bit more of an effort though, and he told himself to up his game— before realising there was little point. After the way she had reacted when he'd inadvertently kissed her yesterday, it was clear that Lena didn't consider him to be anything other than a friend.

If he was honest, he hadn't expected her to. Lena was so much younger than he, and had so much more going for her. She could have her pick of any number of men, so why would she be interested in an old codger like him?

'You're looking smart,' she said, and it took Amos a second to realise that she wasn't being sarcastic.

'This old thing?' He gestured to his sweater with a wry grin. 'I've had it for years.'

'The colour suits you.'

It was a shade Petra referred to as heather, and the plaid shirt was a mix of deeper and lighter purple check, with cream. She'd bought both the jumper and the shirt for him a few Christmases ago, and he thought they were past their best now. A bit like him.

'And you look…' he began, coming to halt when he couldn't find the word he wanted, settling for, 'Beautiful.' She was so much more than that though…

Lena's eyebrows shot up. 'Thank you,' was all she said, but she looked pleased, if a little surprised.

'What do you think we should get for the children?' Amos asked, as the waitress placed their drinks and cake on the table. He looked up at the woman and smiled. 'Thanks, this looks delicious.' Picking up a fork he dug in.

'It's going to be difficult, as their ages differ so widely,' Lena pointed out, popping some cake into her mouth and closing her eyes. 'Gosh, this is wonderful!' she exclaimed.

It was, but Amos was more enthralled by the blissful expression on her face, rather than with the cake he was eating. When she opened her eyes again, they were shining with delight.

'I could get used to this,' she said. 'We ought to make it a regular thing.' Then she blushed. 'I mean, if you want to. You don't have to. I expect you've got enough to be going on with without keeping me company on a regular basis.'

'I agree, we *should* do this again. And I don't have anything else to do, but even if I did, I like keeping you company.' Amos put his fork down and took a steadying breath. He might as well tell her once and for all, so he knew where he stood. 'I like *you.*' There, he'd said it.

Lena's expression didn't give anything away as she replied, 'I like you, too.'

'I mean—' he began, anxious that she didn't think he was just being friendly or polite.

'I know what you mean,' she interrupted, and a slow smile spread across her face.

'Oh, my. Well, that's…er…' Amos stuttered to a halt, his heart thumping.

They were interrupted by Charity calling, 'Hiya, you two! I thought yesterday went really well.' She was making her way towards them. 'I'm off to work, but I thought I'd pop in for a sandwich to take with me. We don't seem to have anything in the fridge.'

'It was good, wasn't it?' Lena beamed. 'Amos and I are going to buy a few gifts for Santa to give out after we finish this.'

'What a lovely idea,' Charity said, then eyed the cake, which had hardly been touched. 'That looks yummy.'

'It is.' Lena pulled a face. 'I wonder if you have any ideas of what we can get for the children? There's quite a range of ages and we're a bit stumped. And if you've got any thoughts on what we could buy for the Honeymead residents, that would be a great help, too.'

'You don't want much!' Charity laughed. 'Let me see…' She tapped her fingers against her chin as she thought.

Amos took a sip of his coffee, thankful for the respite. He had been floundering a bit, after Lena had told him she liked him too, wondering if she meant what he hoped she meant or… Bugger! All this thinking was making his head hurt. He was too old for this nonsense. At his age he should be able to tell someone how he felt about them without all this palaver.

But the problem was, the last time he had told a girl he liked her, was forty-odd years ago and he'd ended up marrying her!

Lena was itching to tell her mum about the play – it was such a big part of her life at the moment and was consuming her every waking minute right now – but she didn't want to spoil the surprise, so when she called into the care home after the shopping trip with Amos, she kept her lips zipped firmly shut.

'Hi, Mum, sorry I'm late, I did a bit of Christmas shopping.' She gave the wrinkled cheek a gentle peck, then sat beside the old lady.

Her mum was lying on her bed, pillows propping up her frail body, and Lena felt the prick of tears behind her eyes when she saw her. Olive looked even more fragile today, if that was possible. Her skin had a sallow tinge to it that Lena didn't like, and her hair seemed even wispier than it had yesterday. Even fully dressed, she was worryingly thin and she didn't look as though she had a scrap of fat on her.

Her mum was fading before her eyes, and there wasn't a damn thing Lena could do about it.

With false bonhomie, she said, 'Why aren't you in the day room with the others? That programme you like is on: you know, the one where you have to guess the answers to cryptic clues.'

Olive shrugged, a tiny movement. 'Don't feel like it.'

'Shall I put the tv on in here, and we can watch it together?'

'Don't bother. I'm not interested.' Her voice was weak and croaky, as though she was struggling to find the energy to speak.

Lena bit her lip. Tears were perilously close to the surface, but she didn't want to break down in front of her mum. There would be time enough for crying later, when…

She coughed to cover the lump in her throat and the pain in her heart, shoving the awful thought to the back of her mind and resolving to try to be cheerful for her mum's sake.

Gently she placed her hand over her mother's limp one, curling her fingers around it. She wanted to squeeze her tight and never let go, but she contented herself with holding her hand, conscious of how it resembled a baby bird with the veins and the bones clearly showing through the stretched-tight skin.

'What's going on?' Olive asked, her voice suddenly stronger. 'I know something is up with you. I can tell.'

There was so much, that Lena didn't know where to start. First and foremost was the knowledge that her mother wasn't long for this world. But she suspected her mum already knew that. Secondly, there was the problem of her loneliness, which would only get worse when her mum passed. Then there was Amos, and the growing feelings she had for him. She hoped he was starting to feel the same way about her, but short of asking him, she couldn't be certain.

'Are you happy, Lena?'

'Eh?' Lena snapped to attention. Her mum sounded like the woman she used to be, strong, determined and capable, and a worm of hope burrowed its way into Lena's heart. Perhaps Olive wasn't as frail as she'd thought?

Something in Lena's face must have given her away because her mum continued, 'I didn't think so. And don't go blaming it on me being in here and not having long to live.' Olive shot her a look, her stare fierce. 'I know I'm dying and so do you, so don't pussyfoot around it.' She held Lena's gaze. 'As I was saying, you haven't been happy for a long time. Not since you retired. You need something to keep you occupied, my girl – and I don't mean looking after an old biddy like me.'

Lena was dumbstruck. This was the most animated she'd seen her mum in a long time. Trust it to be because she was telling her off. Even at this stage in her life, Olive wasn't backwards in coming forwards where putting Lena straight was concerned.

'What do you suggest, Mum?' she asked, thinking that Olive was more perceptive than she gave her credit for. Her mum was also right – Lena *wasn't* happy.

She had moved to Picklewick to live with her, when it became clear that the old lady wasn't managing on her own. At this point Lena had been able to carry on working, mostly remotely with the occasional visit to the office for meetings and to catch up. She'd had a responsible job and had loved it. But a couple of years later, when the company had gone through a restructure and early retirement with a substantial redundancy package had been on offer, Lena had taken it. By this time her mum had needed quite a lot of help, and juggling caring for her mother whilst having such a demanding job was becoming increasingly difficult.

'That's for you to figure out,' Olive said. 'All I know is, that you've gone from being busy all the time, to doing next to nothing apart from visiting me. It's not healthy.' She sent Lena a sideways look. 'Maybe you should think about getting yourself a man?'

Lena gasped. 'What on earth makes you say that? You know I haven't bothered with men much since October was born.'

'Perhaps if you had, you wouldn't be so flaming miserable now. You need someone to share your life with.'

'*You* didn't,' Lena retorted. 'After Dad died, I didn't see you whooping it up with anyone.'

Olive pursed her lips. 'That's where you're wrong,' she said. 'I had my moments. It didn't stop me from grieving for your father, but if I had been lucky enough to find a man I wanted to be with for the remainder of my life, I wouldn't have hesitated.'

'That's just it,' Lena said. 'I've never found the right man. I thought October's father might have been, but it wasn't to be. And I can't say I've missed not being married.'

'Are you working on the premise that you can't miss what you've never had?' Olive asked.

'Not at all. I'm working on the premise that, like you, I haven't found anyone I want to be with.' Unfortunately, a blush began to creep up her neck and into her face, giving lie to her words.

'I still think there's something you're not telling me,' Olive persisted. 'And I reckon it's to do with a man.'

'What on earth gives you that idea?'

'I've seen the way you look at him.'

'Look at *who*?'

'Amos Kelly.'

Lena spluttered. 'I don't know what you mean.'

'I think you do, my girl. And for your information, he looks at you the same way.'

'You're going doolally.'

'My body might be falling apart but my mind isn't,' Olive shot back. 'I've got eyes in my head.'

'We're just friends,' Lena insisted. 'Anyway, even if I did think of him in that way, I'm not sure the feeling is reciprocated. He is still in love with his wife.'

'I expect he is. Just because someone dies, it doesn't mean to say you stop loving them. But it is possible to love more than one person at the same time. If I had met someone after your father died and had fallen in love with him, I would still have loved your father. There would have been room in my heart for both of them. Just as there will be room in Amos's.'

Lena was lost for words, conflicting emotions surging through her. Should she admit to her mum how she felt about Amos? Although she wasn't entirely sure how she *did* feel. She knew she liked him immensely, and found him incredibly attractive. She loved spending time with him, and she was hopeful that their friendship would carry on beyond Christmas. But none of these things, even added together, meant that she was contemplating having a serious relationship with him.

'Okay,' she conceded. 'I like Amos a lot. And I think he might like me. But aren't we a bit old for all that?'

Her mother snorted. 'Don't be daft. You're never too old for love.' She drew in a shuddering breath, and seemed to sink back into her pillows. 'Anyway, I've said my piece. I'm tired now. I think I need to sleep.' Her eyelids drifted shut, and within seconds she was deep in slumber.

Lena sat with her for a while, watching the shallow breaths rising and falling in her mother's skinny chest, and she thought about what she had said, that maybe it wasn't too late, either for her or for Amos. Lena just needed some courage, and some indication that Amos was of the same mind.

The last thing she wanted was to make a fool of herself. She valued his friendship too much for that. He'd said earlier today in the cafe that he liked her, but they'd been interrupted before she could explore what he meant, and then the conversation had moved on and it had been too late to revisit it.

She thought about how nice today had been. They'd almost been like a proper couple, trundling around the little shops in Picklewick, picking out gifts for the residents of Honeymead, working on the suggestions that Charity had given them. It had been fun, and they had chatted and laughed non-stop right the way through the leisurely lunch which had followed.

She had been tempted to invite him back to her house for supper, but decided that he probably had things to do.

And she had wanted to pop in and see her mum, so she'd let it go.

Now, though, she wished she hadn't, because if Amos had joined her for supper, she might have found the courage to ask him if he could ever think of her as more than just a friend. After all, what did she have to lose? If she scared him off, they could simply go back to the way they had been before. And since there was a very strong likelihood that her mum wouldn't need the services of the care home for a great deal longer, Lena wouldn't be visiting Honeymead much, and therefore wouldn't bump into Amos.

However, the thought of not having him in her life hurt her more than she thought possible, and she wrung her hands in worry.

She'd not mention anything, she decided. It simply wasn't worth the risk of losing his friendship. She would have to find something else with which to fill her time and her thoughts, once Christmas was out of the way.

But the problem was, how was she going to fill the hole in her heart – the Amos-shaped hole which she hadn't been aware was there until she'd felt his lips briefly brush against her mouth and his soul brush against hers.

CHAPTER SEVEN

It was one of the acknowledged truths that old age doesn't come by itself, and tonight it had brought insomnia with it to keep it company. Which was why Amos was slumped in an armchair in the snug at stupid o'clock in the early hours of the morning on the day of the nativity play, contemplating his navel in front of the dying embers of the fire.

He stirred briefly at the blarting sound of his great-great-nephew demanding a feed, but soon settled down again when he heard the creak of the floorboards on the landing telling him that Petra had gone to see to her son. He wished he could have fed the baby a bottle to give Petra an uninterrupted night's sleep, but Amory was still being breastfed and she hadn't expressed any milk.

Hark at him, knowing about expressing milk and breastfeeding! Who'd have thought it! He smiled wryly to himself, thinking that this time two years ago, it had been just him and Petra at the stables, with no hint on the horizon of the changes that were about to sweep through both their lives. And he had an unsettling feeling that those changes weren't done with them yet. Him, especially.

One of them would be of his own making, because he was determined to hand the stables over to Petra soon, and not just in principle. He was going to sign the whole caboodle over to her, lock, stock and barrel of oats. It would then be her business, to do with as she pleased, and considering it would be hers when he died, she may as well have it now.

Heck, she and Harry were more or less running it by themselves anyway. All he'd ask is that—

'What are you doing up?' Petra leaned against the door jamb and rubbed her eyes sleepily. 'Do you know what time it is?'

'Two, three…?' He hazarded a guess. 'I couldn't sleep.'

She yawned and padded over to him. He noticed she was wearing socks with cat paws on them, and he thought how young she looked in the soft light of the fire.

'Are you feeling alright?' Her concern was touching.

'Never better,' he said. In a way, he wasn't lying. He did feel good – not physically, because seventy-three came with its own set of aches and pains – but emotionally. Now that he had decided to relinquish his hold on the stables, it was as though a weight had been lifted from his shoulders and he realised it would do him good to make a fresh start in a place of his own.

Petra plopped down into the chair opposite and sighed loudly, stretching her toes out to the fire and wiggling them.

'There's no need to keep me company,' he said. 'Why don't you go back to bed?'

'I'm wide awake, thanks to Amory. He didn't want a feed: the little monster wanted to play. I've put him back down, but no doubt he'll start squawking again in a minute.'

'If he does, I'll bring him down here with me. There's no point in both of us being up, and you need your sleep more than I do.'

'Thanks for the offer, but as I said, I'm wide awake.' She smiled and said softly. 'What would I do without you?'

He nodded sagely. 'You'll manage. Er, I've been thinking…'

'Uh oh!' She looked worried.

'It's nothing bad,' he assured her hastily.

'Go on.' Her eyes narrowed, glittering in the flickering light from the flames.

'I'm going to sign the stables over to you after Christmas. You'll own it outright. It's about time.'

'*What?* No! The stable is yours. It belongs to you.'

It's more yours and Harry's than mine, these days. And it'll simplify things when the time comes.'

'The time–? *Oh…*' Her face fell when she realised what he meant. 'Don't say that.'

'It happens to all of us sooner or later, although I am hoping it will be later. Don't worry, I'm not ill or anything. Just feeling my age, that's all. I should have retired years ago. I'm as much use as a ladder to a fish.'

She gave him a keen look. 'Is that what you think? Just because you don't do the yard work, doesn't mean to say you don't do your fair share. You do loads: the bookings, the accounts, all the ordering, you run the house, you do the shopping, your look after Amory—' She stopped, and her eyes widened. 'Are you saying you don't want to do it anymore?'

'Not in so many words. I'll still help, but you need your own space. And there's something else – I'll be moving out.'

Petra's mouth dropped open and she stared at him, stunned. 'Where will you go?'

'Not far. I was thinking that turning the feed shed into a bungalow might be a good idea. I'll still be on site, but I won't be in your hair. This—' he gestured to the room at large '—will become *your* home. Yours, Harry's and Amory's. Not mine. I'll have my own behind the yard, so I won't have gone far, and I'll be close enough if you need me.'

'A *bungalow?*' Her eyes were wide, all traces of sleepiness having gone.

'Don't you think a bungalow is a good idea?' Amos began to worry. 'I thought it would be better for me, now that I'm getting older. I don't know how long I'll be able to manage those stairs. I mean, I'm fine now, but what about in the future?'

'A bungalow isn't the problem,' she replied shortly. 'That you are thinking of moving out of the farmhouse, is. This is your home, Amos. I can't drive you out of it.'

'*You're* not driving me anywhere. I *want* to go.' He studied her face carefully, and was dismayed to see her eyes fill with tears.

Before she could say anything, Amos leapt in. 'Don't go getting the wrong end of the stick. I want a place of *my* own because you need a place of *your* own. And, as I said, I've got to think about those damned stairs. And the bath. I can barely get in and out of it as it is.'

'We can have a stairlift put in, and what about one of those walk-in baths?'

'And what if you have more children? They'll need their own bedroom, and the farmhouse only has three.'

'We can convert the attic.'

'It's easier to have a purpose-built bungalow,' he countered.

'You're serious, aren't you?'

Amos pursed his lips and nodded. 'I am.'

'Is there anything I can do to make you change your mind?'

He barked out a laugh. 'Anyone would think I'm emigrating to Spain or going on a world cruise for six months. I'll only be just across the way.'

'Is this why you've been out of sorts recently? Although I've noticed that you have perked up since you came up with the nativity play idea.'

Wincing because she'd noticed and he hadn't been as good at hiding it as he had thought, he said, 'Partly,' then paused, before confessing, 'I was beginning to feel useless, old, past it; but as you pointed out, I've been happier since we started planning the play.'

'What will happen once Christmas is over?'

He blinked at her shrewdness. 'I'm hoping I might have something else to keep me occupied.'

'Lena?' she guessed.

He shrugged. 'I haven't yet plucked up the courage to tell her how I feel, and I'm still not convinced she thinks of me as anything other than a friend, so I'm not getting my hopes up too much.'

'It'll work out,' Petra said. 'And although I don't want you to move out of the house, I can appreciate your reasons. Thank you for trusting me with the stables. I know how much it means to you.'

'It means as much to you too, and I know I'll be leaving it in safe hands.'

Tears trickled down her cheeks and she sniffed loudly. 'I love you, Amos. I just want you to be happy.'

'I love you too, precious girl.' His own eyes brimmed with unshed tears as he watched her leave the room.

Lena wanted to squeal with excitement when she peeped into the arena and saw the old folks being escorted to their seats. She felt like a stage director, hiding behind the curtain before it went up, as she watched the auditorium fill up as the punters filed in, and she hugged herself with excitement.

Piano music filled the air, played by one of the teachers from Picklewick Primary, not quite drowning out the murmur of voices, the shuffling of chairs and the scuffling of feet. Amos and Megan were helping William, Charity and Rose to seat the residents, and they were also handing out plastic glasses of mulled wine to keep them warm and to get them in the mood for the singing they would be expected to do later.

The cast was in the barn, having the final touches put to their costumes, some of which had been kindly leant to the stables from the school's dressing up box, and others provided by parents.

Lena caught sight of Olive, and her heart went out to her. Despite the smile on the old lady's face and the pinkness of her cheeks, her mum looked drawn and tired, and incredibly frail. Her eyes were more alert than they had been for a long time, though, which gave Lena some comfort. Olive was clearly enjoying this unexpected treat, and Lena marvelled at how everyone had managed to keep it a secret from her.

Parents and grandparents were beginning to file in, sitting on the plastic seats behind the far more comfortable ones that the care home residents were enjoying, and the level of noise steadily grew.

'Are we ready yet?' Petra asked, sidling up to her and peering around the door. 'Aw, doesn't it look lovely? You and Amos have worked wonders.'

'Not just us,' Lena pointed out. 'You and Harry have done loads, and so have Nathan and Megan.'

Nathan had found a number of large wooden partitions that had been removed from the cow shed when it had been renovated, and had sanded them down and given them a lick of paint, before joining them together to form a backdrop to the manger scene. The manger itself had been loaned to them by the primary school, as well as some other props such as three little painted chests which represented the gold, frankincense and myrrh, and various bits and pieces from the school's dressing-up box. Nathan had also strung together another couple of panels, which he and Harry had painted to look like a brick wall, and they had found an old door for the innkeeper to stand in front of. Megan had painted a sign that said 'Muddypuddle Inn', which hung above the door, and another smaller one saying 'No Vacancies' was nailed to the side of it.

Petra was providing the donkey, the goats (in lieu of sheep) and a pony dressed in an old sheet which had been painted with black and white splodges to resemble a cow and who sported a pair of fabric horns on its head.

Nathan had also rigged up some lighting, and the whole area was awash with coloured fairy lights as well as a large twinkly star that dangled above the manger scene.

With the carols playing in the background, the aroma of mulled wine and hot chocolate in the air, and the huge Christmas tree in a giant pot that dominated one corner of the arena, the place couldn't be any more festive.

Lena was thrilled with the result, and from their expressions, the people in the audience appeared to be too.

She caught Amos's eye, and he tapped his watch then held up his hand. Lena nodded to indicate that she understood the play was to start in five minutes. Most of the chairs were occupied and she didn't want people to begin getting restless, so five minutes was a good shout.

Lena tugged at the skirt of the borrowed elf costume, praying that it wasn't riding up and showing her stripey backside, and said to Petra, 'Can you ask October and Nathan to start lining everyone up in the correct order? I'll wait here to double-check before they come in. Don't forget, we start with the headteacher and the choir first, then as soon as they are in place, the narrator will come in.'

Lena had had the brilliant idea of letting the narrator, a boy by the name of Billy, do all the talking – from announcing the start of the play right through to thanking everyone for coming. It meant that she didn't have to!

Petra had just taken a step towards the barn where all the participants were waiting, when Lena heard her mutter, 'Bloody hell, I don't believe it,' and she felt her heart constrict with worry as she wondered what was wrong.

Petra chuckled. 'There's Walter from Lilac Tree Farm, and he's only got a bloody sheep with him!'

'You can't have a nativity play without a sheep,' the old man said as he came closer, and Lena saw that the woolly creature was on a lead, and he was carrying a proper shepherd's crook. 'This is Flossie. She's one of this year's lambs. I hand-reared her myself, so she's as tame as that there dog.' He pointed the crook at Queenie. The spaniel was standing at Petra's heel and her ears had pricked up when she saw the sheep.

'Nice to see you, Walter,' Petra said, taking the lead from him. 'How are you?'

'Can't complain,' he said. 'Here.' He shoved the crook at her. 'Give that to one of the shepherds.'

'Thank you, that's very kind. Go and take a seat. I'll look after Flossie.' As soon as he was out of earshot, Petra hissed out of the corner of her mouth, 'We are honoured, indeed. Walter hardly ever ventures far from his farm these days, although he did come to the wedding.'

'I remember seeing him,' Lena said. 'Bless him, he doesn't look at all well. I wonder if he will be the next resident at Honeymead,' she added thoughtfully.

'I doubt it. He'll only leave that farm of his when he's in a box. Right, I'll round everyone up. Break a leg,' she called over her shoulder.

Lena waited for the old man to make his way into the gallery and sit down, then she took a deep breath. This was it!

Time to get this show on the road.

As soon as Nathan dimmed the lights in the arena and the headteacher, followed by three members of her staff and the choir of twenty-three children began to take their places, Amos left the gallery in Charity's capable hands and dashed off to the farmhouse to change into his Santa suit.

Praying that it was going well, he hauled the baggy red trousers up over his legs, and stuffed his feet into his black Wellington boots, before shrugging on the oversized jacket and doing it up. Even from here, the strains of *The First Noel* could be heard, and he found himself humming along to the tune, nerves making his hands shake as he hooked the false beard over his ears and donned the jaunty hat.

With a final check in the mirror to make sure he was presentable, he popped a pair of small round spectacles on the end of his nose and hurried back to the arena. He would watch the performance from the office, not wanting either the children or the old folks to spot him until it was time for his appearance.

He was just in time to hear the choir break into *O Little Town of Bethlehem* and see Jospeh lead Mary, who was perched self-consciously on the bemused donkey, towards the inn.

There wasn't a sound made by the audience as the innkeeper told the couple they could bed down in his stable, and even Amos held his breath at the magic of the scene as Mary and Joseph made their way to the makeshift manger, accompanied by the choir belting out *Away in a Manger.*

Three carols, five shepherds, two goats, one sheep (where did that come from, Amos wondered), three wise men riding on the smallest ponies, and an angel later, and the play was drawing to a close to the haunting music and lyrics of *Silent Night.*

Then as the actors took a bow, the audience burst into rapturous applause, scaring the sheep and the goats, who bleated in alarm, although the horses did little more than flick their ears.

The narrator, who had done a brilliant job, waited for the noise to die down before calling for order. Or rather, he shouted 'Oi! Quiet!' to everyone's amusement.

Petra, October and Nathan hurried into the arena to remove the animals, and as they did so, the choir began to sing *Jingle Bells,* the headteacher encouraging the audience to join in.

This was Amos's cue to get into character.

Hoisting a sack of presents over his shoulder with a grunt, he emerged from the office, crying, 'Ho, ho, ho,' and the audience swivelled in their seats to watch him trundle towards the front of the gallery.

Charity and William stepped forward to help distribute the presents to the care home residents while Amos called out their names, then it was the children's turn. He and Lena had decided on book vouchers as suitable gifts for the kids, and he hoped the children would have fun choosing one. The local bookshop had been very grateful for the custom, and would no doubt welcome this generation of readers with open arms.

'Ladies, gentlemen, and kiddiewinks!' Amos cried, once all the presents had been given out. 'Don't go just yet – we have still got the raffle and we've also got mulled wine, mince pies, hot chocolate, Christmas cake and gingerbread men for those who want it.'

It was no surprise to find that most people did and for the next half hour Amos was kept so busy making drinks and handing out delicious goodies, that he didn't have time to partake of anything himself.

Finally though, the audience began to disperse, taking their children with them, and soon it was time to load Honeymead's residents back onto the bus.

'Ooh, I've had a marvellous time!' one old lady crowed, as William manoeuvred her wheelchair across the yard. She was clutching an empty plastic beaker in her hand, and when she caught Amos's eye, she called, 'Is there any more of this wine? It's gone straight to my head!'

Before he could answer, Amos felt a tap on his arm and he turned to see Lena. She was looking flushed, her eyes were sparkling, and he thought she'd never looked so lovely.

'Can you fetch Gerald for me, and maybe ask October if she could bring Princess and one of the bigger horses?' she asked.

'For your mum?'

She nodded.

'Of course. Give me two minutes.'

He scurried off, and was back in less than five, tugging Gerald along behind him.

'I had to bribe him with half an apple,' he said when he reached her. 'I thought your mum might like to feed him the other half. Shall we go inside? It'll be warmer for her in there.'

'You are a sweetheart,' Lena said, giving his arm a squeeze. 'This will mean so much to her.'

October approached, leading Princess, who was trying to eat the hem of her thick jacket, and she also had Storm with her, Chastity's pretty mare.

'Thank you,' Lena said, with a sniffle and a grateful smile.

Amos didn't think he could cope with seeing her cry, not right now, so he chivvied her along with a forceful, 'Ho, ho, ho,' and indicated that she should go ahead of him.

Olive was in her wheelchair, a woolly hat on her head, a big scarf around her neck and a heavy blanket tucked around her legs. She looked old and shrivelled, and she also looked exhausted.

Amos had been about to suggest that maybe Olive lingering in the cold to stroke a furry nose or two wasn't the best idea, but he quickly changed his mind when he caught sight of her expression.

Her eyes were gleaming and there was a determined set to her thin lips, and he guessed that there was little point in trying to persuade her to leave before she had done what she came here to do.

Hesitantly, he inched forward, praying that Gerald wouldn't make any sudden moves. Lena's mother looked as though the slightest thing would injure her irreparably, and he didn't want to be responsible for causing her any harm.

Impatiently, Olive beckoned him closer. 'My arms aren't that long,' she complained, reaching a trembling hand out toward Gerald's whiskery muzzle. 'There's a

446

good boy,' she crooned, rubbing the donkey under the chin.

'I've got some apple if you want to give it to him,' Amos said, passing it to her. 'If you hold your hand like this—' He demonstrated a flat palm.

'I know what to do. I was riding horses before you were born.' And with that Olive expertly fed Gerald his apple.

The donkey took it gently and crunched it up with enthusiasm. Not to be left out, Princess yanked on her lead rope hard enough to reach a discarded paper plate which sat on a nearby chair, and before she could be stopped, she ate it.

'I see what you mean,' Olive chuckled. 'That goat is a menace.'

After she had admired Storm, who snuffled at the old lady and blew gently through her nose, Amos could tell that Olive had finally had enough.

'I'll help you get your mum onto the bus, if you like,' he said to Lena.

'It's okay, William will do it.' She bent down to kiss her mother's cheek. 'I'll see you tomorrow, Mum.'

'I thought you'd forgotten about me wanting to see the horses, or you couldn't be bothered,' Olive said to Lena in a reedy whisper, slumping back into the chair.

She looked absolutely worn out, and Amos was worried. He had an awful feeling that now she had done what she had wanted to, she might allow herself to drift away in the night. It would be a great way to go (who didn't want to die peacefully in their sleep at the ripe old age of ninety-three?) but it would devastate Lena.

'I wanted it to be a surprise,' Lena told her.

Olive chuckled feebly. 'It was that, all right. Thank you, my lovely girl. And thank you too, Amos.'

'It was my pleasure.' Amos meant it. He'd had a whale of a time helping Lena organise the nativity play, and he was filled with a warm glow of satisfaction as he thought of how brilliantly the afternoon had gone. Everyone had thoroughly enjoyed themselves and the behaviour of the children and the animals had been exemplary.

Olive speared him with her gaze. 'Look after her when I'm gone,' she said suddenly. 'She'll need someone to love.'

Lena let out a gasp. 'Mum!'

'I'm tired. Take me back to the bus.' Olive closed her eyes.

Lena looked at him helplessly and Amos gave her a small smile.

'I will,' he promised the old lady, but she didn't give any sign that she had heard.

With a shake of her head, Lena got behind the wheelchair and rolled her mother outside. He could tell she was embarrassed, and he felt for her, but he was also elated. Somehow, Olive had seen into his heart and approved. Maybe she had seen into Lena's, too? Her words gave him hope that there might indeed be a future for the pair of them.

He pottered around, clearing up discarded cups and paper plates, whilst Megan packed up what little food remained. Amos was pleased to see that most of it had been eaten, and he had to admit that Megan had put on a lovely spread.

'Sorry about my mum,' Lena said, coming back to the gallery and picking up an empty cup to drop into the rubbish bag he was holding.

'Don't be. I'm not.' He looked at her, capturing her gaze. 'I intend to keep my promise,' he assured her.

'There's no need. I'll be fine. Sometimes I think she's losing the plot.'

'Your mother is as sharp as a tack.'

'She's dying.' Lena sank onto a chair.

'Yes, she is.' Amos didn't think there was any point lying to her. 'But she could have a while left yet.'

Lena turned stricken eyes up to him.

'She doesn't. I'll be surprised if she lasts the month. What will I do when she's gone?'

Then she burst into tears and Amos promptly dropped the bag he was holding, sat down in the chair next to her and gathered her to him. He wrapped his arms around her, stroking the back of her head with one hand as she cried.

Her heartbreak brought tears to his own eyes, and for a moment he was catapulted back to the terrible grief he had felt when his own parents had died. He knew it wasn't going to be easy for her, but he also knew that it wouldn't destroy her. She would mourn her mother's passing, but the grief would eventually ease, although it would never fade entirely. She would absorb it into herself and hold it close until it became a part of her, a brand on her heart that burnt deep but wouldn't consume her entirely.

Eventually, Lena's sobs became sniffles and she gradually sat up straight and wiped her eyes. 'You must think me such an idiot,' she said. 'Mum is still here and I'm acting as though she's already gone.'

'I don't think you're an idiot at all. I think you're incredibly brave. When Mags was ill, I buried my head in the sand for far too long. I kept thinking that she would pull through, that the latest treatment would be a miracle cure. It was only at the very end, when she had hours left to live, that I believed she was truly going to die. I think my denial made it harder to deal with. You are facing your mum's passing with courage. Yes, it'll hurt, possibly more than anything you've experienced before, but you'll cope. And whenever you need a shoulder to cry on, I'll be here.'

'You're such a kind and lovely man,' Lena sniffed. 'Thank you for making Mum's last Christmas so special. I can tell that she was thrilled.'

'She was, wasn't she? And she wasn't the only one.'

A figure appeared at Amos's elbow and he looked around, expecting to see Petra or Megan. Instead, a stranger was gazing down at them curiously.

'Sorry to interrupt,' the woman said. 'I wanted to

449

introduce myself, and the lady outside said that you were the person I need to speak to. My name is Grace Daley and I'm a reporter with The Picklewick Paper. I've been asked to cover the story. Are you Lena and Amos, by any chance?'

'We are.' Amos spoke for both himself and Lena, as Lena hurried to wipe away the remaining tears.

'I must say, that was a heart-warming performance, and the turn-out was impressive. I love that you thought to involve Honeymead's residents, and I understand that this all came about because your mother is unwell, Lena?'

'She's ninety-three. I wanted to make this Christmas extra special for her.'

'You've certainly done that, and for the others. Have you got time for a quick chat? Our readers are going to love this story. I hope you don't mind, but I took a few photos during the performance.'

Lena swallowed and gave Amos's hand a squeeze. 'See, I told you I'd get the stables some publicity,' she whispered. 'Fire away,' she said to Grace Daley.

The woman sat down. 'Brilliant. Right, let's start at the beginning. How long have you two been married?'

Amos was stunned and for a moment he wasn't able to say a word.

What a wonderful idea, he thought, as the image of him and Lena being husband and wife popped into his head.

What an absolutely wonderful, terrifyingly lovely idea!

CHAPTER EIGHT

'You're daft, you are.' Petra watched Amos give Queenie a wrapped Christmas present, and laughed as the dog tore into it eagerly.

Not to be left out, Tiddles swiped her present with a sheathed paw, then sniffed it suspiciously. The cat didn't look impressed.

They were in the kitchen, and the cat and the dog had been curled up together in Queenie's basket until Amos had enticed them out with a little gift each.

'I've always given the animals presents on Christmas morning. Why should this year be any different?' Amos wrinkled his nose at the baby in her arms, and Amory giggled. 'It's not just good little boys and girls who get presents from Santa,' he said. 'His little face when he saw what was under the tree, was a picture.'

'I'm not sure he knows what's going on. His eyes have been like saucers all morning.'

'You wait until next year. He'll be toddling by then and into everything.'

'Will you still come to the house to see him open his presents?' Petra asked quietly.

'Absolutely! Try keeping me away and see where that gets you. Don't look so worried – there's a long way to go before I move into the bungalow. I haven't even spoken to Isaac or Nelly yet.'

'If you're serious about this, you'd better get a move on. I've heard that they've got more work than they know what to do with. Mind you, I'm not surprised. With him drawing up the plans and with her guys doing the build, they make a good team.'

'Are you trying to get rid of me?' Amos joked.

'Far from it. We don't want you to move out.'

'Yeah, because then you'll have to cook your own Christmas lunch!'

'Not on your life! We're coming to you. You know I can't cook.'

'Speaking of cooking, I'd better check on the turkey. I don't want to incinerate it.' He peered into the oven, but couldn't see a great deal, so he opened the door, wafting away clouds of steam.

'What time did you put it in?' Petra asked.

'Half past four.'

'Please tell me you went back to bed afterwards,' she pleaded.

'No, but I did manage to have a nap in the chair,' he said. 'I'm going to see Lena later, so I don't want to be too tired.'

'God forbid!' Petra joked. 'You might fall asleep when you're canoodling.'

'We don't canoodle.' Amos stuck his nose in the air.

'Well, it's about time you did.'

'Stop matchmaking.'

'I can't help it. You're perfect for one another.'

Amos narrowed his eyes. Ever since the nativity play, when Petra had caught them sharing a celebratory hug after the reporter had gone, she hadn't stopped teasing him.

'If you're going to hang around the kitchen like a bad smell, you may as well make yourself useful and help me prepare the veg,' he said, knowing that the very thought of peeling potatoes would send her running.

'Er, I've got to um…' she said, sidling out of the door. 'I need to change Amory's nappy.'

He smiled as he heard her footsteps pound up the stairs.

Good. Now that he was finally on his own, he'd give Lena a call.

'Happy Christmas,' he said. 'Can you spare a couple of minutes to chat, or have you got visitors?'

'October and Luca have just left. I'm sitting in the chair, with a cheesy Christmas film on the telly, enjoying a glass of sherry before I go to Honeymead for lunch.'

'It's all right for some,' he grumbled jokingly. 'I've been left to cook the dinner all by myself. I'd love to be waited on.'

'I'll wait on you later,' she offered. 'I thought we could have some nibbles for supper. Unless you want to bring a few slices of turkey with you?'

Amos shuddered. 'Good grief, no! One turkey meal a day is enough. We'll be eating it well into next week as it is.'

He grinned. It was so nice chatting with her, sharing easy banter, and he realised that as lovely as this morning had been, and as wonderful as it would be to share lunch with his family, he couldn't wait to see Lena later. Her house was a far cry from the chaos and the busyness of the stables, but it wasn't just the peace and quiet he was looking forward to. He was eager to spend time with *her*.

That reporter had started him thinking, and once the thought was in his head he hadn't been able to shift it.

He wanted to marry again. He was ready to share his life with someone, and that someone was Lena. At his age he didn't want a romance or a love affair, he wanted a *wife*.

All he hoped was that Lena was ready for a husband, because he fully intended to ask her to marry him – as soon as he plucked up the courage!

Lena reached across the dining table and dabbed at the corner of her mum's mouth with a serviette, noting just how little lunch Olive was eating.

Worriedly, she caught William's eye, and he shook his head gently. He knew as well as she did that Olive was fading fast. It had been a struggle to get her out of bed and dressed this morning, but the old lady had been hell-bent on having her Christmas dinner in the dining room with everyone else.

Lena was determined to be cheerful however, not wanting her misery to infect anyone else. She had to admit that William and his team had done a marvellous job in creating such a festive atmosphere for the residents. It couldn't be easy for the staff to give up their own Christmas lunches and time that could be spent with their own families, in order to make the old folks' Christmas Day a happy and memorable one.

The dining room had a small Christmas tree in one corner, and lively festive tunes could be heard playing in the background. The tables had been decorated nicely, with white tablecloths, pretty centrepieces and crackers, and the first thing everyone had done as soon as they were seated, had been to pull their crackers, tell a few jokes and wear their paper party hats.

Even Olive sported a bright pink number perched on top of her head, her wispy hair poking out from the sides, and she had even managed to smile at some of the corny jokes.

But only halfway through lunch, the old lady's eyes were drooping and she was clearly finding it difficult. If Lena had thought Olive frail before the nativity play, she was doubly-so now.

In the intervening days, her mum had been slipping away fast, and every time Lena's phone rang, her heart lurched uncomfortably with fear. Any day now one of those phone calls would be the one she dreaded.

She continued to try her best to persuade her mum to eat, even cutting up the food for her, but Olive simply wasn't interested, although she did have a few sips of water, so at least she was drinking.

Lena tried to keep the conversation going. 'Luca has booked a surprise holiday for October as her Christmas present. They're flying out to Mauritius tonight for two whole weeks. Isn't that lovely?'

Olive gave a tiny nod. 'Lucky girl.'

'She is, isn't she? He thinks the world of her. I wouldn't be surprised if he asks her to marry him while they're out there. We might have a wedding to go to soon. Won't that be nice?'

Olive's gaze flickered to Lena, then she blinked slowly and looked away. Lena made a face, hearing her mother's unspoken belief that she wouldn't be around to attend any such wedding, and she immediately felt guilty. Maybe making small talk wasn't such a good idea.

As soon as the Christmas pudding had been served, complete with flaming brandy sauce, Olive indicated that she wanted to go to her room, so Lena drained her wine glass and stood up.

'Let me help,' one of the care assistants said, and Lena gratefully accepted. Although Olive weighed barely more than a bag of sugar, it still wasn't easy lifting her out of her chair and onto the bed, even with the hoist, and Lena was terrified of causing her any pain or discomfort.

Safely tucked in, after being changed into her nightclothes as she requested, Olive sank back into the pillows with a deep sigh.

'Can I get you anything, Mum?' Lena asked. 'A nice cup of tea?'

Olive shook her head, a small movement, which clearly cost her some effort. 'I just want to sleep.'

And it was at that moment, Lena realised her mum was ready to go, that she had been ready to go for a while. Lena suspected her mum had been hanging on for Lena's sake, not for her own.

Suddenly she understood how selfish she was in wanting to hang on to her mum for as long as possible, and she collapsed into the armchair next to the bed and took hold of her mother's frail hand.

'I'll sit with you for a while,' she said, not wanting to leave, scared that her mum would slip away the second she was gone.

'Go home,' Olive ordered, her voice barely more than a sigh. 'Amos will be waiting.'

Lena had told her that Amos was calling around this afternoon and they were to have supper together, but now she was having second thoughts. What if she went home, and her mum passed away without her being there? She'd never forgive herself.

As though sensing Lena's thoughts, Olive whispered, 'Come and see me tomorrow.'

'But—'

'But nothing. Go home. I'll still be here tomorrow.'

Lena wanted to say 'promise?', but she didn't want to place that burden on her mum, so she did the only thing she could. She kissed her gently on the forehead, and slipped out of the room.

'I thought you weren't going to bring any turkey,' Lena stated, as she unpacked the goodies that Amos had brought with him.

There was so much food at the stables, that he had been worried they wouldn't get through it all, so he decided to share it with Lena. And of course, some of it had to be turkey. Even if they didn't eat it now, Lena could have some tomorrow. He'd also brought a couple of slices of Christmas cake which Megan had made, half a Yule log, some cheeses and pickles, and a loaf of bread that he'd baked overnight. If nothing else, they could have turkey and pickle sandwiches followed by a slice of cake.

Oh, and he'd brought a bottle of wine and some stubby bottles of ale, as well. He poured himself a glass of the ale, but he didn't intend to drink more than one, because he would be driving home later. He wasn't much of a drinker anyway, although he did enjoy a pint or two in The Black Horse, especially when he was playing darts. However, he knew Lena liked wine, and he didn't know whether she would have bothered to have bought herself any since she was spending Christmas more or less alone.

'How did lunch go?' she asked as she put the food in the fridge. 'I take it you're not ready for anything to eat just yet?'

'Good lord, no! I'm not sure whether I'll eat ever again, if I'm honest. It was lovely, especially since it was Amory's first Christmas. He settled for milk and some pureed carrot and swede.' Amos shuddered. It hadn't looked at all appetising, but the little boy had wolfed it down. He certainly had a healthy appetite.

'Timothy and Charity popped in for a few minutes,' he told her, 'But Timothy was on call, and Charity had to go to work, so they didn't stay long.'

'Yes, I saw her at the care home. She looked very festive. She was wearing a jumper with a Christmas pudding on the front, and had Christmas pudding earrings.' Lena looked sad.

'How was your lunch?' he asked, knowing that it would have been a bitter-sweet occasion for her.

'The food was lovely as usual, and the staff made such an effort, but Mum didn't seem quite with it. In fact, I didn't want to leave her, but she insisted.'

'You can't be with her twenty-four hours a day,' Amos pointed out.

'I know, but it could happen any day now, and I want to be there when it does. I know they'll call me when the end is near, but what if they don't realise?'

'They will,' Amos assured her. 'Someone will check on her every few minutes, you know that.'

Lena nodded uncertainly. 'I know, but...' She trailed off.

'Come here,' Amos said, opening his arms wide. 'I think you need a hug.'

When she stepped into his embrace, he breathed in the scent of her perfume and thought how good it was to hold her. It felt right, as though it was meant to be, and he hugged her closer.

She rested her head against his shoulder and hitched in a deep breath. 'Don't worry, I'm not going to cry,' she said her voice slightly muffled.

'I don't mind if you do,' he said. 'I'm just glad that you feel you can share it with me.'

Lena pulled back a little and looked him in the eye. 'You're an easy man to share things with,' she said.

Then she kissed him.

Amos was shocked and it took him a heartbeat or two to recover, but suddenly he was kissing her back, and he marvelled how soft and warm her lips were, and how excited he was beginning to feel, as a fire that he had thought had long been extinguished, burst into flickering flame in his stomach.

Her fingers dug into his hair, pulling his head down as she kissed him passionately, and he lost himself in the sensations coursing through him, conscious only of her mouth, her hands on his back and her body pressed up against his.

Eager to take it further but aware that perhaps now was not the best time, Amos reluctantly drew away. He still kept hold of her, his arms refusing to let go, as he looked deep into her eyes, seeing his own hunger reflected back at him.

'I've been wanting to do that for a long time,' she said, her voice soft.

'Me, too. But, I was scared of losing your friendship.'

'You're not losing anything, you're gaining something. We both are.'

'Are you sure this is what you want?'

'I've never been surer of anything,' she replied.

He knew that this wasn't a knee-jerk reaction from Lena just because she didn't want to be on her own; and he knew her well enough to understand that she would prefer not to be in a relationship rather than be in one just because she might be lonely.

However, he didn't just want a relationship. Amos wanted a deeper commitment, but the question was, did she?

Lena had never married, so what made him think she would want to marry now?

The only way to find out, would be to ask her. But now wasn't the right time. He would wait until the New Year, until things had settled down and life was back on an even keel, and he would ask her then.

But at this moment there was another question he wanted answering, one that he wasn't afraid of asking. 'Can I kiss you again?'

And his whole being burst into flame when she said. 'You better had!'

Where is this heading, Lena asked herself later that evening, after Amos had left and she was able to breathe.

That first kiss had led to many more; so many that it had been a long time before they'd come up for air. And even when the kissing had stopped and they were eating supper, she still hadn't been able to catch her breath.

Every time she looked at him, (which was often, considering she was unable to take her eyes off him for more than a few seconds at a time) her heart skipped a beat and her tummy churned with excitement. She wanted him to hold her and never let go. She wanted to drag him off to bed and make love with him. Hell, she wanted all of him, body and soul.

But she also wanted to take it slow. Jumping into bed with him after just one kiss (okay, many kisses) wasn't her style. And she had been without a man in her life for so long that she worried she was making a mistake.

Because Lena didn't want a friends-with-benefits relationship.

She wanted long-term commitment. And now that she was alone in the house and had space to think, she realised that this situation was going to be an all-or-nothing one. And that meant marriage.

Finally, after all these years, she was ready for it.

She had found the man she wanted to marry.

But the problem was, would *he* want to marry *her*?

CHAPTER NINE

Sleep had been hard to come by for Lena last night. She had lain awake for hours until Christmas Day faded into Boxing Day, restless and unfulfilled, thoughts swirling and dipping through her mind like a flock of starlings preparing to roost.

Five a.m. saw her awake for good, and she was just about to go downstairs to make a cup of tea, when the phone rang.

She didn't need a crystal ball to tell her who was calling, and dread swept through her. With trembling fingers and clammy palms, she answered it.

Nodding once as she listened to the voice on the other end, all she said was, 'I'll be there in fifteen minutes.'

Slowly replacing the phone on the bedside table, she paused for a moment, not wanting to face the reality of what was about to happen but knowing that she must.

This was it. This was the day she would say goodbye to her mother. This was the day she would be without the woman who had nurtured her and loved her unconditionally all her life.

Steeling herself, Lena quickly threw on some clothes, brushed her teeth and splashed water on her face, and in five minutes she was out of the door and sprinting towards her car.

She remembered nothing of the short drive to the care home as she pulled into the silent car park and cut the engine, praying that she wasn't too late.

The air was still, and daylight was a few hours away yet. Cold seeped through her coat as she got out of the car, but it was nothing compared to the chill that had taken hold of her heart, and she wondered if she would ever feel warm again.

As Lena waited to be buzzed in, platitudes tumbled through her mind: her mother had had a good life, she had lived to a ripe old age, time is a great healer…None of them made a scrap of difference when faced with the reality of her impending loss.

William himself unlocked the door. His expression was sombre and he gestured for her to follow him, even though she knew the way to her mother's room blindfolded.

'Yvonne is with her. She's been with her all night, just in case…' he said.

Lena was grateful that her mother hadn't been left alone.

William added, 'Your mum has been asleep since yesterday lunchtime, but at some point in the night she slipped into unconsciousness.'

'Do you think she's in any pain?'

'No, I don't. She's peaceful.' He halted outside her mother's door, before giving it a gentle tap and pushing it open.

Lena's eyes flew to the bed.

Her mother lay on her back, her body barely more than a slight rise under the bedclothes. She appeared to be asleep, and Lena wondered whether she would rouse enough to realise she was there. She hoped so – she wanted to gaze into her mum's eyes one last time, to know that her voice was the last thing her mum heard in this world as she told her how much she loved her and how deeply she would miss her.

Yvonne was sitting by the side of the bed, holding Olive's hand, and Lena gave the care assistant a tearful smile.

Don't cry, she told herself, *don't cry*. She was desperate for her mum not to see how upset she was, but she couldn't hold back the tears and they spilled over to trickle down her cheeks in a steady stream.

'Thank you,' she whispered, as Yvonne got to her feet.

'I'll be outside if you need anything,' she said, patting Lena's arm as she stepped past her.

'Do you want me to stay, or would you prefer to be alone?' William asked.

'Alone,' she said, her voice breaking. 'Does she know I'm here?'

'I'm sure she does.'

Not taking her eyes off her mum, Lena waited until the door closed softly behind her before walking slowly towards the bed. She had to look carefully to see the almost imperceptible rise and fall of her mum's chest and, as she studied her, she saw how long there was between those shallow, fitful breaths.

She did look peaceful though, and Lena took some comfort from that.

'Mum, it's me, Lena.' She bent over the bed, stroking a strand of hair back from the remarkably unlined forehead, and kissing her gently. 'I love you. I just want you to know that.'

'Lena?' Olive's voice was softer than mist, hardly more than a breath in the warm dimness of the room.

'Yes, Mum, it's Lena.' She straightened up as she realised her tears were falling on the white sheet, and she hastily brushed them away and sat down in the recently-vacated chair.

She took her mother's hand in both of hers and caressed it, letting the stillness of the room seep into her, as memories cascaded through her mind.

She had no idea how much time had passed – it might have been minutes, it might have been hours – when her mother's eyes fluttered open and Lena's gaze snapped to her as Olive uttered a gasp.

'Mum? Can you hear me?' Lena croaked, her voice hoarse.

A faint whisper carried to her ears and she rose stiffly, leaning in so close that she could feel her mother's barely-there breath on her cheek. Tears poured down her face as she struggled to hear what her mum was saying.

Another breath. A last sigh. 'Love you too, Lena. You'll always be my little girl.' Her eyes drifted shut.

There were no more breaths.

Her mother was gone.

Amos shifted uncomfortably in his chair, feeling the stiffness in his hips and knees. A cup of tea sat cold and untouched on the side table next to him and the smell of bacon for the residents' breakfast made him feel nauseous. He couldn't face anything, not even tea, not when Lena's mother was dying in the room down the hall.

'Amos?' Charity hurried towards him. 'William told me about Olive. How's Lena coping?'

He shrugged. Although he would have loved nothing more than to go to her and take her in his arms, he knew she needed this time alone with her mum.

'Not good, I suspect,' he said. 'Olive might have had a good innings, but age is irrelevant when it comes to losing a parent. It still hurts like hell.'

'Lena's lucky to have you,' Charity said, and Amos shot her a keen look.

Did everyone think they were an item? And was that what they were, after last night?

'What time do you finish today?' he asked, eager to change the subject.

'Oh, I'm not working today. I heard about Olive and I felt I should pop in, what with October being halfway across the Indian Ocean by now. I thought Lena could do with the support.'

Bless her, Charity's eyes were damp and Amos could see she was upset. 'That's kind of you,' he said.

Charity placed her hand over his. 'I'm sure Lena would rather cry on your shoulder than mine.'

'Get off home – I expect Timothy is waiting. I'll tell her you were here. I'm sure she'll be touched.'

'He is.' She smiled for a moment, then she hesitated. 'Are *you* okay?'

It was sweet of her to ask. 'I will be,' he replied, guessing that she realised seeing Lena so upset would bring memories of Mags's death home to him.

She smiled down at him. 'You make a lovely couple.'

'Eh?'

'Olive told me that the two of you are in love.'

'When did she tell you that?' Amos was flabbergasted.

'The day of the nativity play. She said—' Charity gulped, tears brimming '—she said she could die in peace now, knowing that Lena had you to love and cherish her.'

Amos blinked. 'But what if Lena doesn't *want* to be loved and cherished.'

'Don't be silly, Amos! Of course she does! She loves you.'

'*Lena* told you that?'

Charity frowned. 'No, Olive did. Head over heels in love with you, is what she said. Right, I'll be off. I've already been up to the stables this morning, but if you need me, just shout. Look after Lena.'

'I will,' Amos said to her retreating back.

Fancy that! Had Olive really told her that Lena head over heels in love with him? And if so, how had the old lady known? Had Lena said so? Or was Olive matchmaking?

He was still mulling it over when movement caught his eye, and he saw the forlorn figure of Lena walking slowly down the corridor.

Amos struggled to his feet, cursing his stupidity for sitting still for so long, as he hobbled towards her. He could tell by her face that her mother was gone. She looked pale and incredibly sad, but she brightened momentarily when she saw him.

'I'm so sorry, Lena,' he said, reaching her and pulling her into his arms.

She sank into him, and he felt her tremble as sobs wracked her. There was no need for words and nothing he could say would make her feel any better, so he remained silent and let her cry.

And when her tears eased, he gently wiped her face, and took her home.

'Please stay with me,' Lena pleaded. 'I don't want to be on my own, not today.' She wrapped her arms around her waist and hugged herself. She was freezing, even though the heating was on and the house was warm. It was probably the shock, she thought.

Amos was in the middle of filling the kettle, because what else did one do at a time like this, she mused absently, and as he switched it on, he turned to her.

'I'll stay with you for as long as you want,' he promised.

She would like it to be forever, but... 'Thanks.'

'Sit down, I'll bring the tea in.'

With a deep sigh, Lena wandered into the living room and stared at it with fresh eyes. This was her mother's house – hers now, she supposed – but even though it had been her home since she had returned to Picklewick to live, today it didn't feel like it. Most of the furniture belonged to her mum, and the décor was mostly her mum's taste. Lena hadn't seen the point in changing anything, although she had brought some of her own furniture with her; and a few of October's bits and pieces were also in evidence, although her daughter had taken everything that she had wanted to keep to Luca's house when she'd moved in with him.

'Here you go, a nice cup of tea,' Amos said.

She took it from him and wrapped her hands around the mug without drinking. 'Do you want to know what's strange?' she said. 'Yesterday, if you'd asked, I would have said this is mine, my house, my home, even though Mum still technically owns…*owned*…it. But today, it doesn't feel like mine. From now on, I'll always think of it as *her* house.'

'You're bound to, I suppose. It's full of memories of her. I know I sometimes still see Mags in the farmhouse.'

'No, I don't think that's it…' Lena said. She wasn't entirely sure what she meant, but she knew one thing – she didn't want to live here any longer. 'I want to move,' she said. 'Sell up and buy something smaller. Why do I need four bedrooms? Two will be ample. I want a fresh start.'

'Funny you should say that – I was thinking the very same thing. I'm planning on moving out of the farmhouse and into a bungalow.'

Lena was shocked. 'You are going to leave the stables?' She never would have thought he'd do such a thing.

Amos blew out his cheeks. 'Not exactly. I've told Petra that I want to convert a feed shed into a bungalow. It'll be better for all of us, going forward. Future-proofing, I think it's called. With that in mind, I'm also signing the stables over to her. It'll be hers anyway when I'm gone.' He realised what he'd said, and pulled a face. 'Sorry, that was insensitive.'

'There's no need to tiptoe around me.' Lena took a mouthful of the rapidly cooling tea. 'I think your plan is a sensible one.'

'But maybe you should give yourself time to think about what you want to do? You don't want to make any hasty decisions,' he said.

'I won't do anything yet,' she assured him. There was the funeral and all the legalities to get through first. 'But I'm pretty sure I won't change my mind. Now that you come to mention it, a bungalow sounds perfect.'

Amos was staring at her strangely.

'What?' she asked.

'I'm not sure how to say this, and I know it's the worst timing ever, but… Ah, no, forget it.' He was looking decidedly uncomfortable.

'Spit it out,' she said. 'I won't rest until I know what it is.'

'I wish I hadn't said anything.' He hung his head. 'Me and my big mouth.'

'Amos…?' she warned.

'I was going to suggest that you move to the bungalow with me, but it's the stupidest, most ridiculous idea—'

'Yes.'

His mouth dropped open and his bushy eyebrows shot up to his hairline. He had a good head of hair for a man of his age, she thought absently.

'You will?' He looked stunned.

'I will. But on one condition. I have no intention of being a kept woman or your mistress. I might be old-fashioned and I know that many couples do live happily together without being married, but that's not for me. If I'm going to move in with you, I'll do so as your wife or not at all.' She nearly added 'so there', but instead she pursed her lips, marvelling at how the conversation had progressed so quickly to this point.

Her mum had only just died and here she was, considering selling the family home to move in with a man who hadn't even told her he loved her yet. And – dear god – she had just asked him, in a roundabout way, to marry her.

'You beat me to it,' he said, after a short but very intense silence during which Lena was beginning to think about pleading insanity due to bereavement and buggering off to bed. 'I was going to propose to you, but not for a while,' he added quietly.

'Am I being callous? My mum has only just died and here I am—' She let out a sudden sob, her emotions all over the place.

'No, but if *I* had asked *you* to marry me before you'd had time to come to terms with losing her, then that would be a different thing altogether. I just want to make sure you're not doing anything you regret. I want nothing more than to marry you and I'd call myself the luckiest man in the world if you were my wife, but *love* is what is important here and I love you too much to let you make a mistake.'

He was about to carry on, but Lena didn't let him. 'You love me?'

'I do.'

'Say it.'

'I love you.' He looked nervous and his apprehension touched her deeply.

She put her mug down, took a step closer and said, 'I love you, too. I've loved you for a while. Believe me when I tell you that if we do get married, I won't regret it.' She hitched in a shaky breath. 'It was my mum who made me realise how I felt, and she also made me realise that it's not too late for love. The only thing that was holding me back was Mags.'

Amos's expression clouded. 'Mags? I can understand why, but it's time I let her go. I've clung on to her for far too long, and I know she would have hated that. There's room in my heart for both of you, and although I'll never forget her and I'll always love her, I love you too, and I will for the rest of my life.'

Lena's heart swelled with love, and as she stepped into his waiting arms she thought she heard her mother's voice whisper, 'Be happy, my lovely girl.'

And neither did she think she imagined the gentle stroke of her mother's hand on her shoulder, or the kiss of barely-there lips on the top of her head.

I love you, Mum, she thought, then she was lost in Amos's embrace and the future it held.

This Christmas had been the saddest and the happiest of her life, magical, poignant and wonderful – and with this special man at her side, she found herself looking forward to many, many more.

THE END

About Etti

Etti Summers is the author of wonderfully romantic fiction with happy ever afters guaranteed.
She is also a wife, a mum, a pink gin enthusiast, a veggie grower and a keen reader.

Acknowledgements

My family deserves a great deal of thanks, mainly for putting up with my incessant daydreaming. Love you to the moon and back xxx

Thanks to my lovely editor and friend, Catherine Mills, for her support and advice.

My friends also get a huge hug for all the love and encouragement, even if they don't understand all the wittering on about story arcs!

Finally, I can't go without sharing my heartfelt gratitude to you, my readers.
You make the writing worthwhile xxx

Printed in Great Britain
by Amazon